The Pages of Time

Damian Knight

To Dani,

Hope you enjoy the book.

With best wishes,

Damian Knight

ISBN-13: 978-1514765951
ISBN-10: 1514765950

For Francesca

CONTENTS

Part I
A Clean Slate

1

Present Day

Sam woke with a start. It was dark outside the window of the plane. For a moment he thought he must have slept through a whole day before remembering that they were passing through different time zones. His mum was asleep next to him and had placed a blanket over his legs. A map on the overhead screen showed that they were approaching the west coast of Ireland, several hundred miles south of Iceland.

The cabin crew were in the middle of serving dinner. Sam hadn't eaten anything since the evening before and gratefully accepted a tray covered by a clear plastic lid. He demolished the lamb stew, bread roll and fruit salad without pausing between mouthfuls.

Suddenly a deep tremor rocked the plane. Sam's tray slid off the foldout table and clattered onto the floor. His mum jolted awake, blinked at him and squeezed his hand.

The speaker system crackled into life: 'Ladies and gentlemen, please return to your seats and fasten your seatbelts. It's likely we'll experience pockets of heavy turbulence.'

The stewards and stewardesses stowed their trolleys and strapped themselves into chairs at the front of the cabin. The plane shuddered again. Sam could see the wing bending savagely up and down through the window. 'Is it supposed to do that?' he asked his mum.

She looked out and forced a smile. 'Of course, sweetie. Passenger jets are designed to withstand much worse than this.'

The plane seemed to drop for a second and then regained stability. A series of shocked gasps rebounded about the cabin. Sam tasted lamb stew on the back of his tongue and fumbled in the seat pocket for a sick bag. There was none. He put a hand over his mouth and tried the pocket of his mum's seat. His fingers brushed against something hard and plastic. He pulled it out. It was the smart phone belonging to the man who'd been taken ill in back in Newark, and all of a sudden it started to ring.

Sam glanced across at his mum, his nausea forgotten. 'I don't get it,' he said. 'How can there be any signal up here?'

'Don't ask me, sweetie. You know I'm useless when it comes to that sort of thing. Are you going to answer it?'

He swiped the screen and held the phone to his ear. 'Hello?'

There were three short beeps and then an electronic voice said, 'Trigger activated.'

A loud buzzing sound seemed to come from every-where at once and the lights went out. Someone nearby screamed. The engines spluttered once, twice and failed.

The last thing Sam could remember was a whistling sound that grew louder and louder as the plane fell.

2

Three weeks earlier

It began on a damp evening in August, a month when it should have been sunny and warm. Until the phone call, a seemingly insignificant event that would ultimately alter every aspect of Sam's existence, nothing much was out of the ordinary. He had been sitting in his room, playing online games with Lewis when the internet connection went down. A couple of seconds later the house phone rang in the hall and, assuming it was his friend, Sam picked up.

'Rebecca,' a voice with an American accent said, 'it's Doug. Have you got a minute?'

Doug was Sam's mum's boss at the bank. 'Hang on a sec,' he said, annoyed that anyone could confuse them, and took the handset downstairs.

His mum was leaning over a crossword puzzle at the kitchen table, still in her work clothes with a glass of red wine in her hand. She gave Sam a tired smile and said she'd take the call in the living room.

Sam's dad was draining pasta at the sink. 'Food's ready,' he said through a swirl of steam. 'Can you get your sister?'

'Do I have to?'

'Yes.'

Sam sighed and stamped upstairs. Chrissie's room, which was much bigger than his own, was at the top of their house, located in the converted attic space. He knocked on the door, called her name and, when no answer came, poked his head inside. The room appeared empty at first glance, so he took a step into the Forbidden Realm. At the far end a window overlooked the back garden, across which heavy black drapes were drawn. A pair of scuffed military boots stuck out the bottom.

'Chrissie?' Sam called again.

The drapes bulged and parted to reveal his sister's face.

'What do you think you're doing, runt?' Chrissie glared at him from behind thick black eyeliner. 'I thought I told you never, ever, under *any* circumstances come into my room.'

'What's that smell?' Sam asked, knowing full well. 'Are you smoking?'

She crossed the distance between them in four long strides and grabbed him in a headlock. Chrissie was three years older than Sam, and although he'd grown quite a bit in the last year, she still had an inch over him. He tried to yell, but the sleeve of her baggy cardigan caught in his mouth.

'You breathe a word to Mum and Dad and I'll kill you, I swear it,' she said.

He was beginning to feel dizzy, his face hot with blood. Chrissie's studded metal bracelet dug into the skin of his neck.

'All right,' he wheezed.

She tightened her grip. 'What's that? Can't hear you.'

'All right, I promise. Just let me go.'

'Promise what?'

'I won't tell Mum and Dad. Please Chrissie, let go. I can't breathe.'

She released him at last. Sam stood hunched for a few seconds, gasping for air.

'What did you want anyway?' Chrissie asked.

'I only came to tell you dinner's ready.'

She placed a hand on her hip, tilted her head to one

side and eyed him with contempt. 'Fine then, I'll be down in a minute. Now get out of my room!'

He turned and left, rubbing his neck and muttering curses as he clumped down the stairs. As a rule, Sam tried to have as little as possible to do with his sister. It hadn't always been that way; when he was very young, he'd idolised Chrissie and would have done anything to win her approval. He had happily allowed her and her friends to dress him up and use him as a prop in their games. Unfortunately for Sam, Chrissie's interest in playing families and shopkeepers hadn't lasted long. As the make-believe took a darker twist, he soon found himself the victim of police brutality or hit-and-run incidents. On one occasion many years back, he was held hostage in the cellar, tied to their dad's tool shelf with the lights off. After three hours in darkness, imagining giant spiders crawling along the underside of the floorboards overhead, Sam had wet himself and begun to cry. The lights had come on again and Chrissie entered wearing a balaclava. She'd informed him that her ransom demands hadn't been met and she would therefore have to send a 'clear message', at which point she produced a pair of pliers from the pocket of her dungarees and ordered Sam to put his little finger between the teeth. Not really believing she would do it, he'd done as he was told. At the time the doctors had said Sam might lose the finger, but the wound had healed remarkably well and now, over ten years later, only a thin white scar on the ridge of his knuckle served as a reminder of the incident.

Back in the kitchen, Sam's dad was dishing out food and making a mess. Sam slumped at the table and used his fork to push a piece of pasta around the rim of his plate. After a few minutes Chrissie joined them, reeking of mouthwash and spray deodorant. She slid into a chair on the far side of the table and started chewing at her chipped black nail polish. Finally, their mum returned. Instead of sitting at the table, she remained standing by the door, a manic grin stretched across her face.

'What is it?' Sam asked when it became obvious that was what she was waiting for.

'That was Doug on the phone.' She paused to beam at each of them in turn. 'Do you remember the promotion I went for last month?'

'Of course,' Sam lied. She often talked about work, but he rarely paid any attention.

'Well, I can hardly believe it. The competition was so intense, but Doug said the whole board was impressed with the way I handled the Madsen case and...' *drum roll* '...it turns out I got it!'

'Sweetheart, that's fantastic,' his dad said.

Although Sam's parents tried to hide it, money had been tight for a while now and he'd overheard several hushed conversations containing phrases such as, 'final demand', 'missed payment' and 'tighten our belts'.

'Isn't it just?' his mum said. 'At last a bit of recognition for all the extra work I've been taking on. It'd mean a pay rise too.'

'Well done,' Sam said, imagining new trainers and the latest games console.

'There's something else.' The corners of her mouth dropped slightly. 'The new position isn't at the London branch. If I take it we'll have to relocate near the head office in New York.'

'New York as in America?' Sam asked.

'It's the only one I know of.'

He stared at her silly grin and was about to complain when Chrissie beat him to it. She jumped up, sending her chair clattering back, and planted her fists on the table. 'Impossible, no way!'

'Chrissie—' their mum began, trying to sound soothing and calm.

Chrissie was shouting now. 'Don't waste your breath. God, I hate you sometimes! All you ever think about is yourself.'

Mum looked upset and, as always, Dad jumped in to present a united parental front. 'Look,' he said, 'I know you're upset, Chrissie, but we can talk about this. It's a family decision.'

'There's nothing to talk about, I'm not leaving Lance and there's nothing you can do to make me. I'm almost twenty years old and, in case you lot hadn't noticed, I can do whatever I want. If you want to move halfway around the world then that's your problem. I'm staying here, simple as.'

Lance was Chrissie's boyfriend. They'd met the summer before when Chrissie spent two months travelling in India after her A-levels (one of the happiest and most harassment-free times of Sam's life), but she'd only introduced him to the family a couple of months ago. Although their mother didn't approve, Sam liked him: Lance was far more relaxed than his sister.

Chrissie marched from the room. A couple of seconds later the front door slammed, sending shock waves reverberating through the walls. Sam sat gobsmacked, looking at his parents and knowing there was nothing he could say that would match his sister's outburst.

His dad cleared his throat and smiled weakly. 'Well, son, what do you say? You're with us, aren't you?'

3

Lewis was woken at six in the morning by the pipes in his bedroom wall clunking and his father singing tunelessly in the bathroom next door. He groaned, pulled the pillow over his head and was just dozing off again when the door flew open and he was presented with the unattractive sight of his father wearing only a hand towel that stretched almost but not quite the whole way around his waist.

'Rise and shine, sleeping beauty,' his father said, scratching a hairy shoulder.

Lewis groaned again, rolled over and tried to bury himself under the covers. His father responded by grabbing the duvet by the corner and yanking it from the bed, leaving Lewis squirming like a new-born calf. He then removed the damp towel from his waist, twisted it into a coil and whipped it across Lewis's bare back. Lewis yelped and jumped out of bed. His father stood facing him, feet planted apart to display his nakedness.

'Jesus, Dad, what's wrong with you? Put some clothes on.' Lewis snatched the duvet from the floor and collapsed back on his mattress.

His father turned to leave, flabby white buttocks wobbling with each step. He stopped in the doorway, farted loudly and said, 'Happy birthday,' before slamming the door behind him.

At close to midday, Lewis woke of his own accord. He showered, checked his reflection for increased facial hair density and returned to his room to dress before going downstairs. There was a pink envelope on the kitchen table with his name on it. It contained a card with a picture of a girl in a floral dress and a badge with the words *Super Sweet Sixteen*. Lewis opened the card and a fifty-pound note drifted to the tabletop. The printed message read, 'To a wonderful daughter, wishing you a superlicious birthday!'

Lewis folded the money and slid it into his pocket, then threw the badge in the bin. On his way out, he stuck his head around the living room door. His mother was on the sofa, watching cartoons with Connor, his little brother.

'I'm going to get my results now, Mum,' Lewis said. 'Wish me luck.'

'Luck's got nothing to do with it,' she said without taking her eyes from the television, 'not with brains as big as yours.'

Connor drew a sleeve under his runny nose, succeeding only in smearing snot across his cheek, and gave Lewis a gap-toothed smile.

Lewis tried to ring Sam again on the way to school, but his call went straight to voicemail. Apart from a few students milling around the gates, it was eerily quiet. He waited for a bit, but Sam didn't show, so eventually he went in on his own. It was strange being there without his uniform, and Lewis felt a bit like an intruder as he walked down the empty corridors lined with stripped display boards, his footsteps echoing loudly around him.

A line of tables had been erected in the hall, the scene of many a mind-numbing assembly. Lewis approached the second table from the left, where Mr Dewey, his history teacher, was sitting behind a tented piece of paper on which the letters *D, E, and F* had been scrawled in marker pen.

'Hello, sir,' Lewis said. 'Having a nice holiday?'

Mr Dewey looked like he'd just got in from an all-night drinking session. His wiry hair jutted out at different angles, except for the left side where it lay flat to his head. 'Might be if I didn't have to be here with you horrible lot,' he said, regarding Lewis with bleary eyes. 'Name and candidate number, if you please.'

'Lewis Fisher, 8739.'

Mr Dewey flicked through a box of envelopes on the table, backed up, plucked one out and handed it to him. Lewis turned the envelope over and traced the flap with his fingertip. During the last few weeks he'd had to listen to his father bleat on and on about how Lewis would be the first member of the family to go to university, and all of a sudden he didn't think he wanted to know.

'Were you planning on proposing marriage to that thing, Fisher, or are you going to open it?'

Lewis gulped. 'Yes, sir…I mean no.'

He turned his back and walked away. It was probably like pulling off a plaster: best done quickly. After a deep breath, he ripped the envelope and pulled out the slip inside.

The column of perfect A's and A*'s was blemished in the middle: Geography – B, Spanish – C.

Lewis had never got a B in his life, let alone a C. There must have been some mistake. The school office had probably placed another student's grade sheet in the envelope marked with his name. But no, there in the top corner of the page were Lewis's name and candidate number, as real as the pain from a punch in the nose. He scrunched the slip up and stuffed it in his pocket, already imagining the look on his father's face when he found out.

'Hi Lewis, how'd it go?'

Lewis turned to find Tania, the girl he sat next to in Maths, standing directly behind him. 'Yeah, pretty much as expected,' he said. 'How about you?'

'Straight A's too!' Tania grinned, the thick lenses of her glasses magnifying her eyes to enormous proportions. 'And I was *so* unbelievably nervous, but I'll definitely get into St. Mary's now. My parents are going to be *so* unbelievably proud. Where are you thinking of going next year?'

'Fraser Golding.'

Tania blinked her bushbaby eyes. 'Fraser Golding College? *Really*? I always thought you'd end up somewhere a bit more...academic.'

'Thought I'd stay local,' Lewis said. 'Plus, I've got friends going there. Listen, Tania, you haven't seen Sam anywhere, have you?'

'I think he was out back a while ago,' she said. 'You never know, he might still be there.'

'Thanks,' he said and turned to leave.

As he hurried from the hall, Lewis's phone began to ring. He pulled it out and glanced at the screen: it was his father. Without answering, he silenced the call, slid the phone back into his pocket and shoved open the door that led onto the school's only playing field.

Sam was sitting on the steps directly outside and had to dive out of the way to dodge the swinging door.

'What're you doing out here?' Lewis asked. 'We were supposed to meet out front, remember?'

'Sorry,' Sam said, standing to dust himself off. 'I forgot.'

'Whatever, it doesn't matter.'

'Happy birthday, by the way.'

'Thanks,' Lewis said. 'So, have you picked up your results yet?'

Sam pulled an envelope from his pocket and waved it absently in the air.

'What, you haven't even opened it yet?'

'There's no point,' Sam said, looking off into the distance.

'Don't be like that. Your results can't be that bad...can they?'

'That's not what I'm talking about—'

'Just open it and we can get out of here.'

Sam hesitated, then wrinkled his nose and tore his envelope open.

'Well?' Lewis asked, tapping his foot.

Sam handed him the slip.

Lewis glanced over it and passed it back. 'See, you got a B in Maths. That's all right, isn't it? Stop stressing; it's good enough for Fraser Golding. The plan is still on track.'

Sam shook his head. 'No, Lewis, it's not. My grades won't make any difference.'

'What are you on about?'

'That's what I've been trying to tell you,' Sam said. 'I'm not going to college in September because we're moving to America next week.'

4

The sitting room of Chrissie's house was a place that held many memories. Until last week it had hardly changed over the years, but now a grey rectangle marked the spot above the fireplace where a mirror had always hung. The sofas and much of the larger furniture remained, being too expensive to transport to the States, but it was the missing details that robbed the room of its personality; the absent books on the shelves, the photographs removed from the mantelpiece.

Her mum was going through Sam's suitcase and cross-examining him over whether he'd packed his toothbrush and sufficient quantities of underwear, while her brother grumbled and complained. Chrissie shook her head. Was it really any wonder he acted like such a baby when their mother fussed over him that way?

'Hello, pet,' Chrissie's grandmother said from the sofa. 'How're you keeping?'

'Fine thanks.' Chrissie bent to kiss her cheek, then her grandfather's.

'And who's your companion?'

'Grandma, Grandpa, this is Lance, my boyfriend.'

Lance stepped forward and offered his hand to shake. 'Pleased to meet you both.'

'He has long hair,' Chrissie's grandfather said. 'You're not a hippy, are you?'

Lance looked uneasy. Outside a car horn tooted, saving him from having to answer. Chrissie followed Sam and their parents to the front garden and watched on as they hefted their suitcases into the boot of the taxi. Although she had no desire to join them, she couldn't shake the feeling that they were deserting her.

'Ring as soon as you get in,' she said. All of a sudden her throat tightened and her eyes started to itch. 'I mean it, it doesn't matter what time.'

'Will do,' her dad said. He pulled her close, his mouth next to her ear. 'And keep an eye on Grandpa, okay? You know what he's like.'

Mum muscled him out of the way and took Chrissie's hands in her own. Her mascara had run, leaving dirty smudges beneath her eyes. 'I can't stand leaving you alone like this,' she sobbed. 'Are you sure you won't change your mind?'

'I'm sure. Really, Mum, I'm a big girl now.'

'You'll always be my baby, Chrissie. And there'll be a room for you in the new house any time you want to come and stay.'

'I know.' Chrissie turned to her brother. 'Take care of yourself, runt.'

'Yeah, you too,' he said and grimaced when she hugged him.

Lance came to Chrissie's side and put his arm around her waist. They watched from the gate at the end of the path as the taxi pulled away, Chrissie's mum frantically waving out of the rear window.

'You all right, babe?' Lance asked.

Chrissie nodded, but her throat felt tighter than ever. 'Absolutely, it's just…'

'What?'

'I know it sounds stupid, but I can't shake the feeling that I'll never see them again.'

'You're right,' he said, 'that does sound stupid. Come on, let's go back inside.'

5

Sam sat bolt upright, the sheets of an unfamiliar bed wrapped around his limbs. For a second he couldn't work out where he was and then his memory spluttered into life like an old car on a winter's morning. His parents had slept most of way on the flight, but Sam had stayed up watching films as they journeyed through a night that seemed like it would never end. It was still dark when the plane had landed, and exhaustion had finally overtaken him in the back of the car they rented at the airport. He had no recollection of reaching the house or making his way to this strange bed.

Sam's new room, if this was it, was satisfyingly large, even bigger than Chrissie's attic room back home. A beam of dusty sunlight poked through the curtains, spot-lighting a pile of cardboard boxes. He climbed out of bed wearing only his boxer shorts and found his clothes in a heap on the floor. After pulling on trousers and T-shirt, he padded barefoot to a floor-length window, drew back the curtains and stepped onto a balcony overlooking a wide, tree-lined suburban road. It was so warm that it was impossible to tell whether it was morning or afternoon, or how long he'd been asleep. He took a deep breath. The air smelled different here, rich and somehow earthy.

Sam went back inside, put his socks and shoes on, and set off in search of his parents. He had no idea where he was going, but he could hear voices downstairs so followed them to a large, modern kitchen on the ground floor. His mum was standing with her head in a metallic fridge. She closed the door, looked up and smiled. 'Ah, you're awake. Did you sleep well?'

Sam yawned. 'What time is it?'

'Almost seven in the evening. The Bernsteins have come over to welcome us to the neighbourhood.'

'The who?'

'You know, Doug and his family. They've got a daughter roughly your age.' She handed him a chilled bottle of wine. 'Be a love and take this out. There's pizza on the deck, if you're hungry.'

Their garden back home was little more than a square of grass overlooked by other houses on all sides. This was something else altogether, stretching so far in every direction that Sam wasn't sure where it ended. He'd emerged onto wooden decking covered by a canopy that extended from the side of the house. There was a table in the middle surrounded by wicker chairs. His dad was sitting at the end, shovelling pizza into his mouth. On one side were Doug and his wife, and on the other, with their backs to Sam, their two daughters. Doug stood up, grabbed Sam's hand and shook it so hard it felt like he was trying to dislocate his shoulder.

'So, Sam, decided to join your parents across the pond, eh?'

'I'm not sure I had much choice,' Sam said. He eased his hand from Doug's grip and took a seat at the table.

'Well, I just know you're going to love it here,' Doug

said. 'Let me introduce you. This is my wife, Colette...'
She pushed her sunglasses up onto her head and smiled,
revealing perfect, dazzlingly white teeth. '...and our
daughters, Eva and Nicole.'

'Hi,' Eva said.

She was pretty, with long, dark hair, freckles and a
wide smile. Sam was acutely aware that he was wearing
the same clothes he'd travelled in.

'Nice to meet you,' he said.

'We've met before, as a matter of fact.'

'We have?'

'At one of those corporate parties,' she said, waving a
hand in the air. 'It was a while back, you probably
wouldn't remember.'

A recollection slotted into place. It was a party Sam's
mum had hosted for colleagues five or six years before.
He and Chrissie had been palmed off on a kiddies' table
while the adults got drunk next door. There had been
several other children. One was a serious-looking girl
who wore glasses and had braces on her teeth. She'd
spent the whole time tapping away on a laptop. When
Sam had asked what she was playing, she'd laughed and
told him that she was writing code and video games were
for babies. He hadn't bothered trying to speak to her
again that day.

'You look different,' Sam said. 'Are you still into
computers?'

'You could say that.' Eva pulled a slice of pizza from
one of the boxes and dropped it onto her plate. 'Although
my interests have diversified in recent years.'

'I'm Nicole,' the younger daughter said. She was
about eight years old, had the same dark hair and freckles
as her sister and was gazing up at Sam with her chin
propped in her hand. 'Do you have television in
England?'

'Don't be stupid, Nic. Of course they do,' Eva said.

Nicole ignored her sister's comment and continued to watch him with her brow creased. 'And cars? Because in the movies everyone rides horses and wears hats like this.' She placed her hands by the sides of her head to signify a top hat.

'Yeah, we have cars and televisions,' Sam said, helping himself to a slice of pizza. 'Things have moved on a lot since electricity was installed.'

'I must apologise for my sister,' Eva said. 'She has some kind of birth defect, the doctors say. It's a miracle she does so well with only the single brain cell.'

'Mommy!' Nicole said.

Colette poured herself a tall glass of wine. 'Eva, lay off your sister, will you?'

Eva rolled her eyes and took a large bite of pizza, strings of cheese spilling down her chin. She scooped them into her mouth. 'So, Doug tells me you're starting Montclair High?'

Sam nodded. 'What's it like?'

'The same as anywhere, I guess. Fine if you're popular, not so fine if you're not.'

'And which are you?'

Her eyes widened slightly, then she smiled. 'I prefer not to put myself in categories. I just try to be myself, and if you like it, then great. And if you don't…well that's fine too.'

'I see.'

'All the boys like Eva,' Nicole said. She closed her eyes, puckered her lips and made a series of smooching noises. 'Eva and Trent, sitting in a tree, K-I-S-S-I-N-G!'

Eva shot Nicole a death stare, picked a slice of onion from her pizza and flicked it at her sister. It hit Nicole square in the forehead, where it remained stuck for a second or two before flopping to the tabletop. Sam suppressed a giggle with the back of his hand.

'Mommy!' Nicole said again.

'Stop it you two, or you can wait in the car.'

'But she started it—'

'I'm serious,' Colette said. She drained her glass, refilled it to the brim and placed the empty bottle back on the table.

Nicole scowled and grumbled under her breath.

'Sam, could you get some more wine from the fridge?' his mum asked. 'There's another bottle on the top shelf.'

He stood up. 'Does anyone want anything else while I'm there?'

'I'll have a Coke, please,' Eva said.

'The bottom shelf,' his mum offered, noticing Sam's look of confusion.

He went inside and, once out of sight, flattened his hair and sniffed his armpits: not as bad as week-old PE kit, but hardly alpine fresh. With any luck Eva was sitting far enough away not to have noticed. After collecting another bottle of wine, Sam pulled a can of Coke from a multipack on the bottom shelf of the fridge. He turned to go and then stopped, searched several cupboards until he found a glass and filled it with ice from a dispenser set in the fridge. Carrying the glass, can and bottle, he headed back out.

'Here you go,' he said, passing Eva the glass and can.

She stood up, her phone in her hand. 'Thanks, but something's come up. I've got to go. Maybe I'll see you at school?'

Before Sam could digest what she'd said, let alone reply, Eva had left, walking quickly into the house. He closed his mouth, put the drinks on the table and looked to the others.

'I think I'd like a chocolate shake,' Nicole said. 'Do you have milkshakes in England?'

6

Eva balanced a contact lens on her fingertip. Flinching, she pulled her eyelid back, popped it in and blinked as the basin and medicine cabinet floated into view. Colette had offered to pay for laser eye surgery on several occasions, not that it would be her money, of course. Eva always declined, listing the associated risks. She knew that complications were statistically rare, but the thought of someone slicing the surface of your eye and zapping you with a laser didn't sit right. Colette had sighed with disappointment and said, 'Perfection comes at a cost.'

Eva brushed her hair, smoothed foundation over her cheeks and then applied lipstick, mascara and pencilled in above her eyes until the mask was complete and that familiar stranger stared back from the mirror. Briefly, she entertained the fantasy of scrubbing it all off, back-combing her hair and going to school wearing sweat pants and her glasses. It would be worth the social ostracism just to see the expressions on her friends' faces.

But no, appearances must be maintained. Perfection, after all, came at a cost.

Eva's thoughts were disturbed by the sound of Trent's car pulling into the drive. Last week she'd had to leave the Rayners' house in a hurry after receiving his text. Trent had been at *Jammin' Joe's* on the other side of town, where he often hung out, shooting pool and buying drinks with the fake ID she'd made for him. When Eva had called back, Trent was already slurring his words and shouting down the phone. The bartender had taken his car keys, so Eva had to walk home to collect Colette's car. When she'd arrived some thirty minutes later, Trent was sitting on the sidewalk, his collar torn and his lip bloody. He'd yelled at her for taking so long and Eva had told him he could walk home if he was going to be like that, at which point Trent had apologised. He didn't mean to take it out on her, he'd explained, and it was only because he was mad as hell at the bartender for tearing his shirt when they'd thrown him out, which kind of made sense. But then he'd wanted to go back inside and had that crazy look in his eye that made Eva certain the night would end badly, and somehow – she wasn't quite sure she knew how – she had managed to coax him into the car, then driven him home and helped him into bed, easing off his shoes and tucking a blanket around his shoulders. She'd left him there, with his mouth lolling open and his socked feet poking out the end of the bed, and the next day he had forgotten all about it.

Eva picked up her bag and ran down the stairs, the sound of Colette's snores audible through the door to the spare room. Doug was up and dressed – probably had been for hours – and was talking to Trent on the porch, his cufflinks sparkling in the morning sunlight.

'So, Trent,' Doug was saying, 'you looking forward to the new season? Word on the grapevine is you're going to be number one quarterback.'

'Shouldn't really talk about it, but...' Trent ran his fingers through his hair, his muscles flexing beneath his polo shirt. 'Yessir, it sure looks that way. Been working in the gym all summer, working to improve the athletic side of my game. Think we got a real good shot at the playoffs this year.'

'Glad to hear it, son.' Doug drained his tiny espresso cup and returned it to the saucer in his hand. 'Ah, here she is! Good morning, sweet pea.'

Eva stretched to kiss her father on the cheek as she passed.

'You ready?' Trent asked.

'Uhuh,' Eva said, 'let's go, I don't want to be late on our first day back.'

She climbed into the passenger seat of Trent's car. The floor was littered with fast food wrappers.

'Sorry about the mess,' he said.

Eva wound down the window to let some air in. 'It's okay.'

'My brother borrowed the car Saturday night.'

'Really, I don't mind.'

He slammed the stick into reverse, gears crunching, and swung out onto the road. 'We could always use your car instead.'

'Colette's car, you mean, and, *er*, no we can't. She's getting her hair done today.'

'Fine. Whatever.' Trent reached down, cranked the stereo and then gunned it to the end of the road.

7

By the time the first day of the new school year arrived, Sam was almost grateful, since it offered some relief from the slow death of boredom he'd been dying. It also meant he might see Eva again, which was a definite bonus.

He'd needed to get used to his own company during his first week in Montclair. His mum started her new job the day after they arrived. She was already gone when he woke up in the morning and arrived home late each evening. Sam and his dad had visited a superstore on the edge of town, where they'd wandered around, not really knowing what they needed until they stumbled upon a DIY aisle and his dad had filled the trolley with a range of power tools they'd probably never use. The next day, Sam had helped him put up shelves, but his dad's whistling and relentless optimism about their 'clean slate' soon grated, so Sam retreated to his room. He'd tried unpacking, rearranged the furniture several times over and even stuck up some old posters from home, but they looked lost and out of place, lonely islands of colour on the huge, blank walls.

Sam's mum offered to work from home on his first day at school so she could drive him in, and stupidly he agreed. As they pulled up outside the sprawling, redbrick building on the other side of town, he sank low into the passenger seat and watched as other students congregated in small groups. Most owned cars, got lifts with friends, or cycled or walked. As far as Sam could see, he was the only person driven by a parent.

'Do you want me to come in with you?' his mum asked.

'Are you off your rocker?'

'You'll be fine, sweetie.' She leaned across and planted a wet kiss on his cheek.

Before she could embarrass him any further, Sam grabbed his backpack and jumped out of the car. In front of him a path cut through a worn, yellowing lawn, leading to concrete steps that climbed to a large set of doors. He found the school office just inside and, after a brief induction, was given his individual schedule.

His first lesson of the day was US History, one of the compulsory humanities courses and a subject Sam knew next to nothing about. He left the office with instructions to find Room 24 and walked dazed through a maze of crowded corridors until a bell sounded. On cue the place emptied and he suddenly found himself standing alone. After several minutes of lonely wandering, he came across a janitor fixing a water fountain, who wiped his hands on his overalls and pointed up a flight of stairs. Sam eventually wound up facing a wooden door with the number 24 inscribed on a metal plate.

He peered through the window. The room was almost full and the lesson had already started. Instead of desks, each student sat in a chair with a writing surface fixed to the armrest. Eva was standing near the back, reading from a book. Sam waved through the glass but she didn't look up. All of a sudden the door flew open and he was confronted by a woman with hair tied back so tightly that it stretched the skin around her eyes, which only added to her air of annoyance.

'Can I help?' she demanded.

'Um, is this US History?' Sam said. 'I'm new.'

She lifted her chin and looked down her nose at him. 'So I can see, young man. I am Miss Forbes, and this is indeed US History. In addition to being new, you are also late. Please do not make a habit of it.'

'Sorry,' he said. 'I won't.'

'Do you have a name?'

Sam nodded.

'Is it a secret, or are you going to share it with us?'

'Sam Rayner.'

She clasped her hands in mock euphoria. 'Splendid! Well then, Sam, now that introductions are out the way, would you mind taking a seat so we can resume class?'

Sam looked at Eva. She smiled back, but the places around her were occupied.

'Where should I sit?' he asked Miss Forbes.

'Goodness, child! Must you have everything spelled out for you? How about up front next to Brandon? You can share his book until I find you a copy of your own. Please continue, Eva.'

Sam slid into the chair that Miss Forbes had indicated, next to a bulky boy who looked about twenty-five years old, and dropped his bag on the floor.

'Hi,' he said.

Brandon, the man-boy, glanced briefly in his direction and grunted.

Eva began to read again, her voice clear and steady. 'Theories as to the cause of the Great Depression can be broadly divided into two main categories. Under demand-driven theories…'

Brandon ran his finger along the print as Eva spoke, his face lined with concentration. Sam shuffled his chair closer to see the book. The heading at the top of the page read, *'KENNEDY LAUNCHES RACE TO THE MOON.'*

Although Sam's subject knowledge was poor, he was pretty certain the Great Depression had happened several decades before the moon landings. Lowering his voice, he asked, 'Have you got the right page?'

'Huh?'

'Look, you're on the wrong page. Can't you read?'

Brandon scowled, his cheeks turning a volcanic shade of red. 'What you saying, new boy?'

'Sorry, didn't mean anything by it. It's just—'

'Who's talking?' Miss Forbes snapped. She fixed her gaze on Sam and Brandon. 'I don't know how things worked in you last educational establishment, Sam, but in my class you raise your hand if you wish to speak. Brandon, I would have hoped you'd know better by now. Do you enjoy my company so much that you wish to spend yet *another* afternoon in detention?'

'No Miss Forbes,' he said.

'Perhaps you'd like to read instead?'

Brandon shook his head furiously.

'I'll do it,' Sam said.

'A volunteer, how marvellous! Looks like you're off the hook this time, Brandon.'

Sam took Brandon's book and stood up. 'Miss, which page are we on?'

'If you were paying attention instead of talking, you might already know. Page eighty-nine, third paragraph, beginning, "The Monetarist Theory."'

He found the page, cleared his throat and began. 'The Monetarist Theory, as laid out by Friedman and

Schwartz, was caused by the fall of money supply...'

He had almost reached the end of the chapter when the bell rang, cutting him off mid-sentence.

'Hold on!' Miss Forbes said, raising her voice to be heard over the scraping of chair legs. 'I know it's only the first day back, but it's time to blow out the cobwebs. I expect essay proposals on my desk by Friday next week. Remember, you're Juniors now. This is a big year!'

There was a collective groan and then everyone made for the bottleneck of the door at the same time. After the main squash had passed, Sam filed out and saw Eva standing at a locker a bit further down the corridor. She glanced up as he approached and said, 'Hi, looks like we're in some of the same classes.'

As Sam opened his mouth to reply, he suddenly tripped, stumbled to his knees and remained like that for a moment, as if praying, before there was a shove in his back that tipped him face forwards onto the floor.

He rolled over to see Brandon filling his view.

8

As Sam attempted to rise, Brandon lowered a boot onto his chest and said, 'Stay down if you know what's good for you, new boy.'

A chorus of snickers grew nearby. Sam dropped his shoulders back to the floor. Brandon remained standing over him for a few seconds more, then grinned, lifted his foot and walked away, laughing his head off. Sam waited until he had rounded the corner before clambering to his feet. There was a dirty smudge on the front of his T-shirt, the treads of Brandon's boot clearly visible.

He glanced up, blushing. Several passers-by were still staring, but they quickly looked away and began busying themselves, embarrassed to have been caught up in the spectacle.

Eva stepped forwards after the last onlooker had moved off. 'Are you hurt?' she asked.

'I don't think so,' Sam said, rubbing the side of his head. 'What's that guy's problem?'

'Don't pay Brandon any notice. He's just bitter because he was kept back a year...oh, look at your things!'

Sam glanced down to see the contents of his unzipped backpack – brand new pens, pencils, notebook and calculator – strewn across the floor.

'It's okay,' he said and stooped to pick them up.

'Here let me help,' Eva said and crouched beside him. She reached for a pen at the same moment as Sam went for it and accidentally laid her hand on top of his. Sam felt something pass between them like an electric shock, only pleasant. He opened his mouth without really knowing what to say, when all of a sudden Eva pulled her hand back and drew herself up.

Sam quickly scooped the last few items into his bag and stood as well. 'Sorry. Thanks. I...er...it's...my...'

Eva smiled and tucked a lose strand of hair behind her ear. 'So, how're you finding Montclair? Aside from the particular brand of brain-dead bully we have on offer, that is.'

He smiled back, relieved to have the direction of the conversation taken out of his hands. 'It's good,' he said. 'In fact, no, it's not. It's been pretty much the most boring week of my life, up until today. Your local variety of bully at least adds some excitement.'

'It's not so bad, once you get used to it. I could show you around some time, if you like.'

'*Really*?' Sam asked in a voice that came out embarrassingly high-pitched. He cleared his throat and tried again. 'Really, when?'

'How about Saturday morning?' she said. 'I'll come by your house.'

9

'Sounds like there could be romance on the cards,' Sam's mum said, placing her hand on his shoulder.

He knocked the hand away. 'Seriously, Mum, stop it.'

'I'm only asking. Can't a mother show a little interest in her son's love life?'

'I don't have a love life and, even if I did, the answer would be no. Categorically, unconditionally, definitely *no*.'

She did her best to look offended. 'Well, I think it's nice the two of you are spending time together. I've been so worried about you moping about the house on your own. It would do you good to get out for a bit and meet some people your own age.'

'I have plenty of friends my own age,' Sam said, 'and, as far as I remember, it wasn't my idea to move thousands of miles away from them all.'

This time his mum looked genuinely upset.

'Sorry, you're right,' he said before she could start lecturing him about what a fantastic opportunity the move was. 'I'll make new friends in time. Eva's a nice girl, it's just—'

'She's very pretty, don't you think?'

'I suppose, if you like that sort of thing.'

'And since when do you not like pretty girls?'

'I'm serious, leave it out. I wish I hadn't told you anything now.'

It wasn't just that he was trying to be evasive. If Sam had believed for a moment that there was anything more to Eva offering to show him around than kindness or pity, then those hopes had collapsed faster than a paper bag in rainstorm. All week at school he'd eaten lunch on a table by himself. Eva always ate at the same table and always sat next to the same boy. He was tall, with big muscles and precision-styled hair that suggested he spent a long time in front of the mirror each morning. They were obviously a couple, and Sam had no intention of getting involved in anything complicated.

The doorbell rang and his mum went to get it. Eva was casually dressed with less make-up than she usually wore at school, but somehow managed to look even better without appearing to make any effort. For the hundredth time already that morning, Sam decided that this was a bad idea.

'Did Doug get off all right?' his mum asked Eva.

'Oh yes, he rang this morning to say his flight got in fine.' She turned to Sam. 'You ready?'

'What's the plan?' he asked.

'I thought I'd give you the basic package, historical points of interest, etcetera. It'll cost extra if you want the extended tour.' She smiled at his mum. 'Nice talking to you, Mrs Rayner.'

'You too, Eva. And please, call me Rebecca.'

They stepped from the house into a bright, late-summer's morning. Eva pressed a button on her keys and the lights on a white convertible parked by the road flashed twice. None of Sam's friends back home could drive, although Lewis insisted he knew how and that once he was old enough the test would be a mere formality. Chrissie had taken a few lessons after turning seventeen, but had quickly lost interest, which was probably a good thing for road safety statistics.

As Sam climbed in the seatbelt automatically closed around him, pinning him to the seat. Eva climbed in beside him.

'Is this your car?' he asked.

'Technically no.' She leaned over to open the glove compartment, her hand almost brushing his knee, and took out a pair of glasses which she unfolded and put on. She must have noticed him staring. 'Hey, cut it out!'

'They suit you,' he said.

'Very funny. They make me look like a dork, but contacts make my eyes itch and I need them to drive.'

'No really, I mean it.'

She shot him a sideways glance and started the engine. 'You're a terrible liar, Sam. And no, the car's not mine. Colette's name is on all the paperwork, but she rarely drives it. As long as I finish certain chores, like picking up my sister from ballet class in a couple of hours, then I'm pretty much free to use it whenever I want.'

She pulled away from the house, turned left at the end of the road and, after a few more twists and turns, joined the freeway. There was a light breeze and barely a cloud in the sky. As they drove, the wind whipped and pulled at Eva's hair, causing it to flutter about her head.

'Do you always call your parents by their first names?' Sam asked.

'Always have. It was Colette's idea at first. When I was a kid she used to say "mom" made her sound old, and now it just sounds wrong to call her that, even though Nicole does. Besides, it creates the impression of a structure that doesn't really exist in our family. We each do our own thing. Nicole has her activities, Doug works all the time and Colette…well, she drinks and gets her nails done.'

'And what about you?'

Eva flicked hair from her face. 'As long as my grades are good, whatever I please.'

Sam's parents might have got on his nerves from time to time, his mum with her constant nagging and fussing, and his dad with his good-natured bumbling, but Sam always knew where he stood. They were his parents, never friends or equals.

Before long Sam and Eva had reached the edge of town. The buildings thinned and, shortly after, the road climbed into the hills to the west. The trees that lined Sam's road were more numerous here, and the car darted in and out of their shadows as it sped along. Eventually Eva turned onto a dusty track that climbed even more steeply. She slowed and then came to a stop in a clearing overlooked by a ridge.

'Where are we?' Sam asked.

'Only my most favourite place ever,' she said and got out of the car. 'Follow me; you need to climb for a bit to see it properly.'

She ducked behind a bush and started up a narrow path. Sam trailed after, branches snagging at his trouser legs. The ground consisted mostly of loose rock and dry earth, and every step sent a mini-landslide cascading down the path. He was afraid of falling and lost sight of Eva more than once, only to find her waiting a little further up ahead. At last he emerged onto a ledge some thirty metres above where they'd left the car. He bent over to catch his breath, both hands on his knees.

The whole town was spread out before them like a model. In the distance he could make out the grounds of the school and, on the far edge of town, the ugly bulk of the shopping mall he'd visited with his dad.

'Over there,' Eva said and pointed to the hazy horizon. He stared in the direction of her finger. Far away, sparkling in the sunlight, gaped the jagged teeth of New York's skyline.

'You can only see it on a clear day like today,' Eva explained.

'What's it like there?'

'Big, polluted, noisy. And people are generally unfriendly.'

'Sounds a bit like London,' he said.

Eva inspected the grass behind her and, once satisfied it was dry, sat down, tucking her knees under her chin and folding her arms around her legs. 'Big cities are the same everywhere, I guess. Do you miss it, your home?'

Sam picked a piece of dry grass and, twirling it between his fingertips, sat down next to her. 'There's people I miss. My friend Lewis, for example. It feels weird not having him here if I need someone to talk to, or even just if I'm bored. And there's my grandparents. And my sister too, although I never thought I'd actually miss her. I think what I'm saying is that it's the people I miss more than the place itself. People are what make a place special, I think.'

Eva gazed at him with her head tilted to the side as she considered this, and it took all of Sam's willpower to resist the urge to lean over and kiss her. 'I can see what you mean,' she said eventually, 'but places can be special in their own right too, like where we are now. I used to come here when I was just a kid. Doug was in the army before he worked at the bank and he used to bring me camping on weekends when Nicole was still a baby. I think he was worried I'd get jealous about not being the centre of attention or something like that, but back then, when he didn't work so much, we'd go trekking in the hills all day, just the two of us. We stopped on this ledge for a picnic once. I'm not sure if it was the quiet or just being able to see the whole town from up here, but this place always felt special to me.'

'Isn't that because you first came here with Doug and it reminds you of someone special?'

'Could be a bit, but Doug hasn't taken me camping in years. This place is all mine now. *That's* what makes it special, not the memory of being here with someone else. This is where I come whenever I need space to clear my head and think.'

'Is that often?'

'You'd be surprised,' she said, and dismissed the topic with a laugh.

After that they sat in silence for a long while. The only sounds were the rustle of the breeze caressing the long grass and the faint hum of traffic far below. It felt to Sam as though they didn't need to say anything at all, and he understood what Eva meant; this place was special in its own right, as if it had the power to calm the mind. He lay back in the grass and closed his eyes, aware of nothing but the warmth of the sun and the rise and fall of his chest with each breath.

When he opened his eyes again he wasn't sure how much time had passed. Eva was lying on her stomach watching him, her legs bent at the knee and her feet dangling in the air. She grinned. 'You were asleep.'

'No I wasn't,' Sam said.

'Yes, you were. You make noises like a hibernating bear.' She stood and brushed grass off her clothes. 'I need to collect Nicole soon, we better go.'

Descending the path was even trickier than coming up. They went slowly, Eva in front and Sam struggling with the loose footing behind. At one point he slipped and needed to grab an overhanging branch to stop from crashing down on top of her. After that she took his hand and helped him the rest of the way. Her skin was as cool and smooth as glass, and at the bottom he had to force himself to let go.

They climbed back in the car and followed the track to the road, where Eva turned towards town again. She drove around the outskirts to the mall and parked several hundred metres from its entrance, even though there were plenty of spaces. They entered through a wide revolving door, emerging into bright artificial light and easy-listening music. It was several degrees cooler under the industrial-sized air-conditioning and Sam shivered, the hairs on his arms standing on end. The main atrium was buzzing with weekend shoppers, mostly families with small children and the occasional group of teenagers with nothing better to do.

Sam and Eva rode a lift to the upper level. The doors opened in front of a pharmacy next to a unit with a sign that read, *Rosemary Lipscomb's School of Dance.* Through the glass front Sam could see a row of young girls holding a bar attached to a mirrored wall as they pirouetted and stretched. They were all between about six to ten years old, he reckoned, and wore matching pink leotards and fluffy tutus.

Eva checked her wristwatch. 'We're early still. Her class doesn't finish for another twenty minutes.'

'Where's Nicole?' Sam asked, peering through the window.

'Near the back, hopelessly out of time as always. She has no sense of rhythm, not that it puts her off. Let's eat and come back. There're fast food outlets on the ground floor.'

They doubled back, rode the lift down again and ordered at a burger bar. Sam took his tray and found a place at one of the communal tables.

'So, who's the guy I always see you with at school?' he asked when Eva joined him.

She unwrapped her cheeseburger and took a bite, chewing slowly before swallowing. 'You mean Trent, I think. He's my boyfriend.'

'Oh,' Sam said and sucked on the straw of his drink, making a slurping sound. It was the answer he had expected but not wanted.

'He's a good guy,' Eva said, 'in spite of what some people say about him.'

'And what do some people say?'

She set her burger down in its wrapper and frowned. 'The usual kind of thing is that he's a dumb jock. But anyone who says that doesn't really know him, just the company he keeps. Trent's actually really smart. He's only using sports to get a college scholarship, you see. He wants to study Economics, but if you're lucky enough to be good at something, then why not use it to your advantage?'

'I've never been very good at sports,' Sam said.

'I think the two of you would get along, as it happens. Do you have plans this evening?'

'You mean besides watching TV with my parents?'

'Doug and Colette are away, so I'm having some friends over. You should come.'

They emptied their trays and took the lift back up. As Sam stepped out on the upper level, the door to the pharmacy opened. A large woman wearing an oxygen mask over her nose and mouth appeared in a wheelchair. Her hair hung in dank clumps around her face and rolls of flesh overflowed the sides of the chair. Brandon was behind her, pushing.

'Look,' Sam said, 'isn't that—'

'Hide!' Eva hissed. She grabbed Sam's T-shirt and dragged him into the recessed doorway of a fire escape. It was a squeeze and the metal bar on the door dug into his ribs. Eva pushed right up against him so that their faces were only an inch apart and he could feel the warmth of her breath against his cheek. He bit down hard on his tongue and tried to think unsexy thoughts (his parents kissing / kittens / the bunions on his grandmother's feet) but overriding everything was the scent of Eva's hair, a thick lock of which had fallen onto his shoulder.

'Get me out of here fast, I wants me a smoke,' a rasping voice said. It sounded very close.

'But Ma,' came Brandon's voice, 'the doctor says you mustn't no more, for your health.'

'Nonsense, boy. I ain't letting no hoity-toity physician tell *me* what to do.'

'But Ma—'

'Leave it be, Brandon! You're not so grown I can't still show you the back of my hand.'

There was a ping as the lift doors opened, followed by silence. After a few seconds Eva poked her head out. Cautiously, Sam did the same. Brandon and his mother were nowhere to be seen.

'God, I hate that guy,' Eva said. 'I hope Trent hasn't invited him this evening. You think he saw us?'

'I don't think so,' Sam said.

He turned to see Nicole standing outside the ballet school with her arms crossed and her eyebrows raised.

'Aren't you a bit old for hide and seek?' she said.

10

Chrissie and Lance climbed off the night bus and, holding hands, walked the rest of the way home. Dawn began to break as they made their way up her road, turning the sky a wishy-washy shade of grey and filling the cool morning air with bird song.

'That was a good party,' Lance said as he followed Chrissie up the path to the house and past the FOR SALE sign that had been erected the day before.

'Yeah,' she said, unlocking the front door. 'You hungry?'

He stifled a yawn and shook his head. 'Think I might just hit the sack.'

'Okay, I'll join you in a bit. And keep the noise down: I don't want to wake Grandma and Grandpa.'

Lance mimed zipping his lip, slid his shoes off and crept up the stairs.

Chrissie went through to the kitchen to find her grandfather sitting at the table with a mug of tea in his hand and yesterday's newspaper spread out before him.

'Morning, Grandpa,' she said, wondering what it was about aging that made people go to bed and get up ever earlier.

'Oh, you're awake already,' he said and flattened the few remaining hairs on the top of his head. 'Kettle's just boiled, if you fancy a brew.'

'Thanks,' she said. 'Want a top up?'

He drained his mug, then passed it to her. 'Well, if you're offering, love.'

Chrissie fetched a clean mug from the draining board, placed it next to her grandfather's on the kitchen counter, then dropped a teabag in each and poured in boiling water. She hadn't eaten since the previous evening and, after a night of nonstop dancing, felt ravenous. The fridge was disappointingly bare, however, but close to the back there was a block of cheese that wasn't mouldy yet.

'We're running low on a few essentials,' she said, taking it out. 'I might pop to the supermarket later. Is there anything you need?'

There was no reply.

She turned around. 'Grandpa?'

36

He was staring at her with one eye half closed. The entire left-hand side of his face had sagged, and a stream of spit dribbled from the corner of his mouth.

Chrissie dropped the block of cheese on the floor and ran for the house phone.

11

Raindrops spotted the tarmac as Sam walked up the drive to Eva's house. The air was several degrees cooler than on any night since he'd arrived in America, as though the summer had finally realised its number was up. The house was even larger than Sam's own, which he still occasionally got lost in. As he climbed onto the pillared porch he heard laughter from somewhere inside. He shifted his weight from foot to foot, his finger hovering over the doorbell until he summoned the nerve to push it.

Eva answered. She was wearing heavy eye shadow and had straightened her hair so that it fell like curtains of dark silk. For a moment Sam lost the ability to speak.

'Come on in,' she said, 'you're one of the first to arrive.'

He gave her his coat, which she hung on a hook, and followed her down a hall lined with abstract paintings; random splashes of colour that resembled nothing in real life. There was a high-tech burglar alarm on the wall that looked like something used to operate a nuclear reactor. The place reminded him of an art gallery, expensive and breakable, making Sam afraid to touch anything in case he left smudge marks or damaged it.

At the end of the hall they entered a large, open-plan room. On one side a kitchen was separated by a long breakfast bar, on which an Italian-style coffee machine sat. On the other side a short flight of steps led down to a den, where three low-slung leather sofas surrounded a glass-topped coffee table, all facing a huge, wall-mounted television above a fireplace. There was a long dining table directly in front of Sam that supported an impress-sive selection of drinks and snacks, and beyond this a set of sliding patio doors leading out to the garden.

A few other people were there already, some of whom he recognised from school. Eva led him over to where a boy and girl were chatting next to the dining table.

'Trent, Kimberly, this is Sam,' she said, 'he's just started at school.'

'Hi,' Kimberly said. She was chewing gum and, in spite of the low light, wore sunglasses.

Trent grinned. He had his hair swept into a gravity-defying quiff. 'Hey, guy, want some punch?'

Sam accepted a glass. 'Thanks. What's in it?'

'Orange, strawberry, kiwi, banana,' Trent winked and withdrew a mostly empty bottle of rum from his pocket, 'and my own special ingredient.'

Sam held the glass to his nose and sniffed. The thick pink liquid smelled toxic, but not wanting to seem uptight he took a sip. It was sickly sweet and burned the back of his throat. He coughed and decided he would try to drink the rest as slowly as possible.

'I think he likes it!' Trent said. He turned to Eva and took her hand. 'Come with me, there's something I want to show you.'

'Make yourself at home,' Eva said over her shoulder as she allowed herself to be led away.

Much as Sam didn't want to admit it, they made an annoyingly good-looking couple. He smiled at Kimberley and took another sip of punch. She flashed him a smile back and began fidgeting with her bracelet. 'So, uh, what did you say your name was?'

'Sam.'

'And how do you know Eva?'

'Our parents work together,' he said. 'This house is amazing, don't you think?'

'Yeah, sure. Got a cigarette?'

'I don't smoke.'

'Never mind.' She crossed the room, went out the patio doors and tried to scrounge a cigarette from someone outside, leaving Sam conspicuously alone. Half-wishing he'd stayed at home, he walked over to the den and descended the four short steps. There was a cabinet against the far wall which was lined with DVDs. Sam started flicking through in an attempt to look busy. It contained an extensive collection of Westerns, mostly dating from the 1950s and 60s, and a row of Disney films on the shelf below. He pulled out *Toy Story*, remembering it had been one of his favourites when he was young, and started to read the cover blurb.

'We can watch it if you want,' a voice behind him said, 'but I prefer *Frozen*.'

He turned to see Nicole standing barefoot on the last step. She was wearing pyjamas with a ballet-dancing hippo motif and had her hair tied in bunches.

'Shouldn't you be in bed?' Sam said.

'Don't be a loser, it's not even ten yet.'

'Oh, right. What time do you usually go to sleep then?'

'When I'm tired,' she said matter-of-factly. 'Are you hungry? There's ice cream in the freezer.'

Sam returned *Toy Story* to its place on the shelf. Although he may not have anticipated spending the evening in the company of Eva's eight year old sister, it was better than standing around on his own. He followed her to the kitchen and poured the rest of his punch down the sink. Nicole fetched bowls and spoons, while Sam opened the freezer.

'Not that drawer, the middle one,' she said, perching herself on a stool at the breakfast bar.

He retrieved several large tubs of ice cream. A truck load of sugar probably wasn't the best idea in the evening, but seeing as how Nicole was already wandering around unsupervised at a teenage party, Sam decided it was the lesser of two evils. He draped a dishcloth over his forearm like a waiter. 'We have raspberry ripple, vanilla, cookie dough and chocolate fudge. The cookie dough is a particularly fine vintage. Which flavour does madam desire?'

Nicole giggled. 'All of them please, except vanilla. That's just dull.'

'An excellent choice.' He dished out two healthy servings and handed her a bowl.

'Where's my sister?' she asked between mouthfuls.

Sam glanced around the room. 'Your guess is as good as mine.'

Nicole quickly polished off the contents of her bowl. The doorbell rang as she passed it back for a second helping and Kimberly dashed past to answer it.

Nicole licked her spoon. 'You like her, don't you?'

'Who, Kimberly?'

'Not her, my sister.'

'Yeah, of course,' he said. 'Eva's been really kind showing me around and, you know, making me feel welcome.'

'No, I mean you *like* like her. I can tell.'

There was something unsettling about such awareness in someone so young. It made Sam suspect that, if Nicole could work this out, his feelings for Eva must be pretty obvious to everyone else.

'Does it even matter?' he said.

Nicole helped herself to another serving of raspberry ripple. 'I don't know, you'd have to ask Eva.'

All of a sudden the sound of raised voices came from the hall, followed by shouts and whooping. Sam looked up to see Kimberly return, followed by four boys wearing the matching jackets of the school football team. Last in the line was Brandon.

12

Brandon followed his friends to the den, eyeballing Sam as he went, then slumped on a couch, popped open a beer and took a swig. Froth spilled down the neck of the bottle, dripping onto the cushions.

'Who's that?' Nicole asked.

'I think you should go to bed now,' Sam said.

She dropped her spoon, splattering melted ice cream across the counter. 'I thought you were fun, Sam, but you're just like the others, always treating me like a little kid.'

'You *are* a little kid, Nicole.'

Sam wished Lewis was with him. He needed someone to talk to, someone who had his back. He took his phone out and was about to call his friend when he realised it would be the middle of the night in London. At that moment Trent came in again. His quiff was a flattened mess and there was a strange red line on his nose. Eva wasn't with him.

'Yo, Trent, over here!' Brandon called.

'I think I'm going to go now,' Sam said to Nicole. 'Thanks for the ice cream'

'Don't go,' she said. 'I didn't mean what I said. You are fun really.'

'It's not that. I…I just don't think I should be here. Tell your sister I said bye, will you?'

Sam was at the door to the hall when he heard footsteps approaching from behind. He turned to see Trent's fist flying towards his face and just managed to duck so that it skimmed the top of his head. As he opened his mouth to speak, Trent grabbed him, twisting the material of his shirt, and shoved him back against the wall. Sam's phone flew from his hand and shattered into hundreds of tiny pieces on the tiled floor.

'You were with my girl this morning,' Trent said, spraying Sam's face with specks of saliva.

'I don't know what you're talking about.'

'Don't lie to me, man. Brandon saw you at the mall.'

'Oh, that. That was nothing, just—'

Trent wound up to deliver another punch, but Sam saw it coming and hit him low in the stomach. It took the wind from Trent's body, leaving him hunched for a second.

Someone in the background was chanting, 'Fight! Fight! Fight!'

Trent's next blow landed under Sam's eye, slamming his head against the wall. The world melted to shapeless blurs without sound. As Sam stumbled forward, Trent tackled him, carrying them both to the ground. Sam's chin connected with the floor and the coppery taste of blood filled his mouth. He knew there would soon be pain, but in the moment felt nothing. Instead the taste somehow clarified his senses, washing the fog from his brain. Trent may have been bigger and stronger, but he had also been drinking, and there was no way Sam was going to take a beating without fighting back.

He sprang to his feet and, as Trent rose, punched him in the head. Although it wasn't the blow Sam had intended, it caught Trent square on the ear. He yelped and, for a moment, neither moved, as if they were both confused by this sudden deviation from the script. Trent's face gradually reddened. He let out a deep roar and charged at Sam, his arms whirring like lawnmower blades. Sam raised his hands to shield his face, but only succeeded in deflecting a couple of blows before Trent's fist struck him in the mouth. He went flying back, twisting in the air like a stuntman, and bounced down the steps to the den, finally coming to a rest in a crumpled heap at the bottom.

Sam sat up and dabbed his mouth with his sleeve. It came back smeared with blood. Gingerly, he got to his feet. Trent was on the top step, clenching and unclenching his fists, his breathing ragged and shallow.

Why were they even fighting? Sam wanted to put an end to it. He held his hands out, palms up in the universal gesture of peace, and began to climb the steps. 'Listen, I don't know what Brandon told you or what you think happened—'

A hand clamped around Sam's ankle and yanked it back. Sprawling forwards, he instinctively stuck his hands out to prevent his face slamming into the top step. His momentum took his weight from his standing leg, which shot back, connecting with something soft and fleshy that felt suspiciously like somebody's face.

There was a shout, followed by an almighty crash.

Sam rolled over. Brandon was on his backside on the floor behind him, surrounded by shards of the glass coffee table. He was clutching a gaping cut on his left forearm, his face pale as thick blood pumped through his fingers.

13

Sam walked alone through the night. It didn't matter that he was lost because there was nowhere he wanted to be. Slanting rain lashed against the pavement. A fast-flowing stream had risen along the gutter, washing the first fallen leaves of autumn along like tiny boats. Soon he was drenched, his hair slicked to his forehead and his feet squelching in his shoes. He was beyond caring, though. His body ached and throbbed as countless bumps and bruises surfaced. The cut on his lip had begun to scab, but every twitch of his mouth reopened it and sent a trickle of blood down his chin.

He clenched his fists, digging his fingernails into the palms of his hands. The clean slate was ruined, his only friend in America lost. Now Sam doubted if Eva would ever speak to him again. The idea of going to school on Monday morning made him want to vomit. He hated his parents for forcing him to come with them to this place, and for one dreadful moment he wished they were dead.

After a while the rain slackened off and the clouds parted to reveal mocking stars. Without even meaning to, Sam had wound up at the end of his road. Although he had no idea how long he'd been walking for, he suspected his midnight curfew was long gone. He checked his pockets for his phone, then remembered seeing it smash on the floor at Eva's.

As he approached the house, Sam saw that all the downstairs lights were on and at that point knew he was definitely in for it. He sneaked inside, hoping to make it to his bedroom without being heard, but his mum called his name from the kitchen before he'd even shut the door behind him.

Sam traipsed through, head down, braced for the onslaught. The clock on the wall said it was quarter to two in the morning. His mum was leaning against one of the worktops with her arms folded. His dad was at the kitchen table with his head in his hands.

'Sorry I'm late,' Sam said.

His mum scowled. 'Where have you been? And why is your phone off? I must have called twenty times. You were supposed to be back before midnight and...what's happened to your face? Have you been fighting?'

'It's nothing,' Sam said, 'I'm fine.'

At that moment his dad lifted his head and stared at Sam with puffy, red-rimmed eyes. He looked like an old man.

'What's happened?' Sam asked.

'Chrissie rang a couple hours ago.' His dad's voice was barely louder than a whisper. 'It's Grandpa, Sam. He's had a stroke.'

14

In little more than two weeks after first stepping off a plane at Newark Airport, Sam found himself back there, albeit under entirely different circumstances. This time there had been no warning and no time to pack properly. Like his parents, he had simply thrown the contents of his drawers into a suitcase and flung it in the back of the cab. Chrissie's phone call from hospital had been vague and confused, with no indication of how serious their grandfather's stroke had been. Their only plan was to get back as soon as possible, so Sam's mum had booked tickets on the next available flight.

The airport throbbed with passengers in spite of the early hour. There had been bad weather, a storm moving down from the Arctic Circle, and many later flights into Europe were cancelled or delayed. After checking their bags and passing through security, they queued to have their boarding passes and passports scanned, then filed down a long metal walkway connected to the side of the plane. Sam's throat was parched and his head ached from lack of sleep. More than anything he wanted a shower, a change of clothes and the chance to brush his teeth.

He was greeted by a blast of stale, recycled air as he stepped aboard. The flight was almost fully booked, meaning they hadn't been able to buy seats next to one another. Sam's was at the very back of the plane, some distance from his parents' near the middle. On the plus side, he had a window seat and would be able to watch as they took off. He sat down and peered out onto the runway to see that the sun had risen on a clear and bright morning, shrinking the puddles left by the night's rain.

'Excuse me.'

Sam looked up to see a man standing in the aisle. He had a tanned complexion, black hair slicked away from his forehead and was staring at Sam with dark, bulging eyes that didn't blink.

'I believe you are in my seat,' he said.

Although his English was impeccable and without the hint of an accent, there was something foreign about the way he spoke. Sam checked the stub of his boarding pass and held it out for the man to see. 'I don't think so. I'm in 34F.'

The man checked his own pass. 'Ah, here is the confusion, I think.' He patted the headrest of the aisle seat. '*This* is 34F. You are in 34G, which is booked under my name.'

'Sorry,' Sam said and started to get up.

The man raised a hand and smiled in what was obviously intended as a friendly gesture, but came across more like a wolf baring its teeth. 'Please do not let me inconvenience you,' he said. 'Regrettably, I am a restless flyer and do prefer the aisle seat. Perhaps we could swap?'

'Yeah, if you like,' Sam said and sat back down.

The man unbuttoned his suit jacket, folded it meticulously and placed it in the overhead locker. Then he sat in the aisle seat and took out his phone.

Sam turned back to the window and watched the ground crew finish their preparations. After a while the seatbelt sign flashed on the overhead display and the pilot's voice sounded over the intercom. 'Good morning and welcome aboard this Boeing 757, British Airways flight to London Heathrow. My name is Captain Gavin McGormick. We'll begin taxiing in a moment, so please remain in your seats and keep your seatbelts fastened while the sign is displayed. Today we'll be cruising at an altitude of approximately thirty thousand feet, with an average airspeed of five hundred miles per hour. Our journey should take a little over eight hours. Unfortunately, we've had reports of adverse weather conditions in Europe, so you are advised to remain seated with your seatbelts fastened at all times, should we run in to any turbulence. I shall now pass you over to the capable hands of our cabin crew. Please pay close attention to the safety demonstration, even if you're a frequent flyer.'

A tubby air steward with spiky hair and bad skin took to the floor several rows down. With theatrical twirls of his wrists he pointed out the emergency exits, then began demonstrating the correct procedure for fastening a life jacket.

There was a thud to Sam's left. The man in the aisle seat was upright in his chair, straining against the seatbelt, his body as taut as a guitar string and his bulging eyes unfocused. Blood flowed from his nose, spotting his shirt.

All of a sudden he convulsed violently and then went limp. Sam unclipped his seatbelt, jumped up and hit the button above his head to call for assistance.

The tubby air steward glared in Sam's direction, irritated that anyone had the audacity to interrupt his demonstration. 'Sir, the seatbelt sign is on,' he said. 'Please return to your seat *immediately*!'

Sam pointed to the passenger in the next chair. 'It's an emergency, I think we need a doctor.'

The steward approached, took one look at the man and gulped. 'Stay there, I'll be right back.'

By now several other people nearby had left their seats and others further forward were craning their necks to get a better look. With shaking fingers, Sam loosened the man's tie. Blood was still pouring from his nose. Sam shook him gently, but he was completely out of it. Desperate for something to do but not knowing what, Sam picked up the in-flight magazine and tried fanning the man's face.

The plane stopped taxiing and the pilot's voice came back over the intercom. 'Ladies and gentlemen, my apologies for the delay but a passenger has been taken ill. Please remain seated while we await medical assistance. If there is a doctor on board, please make yourself known to a member of the cabin crew.'

The steward returned, huffing noisily. The man's nosebleed had slowed, however his eyes had rolled back in his head and he was still twitching in his seat.

'What should we do?' Sam asked.

'I've alerted the airport and a team of medics are on their way. Maybe he has a condition or something. I suppose I should check his pockets for any medicine or ID.' The steward patted the man's trouser pockets and then shook his head. 'No, nothing.'

'The overhead locker,' Sam said, remembering that the man had placed his suit jacket there.

The steward reached up, opened the locker, pulled out the jacket and checked the pockets. 'Nothing,' he said again. He looked at Sam and frowned. 'Who travels on an international flight without a wallet? And where's his passport?'

Before Sam had time to consider these questions, a pair of paramedics entered the plane and hurried down the aisle towards them. The first to arrive was a short man wearing a cap with the peak pulled down over his face. 'What happened?' he asked.

'I don't know,' Sam said. 'He just came and sat down next to me and then started having a fit.'

'Move aside, please,' the second paramedic said. He was taller than the first and wore a similar long-peaked cap. As he unfolded a collapsible stretcher, his colleague attended to the man, checking his breathing, taking his pulse and shining a flashlight in his eyes.

'Is he going to be all right?' Sam asked.

'Too early to tell,' the first paramedic said. 'He's unresponsive. We'll need to get him to hospital as quickly as possible.'

The paramedics lifted the man onto the stretcher, placed a blanket over his torso and then strapped an oxygen mask to his face. As they wheeled him off the plane, Sam glanced down at his hands and saw they were covered with dried blood. He gagged, then went to the toilet to wash them, scrubbing away until the water ran clear in the sink.

When he came out the seatbelt sign was on again, so he hurried to his seat. At long last the plane taxied to a runway, where it paused for a moment before accelerating with a force that threw Sam back against his chair. He gripped the armrests and watched the tarmac shoot past in a blur. The plane lurched, its front wheels lifting, and then they were off.

Within seconds the airport had fallen away far below. The plane banked and continued to climb. The sprawling mass of New York passed beneath them and, before long, they were racing out over the sparkling ocean. They rose into a bank of cloud and Sam couldn't see anything for a while until they emerged into bright sunshine. The pilot levelled out and the seatbelt sign blinked off.

After a few minutes Sam's mum came and took the empty aisle seat next to him.

'I'm very proud,' she said when he told her what had happened. 'You could've saved his life.'

'Maybe, it's just...' Something didn't feel right, but Sam couldn't put his finger on what it was. 'I'm just worried about Grandpa, I think.'

'You and me both, kiddo.' She kicked off her shoes. 'Would you like me to sit back here with you?'

'Yes please,' he said and closed his eyes.

His last thought before he fell asleep was of the man's face and the smile that was more like a wolf baring its teeth.

Part II
Rewind

15

February 1969

Michael stirred from his uneasy slumber, imagining his father leaning over, bourbon and cigarette smoke on the old man's breath. 'Okay Pa,' he muttered, 'five more minutes.'

'*Pa*? Where in hell do you think you are, bubble butt? Wake up, it's your turn on watch.'

Michael opened his eyes to see Clyde's outline in the wavering candlelight. Sitting up, he rubbed the sweat from the back of his neck, his fingertips brushing the bump of a mosquito bite.

'C'mon, up already,' Clyde said. He spat a stream of chewing tobacco onto the dugout floor, wiped his lips with the back of his hand and kicked the cot.

'Okay, okay, I'm coming.' Michael swung his feet to the floor and began lacing his boots. 'So, you see anything out there?'

Clyde grinned, displaying a mouth full of brown teeth. 'Nope, so quiet you could hear a gnat fart. Now get your useless behind out of here and let me catch some shuteye.'

Michael pulled his helmet over his sticky hair and lifted his M14 by the barrel. As he climbed the steps he heard the whine of a mosquito and guessed it was probably the same one that had bitten him. With any luck it would feast on Clyde too.

The air was heavy and still as Michael followed the path to the camp's perimeter, offering no relief against the thick humidity of the night. The heat stifled him, even without the oppressive sun beating down. It squeezed on all sides like a straightjacket, making every breath an effort. Michael paused, leaned his rifle against a tree and undid his fly, peering out into the jungle and trying to banish the idea of eyes lurking behind every branch and vine. He whistled *Do Your Ears Hang Low*, droplets of pee splashing against the toes of his boots. It was the tune Eugene used to sing when Michael had been little and afraid of the dark, and it brought him comfort now, as if those notes had the power to ward off evil spirits, even thousands of miles from home and with the earth still freshly turned on his brother's grave. Three months ago, Michael had been back on the farm, the snow so deep that the pick-up couldn't make it up the road. It had taken four hours to wade into town to buy groceries for Pa. That memory now seemed an eternity away, and no more real than the flickering movies played in the mess hall each night. Michael doubted it ever snowed in this god-awful place.

At his post, he unsheathed his combat knife and held it to the moonlight to inspect the shimmering blade. He dug it into the sandbag before him, checked his magazine and adjusted the sights on his rifle. Michael had never been much of a shot. Eugene had tried to teach him a few years back using Pa's old Springfield to knock tin cans off the wooden fence behind the shack. When it had been Michael's turn he hadn't hit a single one, and in the end had trudged back inside to read one of his comic books, the shame of Eugene's disappointment dragging at his feet. At boot camp Michael had been bottom of his platoon during target practice and the first reservations about his decision to volunteer had entered his mind. It was one thing to aim at a paper target down a range and quite another to fire at a human being in the knowledge that if you missed it could well be the last thing you ever did.

'Kill or be killed,' the Drill Instructor had said, and those words had circled Michael's mind like a mantra on every guard duty and patrol since he'd stepped off the plane. When the moment came, Michael's life and those of his comrades could well depend on his ability to put a bullet in a stranger. The prospect scared him senseless.

He lit a cigarette, shook out the flame of his match and took a drag, immediately coughing as his chest rejected the lungful of tarry smoke. Michael had only taken up smoking the week before, since almost everyone here did it and it seemed a good way to fit in. For a while only the drone of insect wings disturbed the night.

Then he heard the noise: a sound so small and out of place that, for a moment, Michael thought his mind was playing tricks on him. But then he heard it again: the unmistakable sob of a child.

He fumbled with the safety catch and swung his M14 futilely in the dark. Doing his best to keep his voice level, he called out.

The sobbing stopped.

Michael dropped his cigarette and stepped out over the bank of sandbags, his rifle rattling in his hands. 'Who's there?' he called once more.

There was faint movement, barely perceptible, about ten yards ahead and then the sobbing started up again.

Michael tried to sound authoritative as he edged further forward. 'This is your last chance. Come on out now, or I'll shoot!'

A voice spoke, high and melodic, punctuated by small wails. Although Michael couldn't understand the words he recognised the fear underlying them. He took a step closer, then another. Sitting at the foot of a tree was a girl with a conical straw hat in her lap. She couldn't have been more than twelve or thirteen years old, he guessed. The girl cowered as Michael approached and lifted an arm across her face.

He lowered his weapon. 'What're you doing out here, little one. You lost? It's okay, I'm not going to hurt you.'

The girl spoke again, her eyes wide, her voice fast and pleading.

'Whoa, slow down. I don't understand.' Michael knelt beside her and held out his hands, palms up. The girl looked at him, narrowed her eyes and buried her head in her sleeve again.

Not knowing what else to do, he patted her gently on the shoulder. The girl cried out as if struck and jumped to her feet, sending the straw hat tumbling to the ground. It took a second for Michael's brain to register the significance of the object she was holding, and by the time he scrambled for his gun it was too late.

She stepped toward him, offering the grenade in her outstretched hand like a gift. As Michael turned to run the jungle lit up behind him. Out of the corner of his eye he was vaguely aware of the girl's slender body coming apart before a wall of fire lifted him off his feet.

16

Present Day

Images came and went, disjointed flashes of illumination, each dripping with ungraspable significance, each separated by numb emptiness, all happening at once and yet separated in a precise order. Days and nights passed in seconds, each heartbeat a lifetime.

The frustration and pain were unbearable. Sam wanted to give up, to leave it all behind and drift away to where there could be no more pain. But the images kept coming, thicker and faster, until he found himself fighting his way back up, struggling towards light on the surface. He felt movement, the pulse of blood in his veins. A burning sensation in his head was accompanied by pain in his back and chest, in his arms and legs. He tried to take a breath, but something was blocking his mouth. Reaching out, he discovered that his hands were tangled, as if tied.

Slowly he opened his eyes. They felt sluggish and gluey, dazzled by the dim light.

'He's awake! He's coming to!' a voice said.

Sam wanted to answer, but whatever was in his mouth gagged his words. His throat felt raw and stripped, as though he'd swallowed a hot coal. He blinked, the world swimming until it finally regained stability.

A heavy-set, middle-aged woman in a nurse's uniform was standing by his side. She was holding a roll of fresh bandage in one hand and a pair of scissors in the other. 'Don't try to move,' she said, her voice shaking. 'I'll fetch the doctor.'

17

Chrissie sat on her usual bench and chewed the ragged, bloody stumps of her fingernails. Her old life felt like a distant dream to which there could be no return. She hadn't smoked since the day of the crash, and only ever left the hospital to return home and change her clothes before coming straight back. There was no room for fun and excitement in this new existence, only a never-ending loop of stress and exhaustion.

Lance slept by her side, his head lolling on her shoulder, his breathing deep and slow. His hair had fallen over his lips, so Chrissie tucked it behind his ear to prevent him sucking it into his mouth. She'd told him over and over that he didn't need to wait with her and should go home, but he never did.

Chrissie yawned and checked her watch: it was almost five in the morning. After easing Lance's head from her shoulder, she stood and stretched, the joints in her elbows cracking as she raised her arms above her head. Lance blinked, mumbled something incoherent and fell back to sleep, his head bumping against the wall behind them. Chrissie felt like she needed something to fend off the tiredness, so set off towards the vending machine at the far end of the corridor, where she bought a white coffee with sugar. It was cheap, watery stuff, but would hope-fully keep her awake. She blew into the steaming liquid and took a sip, wincing as it scalded her lips. A backdraught of nausea suddenly hit her. She dropped the full paper cup in the bin and ran to the toilet. The last person to use it had trashed the place, leaving the taps running and the floor drenched with what she hoped was only water. Before Chrissie could make any attempt to clean up, her stomach cramped again. She flung the toilet seat up and vomited into the chipped porcelain bowl. When there was finally nothing left in her stomach, she stood, washed her hands and face, then scooped water into her mouth and swirled it around before spitting it back in the sink. It was the second time she'd thrown up in a week. Perhaps she was coming down with something.

She returned to find Lance awake and standing outside Sam's room with Dr Saltano and Mary, the large Jamaican nurse who cared for her brother.

'Is something wrong?' Chrissie asked, quickening her pace.

Lance turned, a wide grin on his face. 'There you are, babe. I woke up and couldn't work out where you'd gone.'

Dr Saltano pushed his steel-rimmed glasses up the bridge of his nose. He was a young man with thick black hair and perfect teeth. Chrissie supposed he might be rather handsome if he ever smiled. 'Quite the opposite, Miss Rayner,' he said. 'Your brother has regained consciousness.'

Chrissie felt her knees give way. Lance grabbed her arm and manoeuvred her to the bench.

'Fetch some water,' Dr Saltano told Mary.

'No, I'm fine,' Chrissie said. 'Can I see him?'

'Sam is confused and very weak, which is only natural given the circumstances, however I think the sight of a familiar face might help. He still doesn't know what happened or how long he's been comatose yet, so go easy on him.'

'But he'll be all right now, won't he?'

Dr Saltano frowned. 'After such a severe brain injury it's difficult to tell what cognitive damage he may have sustained, but the good news is that he's able to speak and has some motor function in his arms and legs. Why don't you go on through and see for yourself?'

Chrissie nodded and climbed to her feet.

Lance squeezed her shoulder. 'You can do this, babe.'

She kissed him and followed Dr Saltano into Sam's room. Her brother lay flat on the bed with a pillow propped under his head and a sheet stretched over his lower body. He looked up as she entered, a glimmer of recognition passing over his eyes. Chrissie had spent so many hours at Sam's bedside that she thought she'd grown accustomed to his appearance; the tubes and wires; the buzzing and whirring machines; his pale, waxy complexion and shaven hair; the long, angry scar behind his ear. But seeing him awake, moving of his own accord and breathing without the support of a ventilator, brought every emotion she had felt in that time rushing back. Tears began to pour down her cheeks. She wiped her eyes and sat in the chair at the side of his bed.

'I'll give the two of you a moment,' Dr Saltano said and left, closing the door behind him.

Chrissie reached over and stroked Sam's arm. 'Welcome back, little brother.'

'Where am I?' he asked, his voice a hoarse whisper.

'Hospital. How're you feeling?'

Sam tried to raise his head. He managed less than an inch before he flinched and let it drop to the pillow. 'What happened?' he asked.

'There was an accident. You've been in a coma. Don't you remember anything?'

He scrunched his eyes closed, then opened them again. 'We were in America, I think. Mum got a new job and...I don't know, it all feels so jumbled. Grandpa! Is he all right?'

'He's fine,' Chrissie said. 'He's at home with Grandma.'

'Oh.' For a moment Sam looked lost in thought, then, 'My head hurts. Where am I?'

'Still in hospital.'

'Where're Mum and Dad?'

She felt her eyes brim with tears once more, but tried to give a convincing smile. 'Don't you worry about that right now. You need to rest and concentrate on getting better.'

'What's wrong, Chrissie? Why aren't Mum and Dad here?'

She started to cry at full throttle, unable to hold back any longer. 'You really don't remember, do you? The plane you were on crashed. Mum's in a coma too and...'

'Where's Dad?'

'He didn't make it, Sam. He was killed in the crash.'

18

Sam wished the numbness would last forever, because he knew what was to come after would be much worse.

It didn't.

A hole had been torn in him that could never be filled. His father was gone, taken forever. The news on his mother wasn't much better. She'd suffered multiple injuries and was in a coma like Sam had been, however her vital signs remained weak, indicating little possibility of recovery.

Sam wasn't sure how long he drifted in and out of consciousness. At first the passage of time was confused, day and night blending into one, the seams between one waking moment and the next fuzzy and blurred. He was given drugs for the pain, which helped to blunt his sorrow. His mind was a disorientated mess, as if someone had shuffled the contents of his memory like a deck of cards. Some things were clear and vivid, others ripped from his recollection with nothing but gaps in their place.

He often woke to find Chrissie at his bedside and was glad, since she provided some stability in the constantly shifting landscape of his understanding. Sam's grandparents came to visit too. His grandmother seemed to have shrunk and her skin was withered like an old apple, but his grandfather looked as healthy as ever, almost as if the stroke had never happened. They brought a *Get Well Soon* card signed by people from his old secondary school. Sam barely glanced at it before placing the card on the bedside table.

The next day – or perhaps it was the day after – Dr Saltano came to see him again. By now all of the tubes and wires had been disconnected, except for a drip in Sam's arm, and he was able to sit up in bed.

'How're you feeling?' Dr Saltano asked.

'What do you think?'

If Dr Saltano noticed the resentment in Sam's voice, he didn't show it. 'I know you've been through a lot, but we need to do some tests, if you're feeling up to it.'

'Whatever,' Sam said.

Dr Saltano checked his blood pressure, poked his legs and the soles of his feet with a pin and shone a torch in his eyes. Then he sat on the foot of the bed, produced a small pad from the pocket of his white coat and began jotting notes. Sam watched him, waiting for an explanation. Eventually Dr Saltano put the pad away and folded his hands on his lap. 'There's no easy way to say this, so I'm going to be blunt. You're a very lucky young man, Sam.'

'I don't exactly feel very lucky.'

'Well, statistically you are. You probably don't know this, but of the four hundred and thirty-eight passengers and crew on your flight, only four people made it as far as the hospital, all of whom were sitting in the back two rows of the plane.' He took his glasses off and rubbed his eyes. 'I attended to one, a young woman only a few years older than you. She died of her injuries less than two hours after arriving. Another was a man in his thirties. He lasted a little longer, almost a week, but apart from alleviating his pain there was little we could do. He had a wife and two young children. That leaves only your mother and you, and I'm afraid the probability of her regaining consciousness decreases with each day that passes.'

'No,' Sam said. 'She'll get better, she has to.'

'It isn't my job to give false hope. I know it's hard to hear, but we need to be realistic. You have to prepare for the worst.'

'But there is a chance, isn't there?'

'A slim one, yes. And while there's any chance at all, please rest assured that your mother will receive the best possible care. You should take comfort from your own recovery, which has been quite remarkable given the duration of your coma and severity of your injuries. Your fractured ribs are now all but healed, as is the damage to your vertebrae. With any spinal injury there is always the risk of paralysis, however the tests I've just completed indicate sensitivity in your legs, which is an extremely positive sign.

'What concerns me most is the cranial injury you sustained. During the crash a sliver of metal penetrated your skull and became embedded in the tissue of your brain. We had to operate shortly after you were brought in to remove it. Often such an injury results in scarring to the brain, sometimes leading to a severe deterioration in the patient's cognitive ability and problems such as loss of speech and gross motor movement. With any such injury some degree of brain damage is almost inevitable. That you're able to sit up in bed and talk to me is, quite frankly, something of a miracle. You should be grateful for that.'

Gratitude was the last thing on Sam's mind, but he tried to push the thought away. 'So what happens now?' he asked. 'When can I go home?'

'I've booked you in for an MRI scan in a couple of days, so we'll be able get a better picture of the extent of any brain damage. Should that reveal nothing too untoward then I'm hoping to discharge you by the end of the week. You need to remember it's early days in your road to recovery. You've been in a coma for nearly two months and your muscles have decreased in mass in that time, what's known as muscle atrophy. You'll need physiotherapy to rebuild your strength.'

'I'll do whatever it takes,' Sam said. 'I just want to go home.'

19

Mary arrived in Sam's room holding a metal dish that contained a large syringe.

'What's that for?' he asked, eyeing it suspiciously.

'It's a special kind of dye. When you go for your scan it'll help the doctors see your brain more clearly.' She pulled the plastic cap off the needle, inserted it into the valve of the intravenous cannula in Sam's arm and pushed the plunger. 'I should probably warn you, though, some people say it makes them want to pee. Do you need to go?'

'No, let's just get on with it,' Sam said, and then his bladder went from empty to bursting point in a split second. 'Wait a minute! Actually, I think that might be a good idea.'

After the indignity of urinating into a bedpan, Sam was helped from his bed and into a wheelchair, then wheeled out of the room. Wearing only a hospital gown, he felt exposed and half-naked as a breeze blew against his legs. They left the ward and entered a lift at the end of the corridor. Mary pressed the button for the basement level, then wheeled Sam along another corridor and into a small room. At the far end there was a large, ominous-looking piece of equipment shaped like a giant donut.

A woman in a dark blue uniform was sitting at a computer terminal. She spun round in her chair and gave Sam a wide, reassuring smile. 'Hello, Sam is it? I'm Liz Moore, one of the radiographers here at St Benedict's. Don't look so scared, you won't feel a thing.' She pointed at the giant donut. 'This big old thing is a Magnetic Resonance Imaging scanner, or MRI for short. It's essentially just a fancy magnet that we use to take pictures of your brain. Gives us a better idea of what's going on up there. The scan itself is painless, if a little boring. You're perfectly safe, as long as you're not scared of tight spaces.'

With Mary's help, the radiographer lifted Sam onto a narrow table just in front of the machine. She secured straps over his arms, legs and body, then handed him a switch attached to the end of a lead. 'The scan should last about half an hour. I'll be watching on a screen in the next room. If at any time you feel anxious, unwell or unable to continue, then press the switch and we'll stop.' She handed him a pair of orange ear protectors. 'You might want to put these on.'

Sam lay back, feeling like chunk of meat on a butcher's block. The table lifted and then slid headfirst into the gap in the centre of the machine. A few seconds later the noises started and he was grateful for the ear protectors. It sounded like the world's largest alarm clock going off: a dull, pulsating buzz that went on and on. After what seemed an age the sound stopped and the table withdrew.

'All done,' the radiographer said, loosening Sam's straps. 'We'll pass the images on to a radiologist, who'll interpret the readings and write up a report for your doctor. You should have the results in a day or so.'

In the lift on the way back up, Sam asked Mary if he could see his mother.

'Of course, dear,' she said, 'you've done very well today.'

They entered the ward again but continued past Sam's room. Mary applied the brakes on his wheelchair outside the last door on the corridor and went in ahead. Sam's emotions were a strange cocktail of anticipation, fear and fatigue. It felt like he had run a marathon after the short trip to the basement, and although he wanted to see his mum more than anything, he didn't know what he might find.

Mary came back out and unclipped the brakes. 'Ready?'

'I think so,' he said.

She wedged the door open and wheeled him in. The room was almost identical to his own. Sam's mum was on a bed with a wire that ran to a heart monitor clamped over her finger. She had a strip of tape over her nose and a ventilator in her mouth. There was something so peaceful about her that Sam almost convinced himself she was sleeping and might wake at any moment.

Mary positioned his wheelchair by the side of the bed. 'Here we are then. Would you like me to stay?'

'Thanks, but I'll be fine.'

'As you wish, dear. I'll come back in few minutes and check on you both.'

'Mary?' he said as she was about to leave. 'Do you think I should talk to her? I mean, can she hear me?'

She stopped in the doorway and smiled. 'I like to think so. And if she can then the sound of your voice will be better than any medicine.'

Alone, Sam stroked his mum's hand. 'It's Sam,' he said. 'Can you hear me?'

She didn't move, although her chest continued to rise and fall in time with the valve in the ventilator. He lifted a strand of her hair from the pillow and rubbed it between his fingers. It felt glossy and smooth, like it always had. 'It's going to be all right, Mum. You're going to get better, I promise. I suppose you've heard about Dad by now. I want you to know that I'm going to get better. I'm going to look after Chrissie and Grandma and Grandpa. I won't let anything happen to them, so you don't need to worry. All you need to do is get better and I'll take care of everything else. I love you, Mum, please come back. I just want everything to be like it was before.'

He realised that he was crying, heavy teardrops spotting the white sheets of the bed. From nowhere, a strange, sweet smell like burned caramel filled the room. Sam felt dizzy, his vision quivering before him. It was all too much.

He laid his head on his mum's arm, feeling the warmth of her skin on his cheek, and closed his eyes, wishing there was some way to undo everything that had happened.

20

When Sam opened his eyes again he discovered that he was back in his own room with no memory of how he'd arrived there. He assumed that he must have fallen asleep next to his mum and Mary had wheeled him back, although how she'd been able to get him into bed without waking him was a mystery. The sun had set outside and a light rain pattered against the window. Sam's head ached and his mouth felt fuzzy and dry. He poured a glass of water from the jug on his bedside table and took a sip, but felt sick as soon as the liquid entered his empty stomach.

There was a knock on the door and Mary stepped in. 'Hello again, dear. How are you feeling now?'

'Tired,' he said, 'and hungry. When's dinner?'

'Not for an hour or so yet, it's only just gone five thirty. There's a visitor here to see you—'

'Chrissie?'

'No, a lady I've not met before. She looks very *official*. I told her you need your rest, but she was very insistent.'

He sat up and rubbed his eyes, wondering whom it could be. 'All right then, I suppose you'd better show her in.'

After a minute the door opened again and a woman marched into the room. She was tall and slim, probably mid-thirties, and held her back very straight, as if she practised walking with a book balanced on her head. Her hair, jet-black like her suit, was tied in a tight bun.

'Samuel Rayner?' she asked.

Nobody ever called him Samuel except for his mum, and only then when she was cross. 'That's right,' he said. 'Who are you?'

'Inspector Frances Hinds.' She withdrew a leather wallet and displayed her badge and credentials. 'I'm with CT Command.'

'Sorry, what's that?'

'Counter Terrorism Command, the counter terrorism branch of the Metropolitan Police.' She snapped the wallet shut and returned it to her pocket. 'May I have a few minutes of your time?'

'Sure,' he said, 'I'm not exactly going anywhere.'

'I understand that you were a passenger on British Airways Flight 0368?'

Sam had been so curious about his visitor that he hadn't thought about his parents for a few minutes, and to be reminded was like having a recently healed wound torn open. He fought back the lump that had forced its way into his throat. 'Look, Inspector...'

'Hinds.'

'What's this about?'

She blinked, her stony expression softening. 'I understand it must be distressing to talk about this and, really, I wish there were another way, but I'm afraid we can't wait any longer. Crash scene investigators have been going through the recovered debris, examining evidence and exploring possible causes for the tragic event in which you and your family were involved. I'm sorry to be the one to tell you this, but the crash was no accident. What happened was an act of deliberate sabotage.'

'Sabotage? W-what do you mean?'

'The findings suggest someone interfered with the aircraft's electronics. That constitutes an act of terrorism, which is why CT Command are now involved. Do you remember anything about that day? Anything suspicious? Anything out of the ordinary?'

Sam shook his head. His memory of the crash was weak at best, and he didn't yet have the strength to open the lid on that particular box and begin sifting through the contents.

Hinds took a business card from her pocket and leaned it against the jug of water on Sam's bedside table. 'Here's my number, office and mobile. I understand it must be difficult talking about what happened, especially in light of your own injuries. I had reservations about contacting you so soon, but I'm afraid we had no choice. You're the only witness we've got.' She stopped at the door and looked back over her shoulder. 'Oh, and my condolences for your loss.'

21

Sam sat for a while and stared at the wall opposite his bed. Thoughts fizzed through his head like a shower of shooting stars, each lasting for only a moment before being replaced by another. The crash was no accident. That meant somebody was responsible for destroying his family.

Anger gripped his body, blasting away the remains of any exhaustion. He wanted revenge. He wanted justice. He wanted to get out of this damn hospital and take care of himself rather than having to call a nurse every time he needed the toilet.

Sam kicked off his sheets and started rocking from side to side until he'd built up enough momentum to swing his legs off the mattress. The pain was so great that he had to bite down on his knuckles to stop from crying out. On the third attempt he managed to shift his body around so that he was facing the door with his feet dangling over the side of the bed. He sat still for a few seconds to catch his breath, then wriggled slowly forward, his feet inching down until his bare toes brushed the floor.

Now for the moment of truth.

Sam grasped the frame of the bed and, using every last bit of strength he had left, pushed himself onto his feet. He stood swaying, drenched in sweat, hardly noticing the pain anymore and grinning from ear to ear as a rush of mad euphoria swept through him.

Then, without warning, a memory slotted into place, an image floating up from the shadowy depths. It was a face, a man with a smile that looked out of place, more like a wolf baring its teeth.

It all came flooding back, the truth collapsing over Sam like the bricks of a demolished building. He remembered the flight and he remembered the passenger who had been taken ill. He remembered the man and his smart phone. He remembered the engines dying and the plane starting to fall.

Sam reached for the business card Inspector Hinds had left and realised he was shaking all over. Again, the strange, sweet smell of burning caramel came. The world seemed to pulse; a bubble expanding and then contracting. A bead of sweat ran down his forehead and rolled to the tip of his nose, where it gathered, gaining weight, and then dropped. The hall outside fell oddly silent. He looked down. The droplet of sweat hung in mid-air, suspended at the level of his waist. It was as if someone had pressed pause on a recording, leaving Sam standing in a snapshot of the moment.

Then things got stranger still. Without deciding to, he turned and climbed back into bed, his muscles going through the motions outside of his control. The bed sheet leaped back and wrapped itself over his legs like a living thing. Sam tried to shout for help, but found he had no voice. He was locked in, viewing the last few seconds rewind before his eyes.

The door stuttered open like movement seen under a strobe light; a string of still images shown one after the other, each connected but separate. Hinds walked in backwards. Her twitching moonwalk was like a drawing in a flipbook played back to front. She turned to face Sam, scooped her business card from the bedside table and put it back in her pocket. The images gradually sped up, the gap between each flash of the strobe shortening until they blended into one. Hinds's mouth moved up and down impossibly fast, her spasmodic gestures a blur. After a while she turned and reversed out of the room, then Mary walked in, also backwards. She began to speak, her lips fluttering up and down without sound, before she reversed out too.

Sam was alone again, but still unable to move. The sky outside the window brightened, clouds casting jerky shadows across the walls. Eventually Mary returned, back to front again and dragging a wheelchair. In one dis-jointed movement she heaved Sam out of bed, spun him into the chair and reversed into the corridor, pulling him behind her. People flew past on either side, all walking backwards, their limbs twitching like malfunctioning windup toys.

They reached Sam's mother's room. Mary scooped him up, dropped him roughly on the floor and knocked the wheelchair over. The room started to spin faster and faster until it became a blur, and then he blacked out.

22

Sam came to lying in a twisted heap on the floor next to his mum's bed with his arm bent painfully under his body. A beam of fading sunlight shone through the blinds, highlighting particles of dust dancing slowly through the air. The wheelchair was on its side next to him, one wheel slowly rotating. Sam's head screamed as if his brain had blown a fuse. He sat up and rubbed his shoulder, relieved that he could finally move again.

Mary was standing over him, her face lined with concern. 'Heavens, dear, are you all right?'

'What're you talking about?' he said. 'You just dumped me here. What did you do that for?'

She frowned and righted the wheelchair. 'Now why on Earth would you go and make up a thing like that? I only left for a few minutes, like you asked, and when I came back you were on the floor. You must have fallen out of your chair. Come on, dear, let's get you up.'

She lifted him under the arms and eased him into the wheelchair.

After Mary had taken him back to his room and helped him into bed, Sam sat thinking for a while. He couldn't make sense of what he had seen. It was as if the flow of time had been temporarily reversed, but such a thing wasn't possible. Even so, what Sam had seen hadn't felt like a dream or hallucination; the images had a certain quality, as though a filter had been lifted and for the first time he had seen the world as it truly was. Maybe there really was something wrong with his brain after all.

Dusk began to settle outside the hospital. Streetlights blinked on in the car park far below the window and it started to rain. Sam wanted to eat, sleep and put an end to this horrible day. After a while there was a knock at the door and Mary came back in. 'Hello again, dear. How are you feeling now?'

'Tired and hungry,' he said. 'When's dinner?'

'Not for an hour or so yet, it's only just gone five thirty. There's a visitor here to see you—'

'Chrissie?'

'No, a lady I've not met before. She looks very *official*. I told her you need your rest, but she was very insistent.'

Sam had a strong sense of déjà vu. 'Inspector Hinds again?' he asked.

'Oh, so you know her already,' Mary said. 'In that case I'll show her in.'

He sat up and rubbed his eyes, wondering what Hinds could be doing back so soon. At least it saved him the trouble of having to phone to tell her about the man he remembered seeing on the plane. After a minute or so the door opened and Hinds strode into the room.

'Hello Inspector,' he said, 'good to see you again.'

She stopped, a puzzled expression on her face. 'Have we met before?'

'Yes, of course. You left your card here, remember?' Sam looked across, but the business card was gone. It had probably fallen down the back of the bedside table, or been blown under the bed by a gust of wind. 'Never mind,' he said. 'I'm glad you're here, actually. I was thinking about what you said earlier, about me being the only witness and all, and I remembered something that happened on the flight. There was a man who sat next to me. He had some sort of fit and medics had to carry him off the plane before we took off. He had this smart phone...'

Hinds looked as if she had just swallowed a piece of chewing gum. Her stiff posture gave way and her arms slumped forward, reminding Sam of a wilting flower in urgent need of watering.

'Are you okay?' he asked.

'Huh? Yes, yes. Fine. Did you say something about a smart phone?'

'I was telling you about the man I saw on the plane. He left his phone in the seat pocket next to me. The thing is, I remember finding it just before we, you know, went down. Do you think that could be important?'

'Important? Yes, it could be.'

'Good, I want to help any way I can. Was there anything else?'

She stared blankly at him for a moment, then reached into her pocket, withdrew another business card and placed it next to the jug of water exactly like the first. 'You've been very helpful, Mr Rayner. I'll be in touch. Oh, and my condolences for your loss.'

She left the room shaking her head.

23

In spite of how tired he was, Sam found it hard to sleep that night, and when he did finally drift off his dreams were riddled with nightmares. He saw his dad at the end of the bed, raggedy clothes hanging from his battered body and his hair stuck to his face with dried blood. A part of Sam was relieved, even though he knew it was a ghost. He climbed from bed and went to hug his father, but the ghost began to fade, breaking up like wisps of smoke until Sam was left standing in the dark by himself.

Then he was at his mum's bedside, holding her hand. He stroked her hair, watching the rise and fall of her chest with each assisted breath. All of a sudden her arm moved and her eyelids fluttered opened. Hope bubbled up within him: after everything that had happened, this was a sign that things would work out in the end. His mum removed the ventilator, but as she opened her mouth to speak the rhythmic beeping of her heart monitor suddenly changed to a dull, continuous tone. Sam looked at the screen to see the repeating peaks and troughs replaced by a flat line, and when he turned back she was lying motionless in her bed. Mary and Dr Saltano rushed into the room. Sam yelled at them to do something, but Mary wrapped her arms around his waist and dragged him away, muttering, 'It's too late, dear. It's too late, she's gone.'

Next he was back on the plane. The passenger in the next chair shuddered and shook, his nose pouring blood. Just as the medics arrived the man opened his eyes and, staring at Sam, drew his finger across his throat like a knife. Sam shouted to the other passengers, desperate to warn them. He tried to unbuckle his seatbelt, but it was stuck. Suddenly the engines roared into life, the cabin vibrating as the plane trundled up the runway. He glanced down at his hands and saw that they were covered with dried blood. When he looked back up, every other seat was occupied by a corpse, their clothes tattered and torn, rotting flesh drooping from exposed bones.

Sam woke with the end of a scream on his lips and his heart hammering in his chest. Dr Saltano was by the side of the bed, peering over the top of his glasses. For a moment Sam wasn't sure if he was real or another ghost.

'You were talking in your sleep,' Dr Saltano said. 'Bad dreams?'

'You could say that.'

'Well, I have some news. The results of your MRI are back.' He transferred a steaming paper cup from one hand to the other and opened a brown folder on the bed. It contained several photographs, each showing cross sections of a skull from different angles with various areas shaded in different colours. 'This, as you may have guessed, is your brain. The scan indicates several regions of abnormal structure, particularly in your Parietal Lobe and Basal Ganglia,' he pointed to the prints, 'here and here.'

'I don't get it,' Sam said. 'What does that mean?'

'In itself, not very much. It's likely these abnormalities are the result of scarring caused by the foreign material we removed, however the human brain is an incredibly complicated organ and medical science is only at the beginning of understanding its complexities. There may be profound side effects, but then again you may be able to live a relatively normal life. I'm afraid there really is no way of telling at this stage. All we can do is wait and see.'

Dr Saltano returned the photographs to their folder and lifted his cup to his lips. Suddenly he cried out in pain and dropped the cup to the floor, showering his trouser legs with coffee.

'Are you okay?' Sam asked.

Dr Saltano produced a handkerchief from his pocket and began dabbing the stains. 'They really should do something about that machine. The coffee is always ludicrously hot. Don't worry, I'll send a cleaner in shortly. Now…what was I saying?'

'You said I might be able to live a relatively normal life. Does that mean I can go home?'

Dr Saltano pushed his glasses up the bridge of his nose and nodded. 'You've made extraordinary progress over the last couple of weeks. We'll continue to monitor you closely, of course, which will mean regular checkups and continued physiotherapy but, short of any unforeseen complications, I'm happy to discharge you. The best place for you to continue your rehabilitation is at home. How does that sound?'

This was the best news Sam could have hoped for, but something didn't feel quite right. 'What do you mean "unforeseen complications"?' he asked.

'As I said, there's still a lot about the brain we don't understand. Why, is anything the matter?'

'I don't know,' Sam said, wondering how to explain it without sounding like a nutcase. 'Something happened yesterday after the police lady came to see me. I must have blacked out, I think. I know it sounds weird, but it was sort of like time got scrambled and when I came round it was earlier than before, like everything I was seeing had already happened.'

Dr Saltano gave him a long, hard stare. 'Is this the first time you've experienced anything like this?'

'Yeah.'

'I see. Well, there's an established link between traumatic brain injury and the onset of epilepsy, especially when the patient has experienced bleeding within the brain.'

'I might have epilepsy?'

'It's hard to say. The condition itself is associated with multiple fits or seizures. For all we know what happened could have been a one-off; a consequence of the stress you've been under. I'll arrange for some blood tests and an EEG to monitor your brain activity, but until we can get to the bottom of this I'm afraid I need to take back what I said about discharging you.'

'Please,' Sam said, 'I just want to go home.'

Dr Saltano shook his head. 'Sorry, Sam, but it looks like you're going to be here a while longer.'

24

Sam nodded off after Dr Saltano had left, but this time his sleep was numb and dreamless. When he woke Chrissie was in the chair next to his bed. She had dark circles under her eyes.

'You look like crap,' Sam said.

She gave him a tired smile. 'You're one to talk. Just feeling a bit under the weather, that's all. A stomach bug or something. How're you?'

'Not good, they've changed their mind about discharging me. Dr Saltano says I might have epilepsy.'

Her smile wavered for a second, then she shrugged. 'Well if you do, you do. Whatever happens we'll deal with it together, as a family.'

'But Chrissie, I want to come home.'

'I know,' she said, 'and believe me that's what I want too, but only when you're ready.'

Sam studied his sister's face. There was something different about her, something he couldn't quite explain. 'The police came to see me yesterday,' he said. 'They think the crash could have been part of a terrorist attack.'

'I know,' Chrissie said, nodding slowly. 'They spoke to me as well. I know there're some crazies out there, but *seriously*?' She pinched away a tear that was building at the corner of her eye. 'I don't get how anyone could do that. All those innocent people. Mum. Dad.'

'I didn't remember before, but something came back to me about that day. There was a man on the plane who was taken ill. I think he might have had something to do with it.'

She narrowed her eyes. 'And you told the police this?'

'Uhuh.'

'Well then, I'm sure they're looking into it.' She reached down and took Sam's hand. 'Listen, there's something I need to tell you. I spoke to the doctors on my way in and they're releasing Dad's body from the morgue today. Once I've signed the paperwork, he'll be moved to a funeral home.'

'Oh,' Sam said.

'The thing is, we have to move quickly. I need to start making arrangements for a funeral. It looks like I'll have to book something in the next week or two.'

'But I'm still stuck here. You can't do it without me.'

'We may not have any choice, Sam. They can only keep the body for so long before, you know, nature begins to take its course.'

He jerked his hand away. 'I can't believe you'd even think about this. I need to be there. I need to say goodbye too.'

She pushed her chair back and stood, her lips squeezed together in a thin line. 'You think all this is easy for me, do you? You think this is all just a walk in the park? You might be stuck in here, but I'm the one left picking up the pieces. I'm the one who has to sign the death certificate, I'm the one who has to look after Grandma and Grandpa and I'm the one who has to arrange this bloody funeral. You can be so selfish sometimes, Sam, you know that?'

'Chrissie wait,' he said, but it was too late; she'd already left the room.

25

Chrissie was right, of course. Sam had been so caught up in his own problems that he hadn't even considered how the crash might have affected her, as though he had the exclusive rights on grief. He was sorry for that, but it didn't mean he had to accept missing his dad's funeral.

It was his own fault, Sam now realised. Dr Saltano had been about to discharge him before he'd opened his big, stupid mouth and ruined everything. In fact, when Sam really thought about it, the whole thing was his fault. If he hadn't been back late from Eva's that night, then he might have been home when Chrissie called to break the news of their grandfather's stroke, meaning his family might have managed to catch an earlier flight.

Tears began rolling down his cheeks. He coughed and wiped his eyes with the heels of his hands. There was only one thing for it: he was getting out of this place. If Dr Saltano wouldn't discharge him, Sam would just have to do it on his own. He pulled back the sheet, shuffled to the side of the bed and carefully lowered one leg at a time, trying his best to block out the memory of how painful it had been the last time he'd tried to stand. The chair that Chrissie had occupied a few minutes earlier was in front of him, but frustratingly just out of reach. If he could use it for support, he might then be able to make it to the door. Sam inched forward until both feet were flat on the floor and, before he could change his mind, lunged towards the chair with his arms outstretched.

He caught the armrest with his left hand, but only succeeded in pulling the chair down on top of himself as he crashed to the floor. Lying face down, he made no attempt to move. After a moment he felt wetness on his cheek and thought he'd cut himself until he spotted the paper cup Dr Saltano had dropped and realised he was lying in spilled coffee.

What had he been thinking? Sam couldn't even walk two steps, let alone the distance to the lift outside the ward, and from that to the entrance on the ground floor. Besides, what was he planning to do if he even made it that far? He had no money and no clothes other than his hospital gown. How would he get home?

Like it or not, he was stuck at St Benedict's and would miss his dad's funeral. To top it all off, he didn't even have the strength to pick himself up and climb back into bed. Assuming that nobody had heard him fall, Sam now faced the choice of either calling for help or waiting until someone happened to come into his room and find him, and neither option was particularly tempting. He rolled onto his back and stared up at the polystyrene squares on the ceiling. The pointlessness of his situation reared up and slammed down on him like a wave. There was nothing he could do to keep from crying. He didn't even bother trying to stop it and just lay where he was, sniffling like a baby with tears and snot streaming down his face.

Suddenly he smelled burning caramel. The room shimmered and throbbed. Each ceiling tile ballooned to twice its original size, then snapped back into position like stretched elastic. Sam tried to call for help, but his mouth wouldn't open.

It was happening again.

His body rolled itself over, his muscles moving of their own accord, until he was lying face down in cold coffee once more. A minute or two passed and then he was propelled backwards into the air, as if fired from a cannon, landing on his feet with his backside resting against the bed at the same moment as the chair miraculously righted itself. Next, his body shuffled back and drew the sheet over his legs. After a bit the door opened and Chrissie walked in backwards.

Sam wanted to close his eyes and shut it all out, but there was nothing he could do. Chrissie began lecturing him, her mouth flapping soundlessly up and down, her face angry and red. All of a sudden she seemed to calm down and laid her hand across his legs, palm up. Sam watched his own hand move to link with hers. Chrissie's mouth kept moving faster and faster. At intervals she would pause to look at him, as if listening, and Sam could feel his own jaw wagging up and down in response. Then his head plunged back onto the pillow and his eyelids closed themselves.

A minute ago this was what he'd wanted – to black it all out – but now lying here in darkness, unable to move or open his eyes, was a form of torture.

It was hard to tell how long Sam stayed trapped in his own sleeping body, but eventually his eyes opened and he saw Dr Saltano walk in, also backwards. Dr Saltano shook his head, a stuttering movement, and began to speak. Like Chrissie he stopped every now and then, at which point Sam could feel his own mouth moving as they took turns in a silent, backwards conversation. Suddenly Dr Saltano's face creased with annoyance. He took a dirty handkerchief from his pocket and patted his trouser legs. A paper cup rolled across the floor to his feet, as if carried by the wind. The stains faded from his trousers, forming drops of coffee that fell to the floor and dribbled into a larger puddle. The puddle poured itself into the cup, which when full flew up into Dr Saltano's outstretched hand.

Slowly the images ground to a halt until Dr Saltano stood frozen, holding the paper cup from which a motionless spiral of steam curled. Sam blinked and let out a whimper, his muscles finally answering his commands. Dr Saltano started to speak again. His voice was deep and slurred like one of Sam's dad's old vinyl records played at the wrong setting, but steadily it rose to normal pitch and speed. 'Therrrre maaay beee profound side effects, but then again you may be able to live a relatively normal life. I'm afraid there really is no way of telling at this stage. All we can do is wait and see.'

Sam stared at him, mesmerised. Slowly Dr Saltano lifted the paper cup to his mouth.

'Careful,' Sam said, 'it's hot.'

Dr Saltano hesitated and then blew into his coffee. 'Thanks. It always is from that machine. They really should do something about it. Anyway, Sam, your recovery has been extraordinarily rapid, and I'm pleased to say that there's no need for you to remain here much longer. You've made great progress over the last couple of weeks. We'll continue to monitor you closely, of course, which will mean regular check-ups and continued physiotherapy but, short of any unforeseen complications, I'm happy to discharge you. The best place for you to continue your rehabilitation is at home. How does that sound?'

'Like the best news I've had in ages,' Sam said.

Part III
The Funeral

26

April 1969

Lara descended the steps of her building and emerged into another beautiful spring morning. The sun was gaining height and shortened her shadow to a dark, crisp outline. She unbuttoned her denim jacket, noticing the increased density of freckles that dappled the fair skin of her forearms. Up ahead, a group of girls were playing skip rope, singing and clapping as they jumped. Lara stopped to watch the game, absorbing their joy for a minute before unlocking her car. She had the feeling that it was going to be a good day.

A cluster of grubby, longhaired protesters had formed just outside the gates of Stribe Lyndhurst Military Hospital. Lara honked her horn as she approached, scattering all but a few. A young woman in a floppy hat and Indian beads stood her ground until Lara drove directly at her. The woman glowered and thumped her placard against the windshield as she sidestepped out of the way at the very last moment. *Make Love Not War*, the sign read, although the O of 'love' had been crossed with a vertical line and inverted V to form a CND symbol.

Lara left her car in the car park and strolled up the path, spinning her keys in her hand. On either side flowerbeds bloomed with colour, perfuming the air. She tried to bury the unpleasant incident with the protester to the depths of her mind and not let it ruin her mood. Tensions in the city had grown palpable in recent weeks as public opinion swayed ever further against the war, but, aside from when directly confronted by it, Lara preferred to stay out of the politics. The circumstances by which her patients arrived were not her business. Her job was to help them get better.

She passed through the glass doors and entered the hospital's granite-clad lobby. Unlike many of its decrepit British counterparts, Stribe Lyndhurst was state-of-the-art and pristinely maintained. Built a quarter of a century ago to accommodate wounded from the battlefields of Europe and the Pacific, it now performed the same function for those returning injured from the jungles of Southeast Asia.

Looking into the mirrored rear panel of the lift as she rode her way up, Lara dabbed her lipstick with a tissue and felt pleased at her appearance. Throughout her childhood and adolescence in rural Scotland, her mother had taken frequent pleasure in reminding Lara that she was a bright but plain girl, and she had passed into adulthood rarely bothering with make-up and other adornments, her confidence scarred by that small but recurrent slight. San Francisco had changed all that, freeing her from the constraints of her mother's puritanical put-downs, and in the last six months Lara had found herself thinking, feeling and doing things that she'd never previously imagined possible.

She stepped out on the sixth floor, signed in at the main desk and prepared to start her rounds. The Lincoln Ward stretched over three long corridors that spanned the entire rear half of the sixth floor. It specialised in the treatment of service personnel suffering from a range of stress-related disorders. Each patient had his own room. Those on the first corridor were short-term patients, many of whom would soon be discharged in the expectation that they would be able to return to a relatively normal way of life. The second corridor was reserved for longer-term patients suffering from more acute disorders. Often these men had seen the worst of the fighting and bore proportional physical injuries to boot. The final corridor housed the secure unit, where patients deemed a danger to themselves or others were accommodated. The rooms here were referred to as 'cells'.

After visiting her patients along the first corridor, Lara pushed open the swing doors to the second. Isaac Barclay was leaning against the wall halfway down, talking to Betty Mclean, the new nurse on the ward.

Lara's pulse immediately quickened. Isaac was handsome, charming and one of the leading neurosurgeons in California before his thirtieth birthday. Betty appeared to have noticed that too, and was flirtatiously twisting a lock of long, bottle-blonde hair while staring into Isaac's hazel eyes with a gooey look on her face. Lara sighed and glanced at the rota to check whom she was supposed to see next. Betty looked like what she imagined most men would want in a woman: tall and voluptuous, with a sun-kissed body that she seemed eager to show off.

'Dr McHayden!'

Isaac stepped away from Betty and waved to Lara as he approached. Betty pouted and shot Lara arrows of hate with her eyes, to which she smiled back sweetly.

'Good morning, Dr Barclay,' Lara said. 'Just coming off nights?'

'It shows that bad?'

Checking that Betty was still watching, Lara laughed and laid a hand on his arm. One thing Betty didn't have on her side, when it came to Isaac at least, was an equal intellectual footing.

'It's been a long shift,' he said and moved a little closer. 'You should check in on Michael soon as you can. He's kept the whole ward up most of the night.'

Michael Humboldt was Lara's patient. At nineteen years old, he was little more than a fortnight off the plane in Vietnam when wounded. He'd been caught in a grenade blast during an attack on his camp and had lost an eye, his right arm below the elbow and had received sixty percent burns over the right side of his body. Amazingly, that wasn't the worst of it. In the explosion a shard of shrapnel had penetrated Michael's skull and become lodged in the base of his brain. The field doctor who'd operated to remove it had, understandably, given him a minimal chance of making it through the night. But somehow Michael had survived, and a week later was flown back to the US to begin treatment at Stribe Lyndhurst. The brain injury had left him with epilepsy. He was also morbidly delusional and convinced he could see into the future. In the month since Michael had arrived at Stribe Lyndhurst, he had already tried to kill himself three times, twice in the first week alone.

'Please don't tell me he's actually done it this time,' Lara said.

'He took a penknife from Joe's pocket and tried to sever his carotid artery.'

'Jesus wept! He didn't manage it, did he?'

'Almost.' Isaac gave a wry smile. 'Joe knocked him to

the ground and wrestled it back from him before he could get the blade out. And you know what Joe said when I asked what he was doing with a goddam knife on the ward? Said he didn't know how it'd gotten there. I had to suspend him, of course.'

'Of course,' Lara said. She let her hand slip from his wrist. 'I'll check in on Michael right away.'

'Lara?' Isaac said as she turned away.

'Hmm?'

'I hope you don't think it too forward of me but,' he looked down at the toes of his shoes like a nervous schoolboy, 'do you have plans Saturday evening?'

'Saturday?' She paused just long enough to create the impression she was actually considering it. 'No, I don't believe so.'

He looked up again and smiled. 'They're still showing *Space Odyssey* at the Balboa. I thought we could catch a showing, if you haven't seen it already, that is.'

Lara felt her heart flutter in her chest. 'Not yet,' she said, although she'd seen it twice. 'Pick me up around...'

'Eight o'clock?'

'Eight it is.'

This time Lara really did turn to leave, but before entering the secure unit she stopped by the gate to return Betty's frosty stare with another sunny smile.

Lara found Michael in his cell, gripping the bars on the window with his remaining hand as he stared out. Some of the bandages around his head had been removed, revealing patches of charred flesh. He didn't move until Lara called his name, and then turned with a vacant look in his only eye. 'Dr McHayden, hello.'

'Good morning, Michael.' She noticed there were fresh scratch marks on the side of his neck. 'I hear there was an incident last night.'

'Oh yeah, that.' He frowned and then winced as the muscles in his face stretched unhealed skin. 'Say sorry to Joe for me, would you?'

'Will do. How're you holding up?'

'It hurts.'

'The burns will do for a while yet. I'll look into getting you some stronger cream.'

'Not *that*.' He jabbed the side of his head with his finger. 'In *here*.'

Michael was on enough painkillers to sedate a horse, and Lara didn't want to up his dose again unless she had to. 'I'll see what I can do,' she said. 'In the meantime, I'll prescribe something to help you sleep.'

'Nooooo! I don't want to sleep. Not when there's so much to see.'

'You need to, Michael. To help speed your recovery. By the way, they're going to fit your prosthetic next week. That's good news, isn't it?'

Michael fingered the bandaged stump of his right forearm. 'Doesn't matter. I'll be gone soon enough.'

Lara hadn't seen him this bad since that first week. She stepped forwards and rested a hand on his good shoulder. 'Don't talk like that, Michael, please. I know you're in pain, but your recovery has been quite exceptional so far. Besides, you've got a lot to live for. You need to look to the future—'

'The future? Oh, but I do.' Suddenly Michael had grabbed her by the neck. 'The future is all I think about, Dr McHayden.'

Lara gasped as his fingers dug deeper into the skin of her throat, crushing her windpipe. She should never have allowed herself to get this close, should never have allowed sympathy to cloud her professional judgment.

'Michael, let go,' she croaked, scrabbling at his fingers in vain. 'Please, you're hurting me.'

Lara was beginning to feel faint now. In a few more seconds she would black out. She tried to speak again, but there was no air left in her lungs with which to do so. Michael tightened his grip. Pops of light exploded before her eyes like flashbulbs. She didn't have much time left.

A sudden wave of comprehension passed over Michael's face, his eye widening in shock. He released her and took a step back. At that moment the door flew open and Thomas, the orderly, ran in.

Lara crumpled to the floor, her lungs spasming as she sucked sharp gulps of air. Michael collapsed beside her a second later, thrashing and squirming as pinkish-white foam dribbled from the corner of his mouth.

Isaac burst in as well, nearly knocking Thomas over, then stood and gaped.

Lara clambered to her feet.

'You could've been killed,' Thomas said.

'Lara, what happened?' Isaac asked. 'Are you okay?'

'I'm fine,' she said, not lifting her gaze from Michael. Her hand went to her neck, where she could still feel the bite of his fingernails. 'It was nothing I couldn't handle.'

As Michael's fit subsided, Isaac and Thomas lifted him to the bed and secured leather straps to his arms and legs.

'I'm sedating him,' Isaac said, filling a syringe.

Lara staggered over. Michael's single eye fluttered open and focused on her as she looked down on him. Slowly his lips began to move, the words too quiet to be heard.

'What's that?' Lara asked, bending closer.

But Michael was already unconscious.

27

Present Day

Lewis shivered and pulled his hood over his head. The sky was a miserable blanket of grey and nonstop rain over the last forty-eight hours had left puddles the size of small lakes on the pavement. He wasn't looking where he was going and stepped in one at the end of Sam's road. Swearing under his breath, he squelched the rest of the way there, his left trainer soaked through to the sock.

The FOR SALE sign still stood by the fence, but otherwise the house looked the same as ever. Lewis opened the creaking gate and began up the oh-so familiar path. Over the last ten years he'd probably spent more time at Sam's house than he had at his own, and it felt weird to be back here; a place that, until recently, he'd never believed he would visit again.

Lewis had started sixth-form college in September, going along with the plan Sam and he had devised in his friend's absence. News of the plane crash broke a few weeks later and Lewis's world had been smashed to bits. Not only had he lost his best friend (or so it seemed at the time), but also his surrogate family. Was it really only two and a half months?

He banged on the front door three times and peered through the frosted glass panel until he saw blurred movement on the other side. The person who opened the door closely resembled Chrissie, although minus most of the piercings from her ears and face. Instead of her usual military boots, she wore a pair of fluffy pink slippers. Her hair, which over the last five years had been dyed every colour of the rainbow, was now a mousy blonde. She gasped when she saw him and threw her arms around his neck. The real Chrissie had never shown Lewis the slightest affection in all the years they'd known one another, and he felt distinctly awkward returning her hug.

Eventually anti-Chrissie released him. 'Where are my manners?' she said. 'Come in out of the rain. Can I take your coat?'

Lewis unzipped the dripping garment and passed it over. 'I'm sorry about your dad,' he said.

'Thanks, I know you two were close.' She turned to hang his coat on the end of the banister. 'You're coming to the funeral, aren't you?'

Lewis felt a tear sting his eye and wiped it away while Chrissie was still facing the other way. 'Wouldn't miss it,' he said. 'So…how's Sam holding up?'

'He's alive, and that's the main thing.' She turned back to him and gave a small shake of her head. 'It's just, well, he's been acting so strangely.'

'That's to be expected, I reckon.'

'Yeah, I suppose so. Anyway, you'll see for yourself in a minute. Come on through.'

Lewis's stomach had wound itself into a knot several hours ago and it twisted even tighter as he followed Chrissie to the sitting room. Sam was lying on the couch with his back propped up by several large cushions. The first thing Lewis noticed was how much weight his friend had lost. Sam had never been fat, but now he had shrivelled to skin and bones. His hair had been shaved in a crew cut, under which Lewis could make out a curving scar behind his ear, still angry and red.

'Easy, mate,' Lewis said. 'How's it going?'

Sam didn't respond. Although the television was off, his gaze remained fixed on the screen.

Chrissie stepped forward and shook her brother gently by the shoulder. 'Sam? Lewis is here.'

Sam started and looked past her, blinking as if he'd just emerged from a dark tunnel. 'Lewis, you came!'

'Course I did,' Lewis said.

Chrissie left and, once they were alone, he pulled one of the armchairs closer so he could sit facing Sam. 'I wanted to visit you in hospital, but they said it was family only. Not sure about the new hair style, by the way.'

'No?' Sam ran his hand over his scalp, his fingertips briefly resting on the ridge of the scar. 'Me neither. At least when it grows back it'll cover this.'

'It's not that bad,' Lewis lied. He handed Sam the plastic bag he'd brought. 'Here, I got you some magazines in case you get bored. And Connor made you a card at nursery. It's meant to be an elephant, I think.'

'Thanks,' Sam said and placed the bag by the side of the couch without looking inside.

A moment passed, the silence broken only by the tick-tocking of the clock on the wall. When they were younger and used to have sleepovers, they would stay up all night talking, but right now Lewis couldn't think of a single word to say. He tugged at a loose thread in the seam of his jeans, took a deep breath and slowly let it out. 'You look okay. I mean, I was expecting much worse.'

'The doctors say they're really happy with my recovery, and I've been having physio every day, which helps. A week ago I couldn't even stand up by myself, it's just…'

'What?'

'The strangest stuff's been happening to me,' Sam said. 'I don't really know how to explain it, but I think there's something wrong with my brain. Something happened while I was in hospital and it was like time froze and then started going backwards. But that sounds crazy, doesn't it?'

Lewis rubbed the section of his chin where downy stubble sprouted. 'A little,' he said, 'but I wouldn't worry about it. I think after everything you've been through there'd be something wrong if you felt completely fine.'

'Maybe you're right,' Sam said and relaxed back against his cushions. 'The police came to see me, you know.'

'Really? What did they want?'

'To talk about the crash. They think someone sabotaged the plane.'

Lewis nodded. 'Yeah, it's been all over the news. You can't even bring your phone on a flight anymore. People are saying it's bad for the economy but—'

'The thing is, I remember something about that day.' Sam leaned forwards, the veins around his temples bulging under his skin. 'There was this guy who sat next to me on the plane. He had some sort of fit and paramedics had to come and take him away before we took off. It was him who caused it, Lewis, I'm sure of it. He did this to me. He murdered my dad.'

Lewis squirmed in his seat. It was only natural for Sam to feel angry, he supposed, but that didn't make hearing it any more comfortable. 'What makes you so sure?' he asked. 'I mean, if this guy wasn't even on the plane when you took off, then how could he have sabotaged it?'

'He left his phone in the seat pocket. It started ringing just before we went down.'

Ordinarily Lewis would have told Sam to get a grip, but under the current circumstances it didn't feel like the right thing to do. Instead he joined his friend on the couch, went to put his arm around Sam's shoulders, then stopped and withdrew it. 'Leave this to the police,' he said. 'Stressing about it won't help, and I'm sure they'll catch this guy if there's anything to it.'

'Maybe.'

'There's no maybe about it. You're home now and the only thing you need to worry about is getting better.

We're all here for you, Sam, especially me. Just say if there's anything I can do to help.'

'You don't have a time machine, do you?'

'Afraid not,' Lewis said.

'Then there's nothing anyone can do.'

28

Matthew Rayner's birthday was the first day of December. He would have been forty-eight years old. Last year the family had booked a table at the Indian restaurant on the high street, where Chrissie's father had drunk too much beer and, before the end of the main course, started to sing loudly. Although he was a musician by trade, he had a lousy singing voice. As he'd worked his way through a selection of Elvis's hits, his lip curled back and his eyebrows wiggling, heads had turned and an array of disapproving looks were cast in their direction. Chrissie remembered sinking low into her chair, wishing the ground would swallow her up.

This year she'd spent her dad's birthday making the final preparations for his funeral, which was to be held that weekend. With Sam only a week out of hospital and her grandparents in no state to help, she'd needed to make most of the arrangements herself. Lance insisted she was taking on too much in her condition, but there was no one else to do it and Chrissie was fast becoming used to her role as the responsible adult of the house.

Although arranging a funeral was more complicated than she had imagined, she went about contacting undertakers, selecting a coffin, choosing flowers, booking a venue and sending out invites with a composed efficiency that she'd never even realised she possessed. She had booked the church in the village where her dad had grown up. It would make her grandmother happy and, although he hadn't been religious, it felt right that this should be his final resting place, almost as though he were returning home.

Over the last couple of months, Chrissie had often found herself questioning her own views on the afterlife. After being expelled from secondary school she'd attended a convent for almost three years (her parents had misguidedly believed that the structure would do her good) where Catholic dogma and discipline had given her something new to rebel against. She'd never really bought into the conventional concepts of heaven and hell. The idea of a fluffy paradise in the clouds for the good and some eternally boiling pit of lava where the wicked were punished sounded like tales concocted to scare small children into brushing their teeth and eating their vegetables.

Since the crash, however, Chrissie couldn't help but wonder if death really was the final curtain call she'd always supposed it to be, or if maybe, just maybe, there was some form of existence beyond the grave. Perhaps it was the comfort of imagining that somewhere out there, on some mystical plain beyond human reach, a part of her father lived on. Or perhaps it was awareness of her own mortality sharpened by the new life growing inside her, for out of the sadness an unexpected shoot of happiness had sprouted.

Chrissie was going to be a mother.

On the afternoon of Chrissie's dad's birthday, the family visited her mother in hospital. There was no change in her condition, so Chrissie changed the flowers by her bed-side, combed her hair, painted her nails and left after an hour feeling her usual sense of despondency. Later, she helped her grandmother prepare a special dinner: roast chicken with roast potatoes, veg and gravy. It had been her dad's favourite.

That evening they sat down to eat, Chrissie and Lance on one side of the table, her grandparents on the other and Sam at the head. A sober air hung over them as Lance carved the chicken. They passed round plates without talking, as if nobody had the stomach to verbalise what they were all thinking.

'Sod this,' Grandpa said eventually. He raised his glass of water (alcohol was strictly off the menu since his stroke) and looked around the table, his face breaking into a smile. 'Here's to Matthew. He wouldn't want us all sitting around looking miserable on his birthday, now would he?'

'No,' Chrissie said, remembering her father's drunken antics the year before. 'Here's to you, Dad, wherever you are.'

Lance laid down the carving knife. 'I didn't know him that well, but he always seemed like a cool guy.'

'To Matthew.' Chrissie's grandmother raised her glass and emitted a sob. 'The best son any mother could ask for.'

Sam squeezed her hand. 'And to Mum,' he said, 'wishing you a quick recovery. We want you home soon.'

'Hear, hear!' Their grandfather rapped his walking stick on the tiles. 'To a quick recovery. And to catching the bastards who did this to you both.'

There was a murmur of agreement and then they started to eat. Grandma was an excellent cook, and before long there were five empty plates on the table. Chrissie stood and began stacking them by the sink.

'Babe, I'll do that,' Lance said, rising to intercept her.

'I'm not an invalid.'

He sighed. 'I know, it's just you shouldn't be lifting anything heavy.'

'They're only plates,' she said and continued to clear the table. Lance's comment appeared to have gone unnoticed, but there was no point putting it off any longer. Chrissie turned to face her family. 'Actually, there's another reason I wanted to get us all together this evening. Lance and I have some news. It's still early days, but—'

The phone rang in the hall, cutting her off.

'I'll get it,' Sam said. He lifted his crutches from the side of the table and hobbled to the door.

'What were you saying, pet?' Chrissie's grandmother asked.

'Never mind.' She returned to the table and sat down. 'It doesn't matter.'

Lance stuck his bottom lip out and gave her a dopey, hurt look.

'Not now,' she said and patted his knee. 'There'll be a better time.'

'Who's for pudding?' her grandmother asked after a while. 'I've made apple crumble and custard.'

Sam returned as she got up, his crutches creaking under his weight. His face was pale and his eyes were glassy.

'Who was it?' Chrissie asked.

'Inspector Hinds.'

'Who?'

'The police officer investigating the crash.' Sam teetered in the doorway for a moment, then held himself upright. 'She says she wants to see me again. They may have a lead.'

29

Sam's dad had owned a sizable life insurance policy, and even though the estate agent hadn't removed the sign yet, Chrissie had taken the house off the market soon after the crash. Their grandparents had moved in and Lance had taken up semi-permanent residency in Chrissie's bedroom. Although the house was now full of people, Sam kept seeing ghosts everywhere, long forgotten memories of his parents surfacing at the smallest of triggers.

Inspector Hinds came to visit a couple of days after calling on his dad's birthday. She arrived half an hour early, just as Sam's physiotherapist was leaving, and was followed by two men as she entered the sitting room. The first wore a turtleneck jumper and faded brown leather jacket. He looked to be approaching late middle age, with thin, greying hair and a goatee beard shaped into a sharp point under his chin. The second man was much younger, probably under thirty. He was tall, with close-set blue eyes and neat blonde hair combed in a side parting. There was something strange about the way he walked, and he stopped to look about with mild disgust as he stepped into the room.

Sam reached for his crutches to stand.

'Please, don't get up,' Hinds said. She tilted her head towards the older man. 'This is Clive Kalinsky. He's a forensic artist, one of the best we've got.'

'You're too kind, Frances,' Kalinsky said and smiled.

'And you're too modest. The reconstructions Clive produces have been instrumental in cracking several high-profile cases.' She nodded towards the younger man. 'And Mr Steele here is with the Security Service. He's been assisting us with our investigations.'

'Nice to meet you both,' Sam said. 'Please, have a seat.'

Hinds joined him on the couch, while the men took an armchair each, Steele laying a handkerchief on the cushion of his chair, hiking up the legs of his trousers as he sat and then carefully straightening the creases. Hinds rummaged in her bag and pulled out a thick, heavy-looking lever arch file.

At that moment Sam's grandmother bustled in. 'Heavens, I feel awful about the mess,' she said. 'It's been ages since we last had visitors. Would anyone like a cup of tea? Or some biscuits?'

'No thank you, madam,' Hinds said.

Steele and Kalinsky both shook their heads.

'Or something savoury? I could rustle up some sandwiches, it really is no trouble.'

'Grandma, they said they're fine,' Sam said.

She gave a disappointed huff. 'Well then, if there's nothing you need, I'm going to the shops. We're having spaghetti bolognaise for tea, pet.'

'Okay,' he said and rolled his eyes as she left.

Hinds opened the file and passed it to Sam. It contained page after page of photographs, each cropped around the person's head and shoulders. 'We're interested in identifying the man you say became ill before your flight took off,' she explained. 'I'd like you to have a look over some mug shots to see if there's anyone you recognise.'

Sam began to flick through, carefully studying each picture at first, but turning the pages faster as he went. At last he closed the file and shook his head.

'Don't be too disheartened,' Hinds said. 'It was always a long shot, but you never know. Most of the people in that file have known or suspected terrorist links, but they're only the tip of the iceberg. There're plenty of reasons why the man you saw might not be included. It could be that he's never been arrested before, or is a new recruit—'

Steele cleared his throat. 'That is, of course, if he even exists.'

'Excuse me?' Sam said.

'It would be unwise to rule out any possibility at this stage of the investigation.'

'You think I'm making the whole thing up?'

'I'm not sure,' Steele said, fixing Sam in his cold, blue gaze. 'Why, are you?'

Sam glanced to Hinds for support, but she immediately lowered her eyes and began tugging at one of her earrings, looking like she couldn't remember whether she'd switched the iron off before leaving for work that morning.

Sam felt sweat break out on his forehead. 'Of course not,' he said. 'Why would I do something like that?'

Steele smiled and brushed an imaginary speck of dust from his sleeve. 'As I'm sure you already know, Mr Rayner, Flight 0368 was brought down by an act of deliberate sabotage. We've been aware that certain terrorist fractions have been developing electronic jam-ming devices for some time now, but until recently all of the samples that we've managed to intercept have been concealed as handheld electronic equipment; smart phones, tablets, laptops and the such. All had one flaw in common, namely the inability to perform the function of the gadgets they were disguised as, meaning they could be detected simply by asking passengers to switch their devices on.

'Although this hasn't been released to the press yet, fragments of the jamming device that brought down Flight 0368 were recovered at the scene. What we found was something different, something designed to bypass our security measures. The contraption in question was stowed in the baggage hold. It was checked in and remotely activated during the flight – remotely activated by the smart phone found in *your* hand when emergency crews pulled you from the wreck.'

The conversation was tumbling out of control, and Sam didn't like where it was headed. He heaved himself up off the couch and, without his crutches, stood to face Steele. 'Look, I don't know who you are, barging in here and accusing me of all sorts of stuff. I can see where you're going with this, and I don't appreciate it.'

Steele watched him without a trace of emotion. 'I suggest you sit down before you do yourself harm.'

Sam glared back, but couldn't stop his legs from shaking. After a few seconds he crumpled back to his seat, exhausted.

'That's better,' Steele said. 'I think we all need to calm down. I'm only expounding a theory, but not one that seems likely to me. For a start, I have to ask myself what motive a sixteen-year-old boy would have in perpetrating such an act.'

'And?'

'In all honesty, I can't think of one. The report also states that your mother and father were involved in the crash—'

'My dad was killed.'

Steele paused for a moment and adjusted his cuffs. 'Yes, indeed. And whilst that is extremely unfortunate, it does, however, lend weight to the notion that you had nothing to do with the crash. Furthermore, a key piece of evidence supports your account of events. The closed circuit television recordings from inside the airport have been analysed and, just after take-off, they show what appears to be a team of paramedics escorting a man in a stretcher to an ambulance parked outside the terminal.'

'What do you mean, "appears to be"?' Sam asked.

'I've checked with my colleagues at the CIA and they can't find any record of an ambulance being dispatched to Newark Airport on the day of the flight, which suggests the paramedics were not what they seemed.'

'I…I'm not sure I follow.'

Steele made a clicking noise with his tongue. 'What I'm suggesting is that the seizure was feigned, and this team of so-called paramedics were, in actual fact, part of the plot. If so, it seems certain that everything you witnessed that day was part of an elaborate deception intended to plant both the jamming device and trigger on board the plane. Whomever we're dealing with is both highly organised and well-funded.'

Sam sat still for a moment, unable to move, his head spinning as he tried to take in what Steele was telling him.

'You said there's surveillance footage of them leaving the airport?' he said after a while.

'That's correct.'

'Well, wouldn't it be possible to enlarge the footage to get a better look at this guy?'

Steele smiled, a brief twitch of his lips that contained no humour. 'We've tried that and, unfortunately, it seems they were prepared for such an eventuality. The man on the stretcher was wearing an oxygen mask and the medics used baseball caps to obscure their faces, meaning we weren't able to get a clear shot of any of them. An external camera *did* manage to capture an image of the ambulance's registration plate, but that only led to a twenty-year-old Toyota belonging to an elderly couple in Texas who'd reported the vehicle stolen two weeks earlier. As the only eye witness, your importance to the investigation becomes paramount. Do you remember what the man you saw looked like?'

'I'll never forget as long as I live,' Sam said.

'Good.' Steele settled back in his chair and crossed his legs at the knee. 'Over to you then, Clive.'

Kalinsky took Hinds's place next to Sam on the couch, removed a laptop from his canvas shoulder bag and opened it. 'I'm loading a facial composite programme,' he said. 'We can use it to make a graphical representation of the suspect.'

They spent a few minutes experimenting with faces of different shapes and sizes until Sam found one that roughly matched the man on the plane. He then instructed Kalinsky to make it longer and thinner, with a sharper jaw. They adjusted skin tone and played about with different features, altering the eyes, hair, nose and mouth. In less than fifteen minutes Sam had managed to produce an image that bore a strong similarity to the man.

'What do you think?' Kalinsky asked, stroking his beard.

'Almost,' Sam said, 'but something's not quite right. It's the eyes, I think. Is there any way to make them more…bulging?'

'Like this?' Kalinsky dragged the cursor and the eyes popped out as though they were about to burst.

Sam laughed. 'Too much, back a bit.'

A sudden chill swept over him like a draft from an open window.

Kalinsky glanced across, his eyebrows arched. 'Well?'

'That's it,' Sam said. 'That's him.'

30

Sam heard the door slam in the hall. Steele shot from his seat, elbowed Kalinsky out of the way and twisted the laptop towards him. The handle to the sitting room door turned and Sam's grandmother came in carrying a bag of shopping in each hand. Sam looked back to Steele, who was gripping the laptop so tightly it seemed he might snap it in two.

'You know who it is, don't you?' Sam said.

Steele closed the laptop, handed it back to Kalinsky and stood up. 'Thank you, Sam, you've been a great help. We really must be going now.'

'But you recognise the composite,' Sam said. 'You know who it is.'

'We've already taken up enough of your time,' Steele said. 'I'll be in touch if you can be of further assistance to the investigation.'

Hinds and Kalinsky muttered goodbyes and followed him out of the door, leaving Sam wondering whether or not he'd just imagined the look that had crossed Steele's face.

31

Saturday, the day of the funeral, came as Sam knew it inevitably must. It was a cold, overcast winter's morning with a sky the colour of ash. A film of drizzle coated the windows of the car as it followed the hearse to Sam's grandparents' village in Hertfordshire.

As they pulled up in the lane outside the church, Sam thought back to a holiday many summers ago when, bored and desperate to escape Chrissie for a few hours, he'd set himself the task of building a tree house in the woods beyond the graveyard. His dad had come to inspect it on the last day of their stay. The tree house, which was loosely held together with bent nails and frayed rope, had swayed and creaked under their combined weight, but the look of pride in his dad's eyes as he clasped Sam around the shoulder and congratulated him on his work had been unmistakable. No matter what accomplishments lay ahead in his life, Sam knew he would never see that look again.

There must have been close to fifty mourners waiting outside, only some of whom he recognised. Lance, looking distinctly uncomfortable in an ill-fitting suit that revealed two inches of sock below his trouser leg, opened the car door for Sam's grandmother and helped her out. Sam linked arms with Chrissie and she with their grandfather, and together they followed after, the wind blowing soggy leaves against their legs. It was the first time Sam had been out without his crutches and although Chrissie had pressured him to bring them, he'd flatly refused. On this of all days, he didn't want to be seen as the sick kid.

Auntie Laura, his dad's childless sister, came over. As she hugged them each in turn, Sam noticed that her eyes were swollen. His mum's cousins from Cardiff, the only members of her side of the family Sam really knew, were huddled in a group next to the church doors. There were also a few of his dad's old friends, as well as the surviving members of *Cannibal's Kiss*, the band he'd played keyboards for in the 1990s.

As the pallbearers unloaded the coffin from the back of the hearse, Sam saw Lewis and his parents in the distance. Lewis said something to his mother and then walked over, his hands stuffed deep in his pockets.

'Thanks for coming,' Sam said. 'It means a lot.'

Lewis shrugged. His wild tangle of curls had been flattened and combed into something resembling order. 'It's all right,' he said. 'I wanted to.'

'He always liked you, you know.'

'I liked him too,' Lewis said. 'He was miles more fun than my old man.'

They stood facing each other as people drifted towards the doors.

'I don't know if I can do this,' Sam said eventually.

'What are you talking about? Course you can.'

Sam's hand went to his pocket, searching out a folded piece of paper. 'I wanted to say something. I wrote a few words, but...well, look at all these people. I don't know if I can do it.'

'Mate, you can do anything if you really want to.'

'Are you sure?'

'Never been surer.' Lewis put his hand on Sam's shoulder. 'Good luck. I'll catch you after.'

The pallbearers made their way inside with the coffin balanced on their shoulders and soon the crowd started to thin as people followed after. Sam went to join Chrissie and their grandfather again. On hearing someone call his name, he turned to see Doug Bernstein. Doug had lost weight and grown a beard since the last time Sam had seen him, which, he now realised, was the day they'd first arrived in Montclair; a day when his dad had been sipping wine and guzzling pizza in the sun, so full of excitement at the prospect of their 'clean slate'. It was also the day he'd first met Eva.

'This is hard,' Doug said. 'I'm really sorry for your loss, Sam. I didn't know Matthew all that well, but I'm sure going to miss him.'

'Thanks,' Sam said. 'Is it just you here?'

'Unfortunately so. Things back home have been a little, er, strained. Lots of upheaval. The girls send their best wishes though.'

'Right,' Sam said, unsurprised. 'Say hi to Eva for me, will you?'

'You've got it. Look, I want you to know that if there's anything you need, just ask. I mean it. Rebecca's a friend, not just someone I work with. Until she's back on her feet I want to be here on a personal level for both you and Chrissie. I can't help but feel kind of responsible for what happened.'

'Don't,' Sam said. 'It wasn't your fault.'

Doug scratched the back of his head. 'I appreciate your saying so. Still, I can't help but think that if it hadn't been for her job, then you guys would have never been on that plane.' He handed Sam a slip of paper. 'Here's my address, personal number and email. I'll be working out of London for a few months at the minimum. Call by if there's anything you need, anything at all.'

By the time Sam entered the church, most people had already taken their seats. He didn't think that he could handle any more sympathies or condolences, no matter how heartfelt, so he put his head down and made his way to his place in the front pew alongside Chrissie and their grandparents.

The pallbearers had placed the coffin on a stand at the front and moved away. The organist finished a hymn and, in the silence that followed, the vicar stepped up to the pulpit, staring over the rows of mourners with sad, grey eyes. 'Dearly beloved,' he began in a scratchy voice, 'we are gathered here today to commemorate the life of Matthew Rayner, who was taken from his loved ones far too early in the tragic events of September. Before we have a reading from Sam, Matthew's son, I would like to say a few words from Romans 8:38.' He opened the bible and raised his voice to fill the room. 'For I am convinced that neither death nor life, neither angels nor demons, neither the present nor the future, nor any powers, neither height nor depth, nor anything else in all creation, will be able to separate us from the love of God that is in Christ our Lord. Amen.'

Chrissie glanced across and took Sam's hand, linking their fingers together. She was wearing a simple black dress and shawl, but looked beautiful. Her hair was full and glossy, her cheeks touched with colour. The resemblance to their mother was uncanny. 'Are you sure you want to do this?' she asked. 'You don't have to, you know.'

'Yes, I do. I need to.'

'All right then, let's go.' She helped Sam up and guided him to the aisle, where she released his hand, allowing him to make his way to the pulpit one careful step at a time. The vicar smiled and moved aside so that Sam could take his place.

Sam turned to face the audience, reached into his pocket and pulled out the speech he'd written. A lump rose in his throat. His head began to ache, a fiery drilling at the base of his skull. 'You can do this,' he muttered to himself. 'You will *not* cry.'

Gripping the corners of the pulpit, he looked up. Suddenly the headache was much worse. He rubbed his temples with thumb and forefinger and looked down at the page. The words swam before his eyes, his handwriting incomprehensible.

Sam blinked, trying to clear his vision, and began with what he could remember. 'Matthew Rayner meant different things to different people. To some people he was a teacher, to others a friend, but to me he was simply "Dad".' He paused and looked up again. The colours of the church had become sharper, like truer representations of their actual selves. The scene throbbed, as if a wave of energy were passing through it. Sam detected the sickening stench of burned caramel.

Suddenly the cold, hard stone of the church floor was flickering up to meet him. He saw the impact but felt nothing. Shocked faces crowded around. Through a gap he could see a circle of the vaulted ceiling high above, and then everything blurred and went dark.

32

Sam blinked and the world slotted into focus. He was on the couch in his sitting room, sandwiched between Lewis and his grandmother. They were all in their black funeral wear. Lewis had a plate on his lap and was shovelling shepherd's pie into his mouth. The curtains were drawn and a log smouldered in the fireplace. The television showed a group of Emperor Penguins huddled together against a blizzard.

Sam looked across to his grandmother. 'What happened? How did I get home?'

'You're fine now, pet,' she said. 'Remember what the doctor told you. It's only natural for you to feel a bit confused.'

'What are you talking about?'

Before she could answer, the door flew open and Grandpa burst in. His face was red and he was breathing heavily. 'Switch it over, Maureen. Put the news on!'

She scowled at him. 'Whatever is the matter, Alfred? Calm down or you'll give yourself another stroke.'

'Hush and do as I say, woman. I just turned the radio on to check the football results. There's been another attack!'

Sam grabbed the remote and changed the channel.

A news reporter stood in the foreground, her hair tussled and her expression grim. The scene behind her looked like a war zone: a building in ruins, smoke billowing and lumps of shattered masonry strewn across the pavement. Emergency workers rushed here and there, their faces sooty and their uniforms smeared with blood.

The reporter placed a finger over her earpiece and spoke into a microphone. 'You join us live from central London where, shortly after nine o'clock this evening, an explosion ripped through Thames House, the headquarters of the British Security Service. Early reports indicate a heavy loss of life, although exact figures have yet to be established. An official report from the Ministry of Defence suggests the explosion was detonated from a device concealed in a vehicle in the building's underground car park. Police are believed to be searching for a lone bomber. They consider him armed and extremely dangerous. The public are advised not to approach him under any circumstances.'

The screen cut to a grainy image recorded on a closed circuit camera. It showed a man in a Royal Mail uniform glancing over his shoulder. Although the picture was of poor quality, there could be no mistake. It was a face Sam would never forget as long as he lived. It was the man he had seen on the plane.

33

Chrissie let out a scream that echoed through the church. Lewis strained his neck to see what was happening, but the circle of people swarming around Sam blocked his view.

Somebody shouted, 'Call an ambulance!'

Lewis jumped to his feet.

'What's happening? I can't see,' his mum said, grabbing him by the arm. Lewis shook free and pushed through the crowd until he reached the front.

Sam was lying on the floor, his body convulsing violently. His head thrashed from side to side and his clenched fists pounded against the stone slabs. His eyes were open, but the pupils had rolled up into their sockets. A thin stream of white foam bubbled from the corner of his mouth and dribbled down his cheek.

Chrissie was on her knees, clinging to Sam's hand and wailing. She looked up as Lewis knelt beside her. 'What's happening, Lewis? Make it stop, I can't lose him too.'

Lewis felt like he had to do something, although he didn't know what. Sam was slamming his head up and down so hard that it looked as though he might crack his skull. Lewis reached over and tried to hold him still, but the vicar knocked his hand away.

'Don't do that! It looks like an epileptic fit. You can't disturb him. Move back everyone, give the boy some space!'

Lewis took his phone out of his pocket. He'd switched it off before entering the church and it seemed to take forever to receive a signal. By the time he'd managed to call an ambulance, Sam's twitching and thrashing had slowed. Another minute passed and then Sam sat up, blinking.

Lewis helped him to his feet. 'Come on, let's get you some air.'

Sam nodded weakly. Lewis put his arm around his shoulder and, supporting Sam's weight, staggered from the church. The air outside was bracing. Sam took a breath and straightened his back. Some of the colour had returned to his cheeks.

Lewis realised that he was shaking, and it wasn't just that he'd left his jacket inside. 'Don't worry,' he said, leading Sam to a bench. 'I've called an ambulance. It's on the way.'

'Give me your phone,' Sam said.

'What?'

'I need to make a call. I think something terrible is going to happen. Give me your phone.'

Lewis heard sirens approaching and saw blue lights flashing up the lane. 'Just relax—' he began, but before he could finish Sam snatched the mobile phone from his hand.

34

Sam's mind felt like a shaken snow globe. Gradually the fragmented flakes of his memory began to settle. He remembered sitting on the couch when his grandfather had come dashing in. He remembered the news report. He remembered seeing the building in ruins and he remembered the bomber's face.

There was going to be another attack.

Sam snatched the phone from Lewis's hand. At that moment an ambulance came swinging around the corner, its lights flashing and sirens blaring. It screeched to a halt just outside the gate. The back door flew open and a pair of paramedics jumped out and jogged up the path towards them. Sam reached into his pocket and took out his wallet.

The first to reach them was a girl roughly Chrissie's age. She had a round face with podgy cheeks and an upturned nose. The second paramedic was an older man with a stringy ponytail and long sideburns.

'My friend had some sort of seizure,' Lewis said. 'He was shaking all over and his eyes rolled back in his head and there was foam coming out of his mouth and…'

Sam's wallet seemed full of things he didn't need; a coffee shop loyalty card with only one stamp, an old library membership, the photo ID for his child's Oyster card.

'Sir?' the female paramedic said. 'Young man?'

Sam ignored her and continued rummaging through his wallet.

'How long did this seizure last?' the male paramedic asked Lewis.

'I'm not sure, three or four minutes. Couldn't have been more than five.'

'Any history of epilepsy or Grand Mal?'

'I don't know. I don't think so. He was involved in an accident a few months back, a plane crash. He had a head injury and was in a coma.'

At last Sam found the business card Inspector Hinds had given him. He held it triumphantly in the air.

'Young man, I really think you need to come and sit down in the back of the ambulance,' the woman said. 'We need to do some tests.'

'No! I have to make a phone call!' Sam tried keying in the number, but the phone was locked. 'Lewis, what's your security code?'

Lewis gawped at Sam and snatched his phone back. 'Mate, what's wrong with you? You're acting like a loony. You do realise you just collapsed in front of a church full of people, don't you? You need medical attention.'

'Please, it's important,' Sam said, his desperation growing. 'Just one phone call, Lewis. It'll only take a minute and then they can do whatever they want.'

'You promise?'

'Yes, just one call.'

Lewis shook his head, punched in the code and handed the phone back.

35

As a boy, George Steele had wanted nothing more than to make it as a professional footballer. Growing up, he spent countless hours, day after day, kicking a ball against the garage door until his mother called him in for tea. Football was all he thought about during the day and all he dreamed about at night. And it wasn't just some far-fetched fantasy; George had been good. In fact, he'd been better than good. He'd captained the school team at every level and, as a midfielder, broke every scoring record at his boys' club. Even George's father, one of a long line of military men who expected George to follow in the family tradition, had finally come around to the idea that his son might make something of his obsession when a scout from Newcastle United had spotted twelve-year-old George playing in a local tournament and signed him up.

In the youth development system, where so many promising players ultimately failed, George had thrived. He represented the Under-16s team at the age of fourteen and a year later was drafted into the Under-18s. By the time he signed his first (and only) professional contract, George was an England youth international. People had begun to stop him in the street for his autograph.

It appeared nothing could derail George's rise to sporting stardom. Except, it turned out, for a metallic grey Ford Transit van. It happened while George was walking home from training on a chilly autumn evening. The road had been quiet, but as always, he pressed the button and waited for the green man before stepping onto the crossing. He didn't see the van until it was almost too late. It had swerved and George managed to twist and fling his body out of the way. Although that split-second reaction had probably saved his life, the back tyre caught George's trailing foot, his favoured right foot.

The driver didn't even stop.

Every bone beneath the ankle was shattered, and his big toe had become severed and needed to be surgically reattached. And like that, George's football career, his life's dream that had seemed so close he could almost bask in the warmth of its glow, was snatched away before it had even begun.

After being discharged from hospital George didn't leave his bedroom for three weeks, and when he did emerge he was a changed person. From that day forth he never spoke of football again and, in all the years since, had never so much as watched a game on television.

Instead George channelled his energies into his studies. He went from an average student to the top of every class, and when he left school two years later it was with a scholarship to study Law at Oxford University and a well-concealed limp.

George found student life a disappointment. His peers were, on the whole, pompous and juvenile, plus the halls of residence that he was forced to inhabit felt like abject squalor compared to the immaculate cleanliness of his parental home, forcing George to devote so much of his time to cleaning that it became a distraction from his work. Upon gaining a first class honours degree, George immediately enrolled on a Criminology and Criminal Justice postgraduate course. His dissertation, *The Analysis of Paint Fragments in the Successful Prosecution of Hit and Run Drivers*, received widespread acclaim amongst his tutors and earned him a distinction. There was a general consensus that George had all the makings of a fine barrister. His career appeared mapped out, however he was not destined for the Law. On the same day as he received the letter inviting him to interview for the Bar, he also saw an advert for careers at MI5, and a week later was on the train to London. It was by far and away the most impulsive thing he had ever done.

George spent his first two years at the Security Service on the Intelligence Officer Development Programme, and was able to afford the rent on a studio flat which, while cramped, was clean enough and did not necessitate his taking on a roommate. His meticulous nature and unswerving obedience to rules and procedure meant that he had a natural aptitude for the work. He completed the development programme with flying colours and then signed up for a placement in Northern Ireland. It was here that he had met Esteban Haufner, the only person (aside from his mother) to live up to George's exacting standards of cleanliness, and therefore the only person he had ever truly considered a friend.

Once his year in Northern Ireland was up, George returned to London to take up a new role in Operations and a larger flat in a more desirable part of town. Over the next five years promotions followed in quick succession, and soon George was supervising a small team.

Which is how, six weeks off his twenty-eighth birthday, he found himself sitting at his desk on a dreary Saturday afternoon, rubbing hand sanitizer between his fingers and staring at the facial reconstruction Clive Kalinsky had emailed him. The image gave him the chills, leaving him without a clear plan of action. After all, Esteban was dead.

The telephone rang on George's desk, snapping his attention back to the present. He closed the file and, grateful for the distraction, picked up.

'Agent Steele?' It was a woman's voice; one George thought he recognised.

'Speaking,' he said.

There was a slight hesitation, as sure a sign of weakness as there could be. 'This is Frances Hinds, CT Command.'

'Yes, Inspector. What can I do for you?'

'Look, I know you must be terribly busy, and there's probably nothing to it, but I've received a tip-off about a possible attack on your headquarters at Thames House.'

George straightened in his chair, inadvertently squirting hand sanitizer across the desk. 'Your source?' he asked, mopping the mess with a tissue.

She let out a nervous giggle. 'Well, that's the thing. It's Sam Rayner.'

'The boy?'

'I've just got off the phone to him. It was rather hard to make head or tail of what he was saying, but he seems convinced there's going to be another attack this evening, something about a bomb in the underground car park...'

'Go on.'

'Well, he seemed to imply there was a connection to Flight 0368. He thinks the same man is involved, although how he came by this information he couldn't, or wouldn't, tell me. Like I said, there's probably nothing to it, but I thought I should—'

But George didn't hear the end of the sentence; he had already hung up.

36

Chrissie was in the now familiar position of sitting on a bench in a hospital corridor, waiting for news on her brother. Lance sat to one side and Lewis on the other. Neither had said much since they'd arrived.

In spite of Chrissie's hard work and planning, her dad's funeral had been ruined. They'd finished the ceremony and put the coffin in the ground, but after Sam had collapsed the significance of the event was over-shadowed. It was her own fault, she realised. There was no way that her brother was strong enough to give a eulogy. It had been reckless to even consider it, let alone allow it. But Chrissie was still getting used to her responsibilities. The only person who'd ever depended on her before was herself. Now, as well as the baby growing inside of her, she had what remained of her family to worry about.

Chrissie, Lance and Lewis all looked up in unison as a wide-hipped woman in blue medical scrubs approached.

'Miss Rayner?'

'Yes, that's me,' Chrissie said. 'Is my brother okay?'

'My name is Dr Parker. Why don't you come with me and we can discuss it somewhere a little more private?'

'Can I come too?' Lewis asked.

'It's probably best if you wait here for now,' Dr Parker said. 'We shouldn't be long.'

Chrissie followed her down the corridor to an examination room full of mismatched furniture that looked like it had been salvaged from a skip. Sam was sitting on an orange plastic chair with his back to the door. He didn't look up as they entered.

'Please, have a seat,' Dr Parker said, gesturing to an empty chair of a different size and colour to Sam's. 'I'm afraid the news isn't good, Miss Rayner. I've spoken to Dr Saltano at St Benedict's, and he concurs that the most likely cause of Sam's seizure this afternoon is epilepsy.'

'Epilepsy? I thought that was something you were born with,' Chrissie said. 'How comes nobody picked up on this before?'

Dr Parker folded her arms across her chest. 'A person can develop epilepsy at any stage of life. With an injury such as Sam's, post-traumatic epilepsy was always a possibility. Seizures sometimes occur in patients recovering from brain surgery, but epilepsy is classified by multiple seizures.'

'Multiple seizures?' Chrissie said. 'You mean this is going to happen again?'

Dr Parker sighed. 'I wish I could give you a straightforward yes or no, but there are few certainties with the condition. Your brother could have another seizure tomorrow, next week, next year, or never again. Until it happens – or doesn't – there really is no way of knowing.'

Chrissie glanced at Sam. 'Aren't you going to say anything?'

He shrugged and kicked the leg of his chair with his toe.

Dr Parker reached into her desk drawer and took out a prescription pad. 'What I'm going to do, Sam, is refer you to a specialist.' She scrawled across the top page, tore it off and handed it to Chrissie. 'I'd also like to start him on a course of medication. It's a form of anticonvulsant, a relatively new drug on the market. In many patients the frequency of seizures has been greatly reduced, in some cases ceasing altogether. Unfortunately there are some associated side effects, such as drowsiness or mood changes. If he experiences anything like that we may have to try him on a different medication, but let's not get ahead of ourselves.'

'Thank you,' Chrissie said and put the prescription in her bag. 'Come on, Sam, let's go home.'

He nodded, began to stand and then looked up for the first time since Chrissie had come into the room. 'Hang on,' he said. 'I've got a question.'

Dr Parker spread her hands. 'By all means.'

'I was wondering, is it possible to have visions during a seizure?'

'Why yes, as it happens. There are numerous recorded incidents of epileptic patients experiencing visions or hallucinations, often depending on which part of the brain the episode affects. Sometimes seizures can be accompanied or preceded by a sense of déjà vu. Sometimes people with sensory seizures can see, hear or smell things that aren't really there. Did something like that happen today?'

Sam shook his head. 'No, just wondering.'

'I see,' Dr Parker said. She stood and opened the door for them. 'Well, we're done for now. I've booked you an appointment with a specialist in two weeks' time, so if you have any further questions you can discuss them then. In the meantime, Sam, you need to start taking your pills. And try to get some rest.'

'Okay,' he said and followed Chrissie into the corridor.

'Mind telling me what that was about?' she asked as they made their way back to Lance and Lewis.

'Nothing,' Sam said. 'I'm allowed to be curious, aren't I?'

37

They arrived home late from the hospital. Sam's grandparents were already waiting, having come straight from the church. Grandma had made shepherd's pie and invited Lewis to stay for dinner. They took their plates through to the living room and ate in front of the television. There was a documentary on about wildlife in Antarctica. Sam's grandfather lit a fire and then retreated to the kitchen.

'Mind if I put the news on?' Sam asked after he'd finished eating.

Lewis nearly choked on a mouthful of shepherd's pie. 'The *news*? I never thought I'd hear you say that. Come on, Sam, I'm enjoying this.'

'Just for a minute,' Sam said, picking up the remote. 'Anyway, this is a repeat. I've already seen it.'

The *News at Ten* had just started. They listened to the newsreader discuss the main stories of the day; the price of train tickets was going up at twice the rate of inflation, teachers were planning a strike and there was a scandal after a politician had charged the redecoration of his mistress's house to his expenses account. The final story was a piece about a pensioner who'd opened a centre for stray cats and was set to receive an MBE. Obviously it had been a slow day on the news desk.

Sam felt like a punctured blow-up toy, slowly deflating. All afternoon, while doctors had prodded and poked him, he'd comforted himself with the thought that he might have helped stop another attack, only to discover that what he'd seen was a hallucination; sights, sounds and smells that were the products of his damaged mind. He'd made a complete idiot of himself by calling Inspector Hinds. Worse still, he'd ruined his father's funeral for no reason at all.

Lewis swallowed the last piece of food from his plate and licked his fork. 'You mind changing it back now?'

'Whatever,' Sam said, his finger on the button.

'…and before we go, some breaking news just in,' the newsreader announced. 'Within the last hour an attempted attack on the Security Service headquarters in London has been foiled after a year-long investigation by anti-terror police. A lone bomber was apprehended attempting to bring a delivery truck laden with explosives into the building's basement car park. When police tried to detain the suspect he returned fire and was shot dead by sniper…'

The remote control slipped from Sam's hand and bounced across the carpet.

38

Lewis sat on a stool in Sam's bedroom, staring at him with wide, owl-like eyes. 'But it's not possible,' he said. It was the third time in a row he'd repeated those words.

'I know,' Sam said again and leaned back on his bed. 'I don't understand it myself.'

'But I *heard* you make the phone call outside the church. I *heard* what you said. You said there was going to be a bombing, but how could you possibly know that?'

'It's hard to explain. It's a bit like what I told you after I got out of hospital, about time going backwards, except today it went forwards instead.'

'Yeah, I remember.' Lewis flicked the ring pull on his drink, making a twanging sound. 'But when you said that I thought...well, not that you were making it up exactly, just that your head was a mess.'

'That's what I thought too, but it all sort of makes sense now. Back at St Benedict's I told my doctor about blacking out, so he said they were going to keep me in for more tests, which I didn't want because it meant I'd miss Dad's funeral. But when time got jumbled again, I went back to the same conversation and kept my mouth shut, so they discharged me.'

'You don't think it's epilepsy then?'

'Who knows?' Sam said. 'It's hard to describe, but I got this feeling just before I collapsed like time wasn't a continuous flow, one event after another, but was made up of millions of frozen moments, sort of like the pages of a book. Normally you move from page one to page two, then three and four and so on. In the church it was like my brain skipped forwards a few pages to when we were watching the news in the living room just now. I saw it all when I was unconscious. Most things were the same; there was the wildlife documentary you were so interested in, we were all wearing our funeral clothes still and you were eating shepherd's pie. It didn't make sense the first time around, but now – *after* – it sort of does.'

'Let me get this straight,' Lewis said. 'You're telling me that earlier today, while you were lying on the church floor shaking all over and foaming at the mouth, while I was standing right there watching you, you saw exactly what just happened fifteen minutes ago?' He laughed and rubbed his face with both hands. 'That's the maddest thing I've ever heard!'

Sam laughed too. 'I know how it sounds, Lewis, but I don't know how else to explain it. It's like the damage to my brain caused a glitch in the way I experience time, as if the pages got mixed up while I was having a fit. Not everything was the same, though. The first time Grandpa rushed in shouting about the radio, but just now he didn't. Also there was the news. Last time the attack was centre story and this time it was hardly mentioned.'

Lewis stared at Sam for a moment, his face scrunched. 'You think it's because you warned them, don't you?'

'It's the only thing that makes sense.'

'They said there was an investigation by anti-terror police.'

'What do you expect them to say, that they were tipped off by a brain-damaged teenager?'

'Well no, not when you put it like that.' Lewis rubbed his chin and looked up at the ceiling for a moment. 'You realise what this means, don't you? If you *did* manage to stop the bombing, then you changed what was going to happen. You created an alternate future.'

'If that's what you want to call it.'

'Nobody will believe this,' he said. 'I wouldn't if I hadn't been there.'

'But you were.'

'I know, and I still don't know what to believe.' Lewis stood up and yawned. 'Listen, it's getting late. It's been a long day and talking to you is making my head hurt. Mate, whatever you do, please don't go around telling people about this. They'll think you're off your trolley.'

Sam pointed to the scar behind his ear. 'Hey, at least I've got a good excuse.'

39

Sam watched Lewis jog off, hurdling the larger puddles on the pavement. He was about to close the front door when he noticed a dark car parked on the other side of the road. The windows were blacked out, but its headlights shone through the drizzle. The door opened and a figure wearing a long coat stepped out. Sam squinted in the gloom. The figure – a man – raised an umbrella and crossed the road towards him, then opened the gate to Sam's house and strode up the path. For a second Sam felt the urge to slam the door and run inside. The man stopped and shook his umbrella, spraying water every-where, then lowered it.

'Mr Steele,' Sam said. 'W-what are you doing here?'

Steele gave an awkward smile, as though it was uncomfortable to twist his face into this unfamiliar shape. 'I came to thank you,' he said. 'It appears I'm in your debt, Sam. Your warning saved many lives today, quite likely my own included. My office is in that building. My work means I'm not always there, but today I was.'

Sam fought to keep his jaw from dropping open. 'You're welcome,' he said, 'but you didn't need to come all the way over here just to tell me that.'

'Yes, well...' Steele removed a handkerchief from his coat pocket, wiped his forehead and peered over his shoulder at the car. 'Actually, there was something else. If you could spare a few minutes, there's someone who'd like to meet you.'

'Really, who?'

Instead of replying, Steele stepped to the side and raised his umbrella again, waiting for Sam to join him under it. Sam hesitated, feeling a stab of apprehension in his gut, but he wasn't going to get any answers stood on his doorstep, so he slipped on his shoes and followed Steele out into the rain. Steele led him across the road, opened the back door of the car and motioned for him to get in.

Whatever Sam had expected, it definitely wasn't the prim old lady he found sitting there with her hands folded neatly over the pleats of her tweed skirt. She looked like a baby bird, so small and fragile, and it crossed Sam's mind that Steele had brought his mother to meet him. Sam glanced to Steele for an explanation, but he closed the door and remained out in the rain.

The woman removed her half-moon spectacles and left them dangling on a cord around her neck. 'My name is Lara McHayden,' she said. 'I do apologise for dragging you out in this drab excuse for an evening, but after I'd grilled Steele over his source he finally spilled the beans, so to speak.'

'You work for him?' Sam asked.

She chuckled and shook her head. 'No, not exactly. As of today he works for me. Steele tells me you're a survivor of British Airways Flight 0368?'

Sam lowered his gaze. 'That's right. My parents were also on that flight.'

'I'm truly sorry to hear that. I understand you were injured?'

'A few broken bones, but they're healing.'

She pointed to the scar on the side of Sam's head. 'And what about that?'

'A piece of metal pierced my skull and got stuck in my brain,' he said. 'They had to operate to remove it.'

'And how's that healing?'

'Not so well. The doctors say I've developed post-traumatic epilepsy.'

'Fascinating,' she said, her eyes sparkling. 'From a purely medical perspective, that is. Anyhow, I wanted to thank you in person for what you did today.'

'It said on the news that the bomber was shot,' Sam said. 'Was it the man I saw on the plane?'

She produced a photograph as if from nowhere and handed it to him. It showed a man sitting at a table on cobbled terrace overlooking the sea. He was wearing a loud Hawaiian shirt with a flamingo print. Although he looked several years younger and had a floppy moustache, there was no mistaking those eyes; it was the man from the plane.

Sam's hands started to shake. Suddenly he wanted the photograph nowhere near him, as if he might be contaminated by touching the man's image. He half-passed, half-threw it back to McHayden.

'Is that him?' she asked.

Sam nodded and looked up. The photograph had vanished back from wherever it had first appeared. 'Is he dead?'

'Yes.'

'Good,' Sam said. 'Do you know who he was?'

'Only too well, I'm afraid to say. Esteban Haufner.' She pronounced the name as if it left a bitter taste in her mouth. 'He was a foreign operative for MI6. Three years ago, Haufner was working out of Guatemala, monitoring the activities of drug cartels operating in the area. He went missing on a routine surveillance operation and failed to return to his rendezvous point. After several weeks he was presumed killed in action. Until today, that is.'

'You mean he worked for the government?' Sam asked, unable to quite believe what he was hearing. 'Why did he do it then?'

'We can only assume that he must have been turned at some point: a double agent. Regrettably, it isn't the first time such a thing has happened.'

'Turned? But who by?'

'That, we don't yet know. However, after today, the answer to that question has become a top priority.' She paused, lifted her spectacles to her face and peered at Sam, weighing him up. 'Tell me, are you a patriot?'

The image that came to Sam's mind was of a beer-swilling lout in an England football shirt. He hesitated, unsure of the right answer.

'What I'm trying to ascertain is this: do you love your country? Would you do what it takes to protect Britain and our allies from those who mean to do us harm?'

'Well, yeah, of course.'

'Then what I need to know is how you came by the information you passed to Agent Steele this afternoon.'

'I...I...you wouldn't believe me if I told you.'

'Try me,' she said. 'I have a particularly high threshold when it comes to the unbelievable.'

Lewis had just warned Sam not to tell anyone about his vision, but he got the feeling McHayden would smell a lie a mile off. 'Listen,' he said, 'I know how bonkers this sounds, but I had a seizure this afternoon, during my dad's funeral, and I saw what was going to happen before I called Inspector Hinds.'

'Go on,' she said in a voice like a purr. 'You can trust me.'

'I saw what was going to happen before it had happened. Like a hallucination or something.'

He waited for McHayden to laugh, but her face remained straight. 'Do you mean that you witnessed the bombing?' she asked.

'No, not exactly. I saw what was going to happen from my own point of view later this evening. I was back home and there was a report on the news. There was surveillance footage of the suspect – of Esteban Haufner – and I recognised him from the plane. When I woke up I knew had to do something, so I rang Inspector Hinds as fast as I could. I suppose she must have told Agent Steele what I said.'

McHayden lips curled back in a smile. 'So, there is another.'

'Excuse me?'

She unclasped her hands and smoothed her skirt. 'If what you tell me is true, then that would be quite a useful talent, wouldn't you agree?'

'A *talent*?'

'My dear boy, because of you Esteban Haufner is dead. What you did today saved countless lives and, if you'll forgive me for saying so, brought a small measure of justice for your father.'

Much as it pained Sam, there was no denying the pleasure he'd felt upon hearing of Esteban Haufner's death.

'What I'd really like to know,' she went on, 'is if you think you could do it again?'

'What, have another seizure?'

'Precisely.'

'I don't know. I've been prescribed medicine that's supposed to stop them.'

'Jesus wept! And why on Earth would you want to do a thing like that? If you could control your episodes, then you might be able to help us track the people Haufner was working for. Think of what might be possible if we could harness your ability.'

'I wouldn't exactly call it an ability,' Sam said. 'It's only happened a few times and it's not like I can control it.'

'That may be something we can look into. How would you feel about exploring the matter further?'

'What do you want me to do?' he asked.

McHayden smiled again, her face creasing into craggy terrain of wrinkles, and passed Sam a business card with her name and address printed beneath the crest of the Security Service: a dragon in the centre of a ring of portcullises and roses. 'I'd like you to visit my office next week so we can discuss things in more detail. Shall we say...Monday at four o'clock?'

'Fine,' he said, 'four o'clock, Monday.'

'Splendid!' She rapped the window with her knuckle and Steele opened the door again. He waited for Sam to get out, then closed the door and climbed into the front seat. As the engine growled into life, the back window wound down halfway and McHayden leaned out. 'One last thing,' she said. 'The nature of what we've just discussed is a matter of national security. If you're serious about working with us, then I need your word that the details of this conversation will go no further.'

'I won't tell anyone,' Sam said.

She gave a brisk nod. 'Good, until Monday then. And please be punctual, if there's one thing I can't abide it's lateness.'

The window closed and the car pulled away.

Sam stood watching the taillights retreat into the night, oblivious to the rain pouring down around him.

Part IV
Mastery and Control

40

July 1969

Lara lay on her back in the bunker of the 18th hole, gazing up at the countless pinpricks of light filling the night sky. A shower of green blossomed over a copse of trees to the north, followed by a pop and a fizz as the sound of the firework reached her. She scooped a handful of sand and let the grains sift slowly through her fingers.

'Were you okay in there?' Isaac asked, handing her a champagne flute. Muffled laughter drifted over on the warm breeze as the last partygoers made their way from the clubhouse. 'I can't stand these corporate events.'

Lara rolled onto her side and propped herself up on her elbow. So far it had been the most magical evening of her life. Two months earlier, Isaac had taken on a part-time consultancy role at Bereck & Hertz, a pharmaceutical company based in San Jose, and had asked Lara to their Gala Independence Day Dinner. He'd bought her a strapless black gown, which was the most beautiful dress she had ever worn, and a silver brooch embedded with pearls that probably cost more than her yearly salary. Tonight, Lara had eaten lobster for the first time and drunk enough champagne to make her lightheaded.

'It was wonderful,' she said. 'And so were you, Isaac. I never realised you knew so many people.'

He filled his own glass. 'I doubt if I've met half a dozen of that crowd before today.'

'Still, they all seemed to want a piece of you. A girl could get jealous, you know.'

She could make out him blushing, even in the dark.

'You've got nothing to be jealous about, Lara.'

'Really?'

'Really.' He raised his glass. 'Happy Fourth of July.'

'You too,' she said and clinked her glass against his. 'I could get used to this kind of treatment.'

'You may have to. From what I gather these parties are regular fixtures in the Bereck & Hertz calendar.'

Another firework exploded beyond the trees, yellow this time. Isaac stared over the golf course long after the last golden sparkle had dimmed and settled out of sight. He seemed to have grown increasingly withdrawn over the last few weeks and prone to bouts of introspection.

'Penny for your thoughts?' Lara said.

'Huh?'

'What's on your mind?'

Isaac stared away again, looking like he was holding back. Eventually he sighed and turned to face her. 'I can't shake the feeling that there may be other applications than purely military.'

'Tetradyamide, you mean?'

He nodded and took a sip from his glass. Tetradyamide was Isaac's first assignment at Bereck & Hertz.

The drug had the effect of slowing the passage of perceived time in users. The military, immediately recognising the benefits of improved speed and reactions, had commissioned Bereck & Hertz to push Tetradyamide through the research and development pipeline so that trials with American service personnel could begin while there was still a war to fight. 'Its potential is quite staggering,' Isaac said. 'I really think it could help Michael.'

'*Michael?*'

'It steadied his neurological activity during the tests we did last week.'

'You mean to say you've already *given* it to him?' Lara sat upright and glared. 'How could you, Isaac? He's my patient!'

'And I'm your supervising physician.' There were more bangs in the distance. 'Tell me what's worse, Lara, trying doing something that might help, or sitting on our hands until he kills himself?'

'Is it ethical? The stuff's not even signed off yet.'

'If there's any heat – which there won't be – then I'll take it. Don't flip your wig, baby, he's government property.'

Lara shook her head. 'You're beginning to sound like one of those protesters.'

'You dig?'

She finished her glass, scooped up her heels and stood. 'Not really. Are you sure you're okay to drive?'

'Never better, Daddy-O.'

'Really, Isaac, that's enough now.'

He grinned, got up and swept the sand off his tux before taking her hand. Another firework exploded high above. They watched the last sparks fade to nothing, then turned and walked back to the clubhouse.

41

Present Day

Sam arrived forty minutes early for his appointment, which was no bad thing because he was still uneasy on his feet without crutches. It had been difficult persuading Chrissie to let him out. Although Sam knew his sister meant well, he thought he might lose the plot if he heard the words 'just checking how you're doing' one more time. Chrissie had collected his prescription the day after the funeral, travelling the extra distance to find a pharmacy open on a Sunday, and was insisting that Sam take his epilepsy medication. The pills made him feel slow in the head, sort of like his brain was covered in bubble wrap but, short of revealing what Dr McHayden had told him, he couldn't think of a convincing reason not to take them, so had resorted to hiding them under his tongue and spitting them out when Chrissie wasn't looking.

He took his time as he walked up the bank of the river Thames, watching the dirty brown water swirl below. Although it wasn't rush hour yet, the pavements were crowded and slippery with rain. People in suits hurried by on either side and at one point Sam had to squeeze through a large group of Spanish students, all wearing matching orange backpacks. Eventually he reached the address on Dr McHayden's card: an imposing stone-fronted building decorated with intricate carvings. As he crossed at the lights, Sam realised it was the same building he'd seen on the news the other night, when in an alternate reality it had been no more than a bombed-out shell. It stretched for an entire block, and was set back from the road by a lawn behind a low wall. A pair of revolving glass doors stood under an archway halfway along. Sam entered a gaping lobby where the statues and stone were replaced by glass and steel. His shoes squeaked over polished marble as, feeling clumsy and exposed, he crossed the empty floor towards a security desk.

'You missed the last tour,' said a guard behind an x-ray machine and metal detector.

'I'm here to see Dr McHayden,' Sam said. 'She's expecting me.'

'Oh, official business, is it? Your name?'

'Sam Rayner.'

Humming, the guard ran his finger down a list on a clipboard. 'Ah, here you are,' he said at last. 'I'll ring up and have someone come to collect you.'

He prepared a visitor's badge and then handed it over. As Sam struggled to clip it to his jacket pocket, the lift doors on the other side of the metal detectors opened and Steele stepped out. He was immaculately dressed again, this time in a navy three-piece suit. Sam's mind whirred with questions as Steele showed him to the lift. More than anything he wanted to ask what Dr McHayden had meant when she'd spoken about harnessing his ability – although whatever was happening to Sam felt more like a disability than anything useful – but Steele stared directly ahead as they rode the lift to the third floor, making any attempt at small talk too awkward.

They exited onto a long corridor lined with a thick carpet that dampened the sound of their footsteps. Steele led the way past a row of glass-fronted offices, many with blinds drawn to obscure the view of inside. At the end of the corridor they reached a door with *Dr Lara McHayden* inscribed on a brass plate. Steele knocked and, as Sam followed him in, McHayden looked up from behind a large, varnished wooden desk, pointed to a leather chair on the near side and lowered her glasses.

Sam sat down and glanced about the room. It was lined with dark panelling that matched the wood of McHayden's desk. A drinks cabinet stood against the far wall, separating a pair of tall bookcases that stretched from ceiling to floor and gave the room the musty, comforting smell of a library. A collection of framed qualifications and certificates hung on the wall behind McHayden's desk, as well as several photographs. There was a recent one that showed her shaking hands with the Prime Minister. Next to that was an old, faded print that was slightly out of focus. It had a white line running down the middle where it had once been folded and showed a young man and woman in white coats relaxing against a desk in what looked like a hospital. The man had thick black hair, tanned skin and a curved nose. He was laughing at some long-forgotten joke, his head tilted back and his face creased with joy. The woman was much shorter, with freckles and light hair, and was gazing up at the man with adoration in her eyes. There was something familiar about her, and after a moment Sam realised it was Dr McHayden in her youth.

'A long time ago,' she said, following the direction of his gaze. Her voice was soft and only just audible. 'Believe it or not, I was young too once.' She stared at the photo for a minute, a far-away look in her eyes, then turned back to Sam. 'So tell me, how have you been? Any more seizures?'

'No, I feel pretty good,' he said, 'like I'm getting stronger all the time. My sister keeps hassling me to take my epilepsy pills, though. I tried them once, but it made me feel slow in the head.'

'Not to worry, I'll have you transferred from your doctor and take over that responsibility myself. That way we might avoid any external interference in our work, so to speak.'

'You can do that?'

'Oh yes. To keep your sister pacified I can even supply you with placebo pills which look exactly the same as your epilepsy medication, but contain nothing stronger than sugar.'

'That might be an idea,' Sam said. 'I was having to hide them and then flush them down the toilet just to keep her off my back.'

'Hear that?' she said, turning to Steele, who had taken the chair next to Sam. 'Young Mr Rayner is already mastering the art of deception! You may have a promising future in the field of espionage ahead of you, my dear boy.' She opened a drawer, took out a folder and slid it across the desk. 'Now, I expect you're wondering why I invited you here, but before we can proceed there are a couple of items of paperwork that we need to get out of the way.'

Sam opened the folder. It contained two stapled documents. The print was so small that he had to squint to read it, and when he did he found the language so complicated it was almost unintelligible.

'I assure you, they're both standard documents,' Steele said, leaning over to hand him a metal ballpoint pen.

McHayden cleared her throat. 'If you choose to proceed, then you're about to become involved in a matter of national security. Unfortunately, I need more than just your verbal assurances that what we discuss will go no further. The first document is the Official Secrets Act. The second gives me legal status as your doctor and prevents your records from being shared amongst the medical community. You need to sign each at the bottom, there and there.'

Sam gripped the pen, his hand trembling slightly. After this there would be no turning back. He took a deep breath and, before he could wimp out, signed his name on both pages.

'Excellent stuff,' McHayden said. She swept the documents into the folder and tucked it back into the drawer. 'Now that the formalities are out of the way, we can get down to business. As I think I mentioned the other night, I come from a medical background. For some time now I've led a research group made up of selected government officials, scientists, doctors and independent backers, known as the Tempus Project. The focus of our work has been to investigate the influence certain areas of the brain have on time perception; that is, how people experience the passage of time.' She pushed her chair back and laid her hands flat on the desk. 'You see, Sam, the passage of time, and our perception of it, is not necessarily a constant, linear thing. Rather, it can be highly subjective. I'm sure you're aware of the expression "time flies when you're having fun"?'

'Yeah, of course. It's, like, if you're doing something fun time goes by really quickly, but if you're doing something you hate, like a boring lesson at school, it feels like it lasts forever.'

'Couldn't have put it better myself,' she said. 'As it happens, there's more than an inkling of truth to the saying. Time perception depends on a person's state of mind. As you rightly point out, a pleasurable activity may seem to pass faster than an unpleasant one, even if they both take the same amount of recorded time. In rare cases patients with traumatic brain injuries and those with severe brain disorders can experience profound difficulties judging the passage of time. What may seem like a few minutes to a perfectly healthy person could feel like hours to someone with such difficulties.'

Sam thought back to when he'd just come out of his coma, when days and nights had passed in minutes and events had seemed jumbled, with no logical order. 'So you think I might be one of these people?' he asked.

'On the contrary, dear boy, I hope that you might be considerably more exceptional. Let me tell you a story, if I may.' She leaned back, lowered her hands to her lap and exhaled. 'Several decades ago, during the Vietnam War, I worked with a patient, an American soldier, who was involved in an explosion and suffered an injury in which a piece of shrapnel became embedded in his brain.'

'Like me?'

'Like you. The shrapnel was successfully removed which, given the circumstances of the operation, was quite remarkable. Back in the United States, it was immediately apparent that he had become delusional. He claimed that he was suffering from a form of "time sickness", and that he had become unstuck in time.'

'What happened to him, this soldier?'

She paused to wet her lips with her tongue. 'I'm sorry to say that he took his own life shortly after. The single biggest regret of my career is that we never had the chance to further explore his ability. In all the intervening years I've never given up hope that it might be possible to recreate his condition in another person. Once I was in an appropriate position to secure funding for further research, I established the Tempus Project. Since then I've worked with countless patients, many suffering from abnormalities in time perception and even the occasional oddball who claimed to be able to travel in time, but none who could accurately predict future events in scientifically verifiable conditions. That is, I very much hope, until you.'

'So, what is it that you want me to do?' Sam asked.

She watched him intently. The casual atmosphere in the room had evaporated. 'I don't think you realise the implications of this research,' she said. 'Suppose that you could be trained to channel and focus your episodes, choosing when they occur and exactly how far backwards or forwards you see. It would revolutionise the work of the Security Service. An attack such as the one in which you were injured and your father was killed need never happen again. If we were able to reliably predict future events we could prevent such tragedies before they even happen. If we knew the time and place that an attack was planned, we could act pre-emptively, just like we did when you tipped us off about the bombing of this very building but without the element of luck. You could become the ultimate defence against threats to the nation. The war on international terrorism could be won in one fell swoop. You have a responsibility, Sam, not just to your country but to all of mankind.'

'What about Esteban Haufner and the people he was working for?'

'Catching them would be the first item on our agenda.' Her voice was low, as if she were letting him in on a secret. 'What do you say, my dear boy, are you along for the ride?'

42

The car turned onto a muddy, rutted path that looked like it led to the middle of nowhere. Winter had arrived and although it wasn't late yet, the last daylight had already slipped away. Sam used his sleeve to wipe a circle of condensation from the window and peered out. They were travelling through a dense wood of pine trees that rose high on either side of the path. After a few more minutes they approached a clearing, where a gate was set in a tall metal fence topped with razor wire.

The tyres crunched over frozen ground as the car slowed to a halt. A uniformed guard carrying a machine gun and torch stepped from a small hut beside the gate. Steele, in the driver's seat, opened the window, allowing freezing air to flood in, and presented his ID badge. The guard glanced at it, shone the torch in Steele's face, swung the beam to the back seat where Sam and McHayden were sitting and then opened the gate and waved them through.

After another couple of hundred metres they pulled up outside a low concrete building with a sloping, corrugated-iron roof. A flaking sign on the wall read, *KPP&R Logistics.* Sam stepped out of the car and rubbed his hands together, his breath forming puffs of steam in the air.

'This way,' McHayden said, and began striding towards the double doors at the front of the building. Sam and Steele followed her through into a reception room. There was a waiting area to the left, containing several chairs, a water dispenser with an empty bottle on top and a brown potted plant that had shed half its leaves over the black and white chessboard floor tiles. Against the wall to Sam's right was an old vending machine that looked in desperate need of restocking. Another guard was reading a book at a desk in front of them. 'Evening boss,' he said, dog-earing his page. 'Miserable weather we're having, eh?'

'Good evening, Arnold,' McHayden said. 'Allow me to introduce Sam Rayner. You'll be seeing rather a lot of him, I think.'

Sam fumbled in his pocket for the security badge he'd been given (his half-blinking face and shoulders super-imposed next to the picture of a lighthouse – the emblem of the Tempus Project – and the words, *SAMUEL RAYNER, SUBJECT 102*) and held it out at arm's length.

'Pleased to make your acquaintance,' Arnold said and tipped the peak of his cap. 'Go on down, the others are waiting.'

He leaned to one side and pressed a button under the desk. As he did so, Sam noticed a heavy-looking pistol hanging at his hip and wondered if he ever had reason to use it. There was a faint hissing sound and then the vending machine slid to the side to reveal the interior of a lift. McHayden and Steele stepped in, and Sam followed after. The walls were bare, polished metal apart from three unnumbered buttons next to a dull black plate the size of a sheet of paper. McHayden placed her hand to this and a bar of green light pulsed from top to bottom like a photocopier. She hit the lowest button and the doors closed behind them. There was a jolt, followed by the sensation of movement as they began to descend.

The doors opened on an underground level that was several times larger than the building above, reminding Sam of an iceberg with the main bulk hidden below the water's surface. Everything – walls, floor and ceiling – gleamed pristine white under bright fluorescent lighting, making him wince. A small group of people in lab coats stood talking at the far end, but the sound of their voices was replaced by hushed silence as McHayden approached.

A short, stocky man separated from the rest of the group and came to greet them.

'You must be Sam,' he said breathlessly. His skin was raw with eczema, angry red flakes peeling from his neck and the backs of his hands.

'This is Malcolm Fairview,' McHayden said. 'Malcolm is Head Technician here at the Tempus Project.'

'We're thrilled to have you aboard,' Fairview said, grinning at Sam. 'I can't tell you how exciting it is to finally begin trials with a human subject.'

'Human subject?' Sam said, remembering the wording on his security badge and imagining himself as some sort of living crash test dummy.

'Sorry, probably a poor choice of words. Follow me and we can get started.'

Sam looked to McHayden.

'There's nothing to worry about,' she said. 'Go ahead, I'll be waiting right here.'

He followed Fairview to a small room at the back of the main laboratory, where a table and chair were surrounded by several video cameras on tripods. There was a computer monitor on top of the table, which was connected to a plate with two metal joysticks sticking out, both capped by a red button.

'Seriously, you invited me all this way to play computer games?' Sam said. 'You haven't got the new FIFA, have you?'

'You're actually closer to the mark than you realise.' Fairview unhooked a sizable set of keys from a clip on his belt and unlocked a metal cabinet in the corner of the room. He removed one of the small brown bottles from the rows that lined the shelves and turned back to Sam. 'This is Tetradyamide. The molecule was originally discovered in the 60s, but the formula was lost after the head scientist working on its production went missing. We've been attempting to recreate it ever since I joined the Tempus Project. Early batches were of low purity, but we've made significant progress over the last year or two. This particular batch, I'm rather proud to say, is my own design.' He popped the lid and shook a yellow pill the size of a pea into the palm of Sam's hand.

Sam rolled it between his thumb and forefinger. The little pill felt sticky to his touch. 'Tetra...what did you call it?'

'Tetradyamide. Some of the researchers have taken to calling it "glue".'

'What does it do?'

'Don't look so nervous. We've conducted extensive trials and the drug is perfectly safe for human consumption. You're potentially too valuable an asset to be used as a human guinea pig.' Fairview returned the bottle to its cabinet and locked the door. 'Tetradyamide increases neurological activity in the areas of the brain associated with time perception. I've tried it myself, as a matter of fact, and I'm still here to tell the tale.'

'And what happened?'

'Well, if ingested by a person with relatively normal brain function – which apparently I have, no matter what Cynthia, my ex-wife, might say – it has the effect of slowing time perception. My own experience was of seeing the world pass by in slow motion. To an external observer, a user may appear to think, move and react at an accelerated rate.'

'Let me get this straight,' Sam said. 'You're telling me this pill slows down time?'

'The drug slows the *perception* of time. Its original development was funded by the United States military in the hope of swinging the Vietnam War. I'm sure I don't need to spell out the advantages of being able to think and move faster than your enemy. Unfortunately, early formulations had a number of side effects, such as an intense euphoric "high" and the associated lack of judgement. It's only under the guidance of Dr McHayden that we've been able to fill in some the blanks and, with improved techniques and equipment, refine production to limit most side effects.'

'So what if someone who doesn't have normal brain function takes it, someone like me?'

Fairview rubbed his hands together. 'Ah, now that's where things should get *really* interesting. Bear in mind this is all theory, but the effects should be much more profound. We're hoping the drug will simulate one of the seizures you've experienced, increasing neurological activity in certain areas of your brain. The big difference is that Tetradyamide should stop you from experiencing unintended seizures and, with practise, you should even be able to control them, choosing when an episode comes on and how far into the past or future you wish to travel. At least that's Dr McHayden's hypothesis.'

If what Fairview was saying were true, the pill in Sam's hand could hold the key to controlling his fits, and if that were possible then who knew what else might be? Perhaps he could undo what had happened to his parents.

Without another moment's hesitation, he popped the pill into his mouth and swallowed it down.

'Good lad,' Fairview said and chuckled. 'You know, I had a feeling about you the minute you stepped into the lab.'

'Don't suppose you've ever considered sugar coating those things?' Sam asked, gagging at the bitter chemical taste.

'Duly noted. I'll be back with some water.'

Fairview left the room and returned a minute later carrying a paper cup, which Sam drained in a single gulp.

'I don't feel any different yet,' he said.

'You wouldn't.' Fairview took back the empty cup, scrunched it into a ball and tossed it at a wastepaper basket by the door, missing by some distance. 'The drug takes about ten minutes to enter the bloodstream and the effects then last for between three to six hours, after which they gradually diminish. In twelve hours it should have left your system completely.'

'So...what should I do now?'

'There's nothing to do but wait,' Fairview said. He pulled the chair back from the table. 'Here, have a seat and I'll explain how the test works.' He pressed a button at the back of the monitor and the blocky image of a house with a smoking chimney and picket fence appeared on the screen. Two blue doors, numbered 1 and 2, were set in the front of the house.

'Don't you think I'm a bit old for this kind of thing?' Sam asked, thinking it looked like something Lewis's little brother might have drawn.

'Cutting-edge graphics weren't considered much of a priority, I'm afraid. The programme is a random chance generator. It's essentially like flipping a coin over and over: you've got a fifty percent chance of heads and a fifty percent chance of tails. Behind one of the doors is a smiley face and behind the other is a skull and crossbones. Your job is to find the smiley face and avoid the skull and crossbones, but until you open a door there's no way of knowing which one hides which.'

'Sounds simple enough.'

'Good. Why don't you give it a try? You can choose a door by pressing either button.'

Sam gripped the joysticks and, after a moment's consideration, pressed the button on the left. There was a small musical fanfare and Door 1 swung open, revealing a smiley face. When the door closed a counter in the bottom corner of the screen rolled over to 01.

'Good guess,' Fairview said. 'That's one in a row. Have another try.'

This time Sam pressed the right button. Door 2 swung open to reveal the skull and crossbones. There was an angry buzz and pain shot up his hand from the joystick. He cried out and immediately let go. The counter in the corner reset to 00.

'What the hell was that?' Sam asked.

'Just a little incentive to encourage you to select the correct door. Both joysticks are electrified; if you choose the wrong one you get a mild electric shock. Probably should have warned you about it, but I couldn't resist. Fancy another go?'

'And get shocked again? No thanks. What's the point of it all anyway?'

'The test is designed to improve your close control,' Fairview said. 'If you don't press a button then both doors will automatically open after sixty seconds, but the counter will reset back to zero. Once the Tetradyamide takes effect, all you need to do is make the decision not to open either door, then travel forward sixty seconds into the future to see where the smiley face is hidden. In theory, you should be able to return to the present, select the correct door and thus avoid getting shocked.'

'I see,' Sam said. 'And I thought I wasn't supposed to be a human guinea pig.'

Fairview chuckled again, his round shoulders bouncing. 'Looks like you've got me there. Why don't you relax and wait for the drug to take effect? I'll come back to check on you in a couple of minutes and we can give it another try.'

He left the room and returned to the main laboratory.

Sam let out a slow breath, feeling the muscles in his back loosen, and swallowed. In spite of the water he could still taste the pill in his mouth, gluey and harsh. He glanced about. The walls were tinged with subtle shades of pink and yellow. A warm tingle danced up his spine. The door opened and Fairview came back in, carrying a cloth cap covered in evenly spaced holes with wires poking out. Sam blinked and suddenly Fairview was frozen in mid-step, his entire weight supported on the ball of his back foot and his front foot hovering just above the floor. He blinked again and Fairview inched forwards, the movement jerky and mechanical. It was the way Sam had seen things during his fits in hospital, but without the terror of being locked in his own body.

'How do you feel now?' Fairview asked.

'Good,' Sam said. 'I mean *really* good. It's starting to work, I think.'

'Excellent.' Fairview held the strange hat out. 'This is an electroencephalography cap, otherwise known as an EEG. We'll use it to monitor your brain wave activity during the test. Mind popping it on for me?'

'Okey dokey,' Sam said and laughed. It seemed that the attempts to limit the drug's side effects had not been entirely successful.

Fairview took a tube of gel from his pocket, squeezed a drop onto the end of each electrode and pulled the cap over Sam's head. 'I'll be monitoring the readings from the next room,' he said. 'Remember, both doors open automatically after sixty seconds, so just try to relax and focus on what's about to come.'

He restarted the programme and left, taking up a position at a computer terminal on the other side of the glass panel in the wall. Sam grinned and waved, catching sight of his own reflection in the glass. Fairview gave the thumbs up, so Sam gripped the joysticks and tried to concentrate on taking long, slow breaths.

The doors on the screen remained closed. Sam glanced back at Fairview, but he only circled his finger, leaving Sam with the familiar feeling that he was watching images played under a strobe light. Every separate instant was like a drawing on a page of a flipbook; motionless in itself. It was only when the pages began to turn that the illusion of movement was created.

He closed his eyes and focused on skimming through the pages to the point when both doors would open. Without warning, an image popped into his head. Both doors swung open, with the smiley face behind the left and the skull and crossbones behind the right.

Sam opened his eyes to find that both doors were still closed, so he cautiously pressed the button on the left, ready to snatch his hand away. A fanfare sounded and the smiley face was revealed behind Door 1, just as he'd seen it. The counter in the corner turned over to 01 again.

Sam breathed a sigh of relief as the doors closed. Feeling slightly more confident, he shut his eyes again and scanned forward through the pages. Another image jumped into his mind's eye, and this time he saw the smiley face behind Door 2. He opened his eyes to see that both doors were still closed, so pressed the right-hand button. The fanfare sounded again and the counter rolled over to 02.

On his next go the smiley face was behind the right door again, and after that the left. Every time that Sam closed his eyes he saw what was going to happen a minute down the line, and every time he reopened them to find the smiley face waiting in the same place.

After the sixth correct attempt any sense of uncertainty was gone. This was easy, Sam decided. It was more than just guessing, he actually *knew* what was behind each door before pressing the button. He loosened his grip on the joysticks, no longer afraid of being stung, and kept going, pressing the buttons over and over, faster and faster, revealing smiley face after smiley face.

By the time the counter reached 25, Sam had the sensation of a drill bit grinding through his skull. He looked through the window into the lab, but Fairview only raised his eyebrows and gestured for him to continue. Sam turned back to the screen, wishing he could take a break.

On attempt twenty-nine he felt his concentration slipping. When he closed his eyes he saw both doors open, but before he had time to spot which hid the smiley face, they closed again. Instead of opening his eyes and returning to the present, Sam blundered several pages further forward. Suddenly he saw himself standing between McHayden and Steele in the lift. He let out a startled cry and opened his eyes, only to find himself back in the chair, facing a screen with two closed doors and no idea which hid the smiley face.

Shaking his head, he pressed down lightly on the right button, then changed his mind and pressed the left. There was a buzz and pain shot up his arm. He jumped out of the chair and ripped the cap from his head.

Fairview hurried back into the room. 'What's the matter?' he asked. 'Why did you stop?'

'I've had it with this stupid game,' Sam said, rubbing his hands over his scalp. 'Dr McHayden told me I'd be doing important work, but so far all you've done is wire me up to this stupid machine and electrocute me. Is this how you get your kicks?'

'Now hold on just a—'

'Forget it,' Sam said. 'Where's Dr McHayden? I want to go home.'

43

Sam's headache felt much worse as he sat in the back of the car with his arms folded over his chest. The drilling sensation had grown to a steady thump, like a sledge-hammer against the back of his head, and his mood worsened as they retraced their route through the woods and back onto the road.

After a while McHayden turned to him. 'Penny for your thoughts?'

'You what?' Sam said.

'Never mind. It's something my mother used to say, but then again I didn't like her much. What's on your mind?'

He shifted in his seat. 'Today was a total, utter disaster.'

She gave him a long, steady look that was on the verge of becoming uncomfortable when she broke it with a smile. 'On the contrary,' she said, 'I would describe today as a resounding success.'

'A *success*? How do you figure? Mr Fairview said the game was supposed to improve my control, but it all went wrong and I got stung in the end. How's that a success?'

'My dear boy, while the random chance generator has undoubted benefits in training you to travel more accurately over short periods of time, the primary purpose was to scientifically verify your ability, and you did that with aplomb.'

'Even though I got electrocuted?'

'That was after you had selected the correct door on twenty eight consecutive occasions,' she said. 'The probability of achieving such a score by chance alone is in the region of two hundred and fifty million to one. Furthermore, readouts from the EEG showed massive spikes in your neurological activity before you selected each door. This not only proves the validity of your ability, but the effectiveness of Tetradyamide in inducing and stabilising your episodes. I think we can safely call that a success, don't you?'

'Well, when you put it like that...'

'This evidence will go a long way to confirming the importance of our work to my superiors and gaining continued funding for the next stage of our trials. You should feel proud of yourself, Sam.'

44

By the time they pulled up outside Sam's house, his headache had begun to ease. McHayden placed a hand on his arm as he went to climb from the car. 'A quick word of warning before you go,' she said. 'Although you may not still feel it, the drug will be in your system for several hours yet. In no circumstance should you attempt to manipulate time unless under my direct supervision. Any changes you make in the past could have consequences in the present and, believe me, these might not always work out how you intend.'

'Okay,' Sam said. He stepped from the car, then thought of something and turned back. 'Dr McHayden?'

'Yes.'

'You just said about making changes in the past. What about my parents? What if I could change what happened to them?'

She sucked air through her teeth. 'At the moment you need to focus on mastering your ability in a controlled environment. Remember what we're doing this for, Sam. You have a responsibility far beyond your personal desires, no matter how honourable they might be.'

'But—'

'No buts. I need you to promise me that you won't do anything foolish. The future of the Tempus Project depends upon it.'

He faced her for a moment and then nodded. Nothing could be more important than saving his parents, but at the moment McHayden was Sam's only hope of achieving that.

45

To call the last few months of Eva's life a rollercoaster would be the understatement of the millennium. A closer analogy might be that of a rollercoaster that hasn't been safety checked in fifty years, with seatbelts worn to a loose collection of threads, jutting nails, rusted brakes and tracks rotted to the consistency of sponge cake.

On the night of her party, Trent had led Eva to her bedroom, where what began as a quick kiss had soon turned into his hands all over her body. It wasn't as if Eva wasn't against the idea of sex, just that in her head she had always imagined her first time would be romantic, something special, not some hurried fumble with a houseful of guests downstairs. She had told him to stop, but Trent wouldn't listen, and all of a sudden his touch wasn't gentle anymore. Eva had found herself struggling against him, but he was too strong. She'd lashed out with all her strength, catching him square on the jaw with her elbow. Trent's head had twisted sharply to the side, his body contorting as he toppled from the bed. He'd cried out as the bridge of his nose connected with the corner of the bedside table, knocking the lamp to the floor, and then picked himself up and stomped from the room, slamming the door behind him.

The strap of Eva's dress was torn, so she'd taken a few minutes to change her clothes and reapply her make-up. As she'd headed back down there was a deafening crash, and Eva had dashed to the den to find Brandon sitting among the broken pieces of Colette's coffee table as blood poured out of his arm.

Enough was enough. She had lost her cool and yelled at everyone to get out. After the ambulance had arrived to take Brandon to the emergency room, Eva had gone to bed, crying herself to sleep with the covers pulled over her head.

The following morning, much to her surprise, Nicole offered to help clean up. As they knelt together sweeping shards of broken glass into a refuse sack, Nicole had told Eva that she'd seen Trent start the fight with Sam, which had led to Brandon falling through the top of the coffee table. If Trent's behaviour the previous evening had already broken the back of their relationship, this additional piece of information crippled it beyond cure, and the thought of him ever touching her again now made Eva want to puke.

Once the den resembled its previous condition as closely as was possible, Eva checked her phone. It wasn't even midday yet, but she already had five missed calls, all from Trent. She switched her phone off without listening to her messages and set to work cleaning the kitchen.

Colette still hit the roof when she returned from her weekend at the spa. The coffee table, which Eva had always thought was kind of tasteless, had apparently cost over four thousand dollars. Eva was sent to her room, grounded for a month and had her car privileges revoked and her allowance docked. These were minor inconvenences. What really hurt was having her laptop confiscated, which would reduce her to covert operations in the computer lab at school or on Nicole's desktop, and neither option was satisfactory for her purposes, since the former involved the total absence of privacy and the latter required bribing her sister. That evening Eva finished her homework and went to bed without dinner.

The next day she left home early and walked to school before Trent stopped by to pick her up. She had missed the reports of the plane crash on the news, but everyone was talking about it because Annabelle Sutter, a sophomore, had an uncle who'd been on the flight that had left Newark just before the one that went down. Eva was able to avoid Trent for most of the morning, giving a wide berth to the areas where he and his friends usually hung out between classes, but he finally caught up with her in the lunch hall and grabbed her by the elbow as she queued with her tray.

'Where were you this morning?' he asked. 'I called by your house.'

Eva shook free from his grip. 'I walked instead.'

'Why'd you do that?'

'Because I didn't want to share a car with you.' She turned away, but he grabbed her again and yanked her back. His fingers dug into the flesh of her upper arm. 'Trent, let go,' she said. 'You're hurting me.'

'C'mon Eva, don't tell me you're still mad about Saturday night.'

'Mad doesn't even come close.'

'Then let me make it up to you.'

'Let. Me. Go!' she said, raising her voice. 'I don't want you anywhere near me.'

'You're not going anywhere unless I say so.' Trent's grip grew stronger. By tomorrow a ring of bruises would no doubt surface on her arm. 'You're my girl, Eva, and unless I say otherwise that's the way it's staying.'

'You really want to do this now, here in the lunch hall?'

'Keep your voice down,' he said. 'You're making a scene.'

'A *scene*? I'll show you a scene.' She twisted to face the tables behind them. 'Hey everyone, listen! This is a public service announcement! Trent Armitage is nothing but a jumped-up little bully with anger management issues and I'm officially breaking up with him...' A stunned silence settled over the immediate vicinity. Eva took a breath before continuing. '...*plus* he has a small dick and, ladies take it from me, I mean a real teenie-weenie.' She wiggled her pinkie for good measure.

Trent released her arm and took a step back. He looked like he'd been slapped across the face with a wet fish, his mind struggling to make sense of what had just happened. A small giggle broke out nearby and quickly swelled into a torrent of laughter. Trent began to shake, a slight tremor that started in his legs and grew as it worked its way up his body. He raised his fist, and for a second Eva thought he was going to hit her, but instead he brought it down on her tray, knocking it from her hands, and then spun on his heel. A freshman who was half Trent's size and wearing a sweater probably knitted by the kid's mother stood in his way. As if to prove Eva's point, Trent shoved him in the chest and sent him skidding across the floor on his backpack.

It was the first time in Eva's life that she'd ever stood up to anyone like that. All afternoon it felt as though some previously dormant part of her had awakened and the world was now full of possibility. She passed by Sam's house on her way home, thinking it odd she hadn't seen him in any of their classes. Eva hadn't intended to show him her ledge overlooking the town that weekend – she'd never taken anyone else there before – but it had just kind of happened. Although she scarcely knew him, there was something about Sam that made Eva feel she could trust him, and after what Nicole had told her she felt she owed him an explanation for Saturday night.

However, when she rang the bell nobody answered. Eva pressed again, holding the button down for a full thirty seconds, but still nobody came to the door. She walked around to the living room window. The curtains were drawn, which was strange since it was still light out, so she cupped her hands around her eyes and peeked through a gap. There was no sign of movement and, since the car wasn't in the drive, Eva assumed the family must be out for the day and walked home.

She dropped her school bag just inside the front door and went through to the kitchen to fix a snack. Doug was at the breakfast bar, a tumbler in one hand and a half-empty bottle of whisky in the other. His tie was loose and the top two buttons of his shirt were undone.

'You're back early,' Eva said and opened the fridge.

He looked up with bloodshot eyes. 'Huh?'

'I thought daytime drinking was Colette's speciality.'

'Something's happened.' He drained his glass and refilled it, sloshing whisky all over the counter.

'You hear about the plane crash?' Eva asked. She took out a tub of strawberry yoghurt and went to fetch a spoon. 'Some kid at school has an uncle who was on the flight before. Everyone's talking about it.'

'Rebecca Rayner was on that flight.'

'You mean Sam's mom?' she asked, not quite grasping the implication.

'And Sam and Matthew. Rebecca left a message with the office over the weekend. I only picked it up this morning.'

'They're okay though, aren't they?'

'I don't know, sweet pea.' He shook his head and gazed into his glass. 'It sounds pretty goddam awful. I don't think there were any survivors.'

Apart from her paternal grandfather, who had passed away when she was nine years old, Eva had never been close to anyone who had died. She'd seen Sam only two days before. 'Get out of my house,' had been her last words to him. At that moment she felt her stomach turn. The yogurt fell from her fingers and she ran to the bathroom to throw up.

Events in Eva's life spiralled downwards in a rapid manner. Doug said it was okay for her to stay home from school the next day, but when she returned two days later the mood among her so-called friends had changed entirely. At lunch, the table Eva usually sat at was suddenly 'full' and later, when she saw Kimberly and a few of the girls she was friendly with, they immediately huddled into a small group, snickering as she walked past.

Over the next couple of days the full extent of Trent's smear campaign became apparent as the dumb questions started.

Is it true you had a threesome with Trent and Brandon?

Is it true you have genital warts?

Is it true your father was arrested for possessing indecent images of children?

Is it true? Is it true? Is it true?

After a while she gave up denying the things that were said, instead exaggerating them to even more outrageous proportions.

Just Trent and Brandon? What about the rest of the football team?

Genital warts? You forgot to mention Chlamydia, Gonorrhoea and HIV.

Yep, and it's sure gonna put a dampener on family finances, since sex trafficking was our primary source of income, y'know?

Although it made Eva feel better, such retaliation in no way improved matters and further alienated her from her peers. Her standing at Montclair High was damaged beyond repair, but she found it hard to care.

The news came that Matthew had been killed in the crash, while Sam and Rebecca were on life support. Doug took it especially hard, blaming himself for bringing the family over in the first place. He now drank even more than Colette and hardly slept at night. Eva often woke to the noise of him crashing about on the ground floor. His personal hygiene deteriorated and he started getting up late and arriving home early from work, something Eva had never previously dreamed possible.

Then, in early November, the tension that had been cranking up like two tectonic plates pushing together finally came to a head. For as long as Eva could remember her parents had led separate lives, orbiting each other at a safe, consistent distance, but when Doug came home early to find Colette in bed with Paul, the guy who mowed their lawn, they collided with the cataclysmic force of two planets smashing together. Eva arrived back from another miserable day at school to find her mother sitting on the kitchen floor in a pile of broken crockery, an empty bottle of wine in her hand and tears streaming down her face. Doug's clothes were no longer in his wardrobe and his car had vanished from the garage. Her father didn't come home that night, and when Eva rang the next morning he told her he wouldn't be back at all. He needed space to think, he said, and would be in touch soon. Two days later he called to explain that he was taking a position overseeing a restructure at the bank's London branch and would be staying there for a few months.

Although Eva was old enough to understand the futility of her parents staying together just to maintain appearances, the split affected Nicole badly. She became reclusive and even more sullen than usual, showing no interest in her activities or her expensively assembled collection of toys.

Colette swung between extremes of manic hyper-activity and bouts of debilitating self-pity. On returning home each day, Eva could never be sure whether she'd find her mother vacuuming the skirting boards in high heels and full make-up, or lying in bed wearing the same clothes as the night before. Although it was a situation

Colette had undoubtedly brought on her-self, Eva couldn't help but feel for her. Doug was hardly an innocent party; there was only so much boredom and neglect a person could take before they started to go a little strange in the head.

As December approached the news came that Sam had regained consciousness. With only a week of the semester left, Eva decided she could do with a change of scenery, so she rang Doug to ask if she could come to stay over Christmas. Obviously delighted, he'd booked her a ticket on the next available flight. The fact she'd miss the last three days of school was an additional sweetener.

The flight was less than half full, with airport security still on high alert and electronic devices prohibited on all flights since the crash. Once they touched down, Eva heaved her hand luggage from the overhead locker, elbowed her way past a fat man in a sweat-stained shirt and stepped through the hatch onto the metal ramp that descended into the belly of Heathrow Airport. She felt tired and dirty, her clothes clinging to her body like cobwebs, and wanted nothing more than to shower and collapse into bed for the rest of the day. It seemed to take an eternity to get her passport stamped and then pass through baggage reclaim, but Doug was waiting in the arrivals hall, waving from the other side of a barrier.

'Boy, is it good to see you!' he said and hugged her so tightly she could hardly breathe. He had dark circles under his eyes and was sporting an ill-advised beard on his chin. 'Come on, let's get out of here.'

As he wheeled her case to the car, Eva gave him a less-than-flattering critique of his facial hair and told him it looked like he was working too hard. He laughed as he threw her case in the trunk of his car and said, 'You're probably right, sweet pea, but what else am I going to do to occupy my time?'

'I don't know,' she said, 'have some fun for once? Socialise? Relax? Maybe shave?'

'I was thinking we could do that together,' he said. 'Have some fun I mean, not shave. I'm taking the next few days off work in your honour.'

'I'd like that,' Eva said and climbed into the passenger seat. 'Maybe we could hit a few singles' bars together.'

'Nice try, young lady, but even over here you're not old enough to drink.'

'Maybe not,' she said, 'but I'm closer to eighteen than twenty-one. So, how are Mrs Rayner and Sam doing?'

The good humour washed from Doug's face. 'Not well,' he said. 'It was Matthew's funeral the other week. Sam had some sort of seizure and had to be rushed to hospital, the poor kid. I'm sure he could do with some company. You should look him up while you're here.'

'You know, I might just do that,' Eva said.

For the first time in months the world felt full of possibility again.

46

Sam visited the Tempus Research Facility every day that week and almost grew used to the headaches that accompanied his training. He underwent a bewildering array of brain scans, many similar to those he'd already been through in hospital, and was made to complete several memory tests in which he was asked to repeat an ever-increasing sequence of numbers that were read out to him. He also got to work on the random chance generator again, although only after insisting Fairview disconnect the electrified plates on the joysticks, which he agreed to with a disappointed huff.

With each session Sam felt his ability grow as the Tetradyamide sharpened his senses. On Tuesday he beat

159

his previous score on the random chance generator before the headache got too bad, notching up fifty-two correct identifications, and beat that again the following day with a score of seventy-five. On Thursday he broke the one hundred mark, at which point the counter in the bottom corner of the screen rolled from 99 back to 00 and McHayden stepped into the room. 'That's enough,' she said. 'I think we've proved our point here.'

Sam's training with the Tempus Project left him drained, exhausted and unable to manage anything more demanding than shovelling food into his mouth before falling into bed when he got back each evening. On Thursday he arrived home to find Chrissie and his grandparents sitting around the table while Lance washed up at the sink.

'How was it?' Chrissie asked. 'You look terrible.'

Sam had told his family that he was still helping the police with their investigations, which was true, in a way. Chrissie made no attempt to hide the fact that she thought Sam was overdoing it, but because he hadn't had another seizure since the funeral and made a big show of taking the bogus epilepsy tablets McHayden had given him, there wasn't really much she could say or do.

'I'm fine,' he said, 'just a bit tired. And hungry.'

'There's lasagne in the oven,' Grandma said. 'I wasn't sure what time you'd be back, so we've already eaten, I'm afraid.'

Sam filled a plate from a baking dish and took a seat at the table.

'Any breakthroughs in the investigation yet?' Chrissie asked.

'Nothing solid,' he said, hating himself for lying to her. 'We just went through some mug shots. It was pretty boring, actually.'

She narrowed her eyes. 'I thought you looked at mug shots already.'

Sam put a forkful of lasagne in his mouth and chewed slowly to buy a few extra seconds. 'I did. These ones were different, I guess.'

'Hmmm,' she said, looking unconvinced. 'I don't like the idea of you taking on so much after your injury, especially with your interview tomorrow. You need to be taking it easy.'

Dr McHayden had insisted Sam do everything in his power to portray the appearance of normality, so he'd contacted Fraser Golding College earlier in the week hoping to start his A-levels in the New Year, and had been invited to attend an interview with the Principal on Friday, the last day of term.

'I appreciate your concern,' he said, 'but I'm fine. Really, Chrissie, you worry too much.'

'Well someone's got to. You don't seem very interested in your own wellbeing.'

Lance turned from the sink, a damp dishcloth draped over his shoulder. 'Lay off, Chrissie, he's not a baby anymore.'

'Exactly,' Sam said, 'I just want to get on with my life instead of everybody treating me like an invalid.'

'But you *are* an invalid.' Chrissie reached across the table and took Sam's hand. 'I just don't want you taking on too much. I understand you wanting to go back to college, just like I understand you wanting to help the police. Really, Sam, I understand those things better than anyone, but you need to remember that your health is more important than any of that.'

'I do,' he said, wondering how many promises he would have to make that he didn't know if he could keep.

His grandmother covered the lasagne with aluminium foil and transferred the baking tray to the fridge. 'Oh, I almost forgot,' she said. 'You had a visitor while you were out. A young lady; pretty thing, I must say. Foreign; Canadian or American, I think. Said her name was Eve. Or Evelyn. Something like that.'

Sam paused, his loaded fork an inch from his mouth. 'Do you mean Eva?'

'That's it! Anyway, she left a telephone number on the pad in the hall and asked if you'd call her back.'

Sam returned his fork to the plate. Suddenly he wasn't hungry anymore.

47

Sam woke on Friday morning to the view of snow falling through a gap in his curtains, but when he looked out of the window he saw that it was melting away to a muddy slush on the ground instead of settling. Once again, he hadn't slept well that night, his nerves bubbling over like a shaken fizzy drink. On the first two occasions Sam had tried to call Eva, he'd hung up before the phone even started to ring, but on the third he'd managed to hold his nerve. Doug had picked up and put Eva on, and as soon as Sam heard her voice his anxiety had disappeared, the Night of The Broken Coffee Table instantly forgotten. Eva had said she had plans with Doug in the morning, sightseeing and such, but would love to catch up, so Sam arranged to meet her after his interview by the tube station near Fraser Golding.

Lance drove him to college in Victor, his old Volvo, and Chrissie insisted on coming too. Sam's meeting with Mr Tilbert, the Principal, was at 11 o'clock, after which he'd arranged to meet Lewis for lunch, leaving a couple of hours with Eva before McHayden picked him up for his next session at the Tempus Research Facility. It was by far Sam's busiest day since his injury and, as Victor rattled to a stop outside the gates, he began to wonder if he really was taking on too much. As if reading his mind, Chrissie unclipped her seatbelt, leaned over from the front and asked if he wanted them to wait.

'I'll be fine,' he said.

'Are you sure? We can come back and collect you, if you like?'

'Thanks, but it's okay. I'm supposed to meet someone afterwards.'

'I'd prefer it if you came straight home,' she said and bit her lip in a way that suggested she was holding back.

Lance rolled his eyes in the rear view mirror. 'Chill, Chrissie. He said he's fine.'

'He's my brother,' she said, glowering at him. 'I'm allowed to be concerned, aren't I?'

'I'd better go,' Sam said before he could get caught up in their spat. 'Thanks for the lift.'

He climbed out, his jacket flapping in the cold wind, and made his way towards the entrance. Sam wondered if Chrissie would revert back to the role of sister if their mum ever woke up. She only had his best interests at heart, but he almost missed the sullen bully he'd spent most of his life trying to avoid, compared to this clucking mother hen only three years older than him. It was as if the crash had changed Chrissie more than Sam, and he was the one who'd been injured.

Fraser Golding Sixth Form College educated over two thousand students and was set over a sprawling campus with several different faculty buildings scattered amongst courtyards and sports fields. Sam signed in at the front desk and was given a visitor's badge and directions to the Principal's office.

Mr Tilbert was sitting in a high-backed leather chair that dwarfed his narrow frame. He had a thin, ratty face and a beard that was a blatant attempt to hide an overbite.

There was an executive toy on the surface of his desk: five metal balls suspended from a frame. As Sam entered, Mr Tilbert lifted the first ball and released it, sending the last rebounding into motion. 'Hello. Sam, is it?' he asked. 'Please, have a seat. I've had a quick look through you file and it appears we offered you a place back in April.'

'That's right,' Sam said and sat on one of the cheap, plastic chairs reserved for visitors.

'The thing is, Sam; this offer was conditional on you taking the place in September. It says here that our offer was initially accepted and then later declined.'

'My family moved to America in the summer,' Sam said. 'It all happened at the last minute, which is why I accepted and then had to decline.'

Mr Tilbert studied the file like he was checking a script for his next line, then pursed his lips and emitted a low whistle. 'This presents us with something of a problem, you see. When you declined our offer, your place was automatically allocated to the next student on the waiting list. Unfortunately, at this particular moment, the College is fully subscribed.'

Sam stared at him, unable to believe the man had invited him all the way down here just to say he wasn't going to let him in. 'Please,' he said, 'there must be something you can do. Fraser Golding was always my first choice. Loads of my friends go here.'

'You know, Sam, where your friends go should never be a deciding factor when choosing a sixth-form college.' He paused, rested his elbows on the desk and placed his fingertips together. 'I do, however, understand there have been some *extenuating circumstances* in your case.'

'Extenuating circumstances?'

A jewel set in the chunky gold ring on Principal Tilbert's little finger glittered in the light. 'I'm talking about the plane crash,' he said. 'A truly terrible business.'

'Oh, right, that. What's that got to do with it?'

'Well, when dealing with such a high-profile...' He sniffed, trying to suck the word he was looking for from the air. '...situation as yours, I don't think it would be wise for the College to turn you away. Above all, I have our reputation to consider and, although this is strictly off the record, I might be willing to bend the rules in this instance.'

'You mean you're letting me in?' Sam asked.

Mr Tilbert twisted his ring and smiled. 'You'd have a lot of catching up to do, you realise. You've already missed the first term of the academic year and I wouldn't want you falling further behind.'

'I'll do whatever it takes.'

'Good.' He rose from his chair and offered Sam his hand. 'I'll have a word with admissions and get you enrolled for the new term. In the meantime, I'll have your teachers prepare some work to get you up to speed over the Christmas holidays.'

'Thank you,' Sam said. 'You won't regret this.'

'I sincerely hope not. And remember, if you ever need someone to talk to, my door is always open.'

'Sir?'

'About the, you know, *situation*. I've been told I'm a very good listener.'

Sam thanked him again and left. While he would have loved someone to confide in, Mr Tilbert was just about the last person he would choose.

48

Lewis stood outside the cafeteria with his bag slung over his shoulder. It was freezing and he had to keep stamping his feet to maintain the flow of blood to his toes. He glanced at the clock across the courtyard, set high on the wall of the main building, which was the oldest part of Fraser Golding College and dated back to some point in the late 1800s. Sam's interview should have finished ages ago. What was keeping him?

A group of people passed by on their way into the cafeteria. 'You coming?' Mo, a boy in his Politics class, asked.

'Waiting for someone,' Lewis said.

'Who?'

'My friend. He might be starting after Christmas. He's got an interview with Tilbert the Dilbert.'

Mo made to leave, then turned back, his eyes round. 'Oh, you mean *that* kid, don't you? The one in a coma.'

'His name's Sam. And he's not in a coma anymore, otherwise he wouldn't be here for an interview, would he?'

'Deep,' Mo said, nodding like it all made sense now. 'Catch you later.'

'Muppet,' Lewis muttered, watching him go. He wished Sam would hurry up: it had now been close to two hours since he'd last eaten and his stomach was beginning to rumble.

Lewis still didn't know how to explain what had happened after Sam had collapsed on the day of Matthew's funeral, and it bothered him like an itch in the middle of his back that he couldn't quite reach. Sam had been out every night that week – helping the police with their investigations, he'd said – but when Lewis had managed to corner him and bring it up again, his friend had changed the subject so quickly it was almost suspicious.

A few more people went by, then the door to the main building opened and, at long last, Lewis saw Sam come out and cross the courtyard. Although he wasn't exactly nimble on his feet yet, it was hard to believe that Sam had been on crutches only a couple of weeks earlier.

'What took you so long?' Lewis asked. 'I'm about to faint with hunger here.'

'Sorry, I got lost.'

'You'd get lost in a one bedroom flat. Anyway, how'd it go?'

Sam wrinkled his nose. 'Mr Tilbert made a bit of a song and dance about it. The year's already started, he said, and the college is fully subscribed—'

'Blah-blah-blah. He likes the sound of his own voice.' Lewis mimed a yawn. 'But he let you in, right?'

'Yeah,' Sam said and grinned. 'After the plane crash I think he was more worried about what people would think if he didn't.'

Lewis fist pumped the air. 'Get in! I've got a free period this afternoon, what do you want to do to celebrate?'

'I can't,' Sam said, shaking his head. 'I've got to meet someone in an hour.'

Lewis was slightly taken aback. 'Really? Who?'

'Just a friend from America.'

'A *friend*? I didn't think you were there long enough.'

'Wow, thanks a bunch. I am capable of making new friends, you know.'

'Sorry,' he said. 'I'll drop by your house tomorrow then. Come on, let's eat.'

The cafeteria was filled with noise as people shouted to be heard over one another. Lewis and Sam took a tray each from a stack at the end of a counter and pushed them along a rail as they waited to be served. Lewis chose the fish fingers and chips, and Sam the chicken curry.

'What's the food like in this place?' Sam asked as they took a table in the far corner.

'Better than our last school,' Lewis said, 'but not much.'

Sam took a bite of his chicken curry, grimaced and then immediately spat it into a paper tissue. 'That's repulsive,' he said, pushing his plate away.

'Hey, what would I know? I'll eat anything.'

'True.'

Lewis took a bite of fish finger and chewed with his mouth open. 'So, I've been wanting to talk to you about what happened at your dad's funeral, you know, when you thought you saw that bombing that didn't happen and—' Sam kicked him on the shin under the table. 'Ouch! What was that for?'

'You haven't told anyone about that, have you?' Sam asked, rubbing the scar behind his ear, which was becoming harder to see as his hair grew back.

Lewis hesitated. 'No, I haven't. At least, I don't think so.'

'Which is it, Lewis? You haven't or you don't think so?'

'No, I haven't. What's the big deal anyway?'

'Nothing. You just can't tell anyone, that's all.'

'Whatever.' Lewis was trying his best to be patient, but his friend seemed so different since the crash.

'Please,' Sam said, 'it's important. I need you to promise you won't tell anyone.'

Lewis put his fork down. 'Fine, if it's so Earth-shatteringly important, I promise. There, happy now?'

'Yes,' Sam said, but Lewis noticed that the veins around his temples were standing out again.

49

It was ten minutes after the time Sam had arranged to meet Eva and he was beginning to suspect she might not show up. He'd been feeling uneasy ever since Lewis had so casually mentioned the bombing over lunch. Only days before, under McHayden's watchful gaze, Sam had sworn himself to secrecy on all matters time travel related, but now he realised that this promise had been broken before it was even made, because Lewis already knew what had happened on the day of the funeral.

The weather had worsened and another watery snow-fall wetted the slabs of the pavement. To keep warm, Sam jiggled up and down while staring through the window of a pharmacy and pretending to be interested in a display that showed Rudolf the Reindeer using a branded nasal spray to cure his red nose. He checked his phone after another minute or two had passed: there were no messages or missed calls, but that was hardly surprising, since he'd already checked before arriving. Just in case he did a quick circuit to the other exit of the tube station, but Eva wasn't waiting there either.

Sam tried to picture what she looked like, but the image in his head didn't seem quite right. He knew certain facts, like the colour of her eyes and the shape of her smile, but couldn't fit these together properly, as though he was missing certain pieces of the jigsaw puzzle. What if she'd had already come and gone and he hadn't recognised her? What if she was still angry about the Night of the Broken Coffee Table and had changed her mind? What if Doug had pressured her into meeting him out of misguided guilt or, worse still, pity?

Sam took his phone out again and was about to call Doug's landline when, all of a sudden, he got the unsettling feeling that he was being watched. He glanced up to see an old man on the opposite side of the road who was staring at him with wild, hazel eyes. The man looked like he had been sleeping rough for a very long time. He wore a mismatching collection of filthy clothes and had long white hair that had fused together with his beard to form a single mega-dreadlock. There was something vaguely familiar about him, although Sam couldn't place what it was.

At that moment someone else, a man with hair shaved even shorter than Sam's, raced up the stairs from the tube station and nearly knocked him over. Without apologising, he darted off, and when Sam looked up again the tramp on the other side of the road had vanished.

There was a tap on Sam's shoulder.

'Hey,' Eva said.

'Hey to you too.'

She looked even more gorgeous than he remembered, the puzzle pieces fitting together with devastating effect. Eva could have kept him waiting all day and Sam wouldn't have cared now that she had arrived. He wondered whether or not a hug was appropriate, but she threw her arms around his neck and kissed his cheek.

'You've had a haircut,' she said and released him. 'I like it.'

'Thanks.' He rubbed his head, his fingers resting on the scar for a second.

'It's good to see you. I couldn't believe it when I heard about your dad. How're you holding up? Doug said you had some kind of fit at the funeral.'

'Oh that,' Sam said, knowing he had no choice but to give the revised version of events. 'They think I might have developed epilepsy after the surgery.'

Eva gasped and put a hand over her mouth.

'It's not as bad as it sounds,' he added quickly. 'And I'm on this new medicine which has totally stopped the fits. All things considered, I'm doing well. So, what brings you to London?'

She stopped smiling and sighed. 'I'm staying with Doug for a few weeks. Things back home are a mess of epic proportions and I needed to take a break before I went crazy. Let's get out of the cold and I'll explain all. Where are you taking me?'

'Um, I'm not really sure,' Sam said, realising he'd been so worried about whether or not Eva would show up that he hadn't given any thought as to where they'd go if she actually did. 'There's a little coffee house around the corner. They sell homemade cakes that are pretty good and—'

'How about there?' Eva said, pointing to a pub across the road. 'I feel like something a bit stronger than coffee.'

Sam was about to protest, but Eva slid her gloved hand into his and stepped onto the crossing, dragging him after. The pub was called *The Prince Regent*, and it was shabby but not in a chic sort of way. The exterior was all flaking paint and grubby brickwork. There was a sign above the door with a painting of the Prince Regent himself, a young man in a red military coat wearing an impressive collection of medals on his chest. Although the sign was at least fifteen feet above the pavement, someone had managed to deface it with a wad of chewing gum over each eye and a piece that stretched across the mouth.

Eva shoved the door open, slamming it noisily against the wall. The interior was almost as run-down as the outside, with seat covers faded to a greyish brown, their original colour unrecognisable, and tables cratered by an assortment of ancient cigarette burns. The only other customers were two red-faced old men, who looked like they'd been drinking for several hours already and turned to stare at Eva and Sam as if they'd just walked in dressed as a pantomime horse.

Sam quickly decided this was the kind of place only visited by 'locals' and that they had no business here. 'Maybe we should try somewhere else,' he said, hanging back by the door.

If Eva heard him, she didn't show it and strode purposefully to the bar, leaving Sam with no choice but to follow. A plump, pig-faced woman with eyebrows plucked to the point of invisibility and then pencilled back in was standing behind the bar, watching them with an expression that was not exactly welcoming.

Eva unzipped her coat, loosened her scarf and smiled sweetly. 'Two shots of tequila, thank you.'

The barmaid looked slowly from Eva, to Sam and then to Eva again. 'Can't serve you,' she said.

Sam turned to leave but Eva tugged at his sleeve, pulling him back. 'Why ever not?' she said. 'We're both old enough.'

The barmaid snorted. 'Yeah, right. So you can prove it, can you?'

'Naturally,' Eva said. She took out her purse and, cool as you like, presented a UK driver's licence. The barmaid snatched it from her and held it up to the light, squinting and glancing back and forth between the card and Eva's face. The two old drunks watched on with varying degrees of amusement and hostility. Sam shifted his weight from foot to foot and muffled a fake cough.

Eventually the barmaid lowered the ID and slid it back across the top of the bar. 'Eva Bernstein?'

'That's right,' Eva said, returning the licence to her purse.

'What can I get you?'

'As I said, two shots of tequila and…what do you want, Sam?'

Of the five taps set in the top of the bar, three had upturned glasses over the handles, limiting the choice.

'A cider, I think,' he said.

Eva nodded. 'Okay. Two shots of tequila and two ciders, please.'

The barmaid grunted in acknowledgement, then poured two pints of flat, yellow liquid and a pair of ominous-looking brown shots, which she placed on a tray with a salt shaker and a couple of shrivelled slices of lemon.

'Here,' Sam said and reached for his wallet, but Eva had already pressed a twenty pound note into the barmaid's hand.

'Doug gave me cash and I don't have anything else to spend it on,' she said. 'You can buy the next round of drinks, if you like.'

Sam carried the tray over to the table that looked least likely to collapse. Eva collected her change and joined him. 'Okay, shots first,' she said and handed him a narrow glass. 'Do you like tequila?'

'Sure,' he said, 'drink it all the time.'

'Good, it's my favourite.' Eva poured a small mound of salt onto the back of her hand and passed the shaker to Sam. 'What shall we drink to?' she asked, raising her glass. 'Your dad?'

'No, let's drink to the future.'

'To the future then...and new beginnings, fresh starts and clean slates.'

'The last clean slate I had didn't work out so well,' he said.

She licked the salt off her hand, knocked back the tequila in a single gulp and banged her empty glass on the table. 'Now your turn.'

Sam sniffed his glass. He'd only ever tried tequila once before – when Chrissie had left half a bottle on the kitchen counter and Lewis had dared him to drink some – but this smelled much stronger. It was enough to make his eyes water and Sam wished he hadn't just boasted about how often he drank it. Copying Eva, he poured salt on the back of his hand, licked it and, before he could retch, swallowed down the shot. His throat instantly caught fire, an intense burning that spread down to his stomach and rose into his nasal cavity. He coughed and spluttered, tears flooding his eyes, and banged his glass on the table.

Eva laughed. 'I thought you drank tequila "all the time"?'

'Well, maybe not *all* time.'

'Here, bite on this,' she said and passed him a slice of lemon. 'It helps.'

Sam bit down and grimaced as sour juice filled his mouth. At least it took the taste of tequila away and, after a few seconds, he discovered the burning sensation actually felt quite good. He sipped his cider, which was almost pleasurable by comparison. 'So, where did you get the fake driver's licence?' he asked. 'I've got to admit, it looks pretty convincing.'

'That's because it's not a fake,' Eva said, as if that were explanation enough.

'But…how?'

'There are ways if you know how. I'm good with computers, remember?'

Sam decided against pushing it any further. 'You said things in Montclair were a bit of a mess. How so?'

'Where to begin? Doug and Colette are getting a divorce.'

It was strange for Sam to think that people's lives had moved on in the time he'd spent in a coma and the weeks since waking up. 'Are you okay with that?' he asked.

Eva shrugged and took a sip of cider. 'There's only so long two people can live separate lives while still pretending to be a couple, I guess. It's Nicole I'm really worried about. She may try to pretend like she's super mature and everything, but it's hit her pretty bad. Still, it's not like anyone died or anything…oh, Sam, I'm so sorry!'

'It's okay,' he said. He knew that at some stage he would have to get used to people talking about death, and the last thing he wanted was Eva walking on eggshells around him.

'No, it is most definitely *not* okay,' she said. 'I don't know what I was thinking. Since I broke up with Trent I've gotten more and more used to saying what I think, but whatever, it's not okay.'

'No, really. It…wait, you broke up with Trent?'

Eva leaned back in her chair and gazed at him, her head tilted to one side.

'I'm sorry to hear that,' he said.

'*Really*? Even after what happened at the party?'

'That whole thing with the coffee table was an accident, by the way. Things got way out of hand and…and I never meant to—'

'I know, Nicole told me what happened. I wanted to apologise, but you never showed up at school. It was only later I found out about the plane crash.' She paused, glanced over to the bar and then looked back and smiled. 'Anyway, enough of the doom and gloom. I'm here to drink and it's your turn to buy. What do you say?'

There were hundreds of things Sam wanted to say to her, but the word 'no' was not among them.

The pub was beginning to get busy when, three tequilas and another pint of cider later, Sam and Eva stumbled onto the pavement. The snowy rain had eased off, giving way to a cold, clear night. It was rush hour and the streets were filled with people making their way home for the weekend. In spite of the chill, Sam's body felt as though it radiated heat. Without giving it a thought he put his arm around Eva, and she smiled and rested her head against his shoulder as they walked.

'What now?' he asked as they approached the station.

'I'd like to stay out, but Doug's taking me for dinner. I had a nice time though.'

'Me too, we should do it again.'

'You mean like a date?'

Sam clenched his teeth, certain he'd taken things too far. 'No, not if you don't want it to be. It'd just be… friends catching up.'

'I thought we just did that.'

'Oh,' he said and withdrew his arm from her shoulder.

Eva laughed, grabbed hold of his hand and pulled it back in place. 'Relax, silly, I'm only kidding. I'm free tomorrow.'

Sam exhaled a cidery breath. 'Maybe you could come over to mine then. My sister will be there and—'

Eva rolled her eyes towards the dark sky. 'And here I was thinking you might want to spend time alone with me!'

'I do,' he said, feeling like he was trying to change direction while running on ice. 'We can do something else instead if…wait a minute, you're messing with me again, aren't you?'

'A bit slow, but you get there in the end. What time shall I come by?'

'How about lunchtime?'

'Sounds good. Until tomorrow then.'

In one swift motion Eva put her hands on Sam's waist and, before he knew what was happening, kissed him. His heart did a quick cartwheel in his chest. He leaned in and was about to pull her closer when she broke away, turned and skipped down the steps to the station. At the bottom she looked over her shoulder and waved before disappearing out of sight.

Sam felt a grin that was probably visible from space stretch across his lips. And then he realised he was late to meet Dr McHayden.

50

Sam stumbled home as fast as his drunken legs would carry him, which wasn't very fast. His stomach sloshed with a mixture of tequila and cider that didn't sit at all well and the world seemed to swim and dip with every footstep. At one point he had to grab hold of a lamp post to steady himself. An elderly couple walking in the opposite direction gave him dirty looks and crossed to the other side of the road.

How could he have forgotten about meeting Dr McHayden when the Tempus Project was his only chance of undoing what had happened to his parents? The answer was obvious: when Sam was with Eva, nothing seemed to matter. He got tunnel vision and all else blurred into the background.

He would have liked to rest longer, but McHayden had already told him that she didn't take lateness lightly, so he took a deep breath, waited a couple more seconds and then staggered on again. As he reached the end of his road a bubble of gas rose within him, exiting as a loud cider-and-tequila-flavoured burp. At that moment Sam realised that he wasn't going to make it home in time, so he ducked into the front garden of the house three doors up from his own, where he bent over double and vomited in Mrs Mason's prized rose bushes.

He retched and retched, his stomach cramping until nothing came up but a thick, yellow liquid that stung the back of his throat. After that he stayed hunched for a while, his knees in the mud as he gasped and wiped cold sweat from his forehead. Sam would have done anything for a glass of water, but thankfully the world had begun to spin a little less. He clambered to his feet and peered over the hedge. No one was about, so he crept out of the gate and fled the scene of his crime.

He had just pulled out his door keys when he noticed a familiar dark car parked on the other side of the road. Dr McHayden was still waiting, it appeared, although Sam wasn't sure whether that was good or bad news. He cupped his hand and breathed into it, wincing at the smell of his own breath, then crossed the road. The rear window wound down as he approached the car and McHayden poked her wrinkled, bird-like face out.

'You're late,' she said.

'Sorry. I—'

'What were you doing in the front garden of that house?'

'I…I…'

She sniffed the air, then her eyes widened. 'Have you been drinking? Get in this instant!'

Sam wiped his mouth and did as he was told. McHayden sat staring at him with a gaze that felt as if it would turn him to stone, so he looked down and noticed his trouser legs were muddy and spotted with vomit. 'Sorry, I had to meet a friend,' he said. 'I didn't realise the time.'

McHayden straightened the pleats of her skirt. 'A friend? Am I to understand that this is all a game to you? Your attitude shows complete disregard for importance of the work we have embarked upon. The Tempus Project could change the world, Sam, and you arrive over an hour late, smelling like a beer towel and in no fit state to be of any use whatsoever.'

'Sorry,' he said and realised he was beginning to sound like a broken record. 'It won't happen again.'

'No, it most certainly will *not*. I'm having serious

reservations about your suitability. There seems little point investing further time and effort in your training if you cannot be relied upon.'

Sam tried to swallow, but could already feel tears brimming in his eyes. Without McHayden his hopes of saving his parents were smashed. 'Please,' he said, 'you can't kick me out.'

'I think I must have misheard. Do you really have the audacity to tell me what I can and cannot do?'

'But you need me.'

McHayden raised herself to her full, if limited, height so she could almost look Sam level in the eye. 'My dear boy, it seems you vastly overestimate your importance. The brain scans we completed earlier this week have proved successful in pinpointing the exact location of the scar tissue that causes your ability to manipulate time. Today we began experimental surgery to replicate the results of your injury in animals and if these are successful, which I have every confidence they will be, then human trials can begin within a matter of weeks. Believe me when I tell you there is no shortage of volunteers ready to take your place.'

'But—'

'While finding you when we did was without question a stroke of luck, don't ever believe that you are indispensable. My research existed long before you joined us and will continue to do so long after. Unless you can prove your continued worth then I don't really see what further use you can be.'

Sam's only hope was to beg. 'Please,' he said, 'just give me one more chance. I'm here now. I need this. I'll do whatever it takes.'

McHayden traced her lips with her fingertip. After a while she exhaled loudly and shook her head. 'Against my better judgment, I'm willing to give you another chance, dependant on certain conditions which are, of course, non-negotiable.'

'Whatever it is, I'll do it.'

She relaxed, the wrinkled skin of her face smoothing slightly. 'If we are to proceed together, Sam, then the Tempus Project entirely must take precedence over everything else. That means schoolwork, friends and family. If you are to regain my trust there must be no distractions, no missed sessions and definitely no alcohol. That is my final offer: full commitment, all or nothing.'

Sam had a simple decision: he could either give in to McHayden and accept everything that entailed, or he could get out of the car and leave the Tempus Project behind, and with it the opportunity to control his ability and save his parents.

'Okay,' he said, his shoulders sagging, 'I'll do it.'

She gave a brisk nod of her head. 'Very well then. You are of no use to me in your current state. Go home and sleep it off; we'll resume training tomorrow morning.'

'But tomorrow's Saturday.'

'Yes, I am well aware of that.'

'It's just...I had plans.'

'My dear boy, were you listening to anything I said? If you have plans then I suggest you cancel them. I'll be here tomorrow morning at nine o'clock sharp, and if you're so much as a minute late then our association ends right there.'

'Okay,' Sam said. 'I'll be ready.'

'That is all.' She turned to look out the window. 'You can get out now.'

Part V
Unintended Consequences

51

July 1969

Although exhausted from working nights, Lara had only managed a couple of hours sleep. It was too warm in her apartment for one thing, however opening the window caused the blinds to flap, did little to alleviate the heat and brought the added distraction of noise from the daytime hustle and bustle in the street below. On top of this, Isaac's scent still clung to the fabric of the sheets, a constant reminder of their lovemaking in the hour they shared after she arrived home before he left for work. She lifted the adjoining pillow, held it to her face and inhaled deeply, breathing in his smell. There was no way she would be able to fall back asleep now.

Lara climbed from the bed and, aware that people in the block across the street could see straight in, wrapped the sheet around her naked body. Technically she didn't need to leave for a while yet – it was nearly three hours before her shift started – but she was curious to see what was happening and wanted to be around other people when it did.

After a blissfully cool shower, she dried off and changed for work. There was next to no traffic on the streets of San Francisco as she drove to Stribe Lyndhurst – everyone was glued to their television sets, waiting for news – and she arrived in record time. The hospital lobby was likewise deserted and Lara rode the lift to the sixth floor alone. As she entered the Lincoln Ward she saw a small huddle of medical and clerical staff standing behind the front desk with their backs to the entrance. A foldout table had been erected in the doorway, on which she glimpsed a portable television set with a perilously taut power cable stretching to a socket in the office beyond.

'What's going on?' she asked, joining the back of the group.

Hank Windle, the janitor, leaned on his mop and stroked his bushy moustache. 'Not much, they're still in orbit.'

'Let me know when something happens, will you?'

'You got it,' he said and winked.

Lara signed in and began her rounds. When she reached the secure unit she found that the gate had been left unlocked yet again. It really wasn't good enough, and she would have to raise the issue at the next ward meeting.

Michael Humboldt was the last patient on Lara's rota. She hesitated outside his door. It had taken weeks to build up the courage to see him again after he'd attacked her and, in spite of the improvement in his condition, Lara still felt on edge around him. She opened the door and found Michael sitting on the corner of his bed with a straight back and his hands – one flesh and blood, the other metal and plastic – folded in his lap. His bandages had been removed a month ago and the charred skin of his face was softening from an angry red to a light, bubble-gum pink. He wore a cloth patch over the socket of his right eye and tufts of mousy blonde hair now sprouted from the left side of his head where the follicles remained intact.

As Lara entered, Michael tilted his head to look up at her through his good eye. 'Dr McHayden, you're early! What a pleasant surprise.'

'Hello, Michael,' she said. 'You're looking very well today.'

'I doubt if I'll win any beauty pageants, but I'll take that as a compliment all the same.'

'Which is how it was intended. How're you feeling?'

'Never better.' He stretched his arms out wide, then hugged them to his chest as if embracing himself. 'Dr Barclay's new medication really is remarkable stuff. You will pass on my thanks, won't you?'

In spite of Lara's reservations, it appeared Isaac had been correct in his conviction that Tetradyamide would help Michael. Michael's father had died two weeks earlier, but far from suicidal, he seemed positively upbeat.

'I'll pass that on,' she said, 'if I see him.'

'Come now, Dr McHayden. You think I haven't noticed the way you two look at one another?'

'I really don't think it's appropriate to discuss—'

He rose stiffly from the bed. 'That's a lovely pin you're wearing. A gift?'

Lara's fingers closed around the brooch that Isaac had given her on the day of the Bereck & Hertz Independence Day Dinner.

'I…I…well, yes, it was, as it happens.'

'Beautiful,' he muttered, stepping towards her, his gaze locked on the brooch. 'A truly beautiful thing.'

Lara recoiled, edging back until the door was directly behind her.

Michael took another step closer, hand outstretched, then blinked and looked up. 'I've startled you,' he said. 'I am sorry, Dr McHayden. My mother, rest her soul, used to have one exactly like it. Seeing it takes me back to when I was just a boy.'

Lara lowered her hands to her sides, let out the breath she'd been holding in and smiled. 'That's all right, Michael, no apology necessary.'

'So, you're not watching the daring explorers like everyone else?'

'Maybe later. Unlike some, I actually have work to do.'

'You work too hard,' he said. 'Certain events are too important to be missed. This is one small step for man, one giant leap for mankind.'

Lara frowned. 'Have I heard that before somewhere?'

'No, not yet.'

'Well, it's catchy. I never took you for a poet, Michael. You should write that down.' There was a pause, during which Michael smiled serenely at her. Eventually Lara cleared her throat. 'Anyhow, I should probably be getting back to my rounds. I'll come to check on you at the end of my shift.'

Michael bowed his head. 'Until we meet again, Dr McHayden.'

She laughed, went to rest her hand on his arm and then pulled it away. 'You make it sound like we won't see each other again in years. Really, Michael, I'll be back to check on you in a few hours.'

He gave her the serene smile again. 'If you say so.'

* * * * *

Lara made her way back up the corridor. Even if Michael's recovery was more down to Isaac's intervention than her own good work, it was really only the end result that mattered, and at this rate there was every chance Michael might be able to be moved from the secure unit in a few months' time.

She was approaching the gate when she saw Hank hurrying towards her on the other side of the bars, his face streaked with sweat.

'There you are!' he said. 'I've been searching everywhere. I was about to give up on you, doc.'

'Something the matter?' Lara asked.

'You said to find you if something happens. Well, it has! They're almost there.'

She let herself out and followed Hank through the last two corridors to the front desk. The crowd around the television set had swelled to several times its previous size. Lara stretched on tiptoes but her line of sight was blocked. Drawing in a breath, she squeezed against the desk and sidestepped around the crescent-shaped mass of bodies. On the far side she found Isaac and squashed in beside him.

'Hi,' he said and guided her in front of him to where she had an uninterrupted view of the screen.

'I thought your shift finished already?' she said.

'It has.' He nodded to the television. 'I didn't want to miss this.'

'What's going on?'

'You're just in time, they're on the final descent.'

Lara squinted at the grainy image. Over the last few weeks she'd had the mounting suspicion that her eyesight was deteriorating, but was putting off booking a test. She could just about make out a circular landing pad in the foreground drifting over a crater-marked landscape. A beep sounded at regular intervals over snippets of commentary from the broadcaster and dialogue between the crew and mission control. Lara reached down and squeezed Isaac's hand where no one else would be able to see. She was glad to have found him; together they were about to watch history be made.

'*Sixty seconds…*' a voice announced, '*…down two and a half…forward…forty feet, down two and a half…kicking up some dust…thirty feet, two and a half down…faint shadow…four forward, drifting to the right a little, twenty feet, two and half down…drifting forward just a little bit, that's good…*' Then silence, save for the beeping. '*…Okay, engine stop…we're home, 413 is in…Houston, Tranquillity base here…the Eagle has landed!*'

The crowd erupted in a chorus of whoops and cries. A champagne cork popped nearby. Thomas, the orderly, lifted Lara by the arms, spun her around and returned her to the floor facing Isaac. He hugged her and then quickly released her before anyone got the wrong (or right) idea.

'Did that really just happen?' Lara asked.

'It sure did,' Isaac said.

Someone thrust a paper cup filled with champagne into her hand. She took a sip and savoured the sensation of bubbles fizzing across her tongue.

Isaac also accepted a cup. 'Dr McHayden, there's something I've been wanting to show you.'

Lara glanced over her shoulder. 'What, *now*?'

'I don't think anyone will miss us. Besides, it should be a few hours until they begin surface operations.'

Holding her cup, Lara followed Isaac to the pharmaceutical storeroom. He unlocked the door and switched the light on. The walls here were lined with tall metal shelving units that held the Lincoln Ward's extensive supply of drugs.

Isaac locked the door behind them and turned to her. 'Imagine,' he said, 'by the time our children are adults we'll probably all have been to the moon and back several times over. It'll be like the yearly vacation to Hawaii.'

Lara placed her cup on the nearest shelf and stepped into his arms. 'What do you mean "our children"?'

'Why? You want kids someday, don't you?'

Lara felt her knees give and might have sagged to the floor had she not been holding on to him. Over recent months her feelings for Isaac had matured from a seed of attraction to full-blown love, however until now they'd never really discussed what the future might hold. If there had been a happier moment in Lara's life, she couldn't remember it. She imagined a house in the suburbs, two children – a boy and a girl – and maybe even a dog. She would give up medicine to raise the kids and spend her days baking cookies and making home.

'It's just over here,' Isaac said, smiling down at her.

'What is?'

'The thing I wanted to show you.'

'Oh, I thought that was just code for…'

'Maybe later,' he said and laughed.

Lara watched as he crossed the room to a cardboard box in the corner, sliced the tape around the lid with his keys and then dug down through polystyrene balls like a child playing lucky dip. Eventually he pulled out his prize and held it up.

'What's is it?' Lara asked.

Isaac shook the bottle, making a rattling noise. 'The latest batch of Tetradyamide. It was delivered this afternoon. I've refined production to improve purity by almost thirty-two percent. This batch will make the last lot look like candy.'

'Isaac, that's fantastic!'

'I'm glad you think so.' He returned the bottle to the box. 'Sorry if I've been a bit preoccupied with the whole thing lately.'

'I understand.'

'I'm not sure you do, Lara. The military want to use Tetradyamide to make more efficient killers, but that's not why I started out in this job. I want to help people.'

'And you are, Isaac. Just look at Michael, who sends his thanks, by the way.'

A worried look crossed his face. He ran his fingers through his hair, opened his mouth as if to say something and then closed it.

'What's wrong?' she asked.

'Probably nothing,' he said, shaking his head. 'We should get back.'

Lara linked her arms around his neck. 'I thought you said no one would miss us?'

He leaned forwards to kiss her, but as their lips met there was a knock at the door, the insistent thump of a heavy fist.

'Hold on, I'm coming,' Isaac called.

Lara tried to look as though she was busy compiling an inventory of supplies while Isaac fumbled with his keys and unlocked the door. Thomas was standing on the other side, his fist raised as he prepared to knock again.

'What is it?' Isaac said. 'Can't you see we're stocktaking?'

'You need to come right away,' Thomas said. 'It's Michael.'

Lara dropped the packet of sedatives that she'd been pretending to examine and headed after the two men as they ran towards secure unit.

'What's he done this time?' she asked when she had finally caught up with them.

'It's not what he's done that's the problem,' Thomas opened the door to Michael's cell, 'it's where in hell he's got to.'

Lara stepped in. The bed was neatly made, the sheets folded and tucked under the mattress with military precision. Michael was nowhere to be seen.

Isaac turned to Thomas. 'Call security. *Now!*'

Thomas nodded and ran off.

Lara crossed the room to the bed. Lying on the sheets was the brooch that Michael had shown such an interest in a short time before.

'He can't be far away,' Isaac said, 'and he's hardly inconspicuous. Don't worry, Lara, we'll find him.'

'No.' She reached down, picked up the brooch and slid it into her pocket. 'I don't believe that we ever will.'

52

Present Day

Sam hadn't slept well all week, and once again he tossed and turned deep into the night. Every time he began to drift off he would snap awake again, his mind alert and whirring. Although the Tetradyamide – or glue, as he had come to think of it – should have no longer been in his system, Sam could feel its afterglow; a lingering hum that echoed through his body and out into the world beyond, leaving him wanting more.

Eventually he gave up on sleep and climbed out of bed. The heating hadn't switched on yet and the house was freezing. He pulled his dressing gown over his pyjamas and, in almost total darkness, crept out onto the landing and down to the kitchen.

The digital clock on the oven said it was 04:23. He made toast with chocolate spread and ate leaning against the kitchen worktop, looking out over the blackness of the garden. The clear night sky was dotted with faint starlight in the places where it was able to fight past the glow of the city, and he could just make out the outline of the tree that stood next to the fence.

After finishing, Sam left his plate and knife in the sink, fetched his duvet from upstairs and, wrapping it around his shoulders, curled up on the sofa in the living room. Once again his life seemed to be spiralling out of control, and this time his problems were far worse than the prospect of moving to another country. The previous evening he had seen a side of Dr McHayden that both frightened and repelled him, a ruthless streak that would stop at nothing to get what she wanted. Whatever her true plans were, it was clear that Sam's own wishes melted into insignificance. He was nothing but a cog in McHayden's machine, and if he didn't do what she wanted then it was obvious she wouldn't think twice about discarding him.

At some point he must have fallen asleep, because the next thing he knew the living room was filled with light. He jumped from the sofa and yanked back the curtains, afraid that he'd overslept and was late again, but there was no sign of McHayden's car in the road. The smell of bacon drifted through from the kitchen. Sam followed it and found his grandmother standing over the stove with a frying pan.

'Good morning, pet,' she said. 'What were you doing in the front room? I came in earlier, but you looked so peaceful that I didn't want to wake you.'

'I couldn't sleep so I came down in the night,' Sam said. 'What's the time?'

'Twenty to nine. Grandpa has another hospital appointment this morning, so I'm making bacon butties before we leave. Fancy one?'

'No time,' he said, wishing she'd woken him.

Sam hurried upstairs, picked up his phone from the bedside table and called Eva at Doug's flat. He had tried several times the previous evening, but there was no answer and he remembered her saying that they were going out for dinner. This time, however, the line was engaged, so he jumped in the shower, pulled on some clean clothes and tried again, only to find that the line was still busy.

With no time to keep trying, Sam went back downstairs to see McHayden's sleek Mercedes already waiting outside, so he stuffed his phone into his pocket, grabbed his coat and yelled goodbye as he stepped out of the door.

It was colder than any other day so far that year and large, feathery snowflakes floated down from the sky. He crossed the road feeling strangely calm, as though whatever lay in store for him couldn't be any worse than waiting for it. Dr McHayden was sitting with a leather bound notebook on her lap. She barely glanced up as Sam climbed in next to her.

'About yesterday—' he began.

McHayden raised her hand, palm towards him. 'I have work to do, and I'd rather not have to endure any more excuses, thank you very much.'

The heating system hummed as they drove, wafting warm air around the car. Still tired from lack of sleep, Sam stifled a yawn and stared out of the window. The snow began to fall more heavily as they left the city, and the roads soon became clogged with cars driving well below the speed limit.

By the time they reached the Tempus Research Facility a thin layer of snow carpeted the ground and lined the branches of the pine trees surrounding them. Sam followed McHayden and Steele to the entrance, their shoes leaving muddy prints on the previously perfect blanket of white.

As always, Arnold was sitting behind his desk, reading a book. He looked up and gave a toothy smile as Sam stamped his feet on the mat. 'Looks like we might have a white Christmas after all,' he said, pushing his cap back on his head. 'Looking forward to Christmas, are you Sam?'

'I suppose so,' Sam said, although he hadn't really thought about it until then. It suddenly dawned on him that it would be the first Christmas without his mum and dad.

Arnold must have sensed Sam's discomfort, because he stopped smiling. 'Well, I suppose you're getting a bit old for that sort of thing. How old are you anyway? Seventeen, right?'

'Almost,' Sam said.

'Thought so. My boy, Ross, is about your age. He used to *love* Christmas when he was little, but now—'

McHayden cleared her throat. 'That's enough of the chit-chat, thank you Arnold. We're on a tight schedule after yesterday's setback.'

'Oh, right you are, boss,' he said and pressed the button under his desk.

McHayden stepped into the recessed lift before the vending machine had even finished sliding back and immediately pressed her hand to the black plate on the wall. Sam just about managed to scurry in behind Steele before the doors closed and they began to descend.

They stepped out into a flurry of activity. There were several times the number of people as on any previous occasion. A row of computer terminals had been set up along one of the worktops that ran down the centre of the lab, most of which were in use.

'What's going on?' Sam asked, but McHayden was already striding away down the aisle that led to the back of the long room. He hurried after, eager not to get left behind. There were four metal cages on another worktop by the far wall which Sam didn't remember seeing before. Each was about four feet high and wide, and six feet deep. The first two were empty but the last two contained monkeys, both with their heads bandaged. One lay curled and motionless near the back of its cage, but the other, a chimpanzee, sat close to the front, watching Sam with sad, almost human eyes. It jumped up as they passed, slammed its small black hands against the bars and, baring its yellow teeth, let out a high-pitched shriek.

Sam realised that these poor creatures must be what McHayden was referring to when she'd told him about surgery to recreate his injury in animals, and he shuddered to think about what he had become a part of.

McHayden marched straight to the small room that usually housed the random chance generator. When Sam entered after, he found that the furniture had been changed, the computer screen and joysticks replaced by a wooden table and a pair of foldout plastic chairs. Malcolm Fairview was sitting on one. There were dark circles beneath his eyes and his eczema appeared far worse than two days before, the red flakes now spreading across his forehead and nose.

'Sam, good to see you,' he said and stood up. 'We were expecting you yesterday. Is everything okay?'

'Malcolm, let's not get into that now,' McHayden said. 'Come on, chop-chop, lots of catching up to do.' With that she turned and left, slamming the door on her way out.

Fairview stared after, a bemused look on his face, then shook his head and opened the metal cabinet in the corner of the room. He removed a bottle from the shelves and poured a glass of water from a jug on the table, which he handed to Sam along with a small, sticky pill. 'Sorry, haven't got round to sugar coating them yet,' he said. 'As you've probably noticed, things have been rather busy here lately.'

Sam held his nose and washed the pill down with a gulp of water. 'So, what's happening?' he asked. 'I'm guessing we're done with the random chance generator.'

'Your assumption is correct. Today we'll be attempting something a little different. I want you to travel into the past over a longer period of time, a day or two, to be exact.'

'All right,' Sam said and took another gulp of water, which didn't quite get rid of the taste.

'During the last day or so we've been observing you going about your day-to-day activities.'

Sam spluttered, sending water shooting out of his nose and dribbling down his chin. 'You've been *spying* on me?'

'Spying is such a strong word. I'm sorry if it seems like an invasion of your privacy, Sam, but it's quite necessary for the purposes of this experiment. Believe me when I say I'm not so interested in your personal life that I'd have you watched, no matter what Dr McHayden may think.' He scratched his neck, showering his lab coat in flakes of dead skin. 'The purpose of observing you was to plant a series of subliminal clues: little things you'd see but would probably never notice. I've drawn up a list of times, places and tasks. Once the Tetradyamide takes effect, you need to travel back to the specified time, find the relevant information and then report back to me, okay?'

'Is that all? I thought you'd ask me to do something difficult this time.'

Fairview chuckled. 'Just relax. I'll be back in a few minutes and we can begin.'

Alone in the small room, Sam drummed his fingers on the tabletop as he waited. After several minutes he felt a surge in his chest like a hit of adrenaline and looked down at the table. His fingers blurred together, each hand a fleshy flipper. He lifted his right hand, wiggled his fingers and the gaps between each regained some definition. When he looked down again the sides of the table had become fuzzy, as if he were watching two overlapping images that were slightly out of sync. He looked back up. The whiteness of the walls was tinged with colour, a faint pinkish orange that hung on the edge of his vision.

Fairview stepped back in, a clipboard under his arm. 'Feel anything yet?'

Sam nodded, the world shimmering around him in a sparkling kaleidoscope of colour. 'I'm ready.'

Fairview pulled a sheet of paper from his clipboard and slid it across the table. The action appeared jerky and disjointed; separate instances connected only by the illusion of time. Sam did his best to ignore the sensation, knowing it was only the Tetradyamide, and glanced down at the page. It contained print that swam and swirled. He rubbed his eyes, which brought the words into focus.

There were three short paragraphs. The first read:

> *Friday, 12:15, Fraser Golding College.*
> *There is a girl behind you in the queue.*
> *Blonde hair, green dress.*
> *What colour are her earrings?*

Sam looked up. 'I don't get it.'

Fairview removed the chewed end of a biro from his lips, leaving them stained with ink. 'The day and time are the point I want you to travel back to. Fraser Golding College is the destination and the girl in the green dress is your target. Find out what colour earrings she's wearing and report back to me.'

'But that was just after my interview yesterday. I don't remember any girl in a green dress.'

'Which means she did her job. The girl was a junior operative instructed to pose as a student at your college as part of a routine surveillance operation. Her instructions were to monitor your activities without arousing your suspicion. Naturally she had no idea as to the true purpose of her assignment. Your task is to pass back and observe what you didn't notice the first time.'

'You mean the colour of her earrings?'

'Exactly.'

Sam closed his eyes and tried to clear his mind. At first this wasn't easy with Fairview breathing loudly beside him, but Tetradyamide helped to sharpen his concentration to the point of a needle. His mind was an empty space, a blank canvas for thoughts cut off from bodily sensations. Brightly coloured shapes gradually emerged from the darkness, like you'd see when closing your eyes after staring at the sun too long. The shapes danced behind his eyelids, spinning and multiplying. Slowly they fused together, forming larger, multicoloured shapes until an image revealed itself.

Sam was looking through the point of view he'd had just before closing his eyes. Fairview was standing beside him, clipboard in hand. But this wasn't happening in time; it was a frozen moment captured like a snapshot, a thing both temporary and eternal, a single page in the book.

Sam willed the image to move backwards, a mental sweep of the hand, and it did. One by one images passed, flicking back to earlier pages. He saw Fairview pick up the piece of paper, slide it into his clipboard and walk backwards out of the door. The harder Sam concentrated, the faster the images went. He saw himself enter the room with McHayden and Steele; he saw the monkey in the cage; he saw Arnold, the security guard, on the ground floor just before they got in the lift. And then he was back in the car, looking out the window at snowflakes rising through the air. Soon things began to move so fast that the images became a blur, nothing but flashes of colour shooting by, until suddenly they were replaced by darkness. Sam willed the pages to stop and, just like that, they did.

He was in his kitchen, a knife dripping with chocolate spread in his hand and a plate of toast on the counter.

'Play,' he said, and suddenly it wasn't just an image anymore, he was actually there. A chill prickled his skin. The smell of burned toast hung in the air. A droplet of water fell from the tap and splashed into the sink. He glanced at the clock on the oven. It was 04:25, but as he watched it rolled over to 04:26.

Sam laughed and licked chocolate spread from the knife. He was standing in the middle of last night but, incredible as this was, it wasn't where he wanted to be: there was a task to complete.

After closing his eyes, he swept the images back once again. Briefly, he saw himself on the stairs and then lying in bed. For a while after that darkness was all he saw, but then the splashes of colour returned and Sam realised that he must be passing through the day before. He concentrated on the time on the sheet of paper, 12:15, and as if on cue the images became visible once more as the rate at which the pages flipped back gradually slowed.

Sam was sitting opposite Lewis in the cafeteria at Fraser Golding College. Lewis put an empty fork in his mouth and pulled out half an uneaten fish finger. Sam saw himself stand, pick up his tray and backtrack past the cash registers, joining a queue where a burley dinner lady sucked chicken curry from his bowl with a ladle and slopped it back into a serving tray. The images slowed to a halt.

This was it.

Sam blinked and the canteen filled with the racket of voices and the smells of cooked food.

'What'll it be?'

'Huh?' Sam said.

'What'll it be, fish fingers or the chicken curry?' The dinner lady wiped her hands on her greasy apron and placed them on her hips.

Sam turned to see Lewis by his side. Lewis picked a chip from his plate and stuffed it into his mouth.

'C'mon, sonny,' the dinner lady said, 'there's other people waiting.'

'Never mind.' Sam took a step back to look down the length of the queue. There was a girl in a pea green dress standing four places behind him. She was petite and very thin, almost like a frightened mouse, and so pale that her veins were visible as faint blue lines under the surface of her skin. Her blonde hair fell loosely to her shoulders, covering her ears. She looked up and caught Sam staring. For a second her eyes stretched wide and then she looked away.

'Mate, are you all right?' Lewis asked.

Sam ignored him and walked towards the girl. She immediately turned her back and began rummaging in her handbag.

'Excuse me,' he said.

The girl did her best to pretend she hadn't heard.

Sam placed his hand gently on her shoulder. 'Hello?'

She flinched as she turned to face him, her eyes angry slits. 'What *is* it?' she hissed. 'I'm not supposed to talk to you. Leave me alone.'

'Sorry,' he said. 'I don't want to get you in trouble or anything, I just wanted to ask you a question.'

She glanced from side to side as if wary of being watched. 'And *then* you'll leave me alone?'

'Swear it,' Sam said and crossed himself like a priest. 'I only want to see your earrings.'

'My earrings?' She frowned and pulled her hair back to reveal bare earlobes. 'But I'm not wearing any today.'

'Thanks, that's all I need to know.'

He stepped back and closed his eyes, imagining the word 'now'. A rush of colour swept over him, image after image flooding by. Finally the images slowed and he was left with the one he'd first started with: Fairview standing beside him as he sat on a foldout chair in the Tempus Research Facility.

Sam opened his eyes. 'It's done.'

'Already? You were only away a minute or two.'

'That's all I needed. She wasn't wearing earrings.'

Fairview stuck his bottom lip out and made a mark on his clipboard. 'Well done. After all the speculation I suppose it might take a while to get my head around how this works in practice. So, on to the next task…'

Sam looked down. The second paragraph on the sheet read:

Friday, 15:35, The Prince Regent Public House.
There is a man playing the fruit machine.
He has a tattoo on his left hand.
What does it depict?

He shut his eyes again and cleared his mind. Shapes emerged from the darkness, twisting and expanding until they filled his vision and he was presented with the image of Fairview standing over him, the point of his chewed biro pressed to the clipboard.

Sam focused on the day and time: Friday, 15:35. On this occasion there was no gradual acceleration. Images erupted before him, gushing past like water from a burst pipe. When they finally slowed Sam glimpsed the view of his knees in the mud of Mrs Mason's flowerbed, vomit spots on his trouser legs. Next he saw himself stopping to lean against a lamp post as he staggered home and then walking with Eva to the tube station, his arm around her shoulder. The last image showed a shot glass in Sam's right hand and a small mound of salt on the back of the left.

'Play,' he said again, and the world lurched into motion. An old country and western song sprang up over the sound system. The smell of stale beer filled the room.

Eva looked up from across the table with a puzzled expression on her face. 'What did you just say?'

'I didn't say anything.'

'Yes, you did. It sounded like you said "play".'

Sam looked around the pub. The pig-faced barmaid opened the dishwasher, sending a cloud of steam billowing into the air. The two old drunks were outside, smoking roll-up cigarettes. There was a battered fruit machine in the corner next to a jukebox. A man with a shaved head was standing at it with his back turned as he pounded the buttons.

Sam looked back to Eva. 'Shall I play a song? On the jukebox, I mean.'

'Sure,' she said, 'if you want. Are you going to drink that shot or what?'

'In a minute.' He placed the glass on the table and brushed the salt from his hand. 'Any requests?'

'Surprise me,' she said and downed her own shot.

Sam stood and crossed the room a little unsteadily. He was well on his way to being drunk again without actually having consumed any alcohol. The man with the shaved head shot him a sidelong glance and Sam realised it was the same person who'd nearly knocked him over while he was waiting for Eva at the underground station.

Sam took out his wallet and looked inside. 'Excuse me,' he said.

The man ignored him, just like the girl in the green dress had, and continued pressing the buttons of the fruit machine with his right hand. His left hand was stuck in his trouser pocket.

'Excuse me,' Sam said again, this time louder.

The man froze, his finger on a flashing orange button.

'Have you got any change for the jukebox?'

He took a second to digest Sam's question. 'Yeah, all right,' he said, pulling his left hand from his trouser pocket and reaching for the breast pocket of his jacket. Inked on the skin between his thumb and index finger was a small, blue bird with a forked tail. 'How much do you need?'

'You know what, it doesn't matter,' Sam said. 'Sorry to bother you.'

He returned to the table feeling the man's stare burning a hole in his back.

'So, what song did you choose?' Eva asked as he sat down.

'Sorry?'

'On the jukebox.'

'Oh, nothing. I changed my mind.'

Eva placed an elbow on the table and rested her chin in her hand. 'You really are quite odd, Sam, you know that?'

'In a bad way?'

'Not at all. I find it intriguing.'

Sam closed his eyes and was about to form the word 'now' in his head when he suddenly had an idea. If he left that minute and hurried home, then he might still be able to make his appointment with Dr McHayden, and if he could keep her trust (or, more to the point, prevent himself losing it in the first place) then his position at the Tempus Project would be safe, and with it his continued supply of Tetradyamide.

He opened his eyes, got up and lifted his coat from the back of the chair. 'Sorry Eva, I've just remembered there's something I've got to do.'

'You're leaving already?' she asked, frowning. 'You want me to come with you?'

'I wish you could, but it's something I need to do on my own.'

She sighed. 'How very mysterious. I'm staying with Doug until early January. Will I see you again?'

'Of course, remember about tomorrow—' He stopped short. In this timeline, they hadn't arranged to meet again yet. 'Would you like to come over to my house tomorrow? You could meet my sister.'

'Sure, I guess. What time?'

'How about lunchtime?' Sam said, and then remembered the panic he'd felt at not being able to reach her on the phone. 'Wait, maybe it's best if I call you in the morning to sort it out.'

She glanced at her watch. 'I should probably leave too then. Doug's taking me for dinner and I want to have a bath first.'

'I'll walk you to the station,' Sam said.

'No, it's fine. I remember the way.' And with that she stood up, pulled on her coat and walked out of the pub.

As Sam watched Eva leave, he remembered the softness of her lips against his own during the kiss they would no longer share. Suspecting he'd just made a terrible mistake, he closed his eyes and mouthed the word 'now'.

53

Sam opened his eyes and was presented with the view of his own bedroom instead of that of the back room of the Tempus Research Facility. Lewis was sitting on a stool, his back against the wardrobe and his socked feet on the corner of the bed. Sam blinked and then gasped as the image began to move, just like someone had just pressed play on a paused recording. The slight intoxication he'd felt a minute earlier was gone, replaced by a heavy stomach that could only be the result of a recently consumed cooked breakfast. Rock music thumped through the ceiling from Chrissie's room on the floor above and a vinegary aroma drifted up from Lewis's feet.

'Are you all right?' Lewis asked. He took a bite from an apple in his hand. 'You've got that look again.'

'What look?'

'The same look as you had in the canteen yesterday, just before you started talking to that strange girl. Sort of like you've been hit over the head with a frying pan.'

'That was yesterday?' Sam asked.

'Yeah.'

'So today's Saturday?'

'Yes, genius. And tomorrow's Sunday and the day after that is Monday. That's the way it normally works.'

'Oh,' Sam said, but in fact it made perfect sense. If he'd managed to undo being late for Dr McHayden on

Friday evening, then she wouldn't have ordered him in again on Saturday, which was today. He wasn't at the Tempus Research Facility because of changes he'd made in the past that had altered what was happening right now. This was another alternate timeline.

Lewis swung his feet off the bed and leaned forward. 'What's going on with you? This is about what you told me after the funeral, isn't it, when you thought you stopped the bombing?'

Sam stared back without saying anything.

'Come on, mate, it's me you're talking to.'

After a few seconds, Sam shook his head. 'I'm scared, Lewis. I think I might have got mixed up in something dangerous and—'

He was interrupted by the doorbell.

'Expecting anyone?' Lewis asked.

'I don't think so,' Sam said. 'No, wait, maybe I am!'

54

Eva looked through the falling snow at the little house, then down at the address on the scrap of paper in her hand. It was weird not having her cell phone and having to make do with verbal directions and handwritten maps. She scrunched the paper into a ball, dropped it into her handbag and pushed the gate open. The hinges squeaked as it closed behind her.

She wasn't quite sure what had happened yesterday. Everything seemed to be going well when, all of a sudden, a funny look had come over Sam's face and the mood completely changed. In fact, it was more than just the mood, it was as if Sam himself had changed, the boy sitting across from her replaced by a different person, someone who was desperate to be someplace else. Eva had spent the rest of that evening and most of the morning wondering whether or not she should just cancel, but in the end she decided to give Sam another chance. After what had happened with Trent she hoped it was the right thing to do.

She pressed the doorbell and, a few seconds later, heard footsteps coming down the stairs. Sam opened the door looking dishevelled. He was wearing a black hooded top, faded grey jogging bottoms and a pair of threadbare slippers. No other date she'd been on had started like this.

'You are expecting me, right?' Eva asked, even though she had spoken to him only a couple of hours earlier.

'Yeah, I...' Sam glanced down at his clothes and blushed. '...you're just a bit earlier than I thought. Come in.' He took her coat and then led her down the hall to the kitchen at the rear of the house. 'Can I get you a drink?'

'Yes please, something hot.'

He filled the kettle at the tap. 'Is tea okay? I've got instant coffee somewhere, if you prefer.'

'Tea's fine,' she said and sat down at the dining table.

Sam placed the kettle on its stand, flicked the switch and came to join her. 'Look, I'm sorry about yesterday, running off like that.'

Eva shrugged. 'It's okay, you already apologised on the phone. Did you do whatever it was you had to leave in such a hurry for?'

'Um, yeah, you could say that.'

'Hello,' a voice behind her said. Eva turned in her chair to see a tall, gawky boy standing in the doorway.

'Eva, this is my friend Lewis,' Sam said.

'Hi,' Eva said, 'Sam told me about you.'

Lewis arched an eyebrow. 'Only good things, I'm assuming.'

The kettle clicked off. Sam poured boiling water into a mug, stirred the teabag with a spoon and then scooped it out and flicked it into the trashcan. 'I might get changed,' he said, passing Eva her tea. 'Will you two be all right for a minute?'

'Sure,' Eva said. Once Sam had left the room she turned to Lewis. 'So—'

'I'm worried about him,' Lewis said. He took the next chair and swung round to face her, staring intently.

So much for small talk, Eva thought as she cradled the steaming mug in her hands. 'That's only natural, I guess. It's not every day you lose a parent.'

Lewis shook his head, his curls bouncing. 'It's not just that. Well, it's that *and* what's been happening since. He had a seizure at Matthew's funeral, you know.'

'I heard. Doug, my father, was there.'

'The thing is, when Sam came round again he was acting really strangely. I called an ambulance and was trying to get him to let the paramedics check him over, but he was obsessed about making a phone call, kept ranting about something terrible that was about to happen.'

'He was probably just confused.' Eva sipped her tea. 'There's a kid at my school who's epileptic. She had a fit in gym class once, right in front of everyone. When she came round she didn't have a clue where she was or what had happened.'

'Maybe,' Lewis said and rubbed his chin. 'But I was there. I heard him make the phone call and heard what he said. He was talking to someone called Inspector Hinds. He told her about a bombing that evening, warned her she had to stop it. After we got back from the hospital – this was several hours later – there was a report on the news about a failed terrorist attack on a government building. That can't be just a coincidence, can it?'

'I don't know,' Eva said. 'What does Sam say about it?'

Lewis laughed, but it came out as more of a snort and he didn't smile. 'That's the really strange bit. At the time he told me that while he was having the seizure he *saw* what was going to happen later that evening, like he was psychic or something, and saw us watching the news report just like before, except this time the bombing had actually happened. He thinks he prevented it, Eva. He thinks he changed the future. What really worries me is that he won't talk about it since, and every time I try to bring it up he just changes the subject.'

Eva thought it sounded an awful lot like an elaborate story made up at her expense, but the look of concern on Lewis's face seemed genuine enough.

'It's not the kind of thing I'd joke about,' he said, as if sensing her apprehension.

There was a noise by the door. Eva turned to see Sam standing there, now wearing jeans, a grey jumper and a scowl on his face.

'Lewis,' he said, 'what have you been telling her?'

55

Sam had only been away a couple of minutes, just enough time to change his clothes and brush his teeth, but Lewis had a voice that carried and could probably be heard from the bottom of the garden. By the time Sam was half way down the stairs, he'd already heard enough to realise that another person now knew his secret.

Eva tilted her head to the side and studied him with a neutral expression that made it impossible to read what she was thinking. 'Is this true?' she asked.

Sam exhaled and slumped in a chair. 'Sort of. Basically. Yes.'

'You can predict the future?'

'In a way.'

'Okay.' She pressed her fingers to her temples. 'What number am I thinking of?'

'That's not how it works,' he said. 'You make it sound like I'm a fortune-teller or something. It's not a magic trick and I can't read people's minds. What happens is, I can sometimes see things that haven't happened yet, or go back to things that have already happened. It's only through my eyes, but like seeing through the eyes of a past or future me.'

'I don't believe you,' she said. 'Prove it.'

Sam knew he should just laugh the whole thing off, but the tone of her voice made it sound like a challenge and, in spite of everything, he wanted to impress her. 'What do you want me to do?' he asked.

Eva reached into her handbag and took out a scrunched ball of paper. She hid both hands behind her back and then held them out, fists clenched. 'Which hand is it in?'

'Hang on,' Lewis said, 'I've got a much better idea.' He got up and left the room, returning a moment later with Sam's grandfather's newspaper, which he spread on the table in front of them. 'Here,' he said, jabbing a finger in the middle of the sports section. 'There's a race at Newmarket in less than ten minutes. Call the winner before it starts and you've proved your point.'

'No problem.' Sam went to fetch the portable radio from the kitchen counter, switched it on and spun the dial, skipping past several stations until he found one playing the race. He had never gambled before apart from the school raffle, and he didn't think that counted.

It couldn't have been more than an hour or two since he'd taken Tetradyamide, so it should still have been in his system for several more hours yet. He closed his eyes and focused on the time that the race started, but nothing happened. The only thing he saw was the darkness behind his eyelids.

'So?' Eva asked.

Sam opened one eye, then the other. She was staring at him with a curious smile on her face.

'Wait, let me try again.' He took a deep breath and, holding it in, closed his eyes so tightly it almost hurt. There were no spinning shapes, only darkness and the sound of Lewis tapping his foot under the table. Sam heard the house phone ring twice and then stop. He opened his eyes again. 'It isn't working.'

Eva slapped her knee and started laughing. 'That's a good one! You almost had me going there. *Ooooh, I can see the future,*' she said, putting on a British accent. '*I can see the through the eyes of a past and future me.* It's original, guys, I'll give you that.'

Something wasn't right. Sam had experienced no difficulties when he'd undone being late for Dr McHayden, so what had changed?

'It's because I don't have the drug in my system anymore,' he said.

'What drug?' Lewis asked.

'The Tetra...whatchamacallit...glue. Without the drug I can't control when it happens.'

'You can give it a rest now,' Eva said. 'I'm not biting. I mean, how dumb do you think I am?'

'I'm not making it up,' Sam said. 'I originally took the drug this morning when I was at the lab, but then by leaving the pub early yesterday I changed what happened and created an alternate timeline – *now.*'

Lewis rubbed his face. 'Mate, you've totally lost me.'

'This is an alternate timeline?' Eva asked. 'Doesn't feel very alternate to me.'

'Well, it wouldn't to anyone else. Only me,' Sam said. 'In this reality I didn't take Tetradyamide this morning because I didn't visit the lab as a result of the changes I made yesterday. In this timeline I wasn't late yesterday and we didn't kiss.'

'Excuse me,' Eva said, 'but did you just say we *kissed*?'

'Yeah,' Sam said, feeling his face starting to get warm. 'But that was an alternate yesterday. When I left the pub early I changed everything that happened after.'

'Well,' she said, a half smile creeping across her lips. 'Some things aren't that hard to put right.'

At that moment Chrissie ran into the kitchen, sliding across the floor in her socks. She bumped into the table, knocking over the vase in the centre, which would have rolled onto the floor if Lewis hadn't jumped up and caught it.

'Eva, this is Chrissie, my sister,' Sam said. 'She's not usually in such a hurry.'

'Hi,' Chrissie said and turned to Sam, panting. Her eyes were wide with joy, her cheeks flushed with colour. 'You're not going to believe what's happened!'

'What?' he asked.

'The hospital just rang. It's Mum, Sam, she's woken up.'

56

George had never been short on self-confidence, but even he would never have imagined the way in which the last few weeks had unfolded. After hanging up on Inspector Hinds, he'd followed departmental procedure to the letter. All non-essential personnel were evacuated, leaving only a skeleton crew to maintain the appearance that the building was occupied. George had led a unit including a bomb disposal team to the basement car park, where he had stationed a man on the kiosk at the entrance and positioned four snipers to cover all angles of approach. The rest of his team, five men and three women, crammed into the back of an unmarked surveillance van.

Tempers had simmered during a five-hour wait in stuffy, cramped conditions. After several false alarms, George began to suspect the whole incident might develop into an embarrassing blemish on his record, but then his radio had crackled into life and the man at the entrance informed him a delivery truck was approaching. It seemed to take forever to descend the ramp and lumber into view. The driver pulled into a bay in the middle of the car park – the place where any blast would do the most damage – and killed the engine. A trickle of sweat ran down George's temple and into his eye. He blinked and wiped it away. The door of the truck opened and a man wearing a Royal Mail uniform climbed out of the front cab. George focused the lens, straining to catch a glimpse of the face. Looking the other way, the man walked round to the rear of the truck and was moment-arily obscured by a pillar. George zoomed out. A second later the man reappeared. As he reached for the handle of the back door, he glanced in George's direction.

It was a face that, until a few weeks ago, George had believed he would never see again. His pulse quickened as he raised the radio to his lips and uttered the words: 'Target is green. Engage.'

Four shots rang out, deafening in the enclosed space, and a crimson spray fanned up from the side of the man's head, settling over the back of the truck.

George was first out of the surveillance van. He reached the truck at a sprint and threw open the rear doors. Eight plastic barrels stood before him, each wired to a central detonating device. As the bomb disposal team arrived, George stepped away and slumped against the bumper next to the bullet-riddled body of Esteban

Haufner, the only person he had ever truly considered a friend.

An hour later, George had found himself seated before the Director General. Once the customary handshakes and slapped backs were out of the way, the Director passed him a sealed envelope and said, 'I have an interesting opportunity for you, my lad. Dr McHayden has asked for you in person.'

The existence of Lara McHayden's research was a badly-kept secret within the service. The Tempus Project was funded in part by government research grants and in part by private backers, and as such could operate as an independent enterprise with no official ties to the government. George's achievements would remain out of the public eye, but the potential for career advancement made the offer too good to refuse, and he accepted on the spot.

'Tell me, George,' the old lady had said as he drove her to Sam Rayner's doorstep later that evening, 'what are your views on the subject of time travel?'

George paused for a moment, unsure if this wasn't a test of some kind. 'Not a thing I've given much thought to, ma'am. However, after what happened today, I'm prepared to keep an open mind on most subjects.'

'Good,' she said, gazing out of the window. 'I suspect you'll need it.'

George had been sceptical of the boy's alleged capabilities – like any rational-minded person would be, of course – but then he'd seen Sam on the random chance generator and been forced to stretch the boundaries of what he thought was possible. If George had previously hoped that his skills and past achievements were the main reasons behind McHayden's job offer, he now began to suspect that his prior association with Sam Rayner was a more significant factor.

Now that the boy's ability was scientifically verified, the Tempus Project's activities had been rapidly intensified as years of careful planning and preparation came to fruition. George estimated that he'd managed a total of five hours sleep in a three day period. Tiredness was catching up with all involved and the first hairline cracks had appeared in McHayden's otherwise calm demeanour. On one occasion she'd lost her temper with a technician at the research facility when an ape had been killed during surgery, resulting in a very public outburst. Next week she intended to utilise the boy in a live assignment and, given his value, had instructed George to keep a close eye on him. Such donkeywork was a misuse of George's talents, and most definitely not what he'd signed up for, but when he protested the old lady had shouted him down, insisting there could be no mistakes and that he do the job himself.

So here he was, sat in a company car as snow settled all around, struggling to keep sleep at bay as he watched Sam's house. After finishing the last bite of his sandwich, George swept the crumbs into an empty paper bag and then folded the plastic wrapper until it formed a neat equilateral triangle with sharp corners and straight edges. He stared down at the notepad on which he'd been logging the day's comings and goings. The boy's grandparents, Maureen and Alfred Rayner, had left the house at 10:36 that morning (to attend a hospital appointment, the phone taps had revealed) and were not due back until later that afternoon. That left Sam, Christina Rayner and Lance Asquith, until the boy's friend, Lewis Fisher, arrived at 11:24, and more recently Eva Bernstein at 12:17.

George picked up his camera and zoomed in on the house. The curtains in the attic room were drawn, as they had been all morning, but he could detect intermittent movement behind the windows on the first and ground floors. All of a sudden the front door flew open and several people rushed out, skidding over the icy path. George pressed the shutter release as the group piled into the back of Lance Asquith's dilapidated 1992 Volvo. A cloud of thick, black smoke belched from the exhaust. The car swerved from the curb, engine rattling loudly, and took off, turning left at the end of the road without indicating. George shook his head at this flagrant disregard of the Highway Code, took out his phone and checked the location of the GPS tracker he'd attached under the Volvo's rear wheel arch. A small, pulsating red dot was working its way across the map in a south-westerly direction.

George scanned back through the photographs he'd just captured. Five people had entered the car: Lewis Fisher, Eva Bernstein, Lance Asquith, Christina Rayner and Sam Rayner himself.

The house was now empty: this was the chance he had been waiting for.

George stepped out onto the pavement, pulled on his leather gloves and removed a small canvas bag from the boot of the car. After a quick glance over his shoulder, he crossed the road and made his way up the path. Kneeling at the door, he withdrew a lock pick from the bag. In less than ten seconds he was inside and wiping his feet on the mat. The house looked exactly as he remembered from a few weeks earlier, with the addition of a line of Christmas cards stuck to the banisters in the hall.

He decided to work his way top-down, so climbed the stairs. The attic room was in disarray. Dirty clothes lay discarded across the floor. The walls were plastered with posters, many curled with age. George detected a lingering stench of burned incense that reminded him of his flatmate's room at university. Holding his nose and trying to push the unpleasant memory aside, he strode over to the unmade bed. A silver picture frame comprised of entwined skeletons sat on the bedside table. He picked it up and examined it. The photograph showed Lance Asquith and Christina Rayner on a beach, their arms around each other's waists. Apart from a bad case of sunburn, Asquith looked much the same, but Christina's appearance differed drastically to recent surveillance footage, with dyed hair, heavy black eye shadow and piercings in her nose, lip and eyebrow. George turned the frame over, undid the clasps and removed the back panel. He took a listening device from a zip-lock plastic wallet in his bag, secreted it behind the photograph where the bump would remain hidden by the edge of the frame, reattached the back panel and returned it to the bedside table in the exact position in which he'd found it. Next he crossed the room to a lacquered wardrobe in the corner. Standing on tiptoes, he ran his finger along the top edge. It came back dusty, so he positioned a miniaturised video camera at an angle that would capture the whole room.

After testing both signals, George descended to the first floor. Once he'd bugged the bathroom and each of the bedrooms, he checked his watch. He'd been in the house close to eight minutes and still had the whole of the ground floor to complete. With each passing second the risk of discovery rose. He needed to hurry, so snatched up his bag and trotted down the stairs.

In the hallway he positioned a camera on top of the dresser and a listening device behind the large mirror that hung opposite the front door. Then he stepped into the lounge. This was the room where he'd first met Sam Rayner; the place where he had watched Clive Kalinsky produce the disturbingly accurate facial reconstruction of Esteban Haufner. A large Christmas tree now stood in the alcove of the bay window, decorated in gaudy baubles and multi-coloured tinsel. George placed a camera on the highest shelf of a tall oak bookcase in the opposite corner of the room and hid another listening device in the frame of a photograph that showed Christina riding a carousel as a young child. There was now only one room left and George could be on his way.

Upon entering the kitchen, he immediately froze, paralysed by revulsion. A mountain of washing-up had been left festering in the sink. George could almost visualise the bacteria crawling over it. He felt his stomach turn and a cold sweat spring out on his forehead. How could anyone live like this? Were they animals? He reached into his bag and pulled out a bottle of water. As he tore off the lid, the bottle fell from his shaking hand and spilled over the floor. Cursing, George reached for the kitchen roll on the counter and began to dab up the mess. Exhaustion had left his nerves frayed and raw. He had to pull himself together and do his job. Everything would be fine if he could just think logically. All he needed were two well-hidden places, one with a clear line of sight, and then he could be out of this godforsaken cesspit once and for all.

He stood up, dropped the wad of wet kitchen roll in the bin and drank the remaining water from the bottle in a single gulp. Feeling slightly better, he planted the final listening device behind the skirting under kitchen units and a camera in the gap where the extractor fan met the wall, then checked his phone again. The tracker showed that Asquith's car was now 2.4 miles away and still moving in a south-westerly direction. It was twelve minutes since George had first stepped through the door, which meant that even if Sam and his friends turned around, he had at least that much time before they returned.

He had done it. He was home and dry. He—

The front door slammed.

George snatched up his bag. A set of French doors beside the sink led onto the garden. He tried the handle and found them locked.

Muffled voices were approaching from the hall.

He was trapped.

George reached for his shoulder holster and took out his Glock. The voices were now loud enough for him to make out what was being said.

'...fancy a nice cup of tea, pet?'

'Not half, Maureen, I'm parched...'

Twisting on the silencer attachment of his pistol, George stepped into the nook behind the door.

57

Chrissie looked into her mother's distressed and disorientated face. Her hair seemed thinner and her skin paler, although strangely Chrissie had never noticed this on the many occasions she'd visited while her mum was in a coma.

'But I don't understand, I've never even *been* to America.'

Sam leaned forward and stroked their mother's arm. 'Mum, we were there almost three weeks.'

'Why are you telling me these things?' She brushed his hand away. 'Where's your father? I want to go home now.'

'You can't yet,' Chrissie said. She glanced at Sam, who was staring down at his rejected hand with his mouth hanging open. 'You've been out for a long time, Mum. There's tests and stuff they need to do.'

'So you intend to keep me prisoner, do you? Just wait until Matthew hears about this. Where is he, by the way?'

'He…he's…' Chrissie broke eye contact and took a deep breath. 'He's dead, Mum. He was killed in the crash, remember?'

Their mother laughed, a single, bitter bark. 'Don't be silly, Chrissie. What crash?'

'The crash on the flight back from America,' Sam said. 'Don't you even—'

'Why do you keep saying that? I've told you already, I've never been to America.' She turned her head towards the window and, for a moment, seemed miles away. 'Look,' she said, 'it's snowing. And in the middle of summer!'

There was a knock on the door. Dr Saltano stuck his head in and beckoned for Chrissie and Sam to join him outside. Chrissie stood and kissed her mother on the forehead. 'We've got to go now. We'll come back to see you tomorrow, okay?'

Her mum smiled. 'Okay, sweetie. Can you ask your dad to have a look for my nightie? This one itches.'

'Will do,' Chrissie said, the lie burning in her chest. Sam got up as well, kissed their mother and, shaking his head, followed Chrissie into the corridor.

Dr Saltano blew into a steaming paper cup and smiled at them. 'Well, the good news is she's conscious and doesn't seem to have sustained any loss of speech or motor function.'

'But she doesn't remember a thing,' Sam said. 'She doesn't even remember moving to America.'

'Rebecca is suffering from Post Traumatic Amnesia. The weeks preceding her accident are a complete blank to her and she appears to be experiencing difficulty retaining new information.'

'I see,' Chrissie said. 'And how long will this last?'

'I'm afraid there's no way of telling,' Dr Saltano said. 'Her memory could come back at any time or, in the worst case scenario, never at all.'

'But there must be something you can do,' Sam said. 'She doesn't even seem like the same person. She's so...so angry.'

Dr Saltano pushed his glasses up the bridge of his nose and sighed. 'Sam, you should know as well as anyone that there are no guarantees. The best thing you can do is be patient with her. You need to bear in mind that it could be much worse. She remembers who she is, at least, and recognises the two of you.'

'Thank you, doctor. Let me know if there's any change in her condition,' Chrissie said.

'Of course.' Dr Saltano bowed his head, turned and walked away up the corridor.

'I suppose we should go and find the others,' Chrissie said. 'Have you managed to reach Grandma and Grandpa yet?'

Sam took out his phone, keyed the number and held it to his ear. After a while he lowered it again. 'The house phone's just ringing and ringing.'

'That's strange, they should be back from Grandpa's appointment by now.' As they walked towards the lifts at the opposite end of the corridor, Chrissie linked her arm through her brother's. 'Don't look so miserable, Sam. She's awake, and that's more than we could have hoped for a few days ago.'

'I know, but you heard what Dr Saltano said. Her memory might never come back. This might last forever, and I don't know how many more times I can take hearing her ask where Dad is.'

'Same, but we just have to be patient. There's nothing anyone can do.'

She pressed the button to call a lift. Several seconds passed as they stood side-by-side, arms linked, and then the doors opened. A hospital porter pushed an empty trolley out and they stepped in after.

'But what if there was something someone could do?' Sam asked as he pushed the button for the ground floor, where Lance, Lewis and Eva were waiting.

'What do you mean?'

'I think I can change what's happened, Chrissie. What if I could make Mum better and bring Dad back?'

Chrissie felt tears at the back of her eyes. She was tired of always having to be the strong one. Sam had seemed so much better recently, with no more seizures since the funeral. 'Will you *please* stop talking like that?' she said. 'Dad's gone. The sooner you accept it, the better.'

'But what if he didn't have to be?'

The world seemed to narrow to a point. Sam was still talking, but his voice sounded very, very far away. Chrissie's legs wobbled. She might have fallen if her brother wasn't there to hold on to.

'Are you all right?' he asked. 'You don't look so good.'

She blinked and fanned herself with her hand. 'Yeah, just came over a bit faint for a second.'

The doors opened and Sam guided her to a row of chairs on the other side. Once Chrissie was seated, he crouched in front of her. 'Sorry,' he said. 'I didn't mean to upset you. I just want us to be a family again.'

She felt a sensation like tiny bubbles popping inside her and realised it was the baby moving. 'Don't worry,' she said, placing a hand over her belly. 'We will be.'

58

Sam left the hospital sandwiched between Lewis and Eva on the back seat of Lance's car. As they drove, he felt Eva's hand, cool and dry, slide into his own. He glanced over, saw her smile and squeezed her hand back. Although she'd only been in the country a few days, the fact that she would soon have to return to Montclair filled him with dread, making him want to hold on to each moment in her company as long as he possibly could.

When they reached Doug's block of flats Sam walked Eva to the door. 'Were you okay today?' he asked. 'A trip to the hospital wasn't exactly what I had planned.'

She turned on the top step so that she was an inch or two higher than him. 'I was fine. Things certainly never are dull around you.'

'A bit of dullness might make a nice change.'

The wind blew Eva's hair across her face. She brushed it away and looked down on him. 'I'm really glad about your mom,' she said. 'And it was nice to meet your sister, and Lance and Lewis too.'

'Look, what Lewis was saying earlier about time travel—'

She grinned. 'You don't need to explain, I know when someone's yanking my chain.'

Sam wanted to tell her that every word of it was the truth, but when he opened his mouth he discovered that he couldn't speak the words. The car horn honked behind him. He looked over his shoulder to see Lance circling his hand, motioning for him to hurry up.

'You better go,' Eva said.

'I...I...'

'I'm free next week. I know it's Christmas and you've got a lot going on and everything—'

'No, I'd like that,' he said, his tongue finally returning to life. 'Maybe it's safer if you choose what we do next time.'

'You've got yourself a deal.' She placed her hand on his shoulder, leaned forward to kiss his cheek and then disappeared through the door. Sam stood on the steps for a few seconds and then climbed down to the car.

Some things aren't that hard to put right, Eva had told him. He very much hoped she was correct.

They dropped Lewis off on the way back and drove the last few streets home. Sam could tell something was wrong from the moment he opened the front door. The Chubb lock wasn't on, which meant his grandparents must be home, but the house was freezing and strangely quiet.

Lance stepped in after. 'Whoa! Why's it so cold in here? Is the heating off or something?'

Sam placed his hand on radiator in the hall and felt warmth beneath his fingers. A breeze was blowing through the house. He opened the door to the kitchen. The vase that had been on the table now lay smashed on the floor, flowers scattered amongst broken glass. The French doors stood wide open and a small drift of snow was collecting on the floor. He stepped around the mess, locked the back door and returned to the hall.

His grandmother was halfway down the stairs. 'There you are!' she said. 'I was wondering where you'd all got to.'

'We've been at the hospital,' Chrissie said. 'Mum's woken up.'

Grandma scampered down the last few steps and threw her arms around Chrissie. 'Why didn't you let me know? Can we see her yet?'

'We're going back tomorrow. She's got amnesia and

doesn't remember anything about the accident. You tried to ring home from the hospital, didn't you, Sam?'

'Yeah,' he said. 'Several times. Where's Grandpa?'

'Having a lie down upstairs,' their grandmother said. 'Why do you ask?'

'The door to the garden was wide open. Snow's been blowing in and the wind knocked the vase off the table. Did you forget to close it or something?'

She frowned. 'Not me, pet. I made a cup of tea when we got back, but that was a couple of hours ago. You know what your grandfather's like, it must have been him.'

'Yeah,' Sam said, 'I suppose it must've been.'

Part VI
Retribution and Remorse

59

December 1969 – January 1970

Lara stood at the edge of the party, twisting her diamond ring as she watched other couples slow dance. Christmas had come and gone, the decade in its final throes. They'd spent the holiday with Isaac's parents in Santa Barbara, staying in his childhood bedroom for three nights before driving back to San Francisco. Lara had been consumed by anxiety at the prospect of meeting her soon-to-be in-laws, but in the event they turned out to be a delight. Judy Barclay stood at just five feet zero, making her one of the few people Lara could look down upon. Judy was infectiously optimistic, kept her home immaculately clean and had the same wide grin as her son. The rest of Isaac's looks came straight from his father, Donald, who apart from the greying temples and potbelly could have been his twin.

Lara had found she had something in common with both Judy and Donald, namely increasing concern for Isaac. In the months since their engagement he had become ever more secretive and withdrawn, working longer and longer hours. His hair was limp and greasy, his skin sallow and covered in pimples. Most of the time he seemed jumpy and nervous, often muttering to himself and casting furtive, darting glances about the place.

The short stay in Santa Barbara almost proved too much for him, and Lara had needed to draw on all of her powers of persuasion to convince Isaac not to leave a day early. In the days since their return to San Francisco, she had hardly seen him, apart from when he stumbled into bed in the small hours of the morning only to leave again before dawn.

The band finished a tune and left the stage to a rapturous applause. Lara scanned the hall for the thousandth time that evening. No matter how much she wanted to throttle Isaac on sight, she would have forgiven all had he turned up right then. Instead she caught the eye of Dr Hamilton, Chair of the Board of Trustees at Stribe Lyndhurst. Smiling widely, he sidled over, a canapé in one hand and a martini in the other.

'Ah, Dr McHayden,' he said and popped the canapé in his mouth. 'So glad you could make our little shindig. May I say how ravishing you look this evening?'

'Thank you, sir,' Lara said, noticing there was a stain on his shirt and that his hairpiece was askew. 'You scrub up very nicely too.'

'Too kind, too kind,' he said, showering Lara with crumbs and fish eggs. 'And where is Dr Barclay, might I inquire?'

Lara felt her cheeks burn. 'He was supposed to…well, I'm sure he'll be along any minute.'

Dr Hamilton nodded in feigned sympathy. 'Between you and me, dear, I think he's working too hard. There's a fine line between dedication and overdoing things.'

'If you'll excuse me, sir, I need to visit the little girl's room.'

'But of course.' Hamilton spied a waiter passing by and snatched another canapé from his platter. 'Tell Isaac I'd like a word when he gets here, will you?'

Lara slipped away while Dr Hamilton snared another guest and made her way to the bathroom located in the foyer just outside the main banqueting hall. Two middle-aged ladies were adjusting their lipstick in the gilded mirror above the basins. Lara recognised one as Dr Hamilton's wife, Mary-Anne, but managed to dart into a cubicle before she was forced to endure another Q & A session on her fiancé's whereabouts. She sat down, pulled off the expensive stilettos she had bought especially for the occasion and rubbed the back of her aching heels.

Lara had reminded Isaac about the party on numerous occasions. She had even rented him a tux, polished his good shoes and left everything neatly laid out in the bedroom. Tetradyamide and his consultancy at Bereck & Hertz were becoming an obsession that was threatening to pull them apart.

'Ladies and Gentlemen!' a voice boomed over the loudspeakers in the main room. 'It is now one minute to midnight! Please fill your glasses and make your way to the dance floor.'

'Hurry, Susan. I don't want to miss it!' Lara heard Mary-Anne Hamilton say.

'Just a minute,' her companion said.

'We don't *have* a minute! Here let me fix that…there, you look fine.'

Lara heard the door swing shut. Alone, she lifted her feet onto the seat, wrapped her arms around her legs and rested her chin on her knees. The bang of an early firework sounded far away in the distance.

'Ten…nine…eight…seven…six,' the loudspeaker announced.

She let out a sob. Where the hell was he? It was inexcusable. Was this what their marriage would be like, a lifetime of missed engagements while she made excuses for him? How could he? How the bloody hell could he?

'Five…four…three…two…one…Happy New Year!'

Lara entered the new decade alone, hiding in a toilet cubicle and crying into her hands.

60

Present Day

Sam, Chrissie and their grandparents went to visit his mother on Sunday, and Sam went again by himself the day after. He'd longed to see an improvement in her condition, no matter how small, but if anything she seemed even worse. She couldn't remember them visiting the day before and kept asking to see his father. It soon became too much for Sam to tell her the truth and see her heart break all over, only for her to forget and repeat the process a few minutes later. Eventually he resorted to telling her that his dad had popped out and would be back soon. The lie was a torture he could take so long as she didn't have to share it, but the possibility of having to go through this act for weeks, months or even years terrified him.

After leaving St Benedict's, Sam made his way directly home. Because he'd undone being late for Dr McHayden on Friday, he now had no recollection of how their last meeting had panned out, or if and when they had arranged another, but shortly after arriving back at the house he looked through the living room curtains to see her car pull up outside. The snowfall over the weekend had only lasted a few hours, but it had settled and the temperature outside had hardly risen above freezing point since, leaving the ground a lethal sheet of trampled ice. Sam let himself out of the house and picked his way down the path, over the pavement and across the road.

When he climbed into the car he found McHayden sitting beside him, but instead of Steele there was a man with short grey hair and stubble in the driver's seat.

'Good afternoon,' McHayden said. 'And how are you today, my dear boy?'

'Very well,' Sam said. 'I've had some good news; my mum has woken up.'

'How marvellous! I am *de*lighted for you. I also want to congratulate you on your outstanding work last week.'

'Thanks,' he said. Whatever had happened on Friday had gone well, from the sound of it. 'Where's Agent Steele today?'

'I'm afraid Mr Steele is elsewhere engaged. Instead, we are in the capable hands of Mr Clarke here.'

The man in the front seat glanced at Sam in the rear view mirror with eyes the colour of a stormy sky. A chill shot down Sam's spine. Steele may not have been the friendliest person in the world, but Sam suspected he was going to like his replacement even less.

They arrived at the Tempus Research Facility an hour later. Instead of coming in with them as Steele always had, Clarke waited in the car. As McHayden and Sam walked towards the building together, snow crunching beneath their feet, she turned to him and said, 'You should know that, for the time being at least, your training is over.'

'Already?'

'Needs must. Today will be your first assignment.' She paused before the double doors. 'I know it may seem like a rush, Sam, but you're ready for this. After last week, I have every confidence in you.'

Arnold was behind the front desk, but there were two men Sam had never seen before seated in the waiting area. Both looked roughly McHayden's age. The nearest was short and plump, with rolls of fat beneath his chin that bulged over his shirt collar. He had bushy eyebrows and the skin of his bald head was all rumpled and splotchy. Next to him was a much taller man with thick grey hair, tinged faintly yellow. He sat crooked in his chair, a cigarette with a finely balanced column of ash drooping from his fingers and his long, spindly legs crossed at the knee.

'Gentlemen, my apologies for keeping you waiting,' McHayden said. 'Sam Rayner, may I introduce Montague Phelps of the Ministry of Defence,' she gestured to the fat man, 'and Clive Lanthorpe of Clearwater Industries, one of the principle stakeholders in the Tempus Project.'

Sam grinned and waved, then felt instantly foolish.

Lanthorpe poked his cigarette in Sam's direction, causing the long column of ash to crumble to the floor. 'So this is the young man, eh?' he asked in a voice like grinding stones.

'Indeed,' McHayden said with unmistakable pride. 'If you'd like to follow me, we can begin.'

She led them to the concealed lift on the other side of the room, pressed her hand to the black plate and selected the bottom button. They were greeted by complete darkness when the doors reopened. It was only after McHayden had stepped out that the overhead lighting flicked on and Sam saw the lab was deserted, the caged monkeys nowhere to be seen. They followed McHayden to the small room off the back and took a chair each around the wooden table. Lanthorpe lifted the leather briefcase he'd been carrying to his knees, opened it and took out a large black and white photograph.

'Tell me,' he said and pushed it across the table to Sam, 'do you know who this is?'

The photo showed a man with a round, egg-shaped head devoid of hair. There was a large scar on one side of his face where, long ago, the skin had bubbled and melted. Sam pushed the photograph back. 'No, should I?'

Lanthorpe coughed, a deathly rattle that reverberated in his chest, then reached into his pocket for another cigarette. 'His name is Michael Humboldt.' In one slick motion he produced a silver lighter, lit the cigarette and breathed out a thick plume of smoke. 'This man, Sam, is responsible for the death of your father.'

61

Lanthorpe pulled on his cigarette, the ember blazing as a new column of ash grew.

Sam's throat clenched and his legs started to shake under the table. 'This is who turned Esteban Haufner?' he asked.

'The first item on our agenda,' McHayden said, 'as promised.'

'But how?'

'We've traced components from the smart phone used to trigger the electronic jamming device that brought down Flight 0368 to a company owned by Humboldt,' she said. 'He's a US national, an extremely wealthy individual who made his fortune trading pharmaceutical stocks and mining oil and precious metals in the 1970s. During the 1980s he diversified into drug and arms trafficking, and has been close to the top of Interpol's

Most Wanted list ever since. We came close to catching him a decade ago, since which time he's dropped off the radar.'

'That is until yesterday,' Phelps said. Given the size of his body, his voice was improbably high and squeaky. He folded his arms and leaned back, the chair creaking under his weight. 'Our sources indicate that Humboldt is in South America at present, somewhere in Bolivia, Southern Peru or Northern Chile, where we believe several cells of his organisation are based. Word is that a rendezvous is planned in coming weeks, but we don't know exactly when or where. The whole area is under satellite surveillance and we have drones capable of delivering an explosive device on standby, but all that is rather messy. We want to bring the bugger in alive, if possible.'

'And that's where you come in,' McHayden said. She passed Sam a sheet of paper containing two lines: an email address and, below it, a password – a random string of letters and numbers. 'This is an encrypted email address. We have a team of operatives monitoring satellite footage around the clock. A daily report and clips of any relevant footage will be sent to this address at 8 o'clock each evening. All you have to do is log in, read the report and study any relevant video footage, then relay back and let us know when the target is in place so that a ground team can be mobilised in advance. You don't even need to leave the comfort of your own home to do it.'

'All you want me to do is read daily reports and watch video clips?' Sam asked, thinking it sounded too easy.

McHayden got up, walked over to the metal cabinet in the corner of the room, unlocked it and returned with a brown pill bottle. 'It's even simpler than that, my dear boy. At the moment, all you have to do is *agree* to check the email account each evening. That will set up the conditions whereby you can travel forward from this point in time to tomorrow night and see if Humboldt sticks his neck out. If not, try the next day, and the day after, and the day after that and so on. He has to show his ugly face at some point and, when he does, I need you to tell us exactly when and where.'

She poured a glass of water, popped the lid of the bottle and handed Sam a pill. He placed it on his tongue and washed it down with a swig of water.

Phelps raised his bushy eyebrows. 'So?'

'It normally takes a while to kick in,' Sam said.

The four of them sat in an uncomfortable silence, broken only by the faint hum of the fluorescent lighting above. After several minutes Sam felt the familiar jolt of adrenaline that signalled Tetradyamide taking effect.

He closed his eyes. Coloured shapes sprang from the darkness, twisting and morphing until they blended together to form the scene he'd witnessed just before shutting his eyes. He concentrated on the time when the first report would be sent: 8 p.m. tomorrow. Instantly the image skipped forward to another and another and then, like the fluttering of pages, they sped up to the point where each image was no more than a flash of colour. The whole process was smoother and faster than ever before, as Sam's control improved with practice.

Eventually the images slowed until he was left with the viewpoint of the computer in his bedroom, his hands on the keyboard under the light of his desk lamp. He blinked and flexed his fingers. Rain was beating against the window and he could hear the sound of the television downstairs. The piece of paper McHayden had given him was next to the keyboard. Sam nudged the mouse, brought up a new window and keyed in the email address and password.

A message with a single attachment was waiting in the account. The subject was tomorrow's date: 24th December. He opened the attachment and found a document containing only two words: *NO SIGHTING*.

Sam leaned back, closed his eyes and focused on the same time the following day. Images leaped forward once again, passing in a blur. When they slowed to a stop he was presented with an identical point of view: his hands resting on the keyboard of his computer. For a second he thought that something had gone wrong and he hadn't moved, but then he noticed that he was wearing a Christmas jumper with a snowman on the front. He got up and pulled back the curtains. The night sky was clear and without a drop of rain, so returned to his chair and logged in.

A new message was waiting with Wednesday's date – Christmas Day – in the subject bar. He opened it and found another document with the same two words: *NO SIGHTING*.

Sam kept going, travelling forwards a day at a time. On one occasion he noticed that his fingernails had grown long and rattled against the keys as he typed, but after the next jump they were neat and trimmed. Before long, he'd counted fifteen emails in his inbox, the last few dating from January of next year. All had a single document attached stating that no sighting had been made.

On the next jump Sam discovered that his nose was suddenly blocked and he had a sore throat. The symptoms of a head cold worsened for a couple more days before gradually beginning to clear. By now the dates on the emails were approaching mid-January. Sam would have started at Fraser Golding College and Eva would have returned to Montclair. He jumped forward another day and suddenly found an email with two attachments – a document and a video file – waiting in his inbox.

Sam opened the video and, while it buffered, read the document. It contained several paragraphs of text under the heading:

TARGET AQUIRED
10:37, 18TH JAN, ATACAMA DESERT, CHILE.
LAT: 23° 7' 56.8812" S, LONG: 68° 15' 45.0720" W.

He grabbed a pencil and scrawled the time, date and coordinates on the back of the piece of paper McHayden had given him, which was becoming increasingly grubby and torn. Suddenly it dawned on him how pointless this was; there was no way he could bring paper back to the present with him, or any other solid object for that matter. The only way to carry the information was in his head, and the purpose of the memory exercises he'd completed during his first week at the Tempus Research Facility became clear.

At that moment the video began to play, maximising over the document on the screen. The clip was 1 minute and 48 seconds long, and opened with an aerial shot over mountains. There was a small village in the middle of the screen. The picture magnified until Sam could make out people moving about between the low stone buildings. It zoomed in again, swooping down on two people; a woman and a man. The woman wore a flowing dress and headscarf. The man's head was bare and hairless. Suddenly the crosshairs in the centre of the screen flashed from white to green. The woman and man approached a building with a straw roof. The woman entered. It looked like the man was about to follow when without warning he stopped, turned on the front step and knelt. Even in the low resolution, Sam could tell this action caused him pain. A child, a young girl with a flower in her hair, entered the shot. Running, she jumped into the man's outstretched arms. He scooped her up, twirled her around and went through the door, holding the girl at his hip.

Then the screen went black.

At first Sam thought it was the end of the recording, but the clip had almost a minute left to play. The picture zoomed out, rising, and he realised the blackness was actually dense, oily smoke billowing from the position where the building had just been. In its place was a crater that covered almost a third of the screen, including the space previously occupied by two or three neighbouring houses. He could make out people running on the crater's edge, while others lay motionless on the debris-ridden ground.

Sam watched the clip until it ended, returning to the aerial shot over the mountains with which it had begun, then he closed the file and put his head in his hands. The village had been bombed. The little girl with a flower in her hair was dead, or would be. No matter how much Sam wanted revenge for his father, this wasn't a price he was willing to pay. He began to cry, violent sobs that shook his whole body. Tears streamed down his face, dripping onto his hands and wrists and wetting his sleeves. He couldn't let this happen: there had to be something he could do.

Sam was startled by a touch on his shoulder. Lowering his hands, he looked up. Instead of the walls of his bedroom, he was surrounded by the whitewashed breeze-blocks of the Tempus Research Facility. McHayden was leaning over from the next chair, her hand on his shoulder. 'What happened?' she asked. 'Did you find him?'

Sam straightened up and wiped his eyes with the crook of his arm. 'No.'

'What do you mean "no"?' Phelps said. 'He wasn't there?'

'No, it didn't work. I couldn't do it. I couldn't see the future.'

Lanthorpe thumped his hands on the tabletop and stood, his chair skittering away off the back of his legs. 'Come on, Monty. I've seen just about enough of this circus.'

Phelps shook his head and heaved himself out of his chair. McHayden rose too, moving quickly to block their exit. 'Gentlemen, please. If we could just try one more—'

'Thank you, Dr McHayden,' Lanthorpe said, pushing his way past, 'but you've wasted quite enough of our time as it is.'

62

The car stopped outside Sam's house and McHayden turned to face him. She looked years older, pale and sickly. 'What exactly happened back there?' she asked.

'I...I don't know,' Sam said. 'I did what I always do, but nothing happened. It didn't work.'

'What if you tried too soon? Perhaps the Tetradyamide hadn't taken full effect yet.'

'It's possible, I suppose, but I waited as long as I always do.'

'Hmmm.' She brushed her hair back, exposing grey roots. Suddenly her eyes widened behind her glasses. 'Or a defective batch of pills? It's happened before!'

'Maybe,' he said, and glanced up. Clarke was staring at him in the rear view mirror again. It felt as if those eyes could see straight through Sam's deception. 'I'm sorry if I messed things up.'

'What? It's hardly your fault if the pills were defective,' McHayden said. 'This is a setback, that's all. There's far too much at stake to give up now. Perhaps it was too early to get the MoD involved. We'll keep trying until we have some solid results to work with, evidence they can't dispute.'

Sam nodded and looked down at his hands.

'You tried your best,' she said. 'Go and get some rest and we'll work on what went wrong tomorrow.'

He climbed out, crossed the road and let himself into the house. Once inside his bedroom, he closed the door and wedged a chair under the handle, which was the closest thing he had to a lock. Sam had believed that the Tempus Project offered a solution to all of his problems, a way to undo the event that had destroyed his family, but after today he saw that he would be responsible for the destruction of a Chilean village, with the deaths of dozens of innocent people on his conscience. McHayden had told Sam that his ability would be used for good, but instead he had become a weapon.

He kicked off his shoes and stretched out on the bed. The warm tingle of Tetradyamide still pulsed through his limbs. Dr McHayden had warned him never to manipulate time on his own, but it seemed to be his only way out. With the drug in his veins, Sam's mistakes could become a learning curve and hindsight transformed into decisive action.

He closed his eyes and focused on a day at the end of last summer. It was the day that had changed everything; the day of the crash. Sam wasn't sure how he was going to stop his mum and dad boarding the plane, but was pretty sure he'd think of something once he was back there.

Shapes fused together in the darkness behind his eyelids to form an image of the ceiling. He saw a cobweb hanging in the corner above his bed that he hadn't noticed before. The still frames flicked back, one by one, steadily gaining speed. The dark of night followed the light of day, over and over until Sam was left with vertigo. This was by far the furthest he'd ever attempted to travel in time and the process seemed to last forever. With no way of knowing how far he'd already gone, he began to worry that he might overshoot the mark and come round a baby, sucking a dummy and crapping in his nappy, when all of a sudden he experienced the sensation of running into a brick wall.

He was on his back, surrounded by darkness. It felt as though his body had been put through a cement mixer, every bone ground to dust. He tried to open his eyes, but they were heavy and gluey.

'He's awake. He's coming to!' a voice said.

Sam tried to speak, but an object blocked his mouth. Gradually his vision returned. The light in the place was painfully bright. The outline of a person hovered over him.

'Don't try to move, I'll fetch the doctor,' the voice said. It was Mary, Sam's nurse at St Benedict's Hospital.

63

Dr Saltano rushed in. He placed his cup on the bedside table and turned to inspect the array of monitors connected to the life support system on the other side of Sam's bed. Mary leaned over and eased the ventilator from Sam's mouth. He coughed as his lungs drew air.

'Sam, can you hear me?' she asked.

What was he doing here? Of all the times and places Sam might want to revisit, this was close to last on the list. Ignoring her question, he closed his eyes again and was presented with the image of Mary standing over him with the ventilator in her hand, a string of his drool dangling from the mouthpiece. Sam willed the image to move back and, slowly, it did. In freeze frames he saw Dr Saltano collect his cup and reverse through the door.

Then his vision dimmed and he was left in darkness.

That was it. He couldn't go back any further. The brick wall had returned, blocking the way to the time before he'd woken up. But suddenly Sam understood why. If his ability to manipulate time was the result of his brain injury, then this, his first conscious moment after the crash, would be the earliest he could go. He was at the beginning of the book, the place where the pages of time began. And that left only one possible direction.

Sam threw himself forward. Thankfully, the pages began to turn again, images flowing by in a blur as he left the hospital far behind. The days and weeks that followed roared past as nothing but flashes of light and colour, vanishing too fast to make out any detail. Sam wanted to return to the present, but by now the Tetradyamide was diluting in his blood and he could feel his control weakening.

Slowly the images stuttered to a halt. Sam was lying on his back with a white ceiling above him, but when he blinked and tried to sit up something held him back. He couldn't move. His head felt foggy and his vision was hazy, like he was looking through clouded glass. He tilted his head to the side and a strand of long, greasy hair flopped over his eyes. There was a windowless breeze-block wall where his bedroom door should have been. He tried to move again, but his arms and legs were fixed in place.

Sam managed to lift his head a few centimetres and, looking down the length of his body, saw a dirty hospital gown spotted with blood and urine stains and layers of accumulated filth. His arms and legs were pale and withered, as if they hadn't seen daylight in years. Thick leather straps at his wrists and ankles pinned him to a metal trolley. Wherever Sam had ended up, it definitely wasn't his bedroom.

Straining against the leather straps, he tried to call for help but only managed to produce a feeble croak with vocal cords rusty from lack of use. The restraints dug deeper the more he struggled, causing thin streams of blood to run from unhealed wounds on his wrists and ankles. He gritted his teeth and tried rocking the trolley back and forth. It was a colossal effort on his shrunken muscles, but eventually he succeeded in jerking the wheels on one side an inch or so off the floor, and by swinging his weight in the other direction tilted the trolley even further. He repeated the process, swinging harder and harder until the trolley toppled over with an almighty crash. Sam's head slammed against the concrete floor and he blacked out for a moment.

When he came to he discovered that his situation was now even worse: he was lying on his side, facing a steel security door with his right arm and leg suspended above him by the restraints on the other side of the trolley. Blood was beginning to pool around his temple and run into his left eye.

The sound of heavy footsteps approached from behind the door. There was a rattle of keys, followed by the clunk of a lock sliding back. The door swung open and Clarke stepped into the room.

'Help me,' Sam wheezed.

Clarke crossed the room and lifted the toppled trolley upright again. More footsteps approached, this time the clip-clopping of high heels.

'Where am I?' Sam asked.

Clarke backhanded him across the face with his knuckles. When the stars had cleared from Sam's vision, he discovered that Clarke was gone and McHayden now stood in his place. She looked younger and fresher somehow, as if her wrinkles had been smoothed out.

'Another escape attempt?' she said. 'I had so hoped we were past all that by now.'

'Where am I?' Sam asked again.

She reached out and stroked the side of his face where the impact of Clarke's hand still burned. 'Why, the very same place you've been for the last eleven months: the Tempus Research Facility.'

Eleven months. Almost a year.

Sam could barely take it in. 'But why? Why are you keeping me here?'

'Hush now, do we really have to go through all this again? You know I could never leave you walking about, not with everything you're carrying up there.' She tapped a fingernail on Sam's forehead, scratching his skin. 'Besides, I would so miss our little chats.'

'You can't keep me here,' he said. 'I want to go home.'

She cocked her head to the side, her lips curling into a grin. 'My dear boy, I think you must have bumped you head harder than I realised. This *is* your home.'

64

McHayden took a syringe from the pocket of her lab coat and stuck the needle through the rubber cap on a glass bottle. She pulled the plunger back, drawing up a clear liquid, then removed the needle and flicked it twice. 'Unfortunately there have been issues surrounding the stability of our enhanced operatives,' she said. 'They keep on...what's the word I'm looking for? Oh yes, dying. That's it, they keep on dying. I suspect it might have something to do with the abnormalities we discovered in your cells—'

'Abnormalities in my cells?'

'That's right. I'm afraid we're going to need to extract more bone marrow for testing, but you're used to that by now, aren't you, dear boy?'

Before Sam could say anything else, McHayden jabbed the needle into his arm and pushed the plunger. Tiredness instantly surged over him. Every muscle in his body loosened and his eyelids sagged shut.

All of a sudden he found himself staring at the cobweb on his bedroom ceiling. Sam sat up and rubbed his wrists where he could still feel the bite of the restraints that would hold him in place for eleven months. He had seen a future where things were far worse than he could ever have imagined. By changing a fate in which he would be responsible for the bombing of a village, he had replaced it with one where he would end up as McHayden's hostage. But it hadn't happened yet. Hindsight could still be turned into decisive action.

He picked up his phone and called Lewis.

65

Sam ran downstairs as fast as he could when the doorbell rang, but his grandmother came out of the kitchen as soon as he'd let Lewis in. 'Oh, you're back, pet,' she said. 'I didn't hear you come in. Are you boys hungry? I could heat up some leftovers.'

'We've already eaten,' Sam said before Lewis could accept. 'Haven't we, Lewis?'

Lewis narrowed his eyes, looking like he was about to complain until Sam elbowed him in the ribs. 'Um, yeah, that's right,' he said, puffing his cheeks and resting a hand on his stomach. 'I'm stuffed, couldn't eat another bite.'

'Well, there's plenty in the fridge if you change your minds.'

Sam waited for her to return to the kitchen and then led his friend upstairs. Lewis dumped his coat on the floor and slouched in the chair by the desk. 'You just made me miss out on your grandma's cooking,' he said. 'This better be good.'

Sam lowered himself onto the edge of the bed, took a deep breath and told Lewis everything that had happened.

When he'd finished, Lewis linked his hands behind his head and sighed gently. 'Sounds like you've got yourself in a spot of bother, I reckon.'

'Thanks a lot,' Sam said, 'that's very helpful.'

'Well, you've got two options, as far as I can see. First, you meet her tomorrow as planned and tell her you're leaving the Tempus Project. Convince her you can't do this time travel thingy anymore and you're of no further use to her.'

Sam shook his head. 'I can't see her going for that. And if she analyses the pills – which she will – then she'll know there was nothing wrong with the batch and I was lying to her. What's the second option?'

'You come clean,' Lewis said. 'Tell her the truth about today.'

'The *truth*? I don't see how that's going to help.'

'It might if you can get your hands on more of the drug. Then you could travel back and, I don't know, stop yourself from ever meeting her or something. What if you tell her you've had changed your mind and want another chance at finding this Humboldt guy? She might give you more then.'

Sam thought about it for a minute, then stood up and clapped Lewis on the shoulder. 'You know what, I think that might just work.'

66

George stood at the back of the comms room with his arms folded across his chest. The only sound was the murmur of efficient activity as the surveillance team worked at banks of computer terminals, monitoring trans-missions from the cameras and listening devices he'd planted at the boy's house.

'Sir?'

He turned to find a technician at his side, a man several years his junior whose name always evaded him. 'Yes, what is it…' George snapped his fingers, trying to dredge up the man's name.

'Marshall, sir. There's something you need to hear.'

'Well spit it out, man. No need to be coy.'

'We're recording a conversation, sir. I think it might be important.'

George followed Marshall to a terminal and accepted a pair of headphones. Five minutes later he stood up and adjusted his cuffs. 'I'll need a full transcript.'

'Of course,' Marshall said.

'As quickly as you can manage.'

'I'll get right on it.'

George left him tapping at his keyboard, marched straight out of the room and rode the lift to the third floor. He paused at the door to McHayden's office, squeezed his fingernail into the pad of each thumb five times – no more, no less – and knocked before entering.

She was in her preposterous, over-sized chair, cradling a glass of brandy. 'George, good to see you,' she said and gestured for him to sit in one of the chairs on the near side of her desk. 'I've been meaning to fill you in on this afternoon's debacle. It seems we have a problem with one or more batches of Tetradyamide.'

George remained standing. 'There's nothing wrong with the Tetradyamide.'

'Beg your pardon?'

'We've just received transmission of a conversation between Sam Rayner and Lewis Fisher. The boy has been lying to you, ma'am. The assignment was completed and Humboldt's location was successfully established. Sam got cold feet about the collateral damage and told you he couldn't do it.'

'The little so-and-so.' She drained her glass and placed it on a coaster on her desk. 'And he thinks he can get away with this, does he?'

'Not at all,' George said. 'It seems our young friend is planning to part ways with us. He intends to confess in the hope we'll give him another chance to prove himself. Once he has more Tetradyamide, he'll reverse his initial discovery, meaning we'll have no knowledge of his existence. The consequences for the Tempus Project are...well, I'm sure you can imagine.'

'Quite.' McHayden rose from her chair, paced across the room and refilled her glass at the roll-top drinks cabinet beneath the window. 'You've done well to bring this to my attention, George. Brandy?'

'No thank you, ma'am. I don't partake.'

She shrugged and returned to the desk, swilling a new drink.

'Shall I bring the boy in?' George asked.

'No, not just yet, I think. This information puts us in control of the situation, and at this stage the boy is of greater value if he can be brought back in line.'

'Yes, of course. And what about Fisher?'

The old lady lowered her glass and smiled. 'Well now, if the time comes when Sam requires a gentle nudge in the right direction, then I do believe Lewis Fisher could provide just the incentive we need.'

67

On the evening of Christmas Eve, Sam climbed into the back seat of Dr McHayden's car. He looked across to find her staring straight at him, her eyes unblinking behind her half-moon spectacles. 'I've had the rest of the bottle of Tetradyamide you took yesterday analysed,' she said. 'The results were perfectly normal.'

Sam had spent the whole day worrying about how to play this exact situation. Now that it was upon him, he wasn't sure that Lewis's plan would work, even if he had the nerve to see it through.

'There's something I need to tell you,' he said, placing his hand on his knee to stop it shaking.

'Really?' McHayden took off her glasses and rubbed the lenses with the sleeve of her cardigan. 'Do go on, I'm all ears.'

'I haven't been entirely honest with you, Dr McHayden. I knew the pills would be fine because I *was* able to manipulate time yesterday. There was a video, sent in mid-January. I saw Humboldt and...'

'Yes?' she said, looking completely unmoved.

'He was in Chile, staying in a village and I...I saw a missile hit. There were people everywhere and some got caught in the explosion. I want to get the man who killed my father, but not like that. I didn't want to be a part of it so I lied to you. I told you I couldn't travel in time.'

'My dear boy, do you have any idea how serious this could be? I'm struggling to persuade the MoD and Clearwater Industries not to withdraw funding altogether.'

'I'm sorry,' Sam said. 'I want the chance to make it up to you, to prove to everyone what I can do.'

'What you saw yesterday was only one possible future, one in which we didn't have the opportunity to mobilise a ground team and bring Humboldt in with minimal civilian casualties. Without your intervention, Sam, the event that you just described will still take place. By *not* passing on Humboldt's location you will, in effect, allow what you saw to happen.'

This hadn't occurred to Sam, but if anything it strengthened his bargaining position. 'I can see that now,' he said. 'That's why I'm telling you the truth. Please, Dr McHayden, I can find him again. Give me the chance to make this right.'

She looked across to Steele in the driver's seat. He turned to face them, straightened his tie and fixed Sam in his gaze. 'I'm not sure. The boy has already demonstrated that he cannot be trusted.'

'But I can,' Sam said. 'I promise, I realise my mistake. Humboldt killed my father. I want him just as badly as either of you. Please, I'm begging you, give me another chance. You won't regret it.'

McHayden blinked at long last. 'It's not normally in my nature to be so forgiving,' she said, 'but on this occasion I may be willing to make an exception.'

'You'll let me try again?'

'After Christmas. I'll need to visit Lanthorpe and Phelps this evening, of course, see if I can explain my way out of yesterday's fiasco. From now on, I need you to be completely honest with me, Sam.'

Although it was cold in the car, his hands felt clammy. 'No more lies,' he said. 'I promise.'

'Good.' She narrowed her eyes for the briefest of moments. 'If you and I are to achieve our aims, dear boy, then there will be sacrifices along the way. Tomorrow I want you to think about where your priorities lie. You say that you want revenge for your father, but are you willing to do what it takes to achieve that?'

'Yes,' he said without hesitating.

'Very well.' She nodded to Steele, who climbed out of the car and opened Sam's door for him. 'In that case I'll see you on Boxing Day.'

68

George let Sam out and then climbed into the driver's seat again. Looking into his near side mirror, he watched Sam gawping at the car from the road. After a few seconds the boy turned around, crossed over and began up the path to his house.

George started the engine. 'So,' he said after the initial growl had died down, 'you're letting him go then?'

'Not at all,' McHayden replied, smiling out of the window. 'Sam Rayner is precisely where I want him. Until we are able to successfully replicate his injury, we need the boy compliant.'

'But he doesn't trust us, ma'am. He could run at any time.'

'I very much doubt that.' She flattened the pleats of her skirt. 'What you have just witnessed, George, was an exercise in the art of appearing to give someone the very thing they want most.'

'You mean revenge?'

'I mean hope. If Sam still plans to reverse his initial discovery, then Tetradyamide is his only means of achieving that.'

'I see,' George said. 'And we are his only supply of Tetradyamide. So, to the Ministry of Defence?'

'No. At this stage I have no intention of embarrassing myself any further. We'll continue to monitor the boy around the clock and, as an insurance policy, I want you to prepare a team ready to bring Sam's friends and family in if he shows the slightest indication that he's planning to run.'

'Very good, ma'am,' George said, and steered away from the curb.

69

Sam stepped through the front door and closed it behind him. It was done: Lewis's plan had worked. After Christmas, he would visit the Tempus Research Facility one last time, take Tetradyamide and then prevent McHayden from ever discovering him, therefore putting an end to the mess which he'd made for himself.

The sound of raised voices came from the kitchen. He followed them and found his family seated around the table. Lance stood at the head, carving slices of meat.

'You're back early,' Sam's grandmother said. 'You only left a few minutes ago.'

'Something's happened,' he said. 'They've made some arrests in connection with the plane crash, so they don't need me this evening.'

'Good,' Chrissie said. 'Does this mean you won't have to keep disappearing off every night?'

'I doubt it,' Sam said.

'Well, never mind.' She stood up and went to fetch a bottle of sparkling wine from the fridge, before returning to the chair next to Sam. 'Would you like a glass? We're celebrating. The hospital just called to say they're discharging Mum in a few days. Her condition isn't much better, but at least she'll be home. That's good news, isn't it?'

'Yeah, amazing,' Sam said, and allowed Chrissie to fill his glass. He should have been ecstatic, but something didn't feel right. Perhaps it was the memory of McHayden's face as she'd driven a needle into his arm in the terrible future that awaited him eleven months down the line. Having glimpsed her true nature the other night, he had expected McHayden to reprimand him more severely for lying to her. Although Lewis's plan had gone down without a hitch, the whole thing had seemed almost too easy.

'Aren't you having any?' Grandma asked Chrissie after she had filled everyone's glass except her own.

'No, think I'll stick to water,' Chrissie said. 'I can feel a bit of a headache coming on.'

'Well, I'm not surprised, pet. You've probably been overdoing things lately.'

Lance looked up from the joint of beef he was carving, opened his mouth as if he was about to say something, then caught Chrissie's eye and closed it again.

'Here, let me help,' Sam said, pushing his chair back.

'There's a tray of roast potatoes in the oven,' his grandmother said. 'Could you get a serving dish out of the cupboard?'

Sam crossed the kitchen and froze. Lying on the counter was a strange, cylindrical object, roughly an inch long and the diameter of a pencil. There was a tiny lens at one end. He picked it up and turned around. 'Where did you get this?'

'Get what, pet?' his grandmother asked.

'This!' he said, showing her the object in his hand.

'It's one of your computer game gizmos, isn't it?'

'No, definitely not.'

'Well, I found it on top of your wardrobe while I was cleaning your room, which was an absolute tip, by the way. What is it then?'

Sam placed the miniature camera back on the counter. McHayden had bugged his house. She was probably listening right now, and must have heard every word of his conversation with Lewis the night before. A sickening realisation dawned on him: McHayden clearly had no intention of giving him more Tetradyamide or letting him find Michael Humboldt again. If Sam went with her on Boxing Day, he would probably be setting up the very conditions through which he would become her prisoner for the next eleven months. He felt his knees wobble and had to grip the kitchen counter.

'Dude, are you all right?' Lance asked.

Sam shook his head, then went to fetch the notepad and pen from beside the telephone on the table in the hall.

'What are you doing?' Chrissie asked as he returned.

Sam raised his finger to his lips, opened the notepad and began to write.

70

George was in high spirits. Everything was now in place so that the Sam Rayner situation could be wrapped into a neat, tidy package, which was precisely how he liked things. After returning to Thames House he rode the lift to the fifth floor. Despite the building being almost deserted, Marshall grabbed him by the arm as soon as he walked through the door of the comms room. George glared down at the appendage that dared crumple the material of his suit, noticing the dirt under his assistant's fingernails with added distaste.

'Let go of me,' he said, and growled so menacingly that Marshall released him and took a step back, his mouth a circle of surprise.

It took a moment for Marshall to find his voice again. 'Sorry sir, I was just about to call you. It's all gone quiet at the Rayners' house.'

'What do you mean "gone quiet"?'

'Maureen Rayner discovered the camera you planted in Sam's room. She didn't seem to know what it was, so I didn't want to raise the alarm prematurely. But then a short while ago, over dinner, the whole family just upped and left. Like I said, it's gone quiet.'

George cursed under his breath and peered at Marshall. Did he detect a hint of insubordination in the man's tone? No matter. Any retribution would have to wait: his worst fear had been realised and the boy had fled.

'Sir, what do you want me to do now?' Marshall asked.

'Contact Dr McHayden, then organise two assault teams, one to take Lewis Fisher and the other to take Eva Bernstein,' George told him. 'I'm going after the boy.'

He left the comms room and, jogging back to the lift, checked the application tracking Lance Asquith's car. They were on the move, as he'd suspected.

After stepping out into the basement car park, George broke into a run and jumped in his car, barely registering the stain on the concrete that marked the spot where, on his command, a sniper's bullet had ended his best friend's life. He accelerated out of the building, one hand on the steering wheel and the other clutching his phone, the screen of which displayed a flashing red dot that was steadily working its way south towards central London.

George was less than fifteen minutes from intercepting Asquith's car when the red dot stopped moving. He put his foot down hard, for once ignoring the speed limit. If Sam had ditched the car and was now proceeding by foot, then the chances of catching him diminished by the second.

71

Eva was crossed-legged on her bed with Doug's old laptop balanced on her knees. It was something of a relic and painfully slow, but any internet was better than none.

She opened a new tab and brought up her emails. There was one from Nicole with the subject *Happy Holidays*. It contained an electronic card with a picture of an unhinged-looking Santa Claus attempting to cram himself, sack of toys and all, down a too-narrow chimney. Eva felt a twinge of homesickness. She typed a quick response and clicked the reply button.

It was odd being apart from her sister at this time of year, however with divorce proceedings rumbling on, it looked as though the family Christmas would now be a thing of the past. Nicole was still at an age when the holiday season had lost none of its magic, and a little of that had always rubbed off on Eva, even into her cynical teenage years. Nicole could be a brat sometimes – most of the time, in fact – but she didn't deserve to be stuck with Colette, who would probably spend the coming days blasted out of her mind on a combination of tranquilisers and eggnog. The house in Montclair had been dolled up with fairy lights and plastic snowmen for almost a month, whereas Doug's London apartment was about as festive as a case of sunstroke. He hadn't even bothered to buy a tree.

Eva opened a new tab and, on a whim, typed the words *time travel* into a search engine. Several million results were listed. Most contained links to Sci-Fi sites, however interspersed among these were some reputable scientific sites. She opened one at random and skimmed through the text. Eva had always believed time travel to be about as real as light sabres and little green men, but there turned out to be some theoretical foundation behind the fantasy. Unfortunately, most theories required travelling close to the speed of light or near a black hole, and it seemed unlikely Sam was capable of either feat. The whole thing was obviously just a gag at her expense, but...

She yawned and closed the laptop. Doug was already in bed. Even on Christmas Day he had an early meeting, but had promised to be back before noon. With no reason to stay up, Eva went to brush her teeth, ran a glass of water in the kitchen, then padded back to her room. As she slid into bed she heard a car pull up outside. She had just switched off the lamp when there was a clunk that sounded like a small object striking the window.

Eva sat upright. Was someone outside? No, of course not: her mind was playing tricks. Doug's apartment was on the third floor, after all.

She had just laid her head back on the pillow when she heard the noise again. This time she yanked her bedcovers off and went to the window, her heart thudding in her chest. There was no way she could have imagined the noise twice. She inched the curtains apart and peered into the alleyway that led to a communal garden at the rear of the building.

Sure enough, there was someone out there, lurking in the shadows. Eva fumbled on the table for her glasses and returned to the window. The someone was Sam. When he saw her he dropped a handful of pebbles, dusted his hands on the back of his jeans and waved. She waved back and pointed to the street in the direction of the door. He nodded and then disappeared around the front of the building.

Eva dressed quickly, pulling on the clothes she'd left hanging on the back of a chair. It was kind of corny to turn up throwing stones at her window, but still romantic, not the kind of thing Trent would have ever done.

The smile fell away from her lips the moment she opened the door, however. Standing in a line down the steps behind Sam were Chrissie, Lance and an elderly couple Eva guessed must be his grandparents.

'Hi,' she said. 'I, er, didn't realise you weren't alone.'

Sam glanced over his shoulder, almost like he thought they were being watched, then back to Eva. He looked awful, kind of like he'd stayed up drinking coffee since the last time they'd met.

'Can I…can *we* come in?' he asked.

'Okay,' she said and stepped to the side. It was a lot of people, she realised as they clumped up the stairs, and there wasn't much chance of not waking Doug, but there was a nervousness among the group and, as if by some form of primal instinct, Eva absorbed it and suddenly found herself hurrying the others along.

'What's happened?' she asked once the door to Doug's apartment was locked and bolted behind them. 'Is everything all right?'

'Not by a long shot.' Sam strode over to the window, parted the blinds and stared into the street. After a while he looked back. 'I don't think there's anybody out there.'

'Why would there be?' Eva asked. 'Tell me what's going on, Sam. You're scaring me.'

He let go of the blinds and scooped up her hand in both of his. 'I'm in big trouble, Eva.'

'What are you talking about?'

'Do you remember what Lewis told you about time travel the other day?'

'Not this again—'

'It wasn't a joke,' he said, tightening his grip on her hand. 'After I came out of the coma I started having these weird fits. It was sort of like time got jumbled; I'd be doing one thing and the next thing I knew it was two hours later or an hour before. I had one at my dad's funeral and found myself several hours ahead. We were watching TV and there was a news report about a bombing at a government building that evening. When I came round I was back in the church, so I called the police and tipped them off.'

'I don't get it,' Eva said. 'Why are Chrissie and Lance and your grandparents here?'

'What I'm saying is I couldn't control it at first, but later I was contacted by someone called Lara McHayden. She works for the Security Service, but also runs a research group that has been working on a drug first discovered in the 1960s. She said it could control my fits and channel them, so I'd be able to choose when they happen and how far into the past or future I'd go. She told me I could help catch the people responsible for sabotaging the plane that me and my parents were on. She told me my ability would be used for good, to protect people, but that wasn't true. I've seen what she's got planned, Eva. She wants to recreate my injury in other people, people she can control.'

'So why don't you leave? You know, just walk away.'

'McHayden won't let me. She's spying on my house. That's why we're here, Eva. It's not safe and I didn't know where else to go.

'Wait here,' she said, 'I'll go wake Doug.'

72

After jumping a set of red lights, scraping a stationary vehicle and driving the wrong way up a one-way street, George eventually turned onto the road where the dot had stopped and slammed on the brakes. Lance Asquith's Volvo was parked up ahead, obviously abandoned, the left wheels resting on the curb. George thumped his fists on top of the steering wheel. A day that had promised so much was slipping into catastrophe.

He stared at the empty car for a forlorn minute, his mind blank, when all of a sudden he spotted the road sign: Mulberry Crescent. It took a moment to work out why this sounded familiar and then he cursed himself for being so stupid. Doug Bernstein, Eva's father, owned a flat on Mulberry Crescent. It was the very same address to which he'd just instructed Marshall to dispatch an assault team.

Grateful that he'd made it there first, George climbed out of the car, went around to the boot and pulled out his trusty canvas bag. It appeared as though he'd been granted a reprieve.

73

On Christmas Eve, Lewis and his family prepared for the next day's marathon of food and television by limbering up with a meal of microwave lasagne and chicken wings, eaten off their knees in front of Pierce Brosnan in *Tomorrow Never Dies*. After the film, Lewis helped Connor to hang up his stocking, then went back down to the lounge. His father was on the settee, one hand clutching a tin of lager and the other down the front of his tracksuit bottoms. The mess from supper remained piled on the floor by his feet.

'Here, Your Majesty, let me,' Lewis said, and scooped up the dirty plates.

'Oi, you're blocking the screen!' his dad said, waving him away.

Lewis shuffled back with his head bowed. 'So sorry to inconvenience you.'

'I'll inconvenience you and all in a minute, you cheeky little gobshite.'

As usual, the bin in the kitchen was overflowing, making Lewis suspect that he was the only one who ever changed the bag. He stacked the plates by the sink, tugged the heaving sack out, tied a knot in the top and went to throw it in the wheelie bin outside. This, however, meant passing back through the lounge and between his father and the television screen once more.

'Training for your future career, are you?'

'What's that?' Lewis asked.

'As a bin man. I hear they really value relevant experience.'

'Ha ha, very funny. You won't be laughing when I'm a millionaire.'

'Oh yeah?' He drained the last swig of his beer, scrunched the can and handed it to Lewis. 'I'll be laughing my arse off. Here, stick this in the recycling while you're out there.'

'I'll be laughing my arse off,' Lewis muttered, mimicking his dad's voice as he dragged the bin bag out the front door. Their house was at the end of the terrace, meaning that there was an alley between it and the house to the left. Although both had slightly larger gardens than the other houses on the street, neither technically owned the alley and, over years of neglect, it had fallen into disrepair. When he was eight years old, Lewis had accidently disturbed a fox in the tangle of bushes at the far end, and as a result developed an irrational fear of both the alley and foxes that had lasted ever since.

A cold wind blew round the side of the house, shaking the bare branches of the overhanging trees and filling the alley with dancing shadows. Lewis shivered, wishing he'd stopped to pull on his coat before stepping out. After lugging the bin bag to the alcove near the back, he placed it on the ground and opened the lid of the wheelie bin, but as he bent to pick the bag up again, the plastic snagged on something sharp, causing the bottom to rip open and a stream of rubbish to pour over his shoes.

'Brilliant!' Lewis said, and shoved what remained of the bin bag into the wheelie bin.

He glanced down at his feet. For a moment he was tempted to leave the fallen rubbish where it lay, but he could see a chicken bone in amongst the empty tin cans and mouldy banana peel, and foxes loved chicken. Probably.

There was a rustle in the bushes a few feet away. Lewis froze, his sphincter clenching. There was another rustle and then a wood pigeon took flight from the branch of a tree. Lewis breathed again, shook his head and bent to pick up an empty kitchen roll tube. As he straightened up, the bushes quivered and a person-shaped object emerged.

'Who's there?' he called out, pointing the kitchen roll tube like a sword. 'Don't come any closer, I've got a... a...'

A tramp staggered from the bushes. The man's long coat was a patchwork of stains. He wore a wellington boot on one foot and an old, formerly white trainer with no laces on the other. Lewis flinched as the aroma of stale urine mingled with something suspiciously cheesy hit his nose.

'Sorry, mate,' he said, lowering his impromptu weapon. 'I know it's Christmas and all, but you can't sleep here. There's a homeless shelter just off the High Street—'

'I'm not looking for a place to sleep, Lewis,' the tramp said, speaking with an American accent.

'Oh, that's all right then. Hang on, how do you know my name?'

'There's no time to explain that now. They'll be coming for you in five minutes.'

'Who will?'

'The Tempus Project.'

'The people Sam's working for? Why would they be coming for me?'

'Like I said, there's no time to explain.' He rummaged in his coat pocket for a second, then pulled out an envelope and a small glass container. 'Here,' he said, offering both to Lewis, 'take these.'

Lewis read the letter twice before going back into the house. His dad remained slouched on the settee, now with a fresh can of beer in his hand.

'What took so long?' he asked. 'Get lost out there?'

'You're not going to believe what just happened,' Lewis said. 'There was a homeless person in the alley, hiding in the bushes at the back.'

His dad placed his beer on the coffee table and stood, hoisting the waistband of his tracksuit bottoms over his gut. 'Hope you told him to clear off.'

'I don't think he wanted to sleep there, Dad. He gave me something and then said he had to go.'

'Good God, boy, are you soft in the head or something? They'll tell you anything they think you want to hear just to—'

At that moment the television switched off and the lights went out.

Lewis just had time to hear his dad shout, 'Bloody fuse!' before the front door was blown off its hinges and what sounded like a herd of cattle stampeded into the house.

74

Doug sat on the sofa next to Sam's grandparents. His hair jutted from his head and his bare legs poked out the bottom of his dressing gown. 'You've put us all in danger by coming here,' he said.

'I'm sorry,' Sam said, 'I didn't want you involved in any of this, I just didn't know who else I could turn to. They've got my house under surveillance. We had to get out of there.'

Doug stared at him for a moment, tight-lipped, then shook his head, put his hands on his hairy knees and heaved his large frame from the sofa. 'Well, it's too late, you're here now.'

Chrissie disentangled herself from Lance's arms. 'So, what do we do next?'

'That's a good question,' Doug said. 'It probably isn't much safer here than back at your house.'

'You mean they might've bugged this place too?' Sam asked, instantly regretting everything he'd just told them.

Doug placed a big, bear-like paw on Sam's shoulder. 'Calm down, son. I had the security system installed by an old army pal. It's state-of-the-art. Trust me, nobody's getting in or out of here without me knowing.' He dropped his arm to his side and turned to face the others. 'We can get through this if we keep our heads. Now, I need to know, do any of you have cell phones?'

Chrissie and Lance both nodded.

Sam reached down and felt the bulge of his phone through his pocket.

'Well, switch them off right now,' Doug said. 'They can use the signal to track your position. Might as well leave them here, in fact. You won't be able to use them again.'

One by one they switched off their phones, removed the batteries and lined them up on the table.

'That's a start,' Doug said, placing his own lifeless phone at the end of the row. 'But we've wasted enough time already. We need to leave.'

'Where to?' Eva asked.

'We need to go underground, at least until I can find a way to get us out of the country. That means no phone calls, no credit cards, no record of where we go. Gerald, the Chairman of the bank, has a house in the Scottish Highlands. He's on vacation in Barbados until January, so the place will be empty. It's remote, plus he's got hunting rifles and shotguns if we need to defend ourselves. We'll have to drive overnight to reach it.'

'I'm parked just outside,' Lance said. 'It'll be a bit of a squeeze, but someone could always sit in the boot.'

Doug shook his head. 'No, if they're monitoring your house, they'll know you've run by now, in which case there'll already be an APB on your vehicle. You'll have to leave it here. I doubt we'd even make it out of the city.'

Lance gulped, obviously gutted at the prospect of abandoning his beloved car. 'How are we going to get to Scotland then?'

'We'll have to steal a vehicle,' Doug said. 'Eva and Sam, you fetch some blankets and warm clothing from the cupboard in the spare room while I get dressed. Lance, Chrissie, can you pack up some food and bottled water from the kitchen?'

'No problem,' Chrissie said.

'Good. And let's be quick about this, I want to be on the road in five minutes.'

Sam followed Eva down the hall to one of the bedrooms at the back of the flat.

'Don't worry about Doug,' she said, standing on a chair to reach the top shelf of the cupboard. 'I think he just goes into army mode at the first sign of danger. I'm glad you came here.'

'Really?'

'I'm glad you came to me, I mean.'

'Me too,' he said.

Eva smiled and handed him a rolled sleeping bag. 'Look, I'm sorry if I didn't believe you earlier, it's just…well, the whole thing's pretty unbelievable.'

'Trust me, I wouldn't believe it myself if it wasn't happening to me,' he said. 'The main thing is I know all of you are safe.'

'In a few hours we'll all be safe.'

Sam opened his mouth to say that he hoped she was right, when there was an ear-splitting crash from the main room followed by the sound of splintering wood.

75

George kicked in the door to the flat and strode into the small but tastefully decorated lounge-cum-diner, noting a floor lamp in the far corner identical to one he had at home. The boy's grandparents, Alfred and Maureen Rayner, were sitting on a leather sofa, their wrinkled faces creased even further by fright. Christina Rayner stood a couple of feet in front of him with a bottle of mineral water in her hand, while Lance Asquith gawped at him from the kitchen.

George gauged their reactions with silent satisfaction until he realised that there was no sign of Sam. Fearing that it had all been a distraction, he drew his gun. 'The boy, where is he?'

Christina took a step back. Before she could take another, George sprang forward, caught her by the throat, twisted her around and pulled her close to his body. At that moment Sam emerged from a corridor at the rear of the flat with Eva Bernstein in tow. He stopped dead in his tracks, his mouth hanging open like a broken gate.

George smiled. 'Attempting to run was a mistake but, given the circumstances, one I understand. This need not get any more unpleasant if you come with me now.' Christina let out a small whimper as he raised the gun to the side of her head. 'This is your last chance, Sam. Come now or she dies.'

76

The only option was for Sam to give himself up. He took a step towards Steele and Chrissie. Eva tried to pull him back, but he shrugged her away. 'I'm coming,' he said. 'Please, just let her go.'

Steele snarled and tightened his grip around Chrissie's neck. 'You must think I was born yesterday. She's coming too.'

'Please,' Sam said, 'I'll do whatever you say.' Out of the corner his eye, he noticed Lance. He had a crazed, almost inhuman look on his face, like he might burst from the pressure building inside him. Sam realised what he was about to do a moment too late. 'Lance, no!'

Lance launched himself at Steele. Chrissie screamed as Lance flew through the air. Steele loosened his grip around Chrissie's neck and turned the gun on Lance. There was a dull clunk and the ceramic shade of the lamp next to the sofa exploded. Lance caught Steele's gun arm with both hands and the three of them fell to the floor in a tangle of limbs. There were two more clunks in rapid succession, then Steele was clambering to his feet. Lance tried to rise with him, but Steele brought the butt of the gun down on top of his head and he crumpled over Chrissie.

Steele straightened up. Lance's hand still clung loosely to his trouser leg. He kicked it away and pointed the gun at Sam. 'I've warned you already, there are consequences for…'

They both seemed to notice the red circle staining Steele's crisp, white shirt at the same moment.

'You're hurt,' Sam said.

Steele prodded the area with his fingertip, oblivious to Doug emerging from the bedroom with a metal baseball bat in his hands. 'Not me—' he began, his face expressionless, but before he could finish Doug swung the bat. It struck the back of Steele's skull with a gratifying crack and he toppled forwards, taking out a potted plant on his way down.

77

Sam rushed over and dropped to his knees. Chrissie was lying on her back with Lance slumped over her. Sam rolled him off. Blood flowed freely from a wound under Lance's hair. He groaned and sat up, his head in his hands.

'Are you all right?' Sam asked.

'Forget me,' Lance mumbled. 'Chrissie.'

Sam turned to his sister. She hadn't moved since she, Lance and Steele had fallen to the floor. Her hands were crossed over her stomach. Blood oozed between her fingers, pooling by her side on the wooden floor.

'Chrissie,' Sam said, and slid a hand under her head, tilting it up. Her eyelids fluttered open. She moved her lips to speak, but blood bubbled from her mouth, dis-colouring her teeth. Lance elbowed Sam out of the way. With his back arched, he cradled Chrissie's head in his lap and stroked her hair. When he looked up again tears flooded his cheeks, mixing with the blood pouring from the cut on his head. 'Don't just stand there,' he said. 'Call an ambulance. Someone call an ambulance *now*!'

78

Sam hardly noticed Eva scurry to the house phone and snatch up the handset. The world narrowed around his sister. The others were speaking, shouting, but it was as if he was hearing them from a different room.

'It's okay, babe,' Lance was saying. 'Just hang in there, everything's going to be all right.'

Chrissie's chest heaved as she sucked in a rasping breath. She coughed and spluttered, blood spraying the air. 'No...' she said, '...too late.'

'Don't say that,' Lance said. 'Help's on the way.'

She tried to smile, her eyes flicking between Lance and Sam. 'I love you both, you know that.' She coughed again, more blood rising from her mouth. 'Sam, you can change all this, can't you? Make things different, make it...'

Then her eyes closed and her head flopped to the side.

'No!' Lance cried and buried his face in her blood-soaked cardigan. Sam stood and wiped his hands on his jeans. Lance lifted his head again and stared up. 'She was pregnant, you know. We were going to have a baby.'

Sam turned his back. The same numb emptiness he'd felt upon hearing of his father's death returned, eating through him like rot. Steele was lying a few feet away, face down, his gun by his side. Sam picked it up, rolled the unconscious man over with his foot, then pointed the gun at Steele's head and squeezed the trigger.

79

A cloud of dust puffed from a spot on the floor an inch to the right of Steele's ear. Sam aimed again and prepared to fire, knowing he wouldn't miss a second time.

'You don't want to do that,' Doug said, suddenly by his side. He placed his hand on the barrel of the gun, pushing it down.

'He killed my sister,' Sam said.

'I know, but trust me, this isn't the answer.'

All at once the gun felt impossibly heavy. As it slipped from Sam's fingers, Doug caught it and tucked it into the back of his trousers.

'It would make me feel better,' Sam said.

'Maybe at first, but not in the long run.' Doug placed both hands on Sam's shoulders and looked him in the eye. 'Killing him won't bring Chrissie back.'

Sam sniffed and wiped his nose with his sleeve. 'No, you're right,' he said. 'Only I can do that.'

Part VII
End Game

80

December 1994

Lara climbed the steps to Judy Barclay's Santa Barbara home, pausing to absorb the memory of climbing the very same steps a quarter of a century earlier. Although the paintwork was flaking and the palm tree by the front gate had grown exponentially, little about the external appearance of house had changed over the intervening years. Regrettably, cosmetics and wishful thinking were not sufficient to convince Lara that the same could be said for her.

Judy opened the door clutching a Zimmer frame. She peered at Lara with misty, cataract-clouded eyes before her face broke into a smile of recognition. 'Lara! How are you? Come in, please, come in out of the cold.'

'It's hardly cold, Judy,' Lara said as she stooped to kiss her cheek. 'You should try visiting London this time of year.'

'Oh no, sugar. You won't catch me on an aeroplane at my age,' Judy said, not quite grasping that the invitation had been rhetorical. She was now in her eighties and, although they had been in sporadic contact over the years, this was the first time that Lara had seen her since 1976, when a memorial had been held and the search for Isaac was officially called off.

They set off up the hall at a snail's pace, Judy shuffling her Zimmer frame forward a few inches at a time and then dragging her body after. The interior of the house looked much the same until they entered the living room, which appeared to have been redecorated at some point during the 1980s.

'I was so sorry to hear about Donald,' Lara said, sitting on a brown corduroy sofa.

'Don't be,' Judy said, 'he had a long, full life.'

They stared at each other, both silently contemplating the implication that the reverse was true of Isaac. After a few seconds Judy shook her head and eased herself into a reclining faux-leather armchair. 'So how have you been keeping, sugar? You said in your last letter that you'd given up medicine.'

Lara had started working for the Security Service seven years earlier, around the same time that the steady seep of grey into her hair had become a landslide and she'd resorted to dyeing it. Had it really been that long since she'd last written?

'Not so much given up,' she said, 'as taking an extended sabbatical. My new employment keeps me very busy.'

'Well, I'm glad to hear that. I always try to stay active, otherwise my mind begins to wander, especially at this time of year.'

'Almost twenty-five years to the day,' Lara said, more to herself than to Judy.

'December 31st, 1969.' Judy gazed through the wide window onto the garden and out over the ocean. 'Not a day goes by I don't think about it. It's the not knowing that's the hardest part. I can't stop myself wondering what became of him, or if maybe he's still out there somewhere. At least if I had a grave to tend…'

Lara gulped. Perhaps the real reason she and Judy hadn't corresponded in so long was because it had become too painful. She reached over and patted Judy's gnarled old hand. 'You can't think like that. If Isaac were still alive he'd have been found by now. You need to move on.'

'Is that what you've done, move on?'

'Well, I'm probably better at giving advice than taking it.' Lara tried to force a smile. 'Besides, I have my career.'

'A career is no substitute for a life. Take it from me, you need companionship, someone to grow old with.'

Lara had never married or, for that matter, had a significant relationship since Isaac's disappearance. For a few years after she'd rejected the advances of several other suitors, but as time wore on and her grief warped to bitterness, such advances had become fewer and further between before drying up altogether. 'It might be a bit late for all that,' she said.

'Nonsense, sugar. It's never too late for a bit of happiness. That's why I'm selling this place.'

'Selling the house? But Judy, you've always loved it here!'

Judy swatted the comment away. 'I can't manage the

stairs anymore, and looking after the place has become too much since Donald died. Anyway, I get lonely rattling around here on my own. There's a retirement village only a mile down the road – Pacific Villas, it's called – where I'll have my own room, in-house medical care and plenty of people my own age to talk to. All this,' she gestured around the room, 'is the past, and I can take my memories with me wherever I go.'

'So you've already made up your mind.'

'I saw a realtor last week. The money from the sale of the house will keep me at Pacific Villas far longer than I expect to live.'

'I see,' Lara said.

'Would you like to have a look around? Isaac's old room is just how he left it.'

A part of Lara – the rational part – realised this was probably a bad idea, but the rest of her knew she would never get another chance. 'Would you mind?' she asked.

'Of course not, sugar,' Judy said. 'You take your time and I'll fix us some herbal tea. Which do you prefer, mint or chamomile?'

Judy hadn't been exaggerating: Isaac's room was exactly as Lara remembered from the three nights they'd spent there, right down to the space rocket bedsheets. A row of sports flags remained pinned to the wall, next to a labelled poster of the human skeleton. The room was cleaned regularly, it appeared, without a speck of dust to indicate the continued lack of occupancy.

Lara paced in slow circles, recalling distant, fading memories. Why had she returned to California, and what exactly did she hope to gain? Looking back, Isaac's absence had had more of a formative impact on her life than his brief presence ever achieved. Over the years, Lara had transformed her grief into motivation, climbing ever higher in her career. She was respected at the Security Service. People valued her opinion. They listened when she spoke and followed her commands. The wide-eyed girl with a crush on her supervising doctor was long gone, replaced by a hard-nosed professional who was accustomed to getting what she wanted.

She should have stayed in London, she now saw, where a mountain of paperwork waited under which she could happily bury herself, rather than indulging this pointless pilgrimage to the past.

Before stepping out of the door, Lara paused to gaze around the room one last time. It was only then that she noticed Gray's Anatomy on the bookshelf. It was the same 1958 edition that Isaac had always kept by his bedside. Unable to suppress a final stab of nostalgia, she pulled the book from its place and was surprised when a folded photograph fell to the floor. She bent to retrieve it. The photo showed Lara and Isaac standing at the reception desk of the Lincoln Ward. It was the day he'd announced his consultancy at Bereck & Hertz; a day full of optimism when neither had known what was waiting around the corner. Isaac was caught with his mouth open in mid-laugh, while Lara gazed adoringly up at him. There was a thick white line running between the couple where the photograph had remained folded over the years: a visual reminder of their separation in the time since it was taken.

When Lara opened the book to replace the photo, she discovered that it wasn't Gray's Anatomy at all, but one of Isaac's hardback notebooks hidden in Gray's dust jacket. The earlier pages were filled molecular diagrams and equations, all in Isaac's spidery handwriting and far beyond Lara's comprehension, but these gave way to a diary of sorts, which stopped abruptly a third of the way from the end with the remaining pages left blank.

Lara skimmed back, stopping at a page at random.

June 30, 1969

Today I gave Tetradyamide to Michael for the second time and, as before, the readouts showed that it steadied his neurological activity. Indeed, under the drug's influence he seems calmer and more lucid than at any time since arriving at Stribe Lyndhurst, and I'm beginning to suspect that Tetradyamide may have applications far beyond those I'd originally envisioned.

On a side note, Michael still claims that he has developed the ability to manipulate time, and that the drug actually enhances this! I laughed (which I probably shouldn't have), but Michael told me he could prove it with a deck of playing cards. To humour him, I fetched some. He instructed me to shuffle the deck and deal it face up onto the table. Somehow – and I'm still scratching my head over how he pulled this off – Michael was able to call each card before it was dealt. Whatever the trick was, I doubt I'd have to pay for my drinks again if I could figure it out!

'Lara, sugar, are you okay up there?' Judy called from downstairs. 'The tea's ready.'

'Coming,' Lara shouted. She closed the notebook, dropped it into her handbag and walked out of Isaac's room without looking back.

81

Present Day

They drove in silence, Doug behind the wheel, Sam in the passenger seat, Eva in the back and Steele bound and gagged in the boot. After leaving the outskirts of London they passed through a village where, as the church bell struck midnight, drunken Christmas revellers stumbled from a pub, cheering and singing as they made their way home. Then they were back in the dark of the countryside again, with only the cones of the headlights to reveal the road unwinding ahead. Although Sam had made this journey a number of times, he'd never fully concentrated on where he was going. It had never seemed important before, but now everything hinged on him remembering the way.

His grandparents had taken Lance's car and driven southeast towards the port of Dover, hoping to throw anyone who might be following off the trail. Doug had given them cash and told them to ditch the car and book themselves into a hotel if they made it that far. Lance had refused to leave Chrissie. Sam had tried to persuade him that it wasn't safe to stay in the flat, but he wouldn't budge and with time running out before either the ambulance arrived or someone came looking for Steele, there was nothing they could do but leave him there, weeping and cradling Chrissie's body.

Steele's car keys had been in his jacket pocket. Sam had helped Doug to tie Steele's hands behind his back in an intricate knot that also secured his ankles. At that point Steele had started to come round, voicing an impressive range of threats and obscenities, but Sam had silenced him with a punch to the jaw and then stuffed a tangerine in his mouth, which he went over several times with heavy duty packaging tape. While this might not have been the same as putting a bullet in his head, it still gave Sam some small measure of satisfaction. Eva had kept lookout while Doug and Sam carried Steele down the staircase and loaded him into the boot of his own car.

Rain started to spot the windscreen as they drove. After a while the country lanes grew impossible to tell apart. Sam was beginning to worry that they were lost when, all of a sudden, they passed over a familiar looking bridge and then a gap appeared in the thick border of pine trees to their right.

'Stop!' he yelled. 'This is it!'

Doug hit the brakes so hard that the car skidded and Sam's weight was thrown against his seatbelt. Doug put the gearstick into reverse, backed up and turned onto the muddy, rutted path that looked like it led to the middle of nowhere.

Sam felt the hairs on the back of his neck stand up as they approached the checkpoint in the metal fence.

'What now?' Doug asked, slowing the car to a crawl.

So far Sam had given them only the briefest outline of a plan, because that was all he had. 'Leave this to me,' he said, rummaging in his coat pocket. His fingers clamped around his security badge and he thanked his lucky stars that he hadn't had time to change when he'd arrived home that evening.

The guard stepped from his hut, the fur collar of his coat turned up against the wind, and walked towards them, twirling a torch in his gloved hand. Sam glanced across at Doug and saw him stroke the handle of Steele's pistol, which was still tucked into his trousers.

The guard rapped his knuckles against the passenger window.

Sam lowered it and leaned out, the ID badge in his hand. 'Evening,' he said and tried to give a reassuring smile. 'Bad luck working on Christmas, eh?'

The guard didn't smile back, but shone the beam of his torch into the car. Sam sensed Doug stiffen beside him. The moment seemed to last forever, then without so much as a word the guard turned back to the hut, opened the gate and waved them through.

Sam let out the breath he'd been holding, but they had only cleared the first hurdle and he very much doubted if any ahead would be as easy to overcome.

They continued along the path, turned a corner and there before them stood the rundown exterior of the building where, one way or the other, Sam knew his fate would be decided.

'KPP&R Logistics,' Eva said, squinting at the flaking sign above the door. 'What's that?'

'It's a cover,' Sam said, wondering if any such company had ever existed. 'The lab is beneath it, underground.'

She nodded, as if this were perfectly normal. 'Okay. So how are we getting in? You weren't planning on walking straight through the front door, were you?'

Sam didn't want to tell her that he was making things up as he went along. A metal medical cabinet stood in the depths of that building and, although he wasn't sure how exactly, Sam's only hope of saving Chrissie was to find a way to reach it. 'Look,' he said, 'I appreciate everything you guys have done, but I think you should wait here while I go in.'

Eva blinked and then frowned. 'Sam, I didn't come all this way to let you go in there alone.'

'It's too dangerous, I don't know what to expect.' He turned to Doug. 'I'm going to need the gun.'

'This?' Doug pulled Steele's pistol out and passed it back and forth between his hands as if trying to guess its weight. 'Tell me, Sam, apart from today, have you ever fired a gun before?'

'In a way.'

'What kind of a way is that?'

'You know, video games and stuff. And at a funfair once.'

Doug laughed and returned the pistol to his waistband. 'Then you're crazy if you think I'm giving this to you. You're more likely to shoot your own foot off than hit anyone else.'

'But I can't go in there unarmed,' Sam said.

Doug held him in a steady gaze. 'You don't need to, son. I'm coming with you.'

Eva leaned forwards from the back seat. 'I'm coming too.'

'No, you're not,' Sam and Doug both said at once.

'So you're planning on leaving me here?' she said. There was a thud from the boot of the car. 'Alone. With *him*?'

Doug sighed and shook his head. 'Looks like we're in this together then.'

82

Eva trudged toward the building, thinking it looked more than a little like an abandoned warehouse. The sloping, corrugated iron roof was covered with patches of melting snow from which mini waterfalls cascaded to the ground. The fear she'd felt in the car was replaced by a jittery anticipation, and on some level she felt more alive than ever before, as though the present moment was the only thing that mattered.

Sam stopped just before the double doors and turned to face them. 'Last chance, are you sure you want to do this?'

'Will you stop asking that already?' Eva stepped forward and took his hand. 'We're with you on this.'

Doug grunted behind them and stamped his feet. 'C'mon,' he said. 'It's cold out here.'

Sam nodded and pushed the doors open. Doug stepped in behind and, after a moment's hesitation, Eva followed.

The room she found herself in reminded her of the waiting room of the orthodontist she used to visit as a child, which was not a favourable comparison, since Dr Price had been a clumsy, unsympathetic man who'd left her in agony after each visit, until he eventually went out of business the month before she was due to have her braces removed. A near-empty vending machine stood on one side of the room and a row of metal-framed chairs was bolted to the floor on the other. There was a reception desk straight ahead, where a small man wearing a peaked cap sat with his feet propped up. As they entered he looked up from the paperback novel in his lap, swung his feet to the floor and blinked at them through the thick lenses of his glasses. 'Sam? What are you doing here?'

Sam ambled over and placed both hands flat on the desk. 'Hi Arnold, how's it going?'

Arnold closed his book and shifted his weight back in his chair. 'A bit on the quiet side, but I can't complain. What can I do you for?'

'That's the thing,' Sam said and glanced over his shoulder at Eva and Doug. 'I know it's a bit, er, unusual, but I've got some visitors, colleagues from the States, and Dr McHayden said she wanted me to show them around the lab.'

Arnold frowned and checked his computer. 'Nothing on the rota about that.'

Sam gave a nervous laugh. 'No, I don't suppose there would be. The request came through right at the last minute. All very hush-hush, if you know what I mean.'

Eva gave Arnold her brightest smile, but he shook his head. 'I'm sorry,' he said. 'I'd love to let you in – really I would – but without direct authorisation from Dr McHayden there's nothing I can do.'

'Aw, come on, pal,' Doug said and stepped beside Sam. 'We'll only be a few minutes. Where's your Christmas spirit?'

The friendly expression vanished from Arnold's face. 'Look, I've told you already, without Dr McHayden's permission there's...' His gaze drifted down to the front of Sam's jeans, which, Eva now realised, were smeared with Chrissie's blood. Arnold looked up again and began moving his hand toward the holster at his hip.

In a split second Doug had pulled the gun from his waistband and was pointing it at Arnold's head. 'Think again,' he said.

Arnold made a face like a cat swallowing a hairball. 'You must be out of your minds. You do realise what this place is, don't you?' He looked up at a small, black hemisphere hanging from the ceiling above their heads. 'There're cameras everywhere. You'll never get away with it.'

'With what we're planning, I don't think that'll matter,' Doug said. 'Now get up. Please.'

Arnold pushed his chair back and stood with his arms raised.

'Much obliged.' Doug spun his finger in a circle. 'Now, be a good fella and turn round.'

Muttering, Arnold turned his back on them. Keeping the gun trained on Arnold's head, Doug stepped around the desk, unclipped the holster on Arnold's belt, pulled out the pistol and dropped it in his own coat pocket.

'Good. So, tell me...' He waved the gun in the direction of the door behind the desk. '...what's through there?'

'Nothing, only a kitchen and a lavatory.'

'That'll do,' Doug said. 'Let's go.'

They followed Arnold through to a small room containing no more than a refrigerator, a sink, a kettle and a door that led off to a tiny bathroom. Doug reached into his other pocket and pulled out the remainder of the rope that they'd used to tie up Steele. Then he guided Arnold into the bathroom, instructed him to sit on the floor with his back to the basin and secured his arms to the pipe, while Sam taped his mouth shut.

At last Doug put the gun away and stepped back. 'So far, so good,' he said. 'Keep it up, Arnold, and this will all be over very soon.'

Arnold glared at them over the top of the thick wodge of packaging tape that covered half his face, but he didn't try anything.

'Watch this,' Sam said and led Eva back to the reception area. He reached under the desk and pressed something. There was the hiss of a hydraulic piston and the vending machine slid to one side, revealing a chamber with metal walls.

'Neat,' Eva said and gave a nod of approval.

'The lift takes us down to the lab on the bottom floor,' Sam said. 'That's where they store the Tetradyamide.'

Doug came up behind them. 'I'll wait here in case we have company,' he said. He took his coat off and pulled on the jacket of Arnold's security uniform, which had been hanging on the back of his chair. It was a poor fit; the zipper barely closed over Doug's belly and a couple of inches of hairy forearm stuck out below the sleeves.

'Almost, but not quite,' Eva said. She returned to the bathroom to find Arnold straining against his bonds. He flinched as she entered and stared up at her with a mixture of resentment and guilt. Eva scooped the cap off his head. 'I need to borrow this. You don't mind, do you?'

Arnold tried to complain, but only produced a muted growl through his gag.

'Thanks, thought not,' Eva said. She returned to the reception desk, placed the cap on Doug's head and took a step back to admire the result. 'Perfect,' she said. 'If someone comes, try to hold them up, okay?'

'I'll do my best, sweet pea.' Doug smiled and slid his gun under Arnold's book, which lay tented on the desk. 'You kids better get going.'

Sam was standing in the elevator already, his hand over a black plate set next to three buttons on the wall. As Eva approached, he pressed his palm to the plate and the edges flashed red.

Sam slammed his fist against the wall and turned to her, his shoulders trembling. It looked like he was about to cry. 'Dr McHayden always put her hand on this plate to operate the lift. It must read your palm print or something, but it won't accept mine. I don't know what else to do, Eva.'

'Is there another way down?' she asked.

'What, you mean like a fire escape or something? No, not that I know of. I think we're stuck.'

'Maybe, maybe not.' Eva stepped out of the elevator and went back to Arnold's desk, where Doug was busy cleaning his fingernails with a matchstick.

'That was quick,' he said.

Eva ignored him, nudged the mouse of Arnold's computer and began tapping away at the keyboard, her fingers a blur.

Sam arrived by her side. 'What're you doing?'

'Accessing the elevator's control system,' she said without looking up. 'There must be a way to override the palm scanner in case of an emergency. Most systems have an automatic trigger built in to prevent people using the elevators in the event of a fire. If the elevator is between floors, it will automatically descend to the lowest level. Obviously you wouldn't want someone stuck between floors with a fire blazing through the building.'

'No, obviously not.'

'All I need to do is recalibrate the controls to make the system think the elevator is between floors, then if we trigger the fire alarm it should take us down to the basement level.'

'You can do that?' Sam asked.

Eva stepped back and grinned. 'I already have.'

83

'Are you sure this will work?' Sam asked as he stood next to Eva in the lift.

She gave him a sideways glance. 'I've never done anything quite like that before, but, yeah, in theory it should.'

He didn't like the sound of the words 'in theory' and suspected they were about to trap themselves in the lift, but unfortunately it seemed to be the only way to reach the lab.

'You ready?' Doug called from out of sight in the next room.

Sam took Eva's hand. 'Do it!'

There was a tinkle of breaking glass and then the lights went out and the lift doors closed. Sam held his breath. There was a jolt and they started to move.

The doors opened onto a scene that resembled the engine room of a sinking ship. The only illumination came from dim emergency lighting overhead, which cast everything in an eerie green glow. Water gushed from sprinklers set in the ceiling, spattering off the work-benches and drenching the floor.

'This way,' Sam said and pulled Eva after him. Together they ran down the length of the lab to the small room off the back, their feet splashing through puddles.

The medical cabinet was in the far corner.

'This is it,' Sam said, turning to Eva. 'We made it.'

Before she could say anything he pulled her close and kissed her. As their lips met, Sam knew that everything would be all right again. He would save Chrissie. He would prevent the nightmarish future in which he was kept McHayden's prisoner and stop her from recreating his injury in other people. Except that he now realised that in order to gain these things there was something he must give up. He broke away from Eva and stepped back, holding her at arm's length.

'What's wrong?' she asked.

'Once I get the drugs in that cabinet it will change everything.'

'I thought that's what you wanted.'

'Yeah, but not everything that's happened since the plane crash has been bad. If I do this, if I go back and change what's happened these last few weeks, then you won't remember. You won't remember any of this.'

She brushed his cheek with the back of her hand. 'That's what you're worried about? I might not remember, but it won't change the way I feel.'

'But everything that's happened since you arrived—'

'Can still happen. You just need to come and find me.'

He kissed her again, longer this time. Eventually it was Eva who broke away.

'I don't mean to ruin the moment or anything,' she said, 'but shouldn't we hurry?'

'Good point.'

Sam knelt by the cabinet and tried the handle. The door wouldn't budge. A terrible thought occurred to him; every time he had seen Fairview or McHayden open the cabinet, they had always done so with a set of keys.

'Well?' Eva asked, kneeling beside him.

'It's locked,' he said, wishing Doug was with them. A carefully aimed bullet in the casing of the lock would definitely open the door, but Doug was upstairs, and even if Eva could reprogram the lift to take them back up, all of the computers had already been soaked by the sprinkler system.

'We need to find another way to open it,' Eva said. She turned and ran back into the main chamber of the lab, returning a few seconds later dragging a bulky metal stool behind her. 'Here, try this.'

Sam took it and, gripping the edges of the cushioned seat, swung the stool so the heavy base struck the door of the cabinet. Shock waves reverberated up his arms and a loud clang like someone striking a gong echoed through the room. He lowered the stool to inspect the damage. The door was dented, but remained firmly in place.

Sam swung again and again. On the fourth attempt the bar of the lock snapped and the door flew open. He dropped to his knees and stared inside the cabinet.

It was empty.

84

It had all been for nothing. Everything Sam had done that evening had been in the pursuit of an empty dream, a mirage that from a distance had offered salvation, but once reached turned out to be no more than heat reflecting off the sand. There was no Tetradyamide and therefore no way of undoing what had happened. By trying to protect those he loved, Sam had inadvertently brought about their downfall. Chrissie was dead and there was nothing he could do to bring her back. And now he and Eva were trapped.

He stood and stared at her. Eva's damp hair hung to her shoulders. Water trickled down her face and arms, dripping from her fingertips and chin. She had tried to help him, and by doing so had been dragged into the very heart of the misfortune that had overtaken his life. Sam opened his mouth to speak, but realised there was nothing he could say that would make up for what he had done.

At that moment the sprinklers stopped. With a flicker the green emergency lighting was replaced by the harsh glare of fluorescent tubes. Sam and Eva stepped back into the main lab, water lapping about their shoes. At the far end of the room the lift doors closed and the mechanism began to whirr.

'What's happening?' Eva asked

'They've switched the fire alarm off,' Sam said. 'I think someone's coming!'

85

Sam and Eva crouched behind one of the long work-benches, their arms wrapped around each other. He thought back to the day in late summer when they'd hidden from Brandon at the mall in Montclair, remembering the smell of Eva's hair and the warmth of her body pressed close to his. In the months since he had lost his father and now his sister too, but for whatever time they had left together, Eva was Sam's and he would do everything in his power to protect her.

He peered around the side of the workbench. The sound of the lift's mechanism stopped and the doors slid open. Staring angrily about the room, McHayden strode out with a walkie-talkie in her hand. A guard followed closely behind. He was dressed all in black and had a snub-nosed machine gun slung on a strap over his shoulder. Taking slow, careful steps that sent small waves rippling out, he edged down the side of the lab. McHayden waited by the lift, her hands on her hips as she surveyed the water damage with an air of sadness. 'Sam?' she called. 'I know you're in here. Come out, it's over.'

Eva tugged at Sam's sleeve. 'What can you see?' she whispered.

He turned to her, his finger pressed to his lips, then peered out again.

McHayden waved to the lift and, after a brief pause, Doug staggered out with his hands on his head as another guard drove him forward with a gun in his back. They stopped next to McHayden and Doug raised his head. A line of blood ran down his cheek from a swelling above his left eye.

The first guard took another step closer. In a few more strides he would reach the end of the workbench.

'It's over,' McHayden said again. 'I realised you might try something like this when you decided to run and therefore had all Tetradyamide removed from the lab. Come out, Sam. You have to the count of ten, otherwise your friend here dies and we'll find you anyway.'

'She's got Doug,' Sam whispered to Eva.

Her eyes filled with panic. In the distance McHayden started to count, her voice high and cheery, as if it were a game of hide-and-seek. 'One...two...three...'

Eva tensed like she was about to stand, but Sam put his hands on her shoulders. 'Wait here,' he said, 'I'm going out.'

Slowly he drew himself up and stepped from behind the workbench. The guard edging towards them spun on his heel, cocked his weapon and held Sam in his sights.

'I'm here,' Sam said, moving away from Eva's hiding place. 'You can stop counting.'

The corners of McHayden's mouth curled up in satisfaction. She waved at the guard behind Doug to lower his gun. 'A sensible decision. And how about your little friend?'

'Friend? I don't know what you're talking about.'

'Dear oh dear, must we really continue to play these little games of yours? The lab is rigged with a separate alarm system, Sam. I knew that you were here the second you stepped out of the lift. I've also seen the girl on CCTV, in addition to what you did to Arnold. Congratulations for bypassing the palm scanner, by the way. If there is a flaw in the building's security then it is best I know about it. Now, I'll ask you again: the girl, Sam, where is she?'

Sam locked his jaw and squeezed his lips together.

'Have it your way.' McHayden nodded to the first guard, who was now almost level with Sam. The guard lowered his machine gun to his hip and fired a short burst across the back of the room. The noise was deafening as bullets cracked tiles and ricocheted off metal surfaces.

'No!' Sam yelled and clamped his hands over his ears.

McHayden motioned to the guard and he lowered his gun. Doubled over, Eva rose from behind the workbench, her body trembling. Sam rushed to her side and helped her upright.

'That's better,' McHayden said. 'Haven't you learned yet that it's far easier to give me what I want the first time I ask for it? If only you had done so from the beginning, none of this would even be necessary.'

'Well, you've got what you want now,' Sam said, glaring up McHayden as Eva shivered against him. 'I'm here. I give up. You win, Dr McHayden. You can let my friends go.'

She sighed. 'My dear boy, I'm afraid it's no longer that simple. I had held *such* high hopes for you. We could have achieved so much, working together as one, but you've proved beyond doubt that you would make an inadequate operative. Luckily for you, you still hold considerable value to the Tempus Project for research purposes, and that is the only reason you're still alive.

Your friends, on the other hand, present an entirely different conundrum.' She glanced to the guard nearest Sam and Eva. 'Bring the girl to me.'

He stepped towards Eva with his hand outstretched. Swinging wildly, Sam lunged at him before he could reach her. The guard reacted in an instant, stepping to one side and catching Sam's fist in midair. In one slick, precise movement he twisted Sam around and yanked his arm up high across his back. Sam cried out as his shoulder joint exploded with pain. The guard released him and shoved him in the back, sending Sam toppling forward. For a split second he saw the metal edge of the workbench rushing to meet him before he smashed into it, and the next thing Sam knew he was lying face down on the floor, gulping water.

By the time he'd staggered to his feet again the guard had already dragged Eva kicking and screaming to McHayden.

It was too late: there was nothing he could do to help her. He thought of his grandparents, waiting for news that would never reach them, and of Lance. What would become of him?

Sam reached up and touched his forehead. His hand came back sticky with blood. 'You can't hurt them,' he said.

'No? And why, pray tell, is that?' McHayden asked.

'Steele. Lance has him and unless you release my friends, he'll kill him.'

She gave a rich, hearty laugh that filled the room. 'My-oh-my, you're not attempting to blackmail me, are you? Perhaps you deserve some credit for trying, but if by "hostage" you mean the man locked in the boot of the company car parked just outside this building, then your bargaining position is considerably weaker than you imagine. Lance Asquith was apprehended a half hour ago.

He is the prime suspect in the murder of Christina Rayner.' She reached into her handbag and pulled out a clear plastic evidence bag containing Steele's pistol. 'It was most accommodating of you to return the murder weapon. I'm sure it will prove extremely useful in constructing the prosecution's case against Mr Asquith.'

'Oh,' Sam said, feeling a dark weight grow in the pit of his stomach. McHayden was right: it really was over. He was out of ideas, without a single move to make. Even if he gave himself up, it was now too late to save his family and friends. As McHayden had told him, he should have just given her what she wanted from the very beginning.

'So you see, my dear boy, there really is no point in resisting any longer. You belong to me and, like it or not, together we *will* achieve great things.'

'You're mad,' Sam said.

'Who's to say? Others may call me inspired, and after my precognitive operatives have established a new order of things, there will be few who'll question my authority. Now, returning to the issue at hand, I have your friends to deal with. You realise I cannot allow them to live, knowing what they do.'

'Get screwed, you crazy bitch.'

Her jaw dropped in mock surprise. 'How very rude! I am *most* offended. Still, in a way you've done me a favour, bringing everyone together in the same place at the same time. It makes our dilemma that much easier to solve.' She raised the walkie-talkie to her mouth. 'Mr Clarke, I think it is time to call on your unique set of skills. Bring Lewis Fisher and his family to the lab.'

86

Lewis had no idea how much time had passed since his house had been stormed by six men brandishing machine guns with flashlights attached to the barrels. He'd stood there, paralysed by fear and only vaguely aware of his father crouched by his side, blubbing like a small child who's dropped his ice cream. One of the men had hung back while the others swept through the house. They returned in a matter of seconds, one carrying Connor and another dragging Lewis's mother.

The man who'd hung back now stepped forward and pulled off his ski mask. He had short grey hair and stubble.

'What do you want?' Lewis's father had managed between sobs. 'If this is about the money I owe, then I'll pay it back, every last penny.'

The man had casually lowered his gun, unclipped a black baton with a pair of metal pins sticking out of the top and shoved it into Lewis's father's neck. 'Lewis Fisher?' he asked, turning back.

Lewis stared at his dad's convulsing body for a second before looking up and nodding.

'Good,' the man said, then raised the baton again and pressed it into the side of Lewis's neck.

Although Lewis had never been stung by a bee before, this was what he imagined it would feel like to be stung by one the size of a small family car. Every muscle in his body tensed in the same instant. He was briefly aware of standing on his tiptoes before his legs gave way and everything went dark.

Lewis woke up in the back of a moving van with the hood already secured over his head. Someone was slumped against his shoulder, breathing heavily. Judging by the smell of beer, Lewis reasoned it was his dad. Not wanting to get shocked again, he sat as still as he could manage. With only the thick, itchy material in front of his eyes, there was no way of telling where they were or how long it had been since they'd been kidnapped. Eventually the van turned onto bumpy, rutted ground before slowing to a stop a minute or so later. Lewis heard the back doors open and felt a gust cold air blow into the van. The hood was ripped from his head and he found himself blinking at the face of the man with grey hair and stubble.

Lewis's father stirred, lifting his hooded head from Lewis's shoulder. 'Where am I? And why can't I see?'

'Get up,' the man said, slicing the cable ties around Lewis's wrists. 'They're ready for you.'

'Where're you taking us?' Lewis asked.

The man punched him hard in the face.

Lewis came to as he was being dragged into a lift. His parents were bundled in after him, but there was no sign of Connor. The man with grey hair placed his hand over a black plate, which pulsed green, and then pressed the lowest of three buttons set on the wall.

The doors closed and, a few seconds later, reopened onto a large, rectangular space that was several centimetres deep in water. Standing just in front of the lift, but facing away, were Eva; a large, middle-aged man with his hands on his head; a man in black overalls pointing a machine gun at them and an old woman with frizzy, unnaturally coloured hair, who Lewis realised must be Lara McHayden.

'Welcome,' she said, turning with a menacing grin on her face. 'Please do join us.'

The man with grey hair pulled out a pistol and prodded him in the back with the barrel. 'Move!'

Lewis stepped out of the lift, followed by his parents, and saw Sam standing halfway down the room between two parallel counters that ran its entire length. On the other side of the right-hand counter there was another man in black overalls, also holding a machine gun.

'Lewis,' Sam called, 'are you all right?'

'Having the time of my life,' Lewis called back. The man with grey hair grunted and shoved him forwards until he was in line with Eva and the man with his hands on his head, whom Lewis now remembered seeing at Matthew's funeral.

McHayden clapped her hands together. 'How marvellous, I do so love a reunion! Mr Clarke, would you care to do the honours?'

Clarke, he of the electric shock baton, took a step forward and raised the gun so that the barrel was an inch from the back of Lewis's head. 'Any last words?'

'Yes,' Lewis said, 'I have a letter from Isaac.'

McHayden's grin faltered. 'Excuse me?'

There was a click-clack noise behind Lewis's head as Clarke cocked his gun.

'Wait-wait-wait!' McHayden flapped at Clarke with both hands, like a kitten batting a ball of wool. Clarke sighed and lowered the gun. McHayden turned back to Lewis. 'Who told you to say that?'

'Isaac. I met him this evening, just before your friend here broke into my house, zapped me and then shoved me in the back of a van.'

'That's impossible,' McHayden said. 'Isaac is dead.'

'No. In need of a bath and a haircut, maybe, but very much alive.' Lewis reached into his pocket, pulled out the envelope that the tramp had given him and offered it to McHayden. 'Here, see for yourself if you don't believe me.'

There was a stunned silence as the rest of the group struggled to make sense of what was happening and collectively failed.

'What are you doing?' Lewis's father asked.

'Saving the day,' he said.

McHayden stared at him with unveiled hatred, then snatched the envelope from his hand and turned to Clarke. 'Why wasn't he searched?'

Clarke frowned. 'It, er, didn't seem necessary.'

'For heaven's sake, must I think of everything myself?' She clawed greedily at the seal, ripped it open and pulled out the letter inside.

87

My Dearest Lara,

I know I can never expect your forgiveness, but I ask that you trust in me all the same. Doubtless you have pieced together much of what happened all those years ago, but you have never had my reasons for leaving. Please believe that I did what I had to because it was the only way to protect you.

Michael came back that last week we were together, the day before we left for Christmas with my parents. He threatened to go public about Tetradyamide unless I gave him more of the drug, which would have kicked up such a hornets' nest that I agreed. That was obviously a monumental mistake, but at the time I only had the faintest notion of how powerful the drug could be.

Michael found me again on the evening of New Year's Eve. He was a changed person, like nothing I've ever seen. He had a gun and said he would kill me unless I gave him the formula for Tetradyamide, so I brought him back to my office at Bereck and Hertz. While there I was able to knock him unconscious and then destroy as much of my research as possible before running from California.

I didn't realise back then that I would be running for the rest of my life, but you have seen what Michael has become. He knows that you have successfully replicated Tetradyamide and it is now only a matter of time before he finds out about the boy. God only knows what he will do then.

I urge you to reconsider the path you have chosen, if only for the memory of the love we once shared. You must terminate the Tempus Project and destroy your work on Tetradyamide before it is too late.

Yours forever,
Isaac

88

Nothing Lewis had said made much sense to Sam, but if he was stalling for time it seemed to be working. Eventually McHayden looked up from the letter. The features of her face softened and, for a moment, Sam could make out the young woman he'd seen in the black and white photograph hanging on the wall of her office.

Slowly, a single teardrop trickled down her cheek.

'All those years,' she said, lowering the letter and wiping the tear away with the back of her other hand. 'I… I had no idea.'

'You don't have to do this,' Sam said.

McHayden stared at him. Behind her half-moon spectacles, her eyes were filled with the deepest sadness and regret that he'd ever seen.

Clarke cleared his throat. 'What are your instructions, ma'am?'

McHayden's face gradually hardened. As Sam watched on, the last remnants of the young woman she had once been died before his eyes, leaving only the spiky shell that had crystallized around her in the years since. She scrunched the letter into a ball and dropped it into the water by her feet, where it bobbed for a moment before soaking through and sinking under.

'This changes nothing,' she said.

89

Sam saw Lewis reach into his pocket again. He pulled out a glass vial, twisted around and threw it at Sam. 'Here, catch!'

For a second nobody moved as every pair of eyes fixed on the tiny cylinder rotating through the air. It reached the summit of its arc and, as if in slow motion, began to fall.

'Catch it, you idiot!' Lewis yelled.

At last Sam dived forwards, springing off his toes, his body almost horizontal, his hand outstretched.

And then all hell broke loose.

90

The machine gun roared again and straight away Sam knew he was hit. Pain tore into his thigh like a rabid dog; a burning, gnawing thing that shut out all thought of the object Lewis had thrown. He was flung back against the counter and bounced onto the floor, where he lay for a second, soaking wet and winded, his body gripped by shock. The pain was the worst he'd ever known, a concentrated spear of fire in his left thigh.

Somehow he managed to pull himself into a seated position with his back against the cold, wet metal of the counter. The trouser leg three inches above his left knee was a mesh of red. Behind the opposite counter the guard raised his gun again. Sam met his gaze and saw his own fear reflected back. There was no question that the guard would fire again.

Sam closed his eyes.

91

Sam waited for the end to come as blood pumped out of his leg, thick and fast. When it finally did, a single gun-shot rang out, not the rapid burst of machine gun fire he had expected. He opened his eyes to find that he wasn't dead.

The guard tumbled forward over the counter, a grey, blood-streaked sludge oozing from the top of his head. McHayden was silhouetted by light from the lift, Clarke's pistol directed at the dead guard.

'I need the boy alive,' she said.

Clarke stared back with a glazed expression. He'd probably never had his gun taken from him before. 'And the others?' he asked.

'Kill them. Kill them now.'

As the remaining guard cocked his weapon, Doug spun around and grabbed it. Eva and Lewis's mum both screamed. Doug and the guard grappled, pulling the gun back and forth between them in a desperate tug of war. Clarke threw himself at Doug, but before he got there Justin, Lewis's dad, tripped him and he fell sideways through the open doors of the lift.

McHayden turned towards them, lifted Clarke's pistol and fired two shots into the ceiling above their heads. The group froze in mid-struggle, looking like stone soldiers in a war statue. A small cloud of dust drifted down from the plaster and settled in their hair.

'That's enough,' McHayden said. 'The next shot won't be a warning.'

With Doug and the guard at a stalemate, McHayden was now the only person with a gun. Sam glanced back at the dead guard. Blood and brains spilled over the edge of the counter, dripping onto the floor, but the guard's fingers remained closed around the grip of his machine gun. Sam was beginning to feel light-headed from blood loss. There was no way he could stand, let alone walk, so he swung his legs to the side and sprawled forwards on his elbows. Although the opposite counter was only a couple of metres away, Sam had to drag his whole weight with his arms. Every inch was agony, but somehow he managed to close the gap, leaving a trail of bloody water in his wake.

He glanced back just in time to see Clarke emerge from the lift with a curved blade in his hand. With a graceful flick of the wrist, he drove it to the hilt into Doug's neck. Blood sprayed in a jet over Clarke's suit. Doug made a gurgling noise, released the guard's gun and toppled backwards as Clarke pulled the knife out. Eva screamed again and collapsed next to her father, but Clarke yanked her away and slapped her face. Free again, the remaining guard trained his gun on Lewis and his parents. There were only seconds left for Sam to save them.

His fingers squelching in brains, he pulled himself up on the edge of the counter until he was lying over the guard's body, his weight supported on his good leg. With trembling hands he tried to bend the dead fingers back and jiggle the gun free.

'So, still have some fight left in you?' McHayden said, striding between the counters.

Sam managed to prise the last of the guard's fingers open and pulled the gun to his chest. It only moved a few inches: the strap was still looped around the man's shoulder. McHayden reached Sam as he fought to unhook the strap and dug the barrel of Clarke's pistol into the bullet wound in his leg. Sam shrieked in agony, dropped the machine gun and, as his standing leg folded beneath him, slid to the floor.

'Get up,' McHayden said. 'Get up so that you can watch your friends die.'

Sam stared down at the floor. Nothing had worked. As a last act of defiance he would at least refuse to watch her kill them. Then he saw something bobbing in the water. It was the glass container that Lewis had thrown.

McHayden sneered and then looked over her shoulder to Clarke. 'Bring the others here,' she said. 'I want the boy to see this.'

Sam grabbed the container and rolled onto his back. A bar of thick, silvery liquid wavered inside, sealed under a red screw cap. As Clarke shoved Eva, Lewis and Lewis's parents into view, Sam propped himself up on his elbow, bit the cap and twisted.

McHayden turned back, her sneer vanishing when she saw what he was holding. She aimed the pistol at him again. 'Put it down, Sam.'

'Or what? You'll kill my friends?'

'No, I'm afraid there's nothing you can do to stop that, but I'd rather kill you myself than lose you. Don't push me, dear boy. I'll shoot if I must.'

'Do what you have to,' Sam said and raised the container to his lips.

92

Another gunshot echoed through the lab. Sam's right hand, the hand that had held the container, disintegrated before his eyes. The pain was so acute that he was no longer aware of the wound to his leg. His thumb was still intact, as was his index finger, but in place of the palm there was a fleshy, gaping hole littered with shards of bone and broken glass. Sam's little finger dangled by a flap of skin and the two middle fingers were missing altogether. He gasped and clutched his wrist with his remaining hand to stem the pumping blood.

'Get him something for that,' McHayden said to Clarke. 'I don't want him dying from blood loss.'

Clarke took a handkerchief from his pocket, knelt beside Sam and cinched it at his wrist. Instantly the flow of blood slowed.

McHayden dropped to her haunches to inspect Clarke's work, the pistol drooping lazily from her fingers. 'So, my dear boy, it seems we have reached the end of this particular adventure.'

He looked up at her, his jaw clenched. The glass container, Sam's last chance, was gone. There was nothing else he could say or do.

Suddenly he saw McHayden's face ripple, the wrinkles moving like waves over a body of water. Her skin was tinged a bright shade of orange, which gave way to yellow, then green. The walls of the lab shimmered and sparkled as though millions of diamonds were embedded in their surfaces. A surge of euphoria swept through him; Sam felt stronger than he had in his whole life. The wound in his thigh was nothing but a vague itch, his hand a minor graze.

He sprang to his feet. McHayden recoiled with the disgusted grimace of someone who's just taken a long swig of off milk.

'I have one surprise left,' Sam said.

She stared at him blankly.

He raised his ruined hand. Planted in the wound was a slender dome of glass, under which a small reservoir of the silvery liquid remained. Whatever was in the vial now flowed through him, infused in his blood. It felt like Tetradyamide, only much, much stronger.

'Oh,' McHayden said.

'Yes, my dear girl. Oh.'

The image before Sam froze and then retreated, dropping away like a pebble down a well. Above, below and to either side were countless other images, each laid out in rows like an infinite deck of cards spread across an endless table. Instead of seeing the pages of time strung in a linear sequence like the pages of a book, Sam now saw the true nature of things. There was no order and there was no book. Time itself was the illusion. Below him, he saw the innumerable possibilities stemming from every possible action in his life since the crash. Most of these worlds were similar to his own, but some were so different as to be almost unrecognisable. All, however, were just as real as each other, preserved for eternity in a static plain of existence. There was no free will, because in some alternative reality every outcome from every possible choice he could have made would be played out, again and again and again. All Sam had to do was decide which reality he chose to experience.

In that moment of clarity, he knew what he must do. He scanned the pages beneath him, searching for the fork in the road at which everything had gone wrong. It came straight away, his mind focusing on a single significant moment where a different choice would have changed everything that had happened since, and then tunnelling down on it as the other pages – or cards as he now saw them – blurred away at the edges of his vision.

And in an instant, Sam was on a bench outside the church in his grandparents' village. Lewis was standing next to him in the baggy suit he'd borrowed for the occasion, an expression of concern mixed with annoyance on his face. In his intact right hand, Sam was holding Lewis's mobile phone.

He blinked and the image gained motion. A cold, damp wind blew, whipping at the panels of his suit. He glanced about. A man and a woman in paramedic uniforms were standing to the other side. The man had a stringy ponytail and sideburns, the woman podgy cheeks and an upturned nose.

'If you'll just let us examine you first, then you can make as many phone calls as you like,' the woman said.

The phone in Sam's hand was ringing, as though he'd just dialled a number and pressed call. He held it to his ear. After another ring someone answered.

'Hello,' the voice said. 'This is Inspector Frances Hinds.'

Sam looked past Lewis and up the hill to the church. The big oak doors eased open and Chrissie stepped out. The sight of her brought tears to his eyes.

'What's going on?' Chrissie called. 'Are you all right?'

'Hello? Is anyone there?' Inspector Hinds asked.

Without saying a word, Sam hung up.

Part VIII
After Effects

93

Sam was on his back in the dark, drenched in a cold sweat. He gasped for air and, raising his right hand in front of his face, wiggled his fingers. It felt as though they were all present and accounted for. Instinctively he reached for his bedside table and, to his immense relief, hit the switch on the base of the lamp. He saw that he was in his own bed, but had kicked the duvet to the floor.

It was the feeling of waking from the most terrible nightmare to find that none of it had been real. Sam climbed out of bed, then crept from his room, up the stairs and knocked gently on his sister's door. There was no answer. A swell of panic filled him. He knocked again, this time banging with all his might.

Suddenly he heard footsteps crossing the floor on the other side. The door opened and Chrissie stared at him, her eyes puffy and her hair tangled. Before she could say anything, Sam threw his arms around her and hugged her as tightly as he could.

Eventually she pushed him back. 'What's the matter with you?' she asked. 'It's the middle of night.'

'Sorry,' he said. 'I had a bad dream and couldn't get back to sleep. I just wanted to check you were all right.'

She narrowed her eyes. 'Did something happen to me in your dream?'

'You could say that.'

Chrissie smiled and ruffled Sam's hair, just like their dad used to. 'I'm fine, see? There's nothing to worry about.'

'Okay,' he said and turned to leave, his hand on the banister.

'Sam?'

'Yeah?'

'Happy Christmas, little brother.'

'You too,' he said. He went back to bed and less than a minute later fell into a deep and dreamless sleep.

94

Sam woke on Christmas Day feeling more refreshed than ever before. His grandmother and Chrissie were already up preparing the turkey. He wondered what Eva was doing and whether in this reality she was still staying with Doug. *You just need to come and find me*, she had said. Well, today Sam would celebrate with his family, but tomorrow he would do just that.

He spent an hour peeling potatoes and sprouts with his grandfather and then set the table with their best plates and cutlery. As he stood back to admire his work, Sam realised that something was nagging at the back of his mind, so he sneaked up to his room and switched on the computer.

It didn't take long to find what he was looking for. His first search brought up a memorial page showing thumbnail photos of each of the hundred and twenty-nine people killed in the Thames House bombing. Close to the top was Dr McHayden, staring out from behind her half-moon spectacles. A knot clenched in Sam's stomach. He closed the window feeling an odd combination of happiness and guilt. His friends and family were now safe, but through his inaction Sam had not only signed McHayden's death warrant, but also those of the other hundred and twenty-eight people in the building, innocent people with loved ones of their own.

Sam shut the computer down, telling himself that they were strangers and not worth the lives of his own family and friends. It didn't work, however, and he was left with the familiar empty feeling gnawing away at his insides. Much of what McHayden had told Sam was wrong, but she had also warned that there were consequences to changes made in the past that might not always work out how he intended, and on that point, he had to concede, she seemed to have grasped the truth.

Before eating the family sat around the tree to hand out gifts. Several packages were poorly wrapped and had Sam's handwriting on the labels. He was embarrassed to realise that he didn't remember buying any of them and did his best to hide his surprise at what each contained when it was opened.

As they sat at the table the house phone rang and Sam went to pick it up.

'Merry Christmas,' Lewis said. 'What're you lot up to?'

'The usual, just about to eat. Get anything good this year?'

'Money from my folks. A couple of jumpers, neither of which fit. Listen, I won't keep you 'cos *The Great*

Escape is starting in a minute, but I wanted to check how you're doing, you know, what with it being the first Christmas without your dad and all.'

The relief that Sam had felt upon seeing Chrissie alive was tempered by the fact that his father was still gone. In all of the alternate realities Sam had seen, this was a constant: his ability to manipulate time derived from the same accident that had killed his father, and he could not pass back to before that point. That loss would always be there, Sam supposed, but with time he hoped that he could grow to accept it and, bit-by-bit, that his father's absence might hurt a little less.

'Lewis, you don't know someone called Isaac, do you?'

Lewis paused for a moment. 'You mean that kid I used to sit next to in Geography?'

'That was Ivan.'

'Then no. Why do you ask?'

Lewis had risked his life for Sam, but that had happened in another reality, a place that was inaccessible to everyone else. He would never know what he had done for his friend, and it was probably best left that way. 'Forget it,' Sam said, 'I just wanted to say thanks for everything. I couldn't have got through the last few weeks without you.'

Lewis laughed. 'Hey, what are friends for?'

Sam hung up and returned to the table, where Lance had already carved enough turkey to fill each of their plates several times over. He pulled a cracker with his grandfather. There was a pack of mini screwdrivers inside, a paper crown and a joke. He pulled the paper crown over his head and looked up at his family. 'What's black and white and read all over?'

Grandpa grinned. 'I know this one.'

'Wait a sec,' Chrissie said, 'before we start I've got some news to share.' She glanced at Lance. 'I mean *we've* got some news.'

'What is it, pet?' their grandmother asked.

Chrissie smiled and squeezed Lance's hand. 'I'm pregnant. We're expecting a baby!'

Grandma raised her hand to her mouth and made a squealing noise, while their grandfather stood up and clapped Lance round the shoulder.

'We'd like to call him Matthew,' Lance said, 'if it's a boy.'

For some reason, Sam had no doubt that it would be.

95

Two Weeks Later

George sat in his hospital bed, staring down at the sheet above the spot his right leg would have once occupied. Peculiar, it seemed, that his severed toe, a handicap that had so drastically altered the course of George's life, had now been erased by an even greater injury.

There was a knock at the door. He ignored it, yet after a few seconds the knock came again and the door opened a crack. It was the blonde nurse with braces on her teeth. In spite of George's best efforts to be unfriendly, she appeared to have taken a shine to him. On several occasions he had considered filing a complaint in the hope that she would be replaced or at least take offense; however his only grounds were her seemingly limitless reserves of practical advice and good-natured optimism, and he didn't have the energy to fabricate a story.

'Hello, Mr Steele,' she said and beamed at him. 'How are we feeling this morning?'

'*We*? What are you talking about, airhead? I'm the only person here.'

Her bottom lip wobbled.

George sighed through gritted teeth. 'What is it, nurse?'

She smiled again, revealing a mouth full of metal. 'There's a gentleman here to see you.'

George frowned. His parents had come to visit earlier that week, but they'd gone back to Northumberland the night before. He was at a loss as to who this unexpected visitor might be.

'Fine, show him through,' he said and dismissed her with a wave of his hand.

The door opened again a short while later and George saw a stranger standing at the threshold to his room. The man held a walking stick with a handle in the shape of a dragon's head in one gloved hand and a bunch of tulips in the other. He was primly dressed in a pinstriped suit, shoes as shiny as polished glass and a black fedora hat. A large scar covered one side of his face, where at one time he must have been exposed to heat strong enough to melt the skin.

'Can I help you?' George asked, trying not to wince at the sight of him.

The man regarded him with bright blue eyes that looked in slightly different directions, and George realised that the incident that had scarred his face must have also cost him an eye.

'I certainly hope so,' the man said eventually. He pointed his stick at the armchair by the side of the bed. 'May I?'

George shrugged. 'By all means.'

The man crossed the room and, with great care, lowered himself into the chair, propping his walking stick against the armrest. He glanced at the tulips absent-mindedly, tossed them onto the bottom of the bed, then folded his hands in his lap and watched George with a contented smile. There was something deeply unsettling about this.

'Forgive me for asking,' George said, 'but don't I know you from somewhere?'

'No,' the man said, 'I know all about you, though.' He did not elaborate, but continued watching George with the same contented smile.

'Righty-ho. Splendid. And I don't suppose there's a reason for your visit, is there?'

The man rolled up his sleeve to reveal the metal plate of a prosthetic arm. 'You and I have something in common, George.'

George felt the itch that plagued his missing shinbone return. He would have given anything just to be able to scratch it. 'Look…hold on, I don't believe I caught your name.'

'Michael.'

'I don't know who sent you, Michael, but if this is some sort of counselling session, then you're wasting your breath.'

'Counselling session?'

'You know, "things will get easier with time, take it from a fellow cripple". Believe me, I've heard it all already.'

'No no, that's not it at all,' Michael said. He picked up his walking stick and began scrutinising the dragon's head handle.

'So, why are you here then, if you don't mind my asking?'

Michael looked up, his glass eye catching the light. 'Because, George, I have a proposition for you.'

About the Author

Damian Knight lives in London with his wife and their two young daughters. He works in a library and, being surrounded by books, probably has the best day job ever. When not writing, reading, parenting or working, he often falls asleep fully clothed on the sofa. *The Pages of Time* is his first novel, and will be followed shortly by the second instalment in the series.

If you enjoyed the book, reviews on Amazon and Goodreads would be most welcome. If you would like to be among the first to hear about new releases, please send an email with the subject 'newsletter' to damianknightauthor@gmail.com. Your address will not be shared with third parties and you will only be contacted when a new book is out.

To find out more, visit www.damianknightauthor.co.uk or get in touch on Twitter @dknightbooks.

Acknowledgments

First and foremost, I would like to thank my friends and family, without whose support I could never have completed *The Pages of Time.* I am hugely indebted to my editor, Will Wain. His insight, advice and expertise went far beyond the remit of his job and helped to create an immeasurably better book. I would also like to thank Phil Patsias for his beautiful cover art. Finally, I would like to reserve a special mention to Emmanuelle Banks and Damian Mortimer for their invaluable feedback on early drafts. Look carefully and you'll see your fingerprints all over the pages.

Ripples of the Past
(The Pages of Time, Book 2)

July 1969

The pin of Dr McHayden's brooch snapped the first time
Michael tried to pick the lock of his cell with it, slicing
open the palm of his hand. He stepped away from the
door and looked down. Blood oozed over silver and pearl.
A scarlet droplet seeped through his fingers, splashing
onto the leg of the ill-fitting pair of pants he'd appro-
priated for his escape. Michael smiled and closed his
remaining eye. Pinpricks of colour emerged from the
darkness before him, spinning and spiralling in a jolly
dance. They grew and grew, coming together to form the
picture of the blood-stained brooch in his outstretched
hand.

'Back,' he said, and the picture obeyed. The stain
withdrew from his leg, forming a droplet of blood that,
when complete, floated up like a balloon and crept back

between his fingers. Michael saw himself step toward the door again. The blood on his hand drained back into the cut, which melted closed, and suddenly the brooch was whole once more. He blinked and, like that, the picture was no longer static but the world around; moving, real and filled with sights, sounds and smells. Turning the brooch over in his hand, he inspected the seamless hinge that, just a few moments before, had been broken.

'A truly beautiful thing,' he said aloud, and then laughed, for there was no one to hear him speak.

Going slowly and taking care not to repeat his initial mistake, Michael inserted the pin into the lock again. He'd been right-handed before the explosion that cost him an arm and eye, bringing him to Stribe Lyndhurst Military Hospital in the first place. By comparison, his left hand felt clumsy and poorly coordinated. Applying gentle pressure, he jiggled and twisted, probed and coerced, until eventually the lock popped open with a satisfying clunk.

He pushed the door open and peered out. The corridor was deserted, as he knew it would be. Stepping from his cell, a memory hit him like a blow to the head. Michael had been struck down with tonsillitis when he was six years old. He remembered his mother leaning over, humming a tune and moping his brow with a damp cloth as he lay shivering in bed. A brooch had been pinned to the breast of her dress. It was silver and pearl, and had sparkled under the dim light of his bedside lamp.

The recollection stopped Michael in midstride. He glanced down at the brooch he'd swiped from Dr McHayden's blouse a short while earlier. It was so similar to the one his mother had worn as to be almost identical, however the trinket didn't belong to him, much as he longed keep it. Michael Humboldt was many things, but his mother – rest her soul – hadn't raised a thief.

313

He returned to his cell and, suppressing a stab of regret, placed the brooch in the centre of the neatly made bed. Feeling slightly better, he stepped back into the corridor and limped to the gate at the far end. It had been left unlocked, as he knew it would be, and hung ajar. Michael paused for a couple of minutes to catch his breath and massage the stump of his right arm, where his newly fitted prosthetic rubbed and chafed, then stepped through, closing the gate behind him before he began down the second corridor of the Lincoln Ward.

It seemed strangely quiet, the assorted moans and groans of the secure unit conspicuously absent. Three quarters of the way down, he saw a man in a wheelchair whose entire head had been bandaged. Michael straightened up and approached. The eyes behind narrow slits in the bandage followed him every step of the way.

'Good evening,' Michael said as he passed.

The man neither spoke nor moved.

Michael pushed open the swing doors to the final corridor of the Lincoln Ward. Here, watercolour paintings hung on the walls, suggesting happier climes. The rooms in the final corridor had no locks on the doors, leaving men free to come and go as they pleased. At the far end a small group was sat around a foldout table, shooting the breeze over a game of cards. Michael attempted to stride purposefully by, but as he drew level one of the men – a short guy with a fleshy hook for a nose – called out, 'Holy Moses, what the hell happened to you?'

Michael ignored the comment and continued on his way, but Hooknose jumped out of his seat and caught him by the arm.

'Sorry, pal, didn't mean to offend you. You new here? Say, why don't you join me and the fellas for a hand of rummy?'

Michael shook his head. Although the offer of company was a rare temptation, the timing couldn't have been worse.

At that moment a chorus of cheers erupted at the far end of the corridor, followed by the pop of a champagne cork.

'I better get going,' Michael said, shaking free from the man's grip.

He paced to the end of the corridor, drew himself close to the wall and poked his head around the corner. A large huddle of hospital staff were standing by the front desk, high-fiving and toasting one another with paper cups.

Michael was too late: Apollo 11 was already down and the moment lost.

A couple broke away from the main body of crowd – a man and a woman – and began walking toward him. Jerking his head back, Michael squeezed his body tight to the wall. It was the nurse with bleached-blonde hair – Mclean, her name was – and Hank Windle, the janitor. As the clip-clopping of Mclean's high heels drew closer, Michael heard her giggle and say, 'This way, Hank. I know a place we won't be disturbed.'

Michael turned and made his way back toward the card-playing soldiers once more. Hooknose was staring at him with a puzzled expression.

'You know, maybe I will join you guys after all,' Michael said.

The man continued to stare for another second or two. 'You sure you should be here, pal?'

There was a shriek a few feet behind them. As Michael looked back, Hank lunged at him with outstretched arms, tackling him around the waist and knocking over. Together they tumbled into the table, sending a plume of playing cards erupting into the air.

Michael thrashed to free himself, but Hank rose first and straddled him across the chest, while Hooknose grabbed hold of his legs.

'Keep him still, I'll fetch Dr Barclay,' Mclean said, and ran off.

A card – the seven of clubs – drifted slowly down, settling on Michael's forehead. He closed his eye: with Dr Barclay's miracle drug in his veins, no moment was ever truly lost. Dots of colour sprang forward again, like shooting stars in a night sky. The expanded, merging to form the picture of the janitor sitting astride him, teeth gritted beneath a bushy moustache.

'Back,' Michael said.

The picture began to reverse. The seven of clubs floated up into the air. Hooknose released his legs, while Hank clambered off his chest and dragged him upright. The table righted itself and the dispersed playing cards dropped to its surface, forming neat piles. Hank sprang back, landing on his feet, then lowered his arms and slid his hand into Nurse Mclean's. Michael's view shifted as his body rotated to face the table, where Hooknose, seated once more, was staring at him with the same curious expression.

Facing the wrong way, Michael backtracked to the end of the corridor, squeezed up against the wall and poked his head around the corner again. He saw Hank Windle and Nurse Mclean walk backwards, separate and merge with the group around the front desk. Then things started to speed up. Michael pulled his head back and reversed toward the second corridor. As he passed the card game, his elbow slid into the waiting hand of Hooknose, who uttered a silent sentence before releasing him and returning to his chair. Michael passed back through the swing doors and continued along the second corridor, watched the whole way by the bandaged man in a wheelchair. He saw himself pause and lean against the wall just before the gate to the secure unit, his chest falling and rising with each breath.

'Stop,' he said, and the flickering pictures ground to a halt.

He blinked and the world around him gained motion. Pushing away from the wall, he staggered towards the swing doors as fast as his legs would carry him. 'How do you feel about an outing?' he asked the man in the wheelchair.

Once again, the man said nothing.

'Great.' Michael unclipped the brakes of the wheelchair, grasped the left handle and, resting his prosthetic on the right one, swung the man around and pushed him through the swing doors. 'I could do with a change of scenery myself.'

This time Hooknose barely even glanced up as Michael and his new companion strode past. Without slowing, they rounded the corner at the end of the corridor. The entire staff of the Lincoln Ward stood facing a television set positioned on a foldout table in the doorway behind the front desk. Keeping a wide berth, Michael wheeled the chair past the rapt crowd, through the entrance and out into the hall beyond.

He applied the brakes and then hit the button for the elevator. 'Appreciate your help,' he said to the bandaged man, 'but I'm afraid that, for you at least, our excursion ends here.'

To be continued...

Made in the USA
Charleston, SC
19 July 2016